D0175908

# The Other Half

SEP - 6 2001

Sarah Rayner was born in the 1960s and grew up in Richmond, Surrey. Daughter of children's author/illustrator Mary Rayner and psychoanalyst Eric Rayner (now divorced), she studied English at the University of Leeds. She has worked in fashion P.R., magazines and for the last ten years as an advertising copywriter. *The Other Half* is her first novel.

Sarah can be emailed on tohfeedback@hotmail.com

# The Other Half

Sarah Rayner

ORION

First published in Great Britain in 2001 by Orion,
an imprint of the Orion Publishing Group Ltd.

Copyright © 2001 Sarah Rayner

The moral right of Sarah Rayner to be identified as the author
of this work has been asserted in accordance with
the Copyright, Designs and Patents Act of 1988.

All rights reserved. No part of this publication may be reproduced,
stored in a retrieval system, or transmitted in any form
or by any means, electronic, mechanical, photocopying,
recording, or otherwise, without the prior permission of both
the copyright owner and the above publisher of this book.

A CIP catalogue record for this book is available
from the British Library.

ISBN 075284 142 4

Typeset at the Spartan Press Ltd,
Lymington, Hants

Printed in Great Britain by
Clays Ltd, St Ives plc

All the characters in this book are fictitious, and any resemblance
to actual persons, living or dead is purely coincidental.

The Orion Publishing Group Ltd
Orion House
5 Upper Saint Martin's Lane
London, WC2H 9EA

# Acknowledgements

A big thank you to my family and friends, not just for their direct advice about this novel but also for sharing their lives with me and all their support over the years, without which this would not have been possible. I would especially like to thank Rachel Leyshon for helping to develop the idea in the first place and for her editorial expertise; art director Debbie Fagan for helping with cover concepts and a whole heap more; fellow writers Jenny Greenhalgh, Paula Morris and Caroline Jowett who were an invaluable inspiration; Julie Miller who kept reminding me what a mum would feel; my own mother for her diplomacy and gentle encouragement; my agent Vivien Green, whose enthusiasm matched my own throughout; Donna Brodie from the fabulous Writer's Room in New York; Jane Fior, who steered me early on; plus Jane Wood, Jackie Skippings, Michele Teboul, Anna Bernadetto, Wendy Mandy and Margaret Heffernan. And not forgetting all at Black Cat Agency; my very own 'Robs', Bill Graber, John Scott and PatricknKarl; Anthony Marsland, for taking my photo etc.; and the tantalising J/J-like guys I have known in my time, especially JG, JK, JT, MD, MR and SM, some of whom got away. Have a margarita on me.

SEP – 6 2001

For my mum and dad,
and their other halves

**The mistress. The wife.**

**Each has her own story.**

# 1 Chloë

**There were three** men opposite her, all hard at it. One had been going for ages and had worked up a real sweat. Every stroke was accompanied by a noisy 'ooof'. The other two seemed more blasé. Chloë pressed the buttons and struck up her own rhythm, feeling vaguely self-conscious.

There was something sexual about rowing-machines, she thought, with their rhythmic propulsion backwards and forwards. Particularly the machines at this gym, which had been set up in two groups of three, facing each other, toe to toe. And as she realised this, it seemed the men did too. They all appeared to be looking at her, and trying not to. For the briefest moment, she knew what it would be like to have sex with them all. Simultaneously.

The 'ooof' man was obviously the fittest, a rugby-type with an innate competitive streak, determined to go faster than anyone else, but governed entirely by his own ego. He'd be crap, she decided, her prejudice against muscular, ruddy-cheeked redheads confirmed. To his right, a nice guy. He smiled at Chloë when she caught his eye and looked skywards, as if to say, in camaraderie, 'Why are we putting ourselves through this?' But it was the guy on the far left who looked the most appealing: a slender, long-distance runner's body, a poetic face. And above all – once he'd given her a cursory glance to acknowledge the ludicrousness of their situation – absolutely no interest in Chloë whatsoever.

No matter how hard she worked out, Chloë would never have the kind of physique that was attractive to *all* men, which, of course, was what she wanted. No, she was lumbered with a certain voluptuous appeal that some found irresistible but others found far too much. She had a bosom, she had hips, she had a tummy. And whereas some women seemed to gain a certain something when they 'glowed' in the aftermath of exercise, Chloë simply looked dishevelled and hot – at her unmade-up worst. Occasionally she worried that that was how she looked during sex. A nightmare thought, best not contemplated.

I'm at that point in life, thought Chloë, as she left the gym, where men don't wolf-whistle quite as much as they used to. She remembered her mother arriving home in a fluster one evening when she was in her late forties. 'A driver went "Phwoar!"' she'd said excitedly. 'It's made my day!' Poor thing, Chloë had thought at the time. At eighteen, wolf-whistles were a frequent occurrence. But gradually she had learned that being the recipient of vocalised desire from male strangers was inversely proportionate to age. And although publicly she liked to dismiss whistling as animal behaviour at its vilest, secretly she found it galling to be no longer so readily appreciated. It was one thing to reject attention from admirers deemed unworthy when she received it daily, quite another when it happened only once a month.

A short walk up Battersea Rise and she was home in minutes. Experience had taught her that unless a gym was on her doorstep she'd find any excuse not to go.

'Hiya,' she said, banging the front door. The whole house seemed to shake.

'Hi there,' came a familiar voice. 'Do you want a glass of wine?'

A delicious smell was wafting down the hall. Chloë dumped her bag on the chair kept there because one of its legs was broken and there was no room for it anywhere else, and went into the kitchen. 'Love one,' she said, picking at the spaghetti.

'Stop it!'

'Oh, Rob,' she leant her head on his shoulder and messed his blond hair affectionately, 'what would I do without you?'

He handed her a glass of red. 'Starve,' he replied.

Chloë Appleton was hurtling towards thirty years of age with a speed that made her feel compelled to get a move on with her life. Thanks to a particularly impatient and demanding nature, she'd experienced in that time a *great* deal to distress and irk her. Born to an affluent intellectual couple in comfortable West London, vexation had started at the age of three with the arrival of a younger sibling, a round-faced, fat-limbed baby whom everyone – especially her parents – adored. Until then she'd been the sole focus of their attention and one part of her infant psyche didn't like sharing them. Yet she was also wooed by her new little brother, and far from immune to his charms. Photos of the time showed her veering between anxiety and sisterly affection; one of her father cuddling her while worriedly she squinted at the camera, another of her leaning over Sam and lovingly stroking his plump apple cheeks.

Over the years they'd grown closer, united by the adversity of their parents' divorce. Now he lived in California with his partner Michele, an affable Australian who, Chloë acknowledged, was probably his soul-mate. The patterns of old re-emerged: on one hand Chloë envied them their relationship, yet she enjoyed their company. She missed them both, particularly Sam. Tonight, after supper, she sat down at the desk in her bedroom, shovelled her way through a mountain of papers and logged on to send him an e-mail.

| To: | Sam Appleton |
| Subject: | Spaghetti |

So, bro, how goes it? Has our dreadful cousin gone yet? Did you do that Couples' Weekend Miche had her heart set on? (I have this hilarious vision of you both sitting naked banging drums in the desert as you bond with your Native American Indian souls – correct me if I'm wrong . . .) Or did your good old English cynicism get the better of you and did you risk her wrath by pulling out after all?

At this end all is much the same – still got bargain of a flat, Babe of a job and I'm hardly Chloë No Mates – though occasionally I wonder if something's missing. There must be more to life than getting trashed, overdrawn and not getting laid! Rob and I are getting on fine, but I'm beginning to think there's a limit to how long we can carry on sharing the same space. Sometimes my head feels like a plate of spaghetti (and that's not simply because he's just cooked me some – he's a dear in that way) that could do with unravelling.

I suppose this mood will pass. Anyway, I haven't got time to worry about it all – work's so frantic it's not true. We're heading for the deadline on the next issue – always a total *mare* – plus I'm presenting that proposal I told you about tomorrow. And if that takes off, I'll have heaps to keep me amused. In fact, whilst I'm on the subject, I must finish it before I go to bed, so I'd better stop farting around and crack on!

LOL Chloë:) xox

Chloë still had some work to do, and by the time she'd finished that she was truly tired out, and Rob was already doing his teeth in the bathroom.

'All done, then?' he asked, mouth full of toothpaste.

'Yup.' She reached past him for the Colgate and ineffectually struggled to squeeze the last remnant from the tube. He gargled while she brushed, sharing the basin. Although she occasionally griped about Rob, she loved these moments of intimacy. There was no one she felt more able to relax with, even after all these years – some married couples got on a lot worse, Chloë pondered. In many ways she was lucky: they rarely argued, they gave each other unconditional support, their friends got on like a house on fire.

Ablutions completed, it was time to hit the sack.

'Night, then,' said Rob, disappearing into his room and closing the door.

'Night,' said Chloë. She stripped off her clothes, throwing them in a haphazard pile on the floor where they merely added to the great unwashed. Exhausted, she climbed into bed and turned out the light. Alone again, naturally.

The alarm went off at seven forty-five. Chloë prodded herself to check that she was okay after her workout at the gym. 'Yes, still here,' she muttered. 'Don't seem too achy.' (First sign, talking to yourself.) She listened to 'Thought for the Day', gleaned a soundbite of spirituality, and threw back the duvet.

Kettle on, a not-very-thorough rinse of a dirty mug to make it fit for coffee, feed the always-well-fed-looking cat. This was the last of the Whiskas: she must remember to buy more – and tooth-paste. Why did she never have time to go to the supermarket? Her frenzied lifestyle seemed to force her to pay over the odds for life's essentials at the local Europa.

Rob, dead to the world, wouldn't be up for another hour. Chloë envied his ability to sleep so soundly.

So, what to wear today? She had a meeting with the new publisher at half ten. Her Whistles suit. Shit! She'd splodged Bolognese down the skirt last night. That would teach her not to split separates. A riffle through her cupboard revealed that nothing appropriate was clean. I'll never make it to editor at this rate, she thought. What I need is a wardrobe of natty little numbers, all interchangeable, carefully ironed and perfect for impressing one's superiors.

Over the years she'd commissioned numerous articles about the merits of co-ordinating colours and capsule wardrobes, yet she was still more inclined to purchase clothes because she fell in love with their sheer outrageousness rather than because they fulfilled a useful purpose. This left her with no choice but to wear a ludicrously loud dress that Rob had brought back for her from New York bearing the label Spunky. Normally she liked the way its floral design and vampishly low cleavage made her look like a cross between a seventies check-out girl and a drag queen, but it wasn't ideal for a meeting with someone she had to impress. Still, it was the only thing that was vaguely presentable, and if she pinned the neckline it wasn't too revealing. What the hell? It suited her – in fact, it was more her style than the Whistles suit any day.

'Cool dress,' said her assistant Patsy, when Chloë arrived at the office.

'Thanks,' said Chloë, flattered. With her sparrow-like physique, immaculate dress-sense and incredible, utterly impractical foot-wear, Patsy was the style barometer of the office. Given that the competition in the world of magazines was intense, this was a position that carried some kudos.

'Is it for James Slater's benefit?'

'Whose?' said Chloë.

'James Slater. The new publisher. You're meeting him this morning, aren't you?'

'Oh, yeah,' said Chloë, trying to sound as if it wasn't that important to her. 'He's due at ten thirty, isn't he?'

'Yes,' said Patsy, checking the diary. 'Make sure to walk him past my desk. He's *gorgeous*.'

'Really?' Gorgeous men in women's monthlies were a rarity.

'And married,' Jean, the editor interrupted, 'to one of my best friends. Chloë,' she continued briskly, 'did you finish off proofing that article? The subs are waiting. We're really pushing it.'

'Of course, of course,' said Chloë, fishing in her bag for the hard copy she'd taken home. Where was it? Panicked, she emptied the contents on to the desk. There was her purse, her makeup bag (held together with an elastic band as the zip was broken), her cheque book, a packet of chewing-gum, numerous receipts she hoped to claim as expenses, and a couple of rather squashed and dusty Tampax. No article. She'd been so busy putting together her precious presentation the night before that she must have left it by the computer. First the splodge, now this. Clearly it was going to be one of those days.

'Just make sure to get it to the chief sub before your meeting,' said Jean, striding off with an efficient click of her eminently practical court shoes.

Chloë looked helplessly at Patsy.

'You've not done it?' asked Patsy.

'I have – that's what makes it worse. I was up till midnight finishing it off. But I must have left it at home. Shit and double shit. She'll be furious! I'll have to do it again. Rob!' She suddenly remembered. 'If I ring now I'll catch him at home. He can read me the corrections.' Hurriedly, she dialled the number. One, two, three, four rings, then the answerphone clicked on. 'Rob!' she howled. 'Are you there? Answer me, please!'

No reply.

She was half-way through doing the whole thing again when Rob called back. 'Sorry,' he said, 'I was in the shower. It's just a fluke I saw the message light flashing before I left. What's the problem?'

By the time she'd explained and Rob had read her the changes with the slowness of one who not only couldn't decipher her writing but also didn't understand what he was doing, it would have been quicker do it from scratch, but he meant well so she could hardly be cross. She got the article to the chief sub with moments to spare. Still pumping with adrenaline, she ran back to her desk to pick up her makeup bag and charged through Reception to the ladies'.

*WHACK!* Straight into the arms of a rather attractive man.

'Whoa!' he said. 'Slow up.'

'Sorry,' gasped Chloë. 'Desperate for a pee.'

Oh, no, she cringed, seconds later, sitting on the loo. I just told a complete stranger I was desperate for a pee! How *familiar* of me! Chloë, Chloë, Chloë, what *are* you like?

By now she was so flustered she couldn't pee anyway, so she abandoned the attempt and opted for a rapid repair to her lipstick, a quick spray of Paloma Picasso and a half-hearted washing of her hands, followed by an equally ineffective blast under the dryer. No matter how much profit UK Magazines made, it seemed they were not prepared to invest in hand towels of any description.

'Ah, Chloë,' said the receptionist, when she emerged. 'This is James Slater. He's come for your ten thirty.'

Triple shit, thought Chloë, as she put out her hand to shake his. Inevitably it was the same man.

'Hello,' he said, taking her hand and shaking it firmly.

'Nice to meet you. Sorry, I think my hands are still wet.'

'Good to know you always wash them after peeing anyway,' he grinned.

## 2 Maggie

Upon waking in the morning, before talking, eating, drinking, smoking or getting out of bed, take your temperature, either orally or rectally (consult your medical adviser as to the method preferred), leaving the thermometer in place for at least five minutes.

**Easier said than** done, when you had a husband and six-year-old child to contend with. Maggie yawned and reached over to the bedside table. It was 05.55. She hit the snooze button for Jamie's benefit, put the thermometer in her mouth (what kind of sadistic doctor would insist on putting it up your bottom?) and patiently counted to three hundred. She wondered what would happen if she bit the thermometer. Presumably she'd end up with a mouthful of broken glass and mercury poisoning, and all her efforts at consuming a relatively toxin-free diet would be wasted.

Time up. By now she knew the instructions by heart.

Record your temperature, each morning, by making a dot on the chart at the temperature indicated on the thermometer. As soon as there is more than one dot on the chart, join them together with a straight line in order to bring the temperature record up to date.

Well, it looked like today was the day. Her temperature was down. She was ovulating. Lucky old Jamie. She hit the 'radio on' button. It was so early that *Farming Today* was still on – hardly a seductive choice of programme, but she hadn't the energy to retune.

'Darling.' She snuggled up to him.

'What?' He groaned sleepily.

'And now Humphrey Henderson brings news from Bonn, where farmers are carrying out trials on a new kind of sheep dip suitable for organic herds,' said the gravelly voiced presenter.

Maggie began to give Jamie's shoulders little kisses.

'Jamie . . .' she began again.

'Jesus!' He sat up with a start. 'What's the time?'

'Six o'clock. Relax.'

'I've got to get up.' He threw off the blankets and leapt out of bed. 'I've a string of meetings today. Back to back. Haven't prepared for one of them at all.'

'Oh,' said Maggie, deflated. Maybe it could wait till the evening, although these days Jamie was better at making love in the mornings. Last month they'd missed their chance because Nathan had been up three nights in a row with a raging temperature. It seemed that something was always conspiring against them.

Sighing, she got up and followed Jamie into the bathroom where he was already running water for a shave. She switched on the shower and stepped in. 'So, who are your meetings with?' She had to raise her voice above the sound of running water.

'Nine o'clock I'm seeing Peter Blandford about a fitness supplement he wants to do for *Men*. Ten thirty some woman from *Babe* wants to talk to me about a new idea. Then a lunchtime meeting to go through next year's figures with Susie Davis and Mark Pickles. Then a three o'clock at the printer's to discuss whether we can bring our on-sale dates forward to be more competitive.'

'It sounds all go.' Perhaps it was the destiny of wives to fake sympathy when what they really felt was irritation.

'Blast!' said Jamie, his face now beautifully lathered. 'Is my razor in there?'

'Oh – yes.' Maggie guiltily passed it out to him.

'I thought you had your own,' said Jamie crossly. 'You know how much that bugs me.' His dark hair meant a daily shave was vital, otherwise he looked stubbly by early evening, and though Maggie secretly preferred him this way, he insisted it wasn't appropriate for an executive in his position.

'Nathan pulled it apart and broke the catch,' she explained. 'I haven't had a moment to buy another.'

'You let Nathan play with razors!'

'Yes – before I slip cyanide into his breakfast cereal.' Maggie felt got at. 'Look, he's six years old. I can't watch him every split second – you know that only too well.'

'I suppose so,' admitted Jamie grudgingly. Only last week Nathan, who was worryingly accident prone, had tripped down the stairs while Maggie was at the supermarket and Jamie had been minding him. For a few days they'd thought he'd broken his nose, and Jamie had felt particularly guilty.

At six forty-five Maggie went in to wake Nathan. Getting him up was not always easy, and today he was sound asleep, fair hair tumbled across the pillow, last night's bedtime reading still open by his side. She shook him tenderly.

'Grab me by my wings!' he said, still in the middle of a dream.

What magical world was she wrecking to bring him down to earth? Was he an angel, perhaps? She doubted it. Far more likely he was an insect in mid-flight. Maggie smiled. 'Nathan,' she called softly.

'Grab me by my wings!' he said again, more insistently, and reached out his arms.

'Here,' she hugged him, 'I've got you.'

'Woah!'

'What were you dreaming?'

'Not sure,' said Nathan, puzzled.

Next the ritual fifteen-minute battle to get him ready for the day. Without Maggie's watchful eye, Nathan's teeth-cleaning could become a feeble ten-second encounter with a toothbrush, face-washing could leave a grimy neck or snotty nose, and hair-brushing missing the back of his head completely. School uniform made getting dressed simpler, but there were clean shirts and matching socks to find, and the inevitable loss of a trainer he'd only been wearing the night before.

With so much time devoted to getting her son presentable, Maggie had less energy to spend on her own appearance than she had in the past. She'd always been reasonably comfortable with her looks and still took care about what she put into her body – indeed, she had long been renowned among her peers for her healthy eating habits and unique dress-sense. But though she was a natural clothes-horse, these days she often felt drab. A quick dab of mascara would have to suffice before she flung on her clothes – something comfortable that she could spill food down was vital in her line of work.

Later Jamie left for the office. His publishing house was well over an hour away, in the West End of London, and he had to drive to the station at Guildford and catch the train from there. If he wanted to be early he had to leave by half past seven. At eight thirty another local mum came to collect Nathan – they took it in turns to walk the children to the village school.

''Bye, love.' Maggie kissed him and handed him his packed lunch.

''Bye,' he said. 'Look after Monday.' Monday was his gerbil.

'Of course,' said Maggie, knowing full well she would ignore the animal completely. He had been a gift from her friend Jean, who – to Maggie's frustration – always indulged Nathan somewhat as she had no children of her own. Actually Maggie found Monday a bit too rat-like for comfort, but she had to acknowledge that Nathan loved him, so she'd never had the heart to tell him so.

Back in the house, she leant against the kitchen door-frame, closed her eyes and listened. There was the quiet hum of the refrigerator, the regular *shum, shum* of the washing-machine. Other than that it was silent. It was at moments like these that she persuaded herself she was glad they'd moved out of the centre of

London. Here in Surrey it was much quieter, and though her social circle was tamer, she loved being closer to nature, actually noticing what season it was, waking to the sound of birds rather than the morning traffic. And Shere, the village where they lived, was exceptionally picturesque.

Still, time to get cracking with her work. Literally.

Today she was testing recipes for 'Pulling Dishes', an article for *Men* suggesting meals to help a man to score with a prospective girlfriend. A ridiculous idea, but more fun than some of the dreary suggestions many magazine editors went for. It was really only a way of dressing up old favourites – soufflé, goat's cheese salad, tagliatelli. In an ideal world she'd rather have written something more controversial that drew on her expertise in nutrition and interest in subjects like GM-free methods of production and organic farming. But somehow she'd slipped into producing more traditional pieces because it was easy, the money was good, and Jamie had lots of contacts in the women's magazine world. Anyway, it was fun to write something less academic for a change.

She opened the refrigerator and got out eggs, milk, butter, cheese. Damn! She'd failed to order more milk – and she didn't have enough. It was ridiculous that she could make such a basic mistake even though she'd worked as a cookery writer for years. Normally she was fastidious and her fridge was well stocked. She'd have to nip out to the shop. As she reached for her bag, she sighed: it was obviously going to be one of those days.

A couple of hours later and she had one recipe almost complete – a spiced-up Delia Smith.

### Artichoke Soufflé with Three Cheeses

There's nothing more likely to whet a woman's sexual appetite than a well-risen soufflé. Remember, size matters. But to impress her, don't be fooled into thinking bigger is better. In fact, a small dish with a collar tied around it can look much more tempting. Then you can pile the mixture in high and when it's cooked remove the collar to reveal something quite spectacular.

She couldn't help but laugh at the thought of being seduced by a soufflé. She had a vision of being cajoled into the bedroom for some 'inter-course' and being confronted by the surprising sight of a man, with his penis happily erect and tied with a red ribbon. Blimey! It was only 11.30! Still, she supposed the first test of good copy was that it should do something for the writer herself.

Better calm down, have some coffee. Maggie had been one of the first converts to Continental methods of caffeine consumption. Even as a student, when her fellow undergraduates had been content with the filthiest instant made with – horror of horrors – *dried* milk, Maggie had had a coffee percolator in her room. In the run-down Victorian terraces of Manchester this had been unusual, but in her immaculate, well-equipped kitchen her perfectionism seemed less misplaced. These days, she had one of those espresso makers that went directly on to the gas hob – she had decided years ago that this was the best way to enjoy quality coffee without investing hundreds of pounds in a special machine. And although she and Jamie could probably afford one, her puritan streak balked at such extravagance. Anyway, there was something about the ritual of using a more basic implement that appealed to her sense of authenticity.

Around the house were various tributes to Maggie's ongoing campaign to get things aesthetically right. She would rather slave all hours to strip layers of paint off a cornice herself than hire someone else to do it, lest they chip a vital plaster detail. Equally, she would rather have no paintings on the wall than twee prints that anyone could have or, worse, something by a third-rate artist bought from some Knightsbridge gallery.

Certainly she was not prone to falling for off-the-shelf stockbroker style, unlike some other local women. When she and Jamie had lived in London, their metropolitan friends had all admired her sense of individualism and confidence in her own vision – their home had even been featured in a couple of magazines. However, here she felt that her insistence on using Farrow and Ball paints and real candles on the Christmas tree was probably seen as arty-farty and pretentious. But Maggie wasn't prepared to compromise just to keep others happy and seem less threatening –

it would have meant denying herself the things that gave her most pleasure in life. Sometimes, though, she felt lonely, cut off from kindred spirits and those with more eclectic tastes.

Perhaps it was to fill this gap that she'd recently begun to want a second child – or was it down to a need to re-bond with Jamie now that Nathan was growing up? As a toddler Nathan had been happy to be endlessly cuddled, but now he was inclined to push her away, seeing her motherly affection as cissy. Whatever the reason, over the last few months Maggie had been feeling broody – and with this broodiness came a desire to make love – a desire so strong that at times it seemed overwhelming, despite the passion-killing thermometers. But Jamie had not been in the mood for making love of late. However, Maggie knew it was a tough time for him professionally and she didn't want to seem too pushy.

The coffee failed to do the trick. She still feeling frisky, and no amount of aphrodisiac recipe-writing was going to alleviate that. There was only one thing to do. Go shopping. *Wicked* shopping.

First, damn it, she was going to take a little time getting ready. Experience had taught her that shopping in one's grottiest clothes was a mistake – lines failed to flatter, and even her favourite colours made her look washed out. She went upstairs to the bathroom for a touch more makeup, though Maggie was always subtle in her use of it. Thanks to her flawless skin, naturally fine fair hair and leggy physique, Maggie scrubbed up both well and quickly, and within minutes the mumsy tracksuit had been replaced by a honey-coloured Alberta Ferretti shirt dress that made her look less suburban woman and more Sharon Stone. Settled in her Renault Mégane, she pumped the volume up on the CD player *much* louder than usual, blasting Lloyd Cole – an old favourite from her student days – into the Surrey countryside.

Forty minutes later, she was in Kingston. She swept into the multi-storey, got out of the car, scooped up her bag and flicked on the alarm. First stop John Lewis. She took the escalators to the second floor and turned left. 'Ah.' She breathed a sigh of relief.

There they were. Hanger upon hanger. Push-up bras and basques, F-cups and G-strings, French knickers and firm-hold panties. And the labels – Lovable, La Perla, Lejaby, Fantaisie, Janet Reger – were nearly as delicious as the underwear.

She prowled around, like a lion assessing its prey. Yes! That one. And that one. And those. It had been well worth driving a bit further for all this choice, and it was such a long time since she'd treated herself to a shopping spree purely for her own pleasure. There were some blessings in being a 36B. She might not have the bosom to make a man stop dead in the street, but it was usually relatively easy to find something that fitted. Within minutes her arms were full of lilac silk, black lycra, pink cotton and white lace. Then, on an uncharacteristic whim, she picked up a red and black basque with suspenders and headed for the fitting room.

The assistant counted the number of hangers (ten) and happily agreed to hand her the surplus items through the curtain. The good thing about the changing room was that it was private, well-lit and spacious. The bad thing was that it had three-angled mirrors so that Maggie could see every imperfection. Still, it meant that what she chose would look good when she got home. On previous occasions elsewhere, she had discovered that the mirrors had been designed to make her look three inches taller and two stone lighter than she really was.

In truth Maggie had a very nice body, naturally slim and toned, but she'd always considered herself rather androgynous. She hankered for a more voluptuous figure, a more defined waist, and breasts that hadn't lost their pertness after childbirth. Sometimes she had a vague suspicion that Jamie liked women who were more generously endowed . . .

As she tried on the various items, Maggie was amazed at how the different styles could bring out in her an entirely new persona: white broderie anglaise, and she was pretty, young and innocent (or was she mutton dressed as lamb?); pastel silk, and she was a little more experienced – maybe with two or three lovers under her belt; grey marl, she was doubtless more interested in comfort than sex. In the black lycra G-string and seamless underwired bra, there were several more notches on her bedpost. (Either that or simply a desire to avoid the dreaded VPL.) In the past, although she'd always loved shopping for underwear, she would have opted for something like the latter – the combination was simple and sporty, not too sexually overt. She was hardly the dyed-in-the-wool feminist she'd been in her youth, but the idea of something explicitly raunchy still tended to make her uneasy. But maybe I should push the boat out and be more daring this time, she thought. And it was the black and red basque that made the most overt statement: from virgin to whore in less than a half a dozen shakes of her hips.

Maggie adjusted the straps (who on earth had tits slung *that* low?) and swivelled round, the suspenders spinning out and hitting the mirror. Without stockings it was hard to gauge the full effect, but she had a good imagination. Her nipples were clearly visible through the sheer black glossiness. Was this really *her* reflected in the glass? The result was a tantalising mix of high-class hooker and high fashion, and Maggie felt it was the kind of thing *other* women wore – women she envied for their audacity yet reproached for their lack of discretion. Certainly it was a far cry from her usual purchases and hardly in keeping with her understated style, but . . . there was something about its sensuality – the red ribbon trim, the black-boning, its sheer impracticality – that she found irresistible.

She stood back for a proper look. There was no doubt that it pushed her up and pulled her in to great effect. Anyway, it wasn't as if it was mere Ann Summers' trash. It was DKNY and hardly cheap.

Damn the cost, damn her usual taste, damn feminism, damn the fact that over the last few years shopping had come to mean Waitrose and things for Nathan or for the house Why *should* she be so restrained? For once she would throw caution to the wind. She would explore uncharted territories. She would have it.

And to her surprise, as she handed her debit card to the matronly woman behind the till, who'd clearly seen it all a dozen times before, she felt wonderfully empowered.

If that didn't delight Jamie and do the trick tonight, nothing would.

# 3 Chloë

**The meeting room** was rather large for just two people, with empty chairs ranged neatly around a clear glass table. With the air-conditioning on full blast it was cold. Chloë flicked off the fan and adjusted the position of the projector, ensuring that her acetate presentation was close to hand. Then she laid out several magazines in front of her.

'Would you like some coffee?' she asked.

'Yes, please. That would be great.' James clicked open his briefcase, got out his notebook and pushed up the sleeves of his jacket in a way that asserted he meant business.

Chloë made a mental note: good hands, attractive wrists, not-too-showy watch. She and Rob had often discussed the various components that gave male forearms their unique appeal. She picked up the phone and rang Patsy. 'Could we have coffee for two, please?' she asked. 'We're in the meeting room.

'So,' said James, 'you wanted to talk about a new magazine idea.'

'I have a proposal.'

'Oh?'

'I believe there is a gap in the market for a new women's monthly.'

'Does your editor know about this?' asked James.

Was it Chloë's imagination, or did he sound a little worried about meeting behind Jean's back? Jean had implied that they knew each other socially as well as through work, after all. Chloë endeavoured to put him at ease. 'No, I didn't feel she had to, not yet. What I'm talking about is not a direct competitor to *Babe*.' She took a deep breath and switched on the projector. The first acetate bore the headline 'Background to the market'.

'I appreciate there are many magazines, and in some ways the market is overcrowded,' she continued, expanding on the bullet points highlighted on the screen in front of her. 'It's certainly jam-packed in the teen area, right up to women in their late twenties. *Babe* is just one of those, as you know. It does very well, with its niche firmly established. And there is ample reading matter for women over forty. But I believe there is a gap for women of between those ages, say between twenty-eight and forty.'

'You don't believe this gap's already been filled?'

'I don't.' Chloë moved on to the next acetate, entitled 'The Competition', where she'd listed various existing women's monthlies. 'Your reader of these magazines is perceived as pretty traditional. The expectation is that she is married, with children, or certainly hitched up in a couple. She is into fashion, but not high fashion. She is into supper parties, recipes and gardening. Which is all very well, but I have undertaken some research that shows there is another kind of woman, and she's interested in a lot more than that.'

'Research?' James sounded impressed.

'Yes,' said Chloë, handing him a copy of her proposal document. 'You'll find full details in this, but I'll run you through the basics.' She laid on another acetate. 'I held a number of discussion groups, selecting ABC1 women I know or friends of friends who work in a cross-section of industries, some with, some without children. All of them, without exception, felt there was no magazine that catered exactly for their tastes.'

'So where did you do this research?' asked James.

'At home,' explained Chloë. 'I found it worked well that way. The group could relax over a glass of wine and chat, away from the constraints of the office and family. I provided samples of all the competitive magazines and asked all sorts of questions – what they liked and didn't like about other magazines, what sort of interests they had, what they wanted to see, what they hated, what they loved. And I found that my initial hunch was right. There *is* a gap in the market.'

At that point there was a knock and Patsy came in with a tray. With her hair in several spiky bunches, and wearing a miniskirt and thick platform shoes, she might have made quite an impression, yet she was so busy ogling James that she barely maintained her cool.

'Thank you.' Chloë was afraid Patsy might drop everything.

'My pleasure.' Patsy grinned like a teenager. James was oblivious to her attentions, but it did allow Chloë a few seconds to assess him further. He was well-spoken, she'd already noted, and she guessed he was probably mid to late thirties. Hmm, she thought. He's not really that handsome, certainly no Tom Cruise or Brad Pitt – his features weren't regular and his hair, which was very dark, needed a trim. Actually, he could do with losing a few pounds too. Yet he was one of those men who was very, well, *male*, she thought, and that was undeniably attractive.

'I see,' said James, after Patsy had reluctantly gone. 'So have you some ideas of what this magazine might be like?'

'I do,' said Chloë, forcing her mind back to her proposal. 'I'll give you a taste – you'll find more in my document. It will have more of an edge. It will be for women who like fast cars and high fashion, getting drunk, even taking drugs occasionally. It will be for women who work, but also for those bringing up children. It will be for those who want to know more about politics, social issues and finance. Yes, there will still be food and gardening, but it will offer real, practical advice, featuring something creative to do when you arrive home and there's nothing but a can of tuna and baked beans in your cupboard. It won't have endless features on how to get your man, or titillating peeps at the perversions of

America – we're sick of all that. But it will talk about sex – gay sex, straight sex, dangerous sex, impotence, the lot.'

She paused. 'Above all, it will be exciting, vibrant and bold. It will be upfront, plain-speaking, but fun. That, in my opinion, is where these magazines have got it wrong.' She picked one up. 'Look at the layout and the typography! Dull, dull, dull! The photography? All this soft-focus stuff – it's *so* five years ago.

'Now,' she said, handing him the latest copy of *Wired*. 'This is more like it. The typography, the colour, the photography – ground-breaking! It's the subject that's a turn-off. IT? There's only so much I want to know about that.'

'So computers are for boys?' asked James.

'No, I'd certainly feature some of this stuff, but not a whole magazine full of it. And I'd have it written in a different way. I'd make sure it was less pretentious, less intimidating in its use of language. Though, as I come to think of it, some of the most exciting things in design terms are on the Internet right now. Web graphics are leading the way.'

'I agree.' James seemed infected by her enthusiasm. 'And that's an area where perhaps the men's magazines are one step ahead.'

'Exactly!' said Chloë. 'Look at *FHM*. It's been around a while now, but there are lessons to be learnt from its initial success. And how did they do it? They did more than spot a gap, they virtually *created* one. They saw a type of man and devised a magazine for him, rather than devising a magazine then thinking of the man. That's what we should do. I have my woman firmly in mind.'

'What is she like?' asked James.

'Me, I suppose.'

'Somehow I thought so,' said James, and added, almost as an afterthought, 'Sounds appealing.'

'Well,' she blushed a little, 'I've been working in this business for eight years now, and I still don't think there's a magazine that's exactly me. Anyway,' she focused again, 'I don't want to lose the thread of my presentation.' She went back to her acetates.

'It's okay,' James interrupted. 'I really like what I've heard so far, but I'm rather pushed for time. I'll take this home and read it there. Meanwhile, what, precisely, would you like from me?'

'Gosh.' Chloë was taken aback by his immediate validation of all her hard work. This was something she felt so passionately about, and for months it had been whizzing around in her head. But this was the first time she'd talked to anyone who could work with her to make her ideas a reality. Yes, she'd bounced ideas off Rob, she'd had her discussion groups, but chiefly this was *her* baby.

'I'd like the opportunity to explore it further, but I think I've taken it about as far as I can in my own time,' she explained. 'Now I'd like UK Magazines' help to do that.'

'A new job?'

'In a way, yes.' Chloë was impressed he'd got to the point so fast. 'I was hoping I could be seconded to Special Projects to develop the idea.'

'Well, I'll need to think about that. I presume you'd want to be the acting editor.'

'Yes.' Chloë was flattered he thought her fit for such a key role, though it was the very post she hoped for. 'So I would rather you didn't tell my current editor for the time being.'

'You're taking quite a risk, aren't you, telling me? And at *Babe's* offices.'

'I am, but I really believe in it.' A story came to Chloë's mind and she smiled. 'Recently my uncle bought a sports car, after driving around in sensible little hatchbacks for years. He's seventy-three. "Life is not a rehearsal, Chloë," he said to me. "Don't wait until you're retired to start realising your ambitions." It might be clichéd, but I could see his point. That evening I went home and started to draft a proposal for this magazine.'

James appeared touched. 'I like your thinking. So, tell me, what position are you in here at *Babe*?'

'Features editor.'

'I'm sure they'd hate to lose you. *Babe* has been doing well of late. Yet I dare say they can hire a replacement, and a visionary editor to launch a new project is harder to find. I do warn you, though, we're not talking about a permanent post initially. Until you've put together a sample issue of the magazine, gone through more formal research and tested with potential advertisers, any move would only be temporary.'

'Of course.'

'And I will have to talk to some others about it. I'll come back to you.'

'Fine,' said Chloë, loath to leave the ball in his court. 'Perhaps we could meet for lunch next week.'

'Good idea. I'll call you,' James shuffled his papers and the proposal into his case. 'I'm sorry to cut this so short, it's just I'm booked solid with meetings all day today and there is one I haven't even prepared for yet.'

Briefly Chloë caught a glimpse of a more boyish nervousness behind the capable businessman. She smiled sympathetically as she gathered up her magazines. 'Not at all. I really appreciate that you took the time to see me.'

'Don't forget these,' he said, handing her the acetates. 'Might not be a good idea to leave them in here.'

'God, no, thanks.' But when he passed them to her several sheets slipped out of her hands and onto the floor. Chloë had to bend down to pick them up. As she did so he did the same, and their heads accidentally bumped. Why was she so clumsy?

'I'm sorry,' she apologised.

'No, don't worry, I'm fine,' he rubbed his forehead, then laughed. 'That's our second collision today!'

'God, I am sorry.'

'It was my fault.'

'No, it was mine,' she insisted, opening the meeting-room door and leading him back to reception.

'By the way I like the dress.' He shook her hand again. 'It shows a certain individual style.' He smiled broadly.

She warmed to his compliment. 'Thank you.'

'I look forward to seeing your fashion spreads,' he said, his voice so low the receptionist couldn't hear.

Golly, she thought, was there a slight innuendo in his tone? Surely not! But, later, as she sat back down at her desk, she was sure of one thing. The madness of the morning had left her feeling somewhat light-headed.

## 4  Maggie

**That Jamie wasn't** back in time to help put Nathan to bed was not unusual, but tonight it was particularly annoying. Maggie had been looking forward to an 'early night.'

'Right,' she said, focusing on her son. 'Supper's ready.'

'What is it?' asked Nathan, who was playing with Monday.

'Soufflé.' She'd made a second one, chiefly to verify the recipe but with the faint hope of casting an aphrodisiac spell on Jamie. Quite what it would do to a six-year-old boy she dreaded to think. Nathan, planting Monday in front of him where his plate should go, was oblivious to the X-rated world he was about to taste. The gerbil's nose twitched as he investigated the myriad smells of the table.

'Nathan, Monday's going to have to move so you can eat your supper. He shouldn't be on the table as it is.'

'But he's exploring!' Nathan protested.

'He can explore all he likes once you've eaten,' Maggie handed him a plate with a little soufflé and lots of baked beans. 'Now, take him back to your room.'

'Okay,' agreed Nathan, and scurried upstairs to put Monday into his cage. Sitting back down at the table again, he looked askance at his portion. 'Can I have some more?'

'Eat what you're given first.'

'I will!' retorted Nathan crossly, but a few minutes later he began to slow up, until he stopped completely, leaving a soggy pink mess of soufflé and beans.

Maggie raised her eyebrows at him quizzically.

Nathan raised his own back, and sped up again, slurping loudly. Then he picked up his plate and licked it.

'Nathan!'

But Nathan just smiled. 'Finished,' he said smugly.

Sometimes Maggie felt he had her wound around his little finger.

Once Nathan was tucked up, Maggie ran a bath. She lit some scented candles, put on *Diva* by Annie Lennox, poured herself a glass of red wine and stepped in. Slowly, she lay back, bubbles floating around her breasts and belly. If she sucked in her tummy, the only part of her body that remained out of the water was her breasts. If she pushed it out, she almost looked pregnant. She lifted her feet out of the water and rested them against the overflow. They were slim and straight with no corns or broken nails, and a pleasing pale brown, thanks to a recent week that she, Jamie and Nathan had spent in a Tuscan villa.

She recollected a trip to New York she'd made with Jamie when she was in her early thirties: they'd been staying with friends in Brooklyn Heights and she had borrowed a gym pass to escape the humidity outside. As she was changing after her workout, the most beautiful black aerobics instructor had come into the changing room and started telling her colleagues about another woman she knew with the 'most phenomenal feet in the world'. Until then Maggie had thought that feet were feet were feet.

'Her feet are so pretty!' the instructor had enthused. 'It's like, they're kinda delicate, elegant – like hands, you know? Her toes, gee, they're so long and straight, not like most toes at all. She wears those criss-cross sandals with little knots in them that just accentuate how pretty they are. And, you know, men love her – I've seen it for myself when I've sat next to her in cafés. Men, they stare at her, transfixed, but not at her face, which is pretty cute, or her figure, which is divine. Boy, no! They stare at her feet. All the while they're talking to her, they're staring at her feet! It really is quite something.'

Maggie had never forgotten this woman, her way with words, her enthusiasm for life's minutiae, and she had resolved two things: she would never compromise her aesthetic standards, even over trivial matters, and she would always, always look after her feet.

She took a sip of wine. It was not a particularly expensive bottle (it would have seemed extravagant to uncork one just for her own consumption) but it was a good Burgundy, bought mail order. She took another sip and let it roll over her tongue. Moments like these were all too rare now. And another child would make them rarer. Still, she thought, reaching guiltily for Jamie's razor, she'd never imagined having only one child. If she and Jamie didn't get a move on, Nathan would be too old to play with a younger sibling.

After her bath, she moisturised all over and wandered around the bedroom letting the lotion sink into her skin. She phoned her sister, Fran, for a brief chat, then reached for the shopping-bag and tipped its contents on to the bed. In the glow of the bedside lamps the basque was even more seductive.

Maggie rummaged in her drawer for some knickers. She knew exactly which ones would be right – a satin and lace pair she'd purchased when shopping with Fran, who had persuaded her to buy them, but which she'd never worn. She pulled them on, fastened herself (with extensive swivelling) into the basque and undid the wrapping on a pair of sheer stockings. Carefully she pulled one up over each newly shaved leg, fastened the suspenders and stood up. Finally shoes. She'd a perfect pair of Manolo Blahnik stilettos bought for a Christmas party a few years ago when she'd wanted to impress Jamie's colleagues. The effect was astonishing – a whole new Maggie.

He must have picked up some divine sexual vibe down the A3,

for at that moment she heard a key in the front door and the familiar rustle of Jamie throwing his coat over the bottom banister. Quickly she pulled on a floor-length wrap and ran out to the landing. 'Hi, darling.' She spoke in a hushed voice so as not to wake Nathan.

'Hi,' said Jamie. He looked tired.

'We saved you some soufflé.' She led him into the kitchen. 'Although I'm afraid it's probably past its best.'

Jamie poured himself a glass of wine and leant back against the worktop. 'Phew. That was quite a day.'

'Poor lamb.' Maggie brushed back a stray strand of his hair.

'You smell nice,' said Jamie, inhaling. Suddenly he looked down.

The shoes.

'Ah, yes.' Maggie let the gown fall open. 'I went shopping today.'

'So I see . . .' Jamie paused and took it all in. Would tiredness win? 'Wow,' he said. It seemed not. 'Let's have a look.'

They made love in the kitchen – the first time in ages. And he hadn't had so much as a bite of soufflé, smiled Maggie later as she drifted off to sleep.

## 5 Chloë

**Patsy put her** hand over the mouthpiece. 'It's James Slater,' she whispered. 'Are you in?'

'Oh, er, yes,' stammered Chloë.

A week had passed since their meeting, and she had just begun to wonder whether it would be inappropriate to call him. She picked up the receiver. 'Hello.'

'Hi. Can you talk?'

'Well, a little.' Chloë was in the midst of debriefing her assistant on some simple facts that needed checking in an article and was aware that Patsy was earwigging every word.

'OK, I'll keep it brief. I'm afraid I'm having a frantic week and lunch is going to be pretty difficult.' Chloë's heart sank. Why did men always turn out to be so flaky where she was concerned? But James continued, 'I wondered, I know it's short notice, but I usually play squash on a Thursday with a friend up here in the West End, and he's just cancelled. So I *could* do tomorrow, but it would have to be dinner. Could you make it?'

Could she make it? Of course she bloody could! But she stopped herself from blurting an enthusiastic 'Yes' in the nick of time. She recalled all those books that banged on about the importance of playing hard to get. Maybe it applied in business too. And she remembered her mother's slightly cruel (but accurate) observation that sometimes her natural upfront exuberance could be misinterpreted as 'lacking mystery'. 'I'll just check my diary.' She flicked to the right page. 'My week's looking pretty hectic. Tomorrow, you said . . . Er, what time?'

'I'll probably be through around seven. How about you?'

'I think I can make that.' Chloë tried to sound busy. 'Where shall we meet?'

'There's a nice little restaurant I know on Lexington Street,' he said. 'It's called Aurora, and I think we can bring our own wine, which means we can enjoy something particularly good. How about if I pick up a couple of bottles and meet you there?'

'Sounds great.' Good! Nice and near the office – and two bottles of wine. She hated people who scrimped – but, then, he could probably charge it. It sounded like he knew a thing or two about wine too. How grown up. 'I'll see you there,' she said.

'Look forward to it.'

She put the phone down, and immediately had to get up, all of a fluster, and walk around the office to calm herself.

'So?' asked Patsy, when she sat down again.

'So, what?'

'When are you meeting Prince Charming?'

'Tomorrow. But he's not Prince Charming – it's business.'

'Oh, yeah? Why are you blushing?'

'I am not!' cried Chloë indignantly, going even redder. She didn't really want Patsy knowing she was meeting James in case word got out about her proposal. Why couldn't she ever control her reactions? Her body never seemed to do what her mind wished it to, and constantly gave her away. 'It's work,' she reiterated, hoping Patsy didn't pry further.

'If you say so.'

'He's married!' Chloë protested, trying to laugh it off.

'So was Prince Charles,' Patsy pointed out. 'Didn't stop him.'

'Chloë,' said Rob, with the air of one who knows about human nature, 'you're telling me that this man cancels lunch, rearranges it for dinner, says he's going to buy two bottles of wine and that he's looking forward to seeing you, and you reckon he doesn't fancy you? My dear girl, at times I may find the male psyche hard to fathom, but this seems to me a classic case of get-this-woman-a-tad-intoxicated-on-the-pretext-of-a-business-liaison-so-I-can-try-to-get-into-her-knickers.'

'But he's married!'

'So are half the men I sleep with, darling,' said Rob. They were watching *Ally McBeal*, but the ads were on, allowing two minutes for chat.

'That's different,' said Chloë.

'How, exactly?'

'The men you sleep with obviously want something they can't get from their wives,' said Chloë.

'Dick, you mean?'

'If you want to put it that way, yes. Anyway, it doesn't really matter what his motives are – though I think you're wrong. Mine are quite pure.'

'So why ask me what to wear?' asked Rob, who at times seemed to know Chloë better than she knew herself. 'I'm sure nuns don't give a fig for such worldly matters.'

'Because it's vital I create the right impression.' Chloë was firm. 'This man could help me get my magazine off the ground.'

'Well, just be careful. And if your motives are so pure, I suggest you wear your Whistles suit. That will show him you mean business.'

Chloë had to admit that that was not what she'd had in mind. She'd been planning on something rather less formal. After all, was it such a crime to want look her best? 'Mmm,' she said non-committally, knowing that she'd be gone before Rob got up and saw what she was wearing.

'I just don't want you falling for another inappropriate male,' warned Rob. 'You don't want to end up like her.' He nodded at *Ally McBeal*.

'There's not much chance of that – there's nothing to her! You could have two of her for every one of me.'

'True. But she's always using flirtation to get what she wants professionally and then getting in a muddle because she's not been clear about the distinction between business and pleasure. Now shush. I want to know what happens.'

Perhaps it was a sign of growing maturity that Chloë was finally learning not to be early for dates. (Though she couldn't be too late for this one, as it wasn't a date but a business meeting, of course.) Restless by nature, she'd discovered that the best tactic was to keep herself occupied right up to the last minute. She rattled off a couple of e-mails – including one to Sam – but phone calls were a better idea, particularly to those friends who liked to listen. Once the colleagues who worked near her had gone home, she could natter on and on *ad nauseam*. Before she knew it, it was six fifty-five.

'Claire,' she said, to an old school chum, after they'd been yacking for over half an hour, 'I'm afraid I must go.'

'Let me know what happens,' said her friend supportively.

'I'll phone you,' Chloë promised.

Quick pee, third (but most thorough) repair of the day to her makeup, and she was off. Fortunately it was only a few minutes from Covent Garden to Lexington Street, and though she didn't know the restaurant, she knew which back-streets to cut through. Soho was a regular haunt.

If she checked her appearance in one window she must have checked it in twenty, and by the time she arrived she was convinced she looked a right state. But at least James Slater was there before her. As she walked into the restaurant she could see him through the back window. He was sitting outside, reading at a small round table in the patio garden, having grabbed a prime spot in the last of the evening sun.

'Ah.' He smiled and stood as she joined him.

From the look of the documents before him, she saw he'd been working. He bent to put them away in his briefcase, and as he sat back up he ran his hands through his hair to sweep it away from his face. Seeing him away from the office, in the sunshine, with the prospect of dinner in this enchanting restaurant made Chloë view him differently. God, he *was* attractive! Although she pushed the thought away, she couldn't help it: she felt like she'd been punched in the stomach by a whoosh of desire. Still, she reminded herself, I'm perfectly safe. He's married.

'How are you?' he asked.

'Oh, I'm well.' As if she was going to admit she was all of a jitter. 'And you?'

'I'm fine,' said James. 'Would you like a glass?' He pulled a bottle of white wine, dripping, from an ice bucket. It looked invitingly cool, the perfect antidote to her unexpected nerves. 'Or, if you prefer, we could order a bottle of red? They've got their own wine list now.'

'No, that looks lovely.' Chloë watched as he poured the pale golden liquid into her glass with a satisfying 'glug glug'. There was something about white wine on a warm summer evening – red just wasn't the same. She took a sip.

'Chablis. Rather good, isn't it?'

'Yes,' Chloë agreed, thinking that anything other than Liebfraumilch would have done at this precise moment.

'So,' said James. 'Busy day?'

'Oh, the usual.' She was glad to focus on work. 'We've just gone to press so this time of the month isn't too bad – it's always worse towards the end. Today has been quite fun – commissioning articles and brainstorming ideas with my assistant. How was yours?'

'Actually, rather good. I had a meeting I was dreading at our printing house. I'd expected it to be a nasty confrontation, but in fact it went rather well. And,' he paused, 'I spoke to Vanessa Davenport, the Special Projects Manager.'

'Yes?' said Chloë, in trepidation. She'd seen this thin-faced, imposing-looking woman gliding around UK Magazines. Her reputation for making or breaking a project – and a career – was legendary.

'We had lunch yesterday, so I brought up your magazine idea, and she would like to meet you with a view to taking it further.'

Chloë was so thrilled could barely restrain herself from clapping her hands.

'One thing she did insist on, though, was that you make up some kind of dummy.'

Chloë reached for her bag. It was all was so exciting! 'I may sound like a presenter from *Blue Peter* . . . but here's one I prepared earlier.' She pulled out a mocked-up magazine and laid it on the table. 'The reason I didn't do this before is that most dummies I've worked on have tended to be made up of cuttings from other magazines. But what I have in mind is something so different that I wanted you to consider the concept in theory before seeing something definite. Also, to be perfectly frank, I wanted to establish you were interested first.'

As James began to flick through the dummy, Chloë sipped her wine. It rapidly imparted a warm glow.

Eventually he looked up, beaming. 'This is great – not the usual approach at all! I think Vanessa would love it. You two should get together as soon as possible.'

Chloë's confidence grew. 'You'll see,' she leaned over the table enthusiastically, 'that because I believe no magazines get it right currently I've hardly used any examples from British women's monthlies. Instead I've taken cuttings from a range of different publications – like this US magazine, *Bust*, and run-outs from the Net, club flyers, even book jackets and album covers. What you've got here is more of an indication of layout – the kind of photography and typography I have in mind. I've given a range of article ideas separately.' She handed him a second document.

James paused at a spread in the dummy. 'I like this.'

'It's from a US website – *ChickClick*. Wicked cartoons, don't you think?'

'Yeah. Why is it that women's magazines are so humourless?'

'God knows!' said Chloë, relaxing. 'If I want a laugh, I'd rather read some of the men's. Maybe people think women are miserable buggers.'

'Well, maybe not *all* people,' James said. '*You* don't seem a miserable bugger to me. But I do agree the magazine industry could be accused of such.'

'It's not that I don't have my ups and downs,' explained Chloë, 'and I believe there's a time and a place for looking at serious issues – in fact, I think that's really important – but to me life's not worth living if you can't have fun, at least *occasionally*.'

'Hmm . . .' said James, and looked at her. Their eyes locked for just a bit too long. His were the most amazing deep hazel. He glanced away. 'It's strange,' he muttered, then added, frankly: 'You remind me of someone.'

'Really?' Chloë was surprised he'd say such a thing. The conversation appeared to have taken a personal turn. 'I thought I was unique.'

'Well, I'm sure you are.' James laughed, and looked at her again for a bit too long. God! Did he know what that did to a woman? Chloë's stomach lurched. 'But you *do* remind me of someone.'

'Don't tell me,' said Chloë lightly, 'I remind you of your wife.'

'Who told you I was married?' James sounded disarmed. Clearly he hadn't known that she knew.

'Jean, I think. I gather she and your wife are friends.'

'Ah, yes, Maggie and Jean go back a long way. But, no, you're nothing like Maggie.'

Chloë didn't know how to take this, but curiosity got the better of her. 'Who, then?' she quizzed.

'A girl I once knew.'

'Oh.' Chloë was fazed.

'Broke my heart, though I didn't admit it to her or anyone else at the time. But enough of that. You're not here to hear about my problems. And, anyway, it was years ago. More wine?'

'Yes, please.' What kind of problems? He seemed the picture of a man who had it all. But Chloë wasn't a journalist for nothing. She wanted the whole story. Even more so because the longer she sat there, the more appealing she found him. In a way it was quite nice that he was unavailable – it allowed her to be really nosy. *And* she reminded him of an ex-girlfriend! How intriguing. Maybe Rob was right – maybe James did fancy her . . . Still, the indirect approach was probably the way to get him to reveal more about himself, so she shifted the conversation in a different direction.

Perhaps she could lead him back to this later. 'Let's order,' she prompted. 'I'm starving!'

Over the starter they talked more of the magazine. James explained that although he was happy to give it his blessing she would have to get first Vanessa then the board to back her before she could go ahead. And while Chloë knew that she had a lot further to go, she couldn't help but feel a burst of pleasure and boosted by his support of the project. By the time they finished the first course, she felt on a complete high. Indeed, she was flushed and needed a breather.

'Just going to powder my nose,' she said. 'Back in a minute.'

As she got up, James's mobile rang. He fished it out of his brief-case and looked at the number calling. Over his shoulder, Chloë glimpsed it too.

*Maggie*, it said.

# 6 Maggie

**Damn Jamie and** his sports equipment! Why couldn't he ever tidy it up instead of just throwing it in the hall cupboard after using it? It meant that Maggie, who was searching for her trainers, could never find anything.

Ah, there they were.

It was over a week since her shopping spree, and Maggie was pretty sure she wasn't pregnant. She had all the signs of a pending period, so although it was another three weeks until she was due to ovulate again, she had decided to adopt an additional strategy in the meantime: get fit. She'd considered joining a health club, but Maggie wasn't really an aerobics class person. All that communal activity wasn't her scene, and she rarely felt physically pushed. No, she'd rather be in control of her own regime, able to decide when and where she would exercise. It was just a question of disciplining herself. She pulled on the trainers and lifted one foot on to the towel rail of the Aga to stretch her hamstring. Leaning forward, she was glad to discover she was still quite flexible. She stretched the other leg, then her calves, and finally her upper arms, gently pulling each over and behind her head.

Outside on the gravel drive she jogged up and down, inhaling and exhaling to get used to the rhythm, then set off down the lane. She decided to follow her old route, thinking she would only manage one circuit.

Ah, the blue, blue sky, the fresh air pumping in and out of her lungs, the sound of her feet on the tarmac – this was why she loved running. She flew past neighbouring cottages with their lovingly tended gardens – it was little surprise that Shere had won several 'Best Kept Village' awards. She pounded up and over the wooden footbridge by the ford, alongside the row of vegetable patches by the river, and as she raced on through the main street, past the antiques shop and tiny museum, the White Horse and local post office, and out on to the country roads, Maggie surprised herself. Maybe she wasn't so unfit, after all.

Why would anyone want to use one of those silly machines, she thought, when they could have this – contact with the outdoors, that feeling of being part of the bigger scheme of things, be at one like this with nature?

There was something about going to a gym that had always struck her as phony – all that rowing and running and stepping on equipment made specially, surrounded by MTV and macho metallic décor and other people puffing and panting. Really these forms of exercise should be enjoyed in their original guise, on rivers, in lanes, up hills, come rain or shine.

Spurred on by appreciation of her surroundings, Maggie ran up the hill, with fields of ripening corn on either side of her. It was so rejuvenating being among growing things! Then it was through the woods and past the farm, with its comforting whiff of cow-dung and hay. This was where she bought her free-range eggs direct from the farmer's wife every week.

I really *must* get a commission for that piece I want to do on factory farming, she berated herself. Instead she was writing an uninspiring feature on Christmas cakes for the October issue of a magazine aimed at the kind of women who planned menus months ahead of the festive season. The subject didn't stimulate her. But Jamie's always on about how we need the money, she thought. If I have to compromise and bash out quick and easy articles that need little research to maximise my income, it's partly his fault. Perhaps we should never have mortgaged ourselves up to the hilt like we have.

Now she was energised by frustration too, and she headed back into Shere at an impressive speed. She had plenty of stamina, and before she knew it, she'd done two circuits – four miles. As she rounded the corner back into the village for a second time, a car passed her, and the woman driving gave her a friendly toot to encourage her. Maggie waved appreciatively.

Panting, she ran back up the drive, and slowed her pace to a walk. Well, she concluded, pushing damp hair off her forehead, maybe it wouldn't take ages to get back to the level of fitness she'd previously enjoyed. Before Nathan was born, she'd even run the London Marathon once.

Later that afternoon Maggie had to go in to Guildford to pick up a book she'd ordered to help with the cake article.

'I think I saw you earlier,' said the woman in Waterstone's as she checked the computer screen.

'Oh?'

'Running,' she said. 'In Shere, a couple of hours ago. I hooted at you.'

'Oh, yes,' replied Maggie. 'That was me.'

'You were running *very* fast.' The woman was full of admiration, and Maggie was flattered. 'You looked so much better at it than me! But, then, I'm a lazy old cow, so what can I expect? I drive everywhere.'

Maggie smiled. The woman was about her own age, with a bright, open face and messy chestnut hair – like a russet-coloured Old English Sheepdog.

'Do you live in Shere?' asked the woman. 'I've just moved there myself.'

'I do,' said Maggie, thinking how nice this woman looked. Perhaps at last there might be a kindred spirit in the village. 'In the big white house, on the corner.'

'That lovely Georgian one?'

Maggie was even more pleased. 'You must come over.'

'I'd love to. I don't know a soul round here yet.' She put out her hand. 'My name's Georgie.'

'Maggie,' said Maggie, shaking it. 'In fact,' she added, with unusual impulsiveness, 'what are you doing on Saturday night?'

That evening, Thursday, was traditionally Jamie's squash night. Maggie was more than happy for him to meet up in town with his old friend, Pete, once a week. She believed that letting him vent his work frustrations on a tiny ball within the confines of a squash court saved her a lot of aggro. Quite often she took the opportunity to visit her sister in Leatherhead.

Maggie and Fran were close, but their relationship had always been marked by a healthy sibling rivalry. There was only a year between them – Maggie was the elder – and in a pale-skinned English way they looked alike, although Maggie, with her fairer hair and paler blue eyes, was prettier. It was no coincidence that both had married successful men within a couple of years of each other. Indeed, it was partly when Fran saw Maggie being the focus of everyone's attention at her wedding to Jamie that she had decided Geoff was the man for her. Then Maggie had Nathan, and six months later Fran's son, Dan, was born.

Dan and Nathan got on well. Their closeness in age was a godsend: Maggie and Fran enjoyed each other's company while the two boys played together. As the boys thudded about in Dan's bedroom overhead, Maggie and Fran settled down for a chat in the kitchen.

'So,' Fran stretched out her long legs and propped her trainer-shod feet on another chair, 'how's your week been?'

'Okay,' answered Maggie. Then, realising this sounded rather downbeat, she went on more positively, 'Yes, actually, rather productive. I had a fun piece on aphrodisiac recipes to do for *Men*, and Jamie and I have been getting on a bit better.'

'Good. I told you, he's just working too hard. Any sign of it letting up?'

'Oh, I don't know about *that*,' said Maggie resignedly. 'A

leopard and his spots, you know. But at least he's been a bit more communicative recently.'

'Excellent.' Fran, who was a part-time teacher, sometimes sounded like she was giving Maggie's life school grades. 'So does this mean you've been having more sex?'

Maggie smiled at the memory of their kitchen exploits. 'Yes, as a matter of fact, we have,' she said, without volunteering lurid details. She always felt slightly embarrassed talking about sex with her sister, who seemed to show no such reserve. On the contrary, Fran always appeared to relish telling Maggie how well she and Geoff got on 'in the sack'. It made Maggie feel a bit inadequate.

'Mum,' Nathan came in and interrupted, 'I want to watch *Star Wars* and Dan won't let me.'

'Oh, darling, I don't know if we've got time,' said Maggie.

Fran looked at her watch. 'It's only half six. Dan!' she yelled. 'Come here!'

Dan came into the kitchen sheepishly. That tone meant trouble.

'How often have I had to tell you that when someone comes to our house you must be nice to them because they are the guest?'

'Nathan's not always nice to me when I go to his house,' Dan retorted. 'Last time he said I had to watch what he wanted because it was his video.'

'Oh, for goodness' sake, boys!' said Fran. 'I don't care what Nathan does in his house, but when he's here you play it by my rules, and I say you've got to be nice to your guest. Now, scoot!'

The boys left the room, Dan stomping, Nathan grinning.

'Ooh,' exclaimed Maggie, 'I forgot. I brought some food. It's in the car. I thought you and I could have it for supper. I'll just go and get it.'

She returned with a big saucepan clutched to her breast and a couple of packs of fresh pasta balanced precariously on top.

'Here, let me help.' Fran scooped up the pasta.

'It's *tagliatelli al amore*,' explained Maggie, putting down the pan.

Fran lifted the lid. 'Mm, smells delicious.'

'Seafood sauce with oysters. Designed to woo a woman virtually all on its own.'

'So this is one of your aphrodisiac recipes?'

'Indeed, it is – the second batch, to test I've got it right.'

'I'll put some on one side for Geoff. Can't have him slacking!'

'Of course not,' said Maggie, as an unwelcome image of Geoff and Fran making love popped into her head. She wondered if they had sex every night. It sounded like it, but surely not. 'Anyway, these things are best eaten fresh. Shall we heat it up now?'

'Let's have a glass of vino first,' said Fran. 'The boys can have their fish fingers in front of the telly.'

A couple of hours later they were still in the kitchen, enjoying that glorious full feeling. Fran picked up the bottle. 'One more?'

'I'd better not – I'm driving.'

At that moment Nathan and Dan burst in.

'Mum,' said Nathan, kissing her, 'can I stay the night?'

'Good Lord!' Nathan rarely kissed her these days. 'I thought you two were at each other's throats.'

'Oh, no,' said Dan sweetly. 'Nathan wants to share a bath so we can have a go with my special intergalactic bubble wash.'

'We ought to get back for Daddy.'

'Oh, he'll be all right,' encouraged Fran. 'Why don't you both stay over?'

'Go on, Mum, *please*,' whined Nathan.

'Go on, Auntie Maggie.'

'You could have some more wine then.' Fran wouldn't relent either. 'I'm sure Jamie can look after himself.'

Maggie looked at the bottle. It was so rare, these days, that she ever had more than a couple of glasses. And she and Fran were having rather a good time setting the world to rights. They had been having a satisfying rant about Tory sleaze and were just getting into their stride. 'Oh, okay,' she conceded. 'But, Nathan, no mucking around in the morning. We'll have to get up earlier to get you to school in time.'

'You're a lovely mummy,' said Nathan, and thundered upstairs again.

'Start running the bath!' yelled Fran after them.

'Obviously the oyster feel-good factor,' said Maggie. She reached for her bag and rummaged for her mobile. 'I'd better let

Jamie know we won't be home.' She dialled his number. 'Hi, it's me – I'm still at Fran's.' She could hear the sound of people laughing and chatting in the background. 'Where are you?'

# 7 Chloë

**By the time** they'd finished their main course, Chloë and James had shared the best part of two bottles of wine and Chloë was feeling mellow, woozy and well fed. Not being one to hold back, particularly after several glasses, she had given James the low-down on her life. She'd started with her diploma in journalism and career history, progressed to where she lived and her relationship with Rob, explaining how they'd been flatmates for nearly seven years and that Rob was gay. 'We get on brilliantly,' she said. 'Sometimes I think I'm closer to him than some of my straight friends are to their partners, but maybe that's *because* there's nothing sexual between us.' She wound up with her current single status – though she was careful to make it sound very short-term.

When it grew dark, the waitress came out and lit small candles on the tables. James shifted his chair a bit nearer, and as the atmosphere grew more intimate, Chloë questioned him, only half aware that her directness was rather exciting to a certain kind of man. Indeed sometimes, though she didn't do it deliberately, her frankness proved her most powerful weapon of seduction, refreshing and irresistible at the same time. She led him to reveal where he'd grown up (Sussex), that he'd a sister (older) and which university he'd been to (Exeter). Silently congratulating herself on her discoveries, she brought him back to the subject that had intrigued her earlier.

'So,' she reached over him to pour them each a final glass, 'tell me about this ex, then. Why do I remind you of her?'

'I'm not sure.' He frowned.

Chloë waited.

'You just look a bit similar.'

'Really? What was she like?' Chloë fished blatantly. It was always interesting to find out how she was seen by others.

'Oh, you know, smallish, about so high . . .' He gesticulated at some vague non-height. 'Curvy, sort of voluptuous.'

'You mean she was fat?' Chloë instinctively heard a criticism.

'No, not at all. Just very, well, you know, hour-glass. What I think of as a real woman.' He twisted his glass. 'Not convention-ally pretty, but kind of sexy. At least, I thought so. And dark – like you, I suppose. But what really reminds me of Beth is your energy, your vibrancy. You're a bit like her – sort of feline . . . and you have a similar spark.' He looked directly into her eyes. 'It's quite something.'

Chloë was speechless. She was fascinated, flattered and frightened all at once. Clearly Rob *had* hit the nail on the head. For all her self-doubt, she knew when someone was attracted to her – and now James had as good as said he was. She needed a few minutes to ground herself: she hadn't expected him to reveal quite so much so fast. She switched to the other subject she wanted to know about.

'So what's your wife like, then?' In some bizarre way Chloë hoped he would start gushing about her. If he was clearly unobtainable, she could prevent herself rushing in headlong. But no such salvation presented itself.

'Maggie? She's, um, very different.'

'What, physically?'

'Yes. In that way she's *completely* different. She's quite tall. Blonde. Leggy. You know, sort of naturally athletic-looking.'

'Sounds lovely,' said Chloë, genuinely. It was the way she'd always wanted to look.

'And she's, well, reserved, I suppose. Not introvert exactly . . . just contained. Sometimes I'm not sure what's going on with her.'

'Oh.' Chloë was confused, but curiosity had her on the edge of her seat. 'What made you go for two such different women? Beth, I mean, and her?'

'In all honesty I don't know,' said James, and then, candidly, continued, 'I suppose I may have been a bit on the rebound from Beth when I met Maggie, though I certainly didn't realise it at the time. I'd finished with Beth, after all.'

'Why?'

'I guess I got scared. Found her too much in some ways . Then, when I met Maggie, she seemed less of a handful, less up-front, more manageable. Oh, she had her passionate beliefs – her vegetarianism, her feminism and so on – and I loved that. But emotionally she was a lot less demanding – more *English*, if you know what I mean. So we started seeing each other and, well, one thing led to another, and here I am.' He stopped. 'Actually, that's not quite true,' he corrected. 'One thing did lead to another, but not in quite the way I'd planned. Maggie got pregnant, you see.'

'What? *Before* you got married?'

'Well, not exactly. We got married when we found out she was pregnant.'

'But wouldn't you have got married anyway?' Chloë was breathless with anticipation. All these revelations!

'I'm not sure,' admitted James. 'I mean, it's not as if I didn't love her – I did. Still do. We'd been living together for a couple of years, all her friends and her sister were settling down, and then, wham! She gets pregnant. We were using the rhythm method at the time.'

'So how old were you both, if you don't mind me asking?' enquired Chloë.

'I was thirty-one, she was thirty-two. It was nearly seven years ago.'

'I *see*,' said Chloë knowingly.

'What?'

'It's just it never ceases to amaze me,' Chloë burst out, 'how many women seem to get *accidentally* pregnant in their thirties. Until then they can find their way to a packet of condoms or the pill with their eyes shut, then, "Abracadabra!" They forget all about them.'

'That's rather unsympathetic of you.' James seemed taken aback.

'Well, actually I understand completely,' said Chloë. 'I'm not saying it from an unsupportive stance. I'm twenty-nine and I've been feeling a bit like that myself. There we all go, trundle, trundle, through our twenties, having one relationship after another, perhaps shagging around a bit, no great pressure to settle down . . . then oops! before we know it, we're thirty. Time's running out. But only for us women. And men barely notice anything has changed. They're happy to trundle on for as long as they feel like it. Enjoying relationships, yes, but unwilling to commit to anything more. So we resort to that time-honoured tactic – the *accidental* pregnancy. We may not acknowledge it even to ourselves, but our motives are more complex than they seem.'

James raised his eyebrows. 'You have a point. I suppose I have always wondered about that. But Maggie had very strong principles about certain things and she said there was no way she wasn't having it.'

'Anyway,' said Chloë brightly, suddenly feeling she might have opened a can of worms, 'I'm sure you're glad about it now, aren't you?'

'Yes . . .' James sounded hesitant. 'I mean, I don't regret having Nathan, not at all. I love him to death. And Maggie's a great mum. It's just . . . sometimes I think about it.'

'Think about what?'

'About what might have happened if I'd stayed with Beth.'

'You'll probably never know.' Chloë felt sympathy for this woman apparently so like her. 'You can't turn back time. Where is she now?'

'She moved back to New York years ago. She's married with two children.'

At that moment the waitress stopped at their table. 'Dessert?' she asked.

'I'd like a coffee,' Chloë stated, without waiting for James to contemplate whether he wanted any pudding. She was feeling decidedly tipsy and thought she'd better sober up, pronto. Or was it all the emotional honesty and sexual tension in the air?

'I'll have one too,' said James, and the waitress left.

'You'd better be getting back soon. What time's your last train?' Her conscience was niggling slightly. Perhaps she shouldn't have brought all this up.

James looked at his watch. 'Oh, I've ages yet.'

'Won't Maggie be expecting you?'

'No. She rang to say she's staying at her sister's tonight with Nathan.'

Chloë's heart missed a beat. Oh, my God! She *was* in deep. 'I think I fancy a cigarette.' She only smoked when she was nervous, or on occasions of enormous social recklessness.

'Me too. Have you got any?'

'No.'

'I'll go and get some,' volunteered James.

'Do they sell them here?' asked Chloë.

'I'll go to the pub,' James got up. 'Wait here.'

And before she had time to argue, he'd gone.

Two coffees and four cigarettes later, Chloë and James tumbled out on to the pavement. The August night was still warm, and Soho was buzzing. As they cut down Windmill Street and on to Shaftesbury Avenue, people were laughing and chatting every-where. The theatres were emptying, and the excited exchanges of tourists mingled with the more cynical critiques of locals. The lights of Piccadilly, the smell of the city, the energy of the crowds – it was central London at its most intoxicating.

'So what now?' asked James and, to Chloë's horror and delight, grabbed her hand.

Chloë tried to be firm. 'I think this is when I should go home.'

'So should I,' said James, but his expression said the opposite. 'But I haven't been out late like this for ages. Shall I tell you what I'd really like to do?'

'What?' She was afraid she already knew the answer.

'Go to a bar.'

Chloë, who was already pretty drunk, though by no means out of control, realised that she should accept the compliment of James' obvious attraction to her and run. But he's so sexy! her hedonistic alter-ego argued. Surely one more drink wouldn't hurt. She felt his hand in hers – it was as if an electric connection was shooting up her arm. It fuzzed her brain and sent rationality running for the hills. What the hell? You only live once.

'Okay.'

James led the way to The Player, a late-night club on Broadwick Street that barely advertised its existence outside. Down a flight of stairs and in a cellar, the atmosphere was sultry and smoky, the vibe cool. The dim red glow of the lighting made everyone appear their most beautiful – seduction hung in the air. Clearly it was designed for an élite who knew precisely where to go when their evenings didn't stop dead at eleven and the night was yet full of possibilities.

'What'll it be?' he asked, leaning against the counter. Chloë squeezed in next to him, acutely aware of his presence by her side.

'A margarita,' she said. Nothing beat tequila when she was in that bad-girl mood. 'No salt.'

'I'll join you,' said James and, with the assurance of a man who could get the attention of anyone he chose, signalled to the girl behind the bar. 'Make them large ones, in a tall glass.'

'Cheers,' he said, when the drinks arrived.

'Cheers.' Chloë clinked his glass and looked him in the eye. For a second she thought he was going to kiss her right then.

''Scuse me.' A drunken media exec pushed her out of the way in his keenness to get served, nearly knocking her drink flying.

'Shall we go and sit down?' asked James, and they headed for a table surrounded by low sofas.

Chloë took a seat. She noted that although he could easily have sat on his own sofa, James sat next to her. Again, she was conscious of his physicality, the crisp white of his shirt, the crumpled linen of his trousers, the polished leather of his shoes. By contrast her own outfit seemed particularly frivolous and girlie, but she quite liked that. She wondered how he looked in out-of-work clothes. Suits made it hard to place a man. But somehow she knew that whatever his taste, she was bound to approve.

James picked up on her thoughts. 'Great shoes,' he said.

'Thanks.' Chloë held her legs out in front of them so they could both admire her sandals' offbeat shape. As she swung her legs down, she manoeuvred slightly closer to him. 'Is that all that's great?' she asked.

'I think you know the answer to that.' James began to stroke her arm, with tiny movements of his fingers at first and then, as Chloë didn't rebuff him, with more assured motions of his whole hand. He edged closer to her. Almost before she knew it, they were kissing. Softly at first, then more intensely, and finally with full, caution-to-the-wind passion. The couple sitting opposite, the people at the next table, the woman whose elbow Chloë accidentally bumped off the back of the sofa behind her, none of it mattered. It was sensual, magical, heavenly. He ruffled her hair (she had good hair for ruffling – her unruly curls meant that men weren't worried about messing up some prissy style). Wives, work, principles, conscience, even tomorrow – none of it had any relevance. There were only the two of them, here, now.

And now she *did* want to go home. But not alone. So she pulled away from him, just enough to speak. 'Mmm,' she said, in a way that unashamedly expressed her appreciation of the experience. She reached forward for her cocktail, and as she did so, he ran his hand up her back, then inside her top. Fuck! When was she going to outgrow this sort of behaviour?

He smelt gorgeous – *irresistible* – and she kissed him again. Desire overwhelmed her. 'We could leave,' she said moments later.

'We could.' James took a large gulp of his margarita. 'C'mon.' He pulled her to her feet. 'Let's go.'

Chloë drained her drink and, as they left, slung the glass on the bar.

Her flat was on his way home, and things got even more heated on the way back in the taxi. Inevitably, he invited himself in 'for coffee' – the very thing she wanted too. Fumbling, she dropped her keys in the porch, and as she bent to pick them up, level with his crotch, she thought she could see he had a hard on.

Inside the flat, he pushed her up against the wall in the hall and kissed her again, more intensely still, urgently.

'Sshh! We'll wake Rob!' she whispered, took his hand and led him into the bedroom.

Immediately they fell on the bed and within seconds he'd removed her top, her skirt, her shoes. She undid his belt, his trousers – yes, he did have a hard on – and they kissed all the while. She had no lipstick on now, that was for sure. They shouldn't be doing this – but hell! She'd left resistance somewhere in Soho.

He slid his hand into her knickers – wow – that was it, there! Blimey, he certainly knew where everything was – and then, because what he was doing was *so* good, *so* delicious, she let him peel off her underwear and kiss her there too. He seemed content to do it for ages – bliss – knowing just when to be gentle, when to suck harder . . . and not to stop too soon, but to carry on . . . and on . . . She was going to come any minute – any second – now, **NOW!** (Christ! The noise – Rob!) And then she wanted it all, inside, and there was no point in stopping and, anyway, she didn't want to.

At four in the morning she woke, after about an hour's sleep, needing a drink. James was asleep beside her, his arm flung over her shoulder. Gently she lifted it off and slid out of bed, hoping she hadn't disturbed him. When she returned, he was awake and half sitting up. The room stank of sex. Lord, she could barely walk!

'You are one of the horniest, sexiest, most gorgeous women I have ever met,' he said, grabbing her and pulling her back into bed.

'Thank you.' At that moment Chloë felt gorgeously, hornily

sexy, head to toe. 'You're okay, too.' And to show she meant it, she slid slowly under the covers and licked down his chest – that oh-so-male broadness – down his belly. Down. Down.

Later, much later, she called another taxi so he could go home and change. And, later still, she bade him farewell on the doorstep, hastily slung-on silk petticoat exposed to the early-morning light of Battersea Rise.

# 8 Chloë

**It hurt.** It really hurt. With every pulse, the back of her head throbbed. She could feel the blood pumping round. White wine, red wine, tequila. Ouch. it was 7.45 a.m. Friday . . . Fuck.

Even Radio Four seemed loud.

Nurofen.

If she took Nurofen on top of that lot, it would mean she was a drug addict. She had one rule about drugs: wait for the last ones to wear off before taking more. Except tea – that didn't count.

Chloë tiptoed into the kitchen. God – it was a mess! She was glad James hadn't seen it. As she stood waiting for the kettle to boil, she cast her mind back to the night before. What had she done? What *hadn't* she done? She'd had sex. She'd had sex with a married man. And she'd not just had sex with a married man, she'd had sex with a married man who, while he wasn't her boss, could play a vital role in getting her ambitions off the ground. She tried to reason. Lots of people had to approve her magazine concept aside from him. And she hadn't slept with him because of that. But she could hear a voice – partly her mother's, partly her own: *'Now you're one of those women.'* What women? *'One of those women who sleeps with men to get what she wants.'* But that hadn't been why she'd slept with him.

Chloë poured the water into the mug. God, she felt awful. She opened the fridge, sniffed the milk – still OK – poured it into the tea, and returned to her room trying desperately to get her act together.

It had been great sex, though.

Mmmmm. Even through her hangover, she felt a warm, sensual rush as she recalled it. Her fingers still smelt of him, them.

Fuck!

It had been lovely. Why was it so . . . so *good* with some people? It wasn't that it wasn't good with others – Chloë tended to enjoy sex with most of the men she slept with, especially now that she was older and more confident about saying what she liked – but there were a few with whom it was just . . . well . . . better. More . . . Fun? Yes. Passionate? Yes. Daring? Yes, that too. She remembered his touch. Stroking her right from her feet, slowly up her thighs, over her hips, in at the waist, up to her breasts, circling there, teasing – oops, she was getting turned on all over again – stroking her neck, then her hair . . . his mouth, kissing . . .

*That* was why she'd done it. That kissing. That was how it had started. Or was it that because she'd thought he was safe – because he was married – she'd been less guarded, more at ease? Then there was the tequila, of course. And the things he'd said about that woman in America, his ex. And he *had* seemed to really like Chloë, to fancy her. And, damn it, she really liked him. It had been a lovely – no, *unforgettable* night. They had got on so well – he'd been so open and easy to talk to. So interesting, so interested in her, so charming, so sexy . . .

Better have a shower. Go to work. She *had* to go to work. Shit! Would she see him? Would everyone be able to tell?

Round and round, the thoughts went. Bong, bong, went her head. It was a weird combination – the bus to work (normal), the hangover (not unheard-of), the lack of sleep on a workday (unusual but something she had done before), the *I-went-out-for-dinner-with-the-publisher-of*-UK-Magazines-*to-discuss-my-idea-which-he-likes-who's-married-with-a-child-and-we-slept-together-and-he-was-gorgeous-and-it-was-great* (a totally new scenario). It was all so recent, so complicated, so awful, so fantastic, it was totally beyond her powers of comprehension.

'Bloody hell!' said Patsy, as Chloë plonked her bag on her desk. 'What happened to you?'

'Nothing.'

'You look like shit.'

'Thanks,' said Chloë.

'Bacon sandwich?'

'Um.' Chloë thought for a moment. 'Good idea.' She fumbled for her purse.

'It's on me,' said Patsy, and bounced out of the office, trendy velcro wallet in hand, looking sickeningly healthy. A little later she returned with a white paper bag, grease seeping through already.

'You're a doll,' said Chloë, peering into the bag. It looked foul. Could this really help? She took a bite. Delicious. Brown sauce squidged on to the article she was trying to focus on.

'So,' chivvied Patsy. 'Tell all.'

Ten minutes had given Chloë the time to fabricate a tale. 'Rob,' she said. 'His birthday. You know. His crowd – they love to party. We hit Soho.'

'You're such a fag hag!' laughed Patsy. 'And I thought you'd had a shag.'

'Ha!' feigned Chloë. 'Not bloody likely. Well . . .' She rummaged in her in-tray for authenticity. 'What's on today?'

She got through the day with the help of several cans of Red Bull and Patsy, who fended off callers with a heroism that would have made Robert the Bruce proud. At lunchtime they resorted to their favourite hangover cure – shopping at the Top Shop superstore in Oxford Street, and Chloë, who didn't really have the energy to remove her clothes again, waited patiently on the big satin chairs outside the changing room while Patsy tried on endless funky yet affordable outfits.

There was one call that afternoon, however, that Chloë did take. Not least because it came through internally on her direct line so she didn't have any choice.

'Chloë?' It was a woman's voice that Chloë didn't immediately recognise.

'Yes?'

'It's Vanessa Davenport here. Is now a good time?'

'Er, um, ish.' Chloë glanced over at Patsy, who was busy typing but whose gossip radar was legendary.

'I've just had a word with James Slater.'

Chloë's heart lurched.

'He showed me your proposal and says you've made up a dummy. I thought we ought to meet for a chat.'

'That would be great.'

'Obviously James can recommend ideas to me,' Vanessa explained, 'but it's me you'd be working with, should we decide to take on the project.' Chloë understood clearly what she was saying: *You might be in with James, but you'll have to win me over too.* As Special Projects Manager it was Vanessa's job to handle the day-to-day business of launching new titles. 'How about lunch next week, say, Tuesday?'

'Lovely,' said Chloë.

'I'll ring you in the morning and we'll arrange somewhere then.'

When Chloë hung up, she couldn't help but wonder what James had said about her. Presumably it was good or Vanessa wouldn't have phoned – and she must have been on his mind to contact Vanessa in the first place. She wondered if he was as hungover as she was. Would he ever call her again? She doubted it – surely he'd only been able to get away like that for one night. So, would their relationship be purely business from now on? Would the fact that she'd had sex with him affect his professional dealings with her? She hoped to hell not. Would he tell his wife? She felt a pang of remorse at the prospect, then told herself that of course he wouldn't. But his wife might find out anyway. Some women just *knew*. Horrors – what if she came round and confronted her? Worse, if she confronted her in the office. In front of Patsy,

Vanessa, Jean and everyone. Imagine if she (Maggie) grabbed her (Chloë) by the hair and tried to throw her down the stairs! Or, what if James was so bowled over by Chloë's sex appeal and intelligence that he decided to leave Maggie at once? Indeed, what if he turned up on her doorstep in Battersea later that night with a suitcase and hang-dog expression?

Chloë's mind was in overdrive. She wanted to call him, but what would she say? And with Patsy tip-tapping away right by her – not to mention all the other complications – even Chloë knew that it would be foolish in the extreme. She bit her lip. For once she must curb her inclinations to talk about anything, although every bone in her body itched to confide in someone. It would have to wait until she got home. There she knew she could off-load it all on Rob. So, once she'd clarified that he was going to be in – 'Of course, girl!' he said. 'It's Friday! *Frasier* and *Friends*' – she put the kibosh on any further attempts to clarify her whirling thoughts and busied herself sorting through the piles of press releases in her pending tray.

Back at home, Rob and Chloë curled up on the sofa with the cat snuggled in a contented half-moon in his favourite spot between them, and waited for the delivery of a fifteen-inch extra crunchy, deep-pan, supreme pizza.

'So,' said Rob, 'was that you I heard crashing around the hall in the small hours? Either you were so pissed you were making enough noise for two or you had a man with you. Please tell me it was the former.'

'I think we'd better set the video,' warned Chloë.

'Oh, my God!' screamed Rob theatrically. 'That means trouble! You did, didn't you? You brought him back here! You did. Oh, Lord! You went – what? All the way? You actually slept with him?'

'Yes,' admitted Chloë.

'So . . .' said Rob eagerly. 'Was it good?'

That was what she loved about Rob. He was very non-judgemental. Perhaps it was because his own behaviour was pretty reprehensible at times that his moral code was so flexible.

'The best,' sighed Chloë.

'Aggggh!' shrieked Rob. 'This warrants a glass of wine.' He virtually skipped into the kitchen. Sex, scandalous sex, forbidden sex – he was in his element. 'Want one?'

'I couldn't.' Chloë shook her head. 'But you go ahead.'

Once Rob had settled back down with his glass and Chloë had set the video for Channel 4, she began. 'So we met at this little restaurant in Lexington Street—'

'Stop, stop!' Rob held up his hand. 'I want to know what you were wearing!'

'Ah, yes,' said Chloë, conscious it hadn't been the Whistles suit. 'That, um, criss-cross turquoise top, that black lace skirt and my Miu Miu sandals.'

'That criss-cross top that makes your boobs look like the best in Christendom?'

'The very same,' Chloë admitted.

'Shit. You're *irresistible* in that. Almost enough to turn me straight. Jesus, woman, you are so naughty! I warned you, dress like you mean business.'

'Anyway,' Chloë ignored this, 'so I arrive at this restaurant – Aurora, do you know it?'

'Indeed I do. Great menu and fab homely décor. Hangout of the discreet media in-crowd. Good choice – his?'

Chloë was proud to be mixing with someone who knew such prestigious venues. 'Yes.'

'And what was he wearing?'

'A suit.'

'More!' cried Rob. 'I want more! Precise, girl, be precise.'

'Okay, okay. A navy linen suit – didn't see the label, but it looked expensive – only he wasn't wearing the jacket, he'd taken that off when I arrived – and a white cotton shirt. He had his sleeves rolled up.'

'Could you see his forearms?' gasped Rob.

'They're to die for.'

'Oh, my God! I'm feeling horny already.'

'So he pulls this bottle of wine from the bucket, dripping—'

'How erotic!'

'—and offers me a glass.'

'Which you guzzle 'cos you're a bit nervous and, anyway, you always knock back the first glass rather quickly.'

'Exactly,' said Chloë. He knew her so well. 'And then we discuss the magazine.'

'Oh,' said Rob, sounding deflated. 'Cut that out. We'll come back to that. I want the sex – now!'

'Okay.' Having been restraining herself all day, Chloë was glad to cut to the chase. 'So then, he starts to look at me strangely, you know a bit too long, and he begins confessing about this ex-girlfriend of his in New York, Beth, her name was, and says how I remind him of her, how I've got the same spark, and that he, well she broke his heart, though he left her and . . . to be honest, Rob, it sounded like he was still in love with her and not in love with his wife at all!'

'No!' exclaimed Rob.

'Well, that's what's he *said* . . . Though I suppose he could have just been saying that.'

'Um,' said Rob, a cynical tone creeping into his voice. 'It's amazing what some men come up with to get their end away. But we'll analyse later. I want gore! So tell me – did he have a big willy?'

'Of course,' said Chloë.

'Thick?'

'Very,' grinned Chloë. 'In fact pretty thick *and* long.'

'I am *so* jealous!'

'Don't you want to know what he did with it?'

'Oooh, no, all that heterosexual stuff. Makes me feel a bit squeamish. I suppose you could tell me about giving head though. I can cope with that. So, did you?'

'I did.'

'Before, or after, he did it to you?'

'How do you know he did it to me?'

''Cos you'll never let a man get away without doing it, you love it so much.'

'True. Anyway, I like to make sure a man has earned it.'

'How many shags?'

'Two,' said Chloë. 'But they lasted for hours. Or, at least, a long

58

time. The first was all, you know, heated, the second more slow and sensual.'

'Did he take you from behind?'

'Rob!'

'Well, did he?'

'Yes, actually, he did – at some point during the first time. But the second time he didn't – we just well, looked into each other's eyes.'

'Oh boring soppy stuff,' said Rob. 'I suppose you came together too!' Chloë's expression obviously said they had. Rob stopped and looked at her a bit more seriously. 'Oh dear.'

'What?'

'You're not hoping this is more than a one-night stand, are you?'

'Of course not!' Chloë lied.

'Good.' Rob sounded relieved. 'Because what with his being married, your publisher and all, it would be a *disaster* to take this any further.'

Chloë knew that was true. But, God, when she thought of him deep inside her, watching his face as he came, she couldn't bear for it never to happen again.

# 9 Maggie

'**Who did you** say was coming tonight?' asked Jamie. He was sorting the silver.

'I've told you,' said Maggie impatiently. She was concentrating on chocolate mousse, which was at a crucial stage. It was not a good moment to interrupt a perfectionist.

'Tell me again.'

Why couldn't he listen the first time? 'Jean and Simon, William and Liz, Alex and Georgie.'

'Alex your old flame?' asked Jamie. 'I thought his wife was called Stella.'

'She is. Or rather was. They're divorcing.'

'Really?' Jamie was surprised. 'Why?'

'I don't know the full story.' Now the mixture was ready. Skilfully Maggie poured it into eight glass bowls. 'Perhaps we'll find out more this evening. Never liked her much, anyway. Thought she wasn't right for him – too out for herself.'

'You were always so nice to her.'

'I know,' admitted Maggie. 'I didn't want her to be threatened by me.'

'Was she? She didn't seem the insecure type.'

'I don't know,' said Maggie. Then, abandoning false modesty, 'Alex always said she was.'

'Oh?' Jamie sounded miffed – just the response Maggie had intended to engender. He'd been rather preoccupied the last couple of days, and had shown little interest in the supper party to which she was looking forward enormously. 'He's still got a bit of a thing for you, hasn't he?'

Maggie felt guilty for winding Jamie up. 'Not really. Anyway, I met this really nice woman in the bookshop the other day. She's just moved in round the corner so I thought I'd ask her along to even up the numbers. You never know, they might take to each other.'

'And she's called Georgie.' Jamie had finally got it clear. 'So, why's she moved here? Not much of a place for a single woman.'

'Maybe she likes the country.' Maggie resented the implication that the area was only suited to the dull and married. 'I gather her job has just been transferred to Guildford. She runs Waterstone's there.'

'Hmph. A bookworm. Sounds right up Alex's street.'

'Why are you always so foul about him?' asked Maggie, carefully placing the bowls in the fridge. But she knew very well. Alex had been the major relationship of her student years and they had always had a soft spot for each other. Then, years later, only weeks before her wedding, Alex, who was completely ignorant she was pregnant, had asked Maggie to get back together with him. She'd never told Jamie, but she thought he knew that Alex had carried a torch for her right up until the last minute.

'Actually,' she said pointedly, 'Georgie seems really good fun.' She checked her watch. 'They'll be here in half an hour. Have you finished?' Jamie grunted. 'Then you'd better put Nathan to bed while I get changed.'

Fifteen minutes later she was showered and sitting wrapped in a towel at the dressing-table, feeling far more in control of everything.

'There,' said Jamie, patting his face dry as he emerged from the bathroom to join her. As Maggie put the final touches to her makeup, she watched his reflection as he got ready.

The ritual was virtually the same as it was each morning. First, he dried himself thoroughly – the bathroom was too steamy, he always maintained. When he'd finished he dropped the towel on the floor.

'Oh, hang it up, Jamie,' she cajoled.

He did as he was told. Now he rummaged in a drawer for a clean pair of underpants. As he pulled on the fitted boxers she smiled: they were the black Calvins she'd given him for Christmas. Next he selected a pair of trousers – an almost new pair of chinos – and a shirt. He pulled on the trousers and zipped the fly. Then, with a *swoosh!* he removed the belt from his Paul Smith work suit, and threaded it through the chinos. He'd got it on the last hole, she noted. Oh dear, was he getting too tubby? That was followed by his socks (*after* his trousers – apparently an ex-girlfriend had told him years ago that the sight of a man in his socks and underpants was hilarious, so it was a combination he'd avoided religiously since). No, she thought, even though he had put on a couple of pounds in the last year or two – probably thanks to her moreish cooking and an increasing number of business lunches – he still had that certain something. He was broad-shouldered enough to retain that pleasing V shape that made his outline so different from hers. Yes, she thought fondly, he's still a very attractive man.

'Inside or out?' he asked about the shirt, tucking and untucking it.

She realised with a jolt that he was dressed and ready before she was. 'Out,' she advised.

He left the room and went downstairs, while she got out her clothes. Tonight, she decided, beneath a navy shift dress, she would wear the new basque.

At a quarter to eight the doorbell rang. It was Jean and Simon, as usual meeting a deadline with time to spare. Jean looked chic in black chiffon; Simon – who, bless him, wasn't ageing so well, having lost most of his hair, his best feature – had made the effort and put on a suit. Fifteen minutes later William and Liz arrived, equally smart, then Georgie, in a pretty floral dress, and finally Alex. Typically, he was half an hour late, and he hadn't dressed up at all. In fact, he looked rather scruffy. But as he grinned at Maggie winningly, told her she looked ravishing and handed over not just wine but her favourite dark Belgian chocolate, she decided to let him off. Alex could get away with murder, thanks to his naughty-boy charm.

When all the guests were gathered, drinks in hand, nibbles in reach and introductions over, Maggie began to relax. Because she was sure that every last detail had been taken care of and she was in the company of her oldest and best friends (bar Georgie), it didn't take as long as usual for her to lose her initial reserve. She turned to Jean. 'How's work?'

'*Exhausting,*' sighed Jean. Maggie knew that really she loved being editorial queen, and that long-suffering was part of her natural disposition. 'You know how it is. And I must say, though I have a good team, at times I *despair* of some of my junior subs. Call me old-fashioned, darling, but it does seem education ain't what it used to be. I'm constantly picking up grammatical errors at the eleventh hour! And the spelling! I was thinking on the drive down here, *please* make sure Nathan goes to a good secondary school, won't you? I couldn't bear it if he can't tell his arses from his asses! Only last week I picked up a classic error in an article about agoraphobia. We'd split 'therapist' over two lines into 'the' and 'rapist' – changed the meaning of the interview completely. Had to get my features editor to go through it with a tooth-comb. Actually,' she turned to Jamie, 'didn't you come in and see her while I was out the other day? What was that all about?'

'What?' Jamie jumped to attention.

'Chloë,' Jean clarified. 'Chloë Appleton. Didn't you come in to see her last week?'

'Oh, er, yes. I thought it'd be a good idea to introduce myself to the senior members of staff at UK Magazines. I'm eventually hoping to get round them all. Information gathering, you know.'

'Gosh, how *thorough*,' said Jean. 'Sounds a bit over-keen to me, though. Just like when you've got a new car. For the first few weeks you're out there cleaning and polishing every Sunday but sooner or later you're back to your old ways. I'm sure that once you've talked to more than one features editor, you'll feel like you've talked to them all.'

'Doubtless that's the case. But so far I've found it most enlightening. So,' Jamie turned to Georgie, 'all this magazine chat must be rather dull for you. How's life in the fast lane at Waterstone's?'

Maggie winced. She could recognise Jamie's sarcasm all too easily. She hoped it would pass Georgie by.

'You'd be surprised.' Georgie grinned. 'It's just one earth-shattering crisis after another. "Are the stocks on *Roget's Thesaurus* running low?" "Have we got that order in for Mrs Bradshaw yet? She's rung twice already today." "Can we persuade that obscure local author to do a signing to boost sales?"'

Maggie warmed to Georgie even more. She liked a woman who didn't take herself too seriously. She glanced over at Alex. From the way he was leaning forward listening eagerly, it looked as if he might rather like her too.

'How did you get into the book world?' asked Jamie.

'I kind of fell into it,' said Georgie. 'It wasn't some major career plan. It was just the first job I got after college.'

'Know the feeling. But you must be pretty good at it. Maggie said you're in charge of Waterstone's in Guildford. It's one of their biggest branches, isn't it?' Clearly he was prepared to be more charming now Georgie had revealed that she wasn't a member of the highbrow literati.

'It is. I do like a book that's easy to read and I quite like working out what is going to sell and what isn't. But what I most enjoy is the people side, managing my staff. They're a really nice bunch.'

Maggie could see she'd be good at that.

'Well, you're obviously getting something right,' continued Jamie. 'Waterstone's seems to be doing rather well. I must admit, I love it in there.'

'You do?'

'Oh, yeah,' he said. 'It's very user-friendly.'

'I'm glad you think so.' Georgie relaxed visibly at his compliment. 'Some people give us a lot of flak.'

'But they probably want to keep book-selling in the Dark Ages. There are plenty of people like that in the magazine world too. Aren't there, Jean?'

'Indeed there are.' Jean nodded.

Maggie listened while Jamie drew Georgie out, helping her feel at ease among a group of strangers. He could be such good company when he wanted to be, she thought proudly. It was one of the things that had first attracted her to him – his social grace.

'Anyway, everyone,' interrupted William, 'we've got an announcement to make.'

'Oooh, goodie!' exclaimed Jean, clapping her hands. 'I love announcements.'

'We're having another baby.' Liz beamed.

Maggie felt a jolt of both pleasure and envy. 'Congratulations,' she said warmly. 'When's it due?'

'I'm four months,' Liz lifted up her flowing top to reveal a small bump, 'so, just before Christmas.'

'How *wonderful*,' said Jean. She was always far too much in demand to spare time for a child so had never wanted her own. Still, at least she was honest about it, she was always happy for others, and Simon didn't seem to mind.

'Well,' said Liz, turning to Jamie and Maggie, 'when are you two going to have another?'

'Actually we're trying now,' said Maggie. Such an intimate revelation was unusual for her, but these were her dearest friends.

'Oh, how exciting!' said Liz.

'That's half the fun, isn't it, darling?' William kissed his wife. 'So, Jamie, looking forward to being a father all over again?'

'Um,' said Jamie. 'All those late nights. Can't wait.'

'But it'll be worth it,' Liz prompted.

'I suppose so.'

Maggie looked at him. Was he sounding a bit detached? Not as happy at the prospect as she was? She took a sip of wine and galvanised herself. Somehow, being surrounded by her friends gave her the courage to say what she might otherwise have avoided. 'I think I'm keener on the idea than Jamie,' she said, hoping he would contradict her. When he didn't, an awkward silence filled the room. Maggie was devastated. The silence seemed endless, but she was too upset to speak.

Eventually Simon came to her rescue. 'Oh, Jamie, I'm sure you'll come round when it's born,' he said.

'Just think how much pleasure Nathan gave you when he was really small,' Jean reminded him. 'I've never seen a father more in love.'

'True,' admitted Jamie. 'I guess I'm just a bit fraught at having to deal with it all and a new job. I worry about the money, too. Running this place costs us an arm and a leg as it is.'

'Oh, goodness!' cried Jean. 'Look at you both! Huge house in the country, both of you working – *surely* you can afford it. Women in council flats have dozens of children on a tenth of your income.'

'And they're pretty miserable,' said Jamie.

'I'd better get on with the dinner.' Maggie got up, thankful to leave the room.

'Can I lend a hand?' asked Alex.

'Yes.' She could do with the support in more ways than one. Jamie's admission had left her bruised and vulnerable.

In the kitchen Alex held out the tureen while Maggie sloshed in the soup. 'Don't worry,' he said. He knew her so well she didn't have to explain how she was feeling. 'You always said Jamie is lousy at stress. He'll be all right once he's settled into his new job.'

'Yes, of course he will,' Maggie said quietly, trying to convince herself. 'Anyway,' she changed the subject – laying bare her soul was not her strong point, 'what do you think of Georgie?'

## 10 Maggie

**As Maggie drifted** in and out of sleep the next morning, a faint sadness tinged her dreams. And when she woke fully, the feeling grew heavier, so that a small movement to brush away silent tears was her first conscious action of the day. It took a few seconds for her to remember why.

Jamie.

The supper party had been a great success. The food had been immaculately presented and delicious, and her guests had got on superbly. Jean had drunk too much, but that was nothing new. Saturday night was the one opportunity she had all week to kick off her eminently practical court shoes and let her neatly bobbed hair down, so to speak. The relief, however short-lived, of not having to be a dynamic editor meant she had knocked back a couple of glasses too many and had released her tension in a series of spleen-venting outbursts on completely unrelated subjects, many of which she knew little about but on all of which she had a strong opinion. Finally she'd fallen asleep on the sofa, snoring in a very un-chic fashion while everyone else continued chatting around her.

William had been his usual gregarious self, and had diplomatically dropped the subject of Liz's pregnancy, using her instead as a foil for amusing tales of their university days with Maggie and Alex.

'Remember that row we had about M & S food?' he'd reminded Maggie. 'How I sent you the container and highlighted the ingredients just to prove their meals weren't full of additives?'

'I do,' Maggie had retorted. 'But I seem to recall what really got my goat was the way you were prepared to spend half your grant on pre-prepared food—'

'—when the miners were on strike and starving!' William had finished for her, laughing. 'Though Arthur Scargill always looked pretty well fed to me, I must say.'

The real hit of the night, however, had been Alex and Georgie, who had bonded quite noticeably over a shared passion for foreign film and a mutual loathing of Martin Amis's books, and finally Alex had offered to give Georgie a lift home.

Maggie couldn't help feeling a little put out when she recalled their chemistry. She'd done a marvellous job of disguising her own feelings all evening, and had been the charming host she was known to be, but underneath she was smarting from what Jamie had said. Watching her old boyfriend flirt with someone else had only made her feel worse.

Not that Alex hadn't been nice to her – he was always good at dealing with other people's upsets. Helping to smooth ruffled feathers came naturally to him and he'd taken several opportunities to check that she was okay, jumping up from the table at the end of each course before anyone else had the chance to carry out the dirty dishes. That way he could grab a few seconds alone with her in the kitchen. But Maggie was too intent on serving up the perfect meal and making sure everyone had a good time to be drawn into discussion about her emotions, so she'd deflected his enquiries with a repeated 'I'm fine'. Instead she'd numbed the hurt with a couple of extra brandies, which was unusual given her abstemious nature and had simply deepened her post-party blues.

Seeking solace from the person who had caused her pain, she reached over to touch Jamie's dark hair. It was beginning to curl around the nape of his neck, she noticed, and could do with a trim. He was still sleeping, tucked almost entirely under the crisp white cotton sheets, his back to her, a familiar early-morning pose. They both found sleeping too close stifling and claustrophobic; he'd always said it made him hot. Indeed one of the prerequisites of their new home when they'd moved to Shere was that it should have a bedroom big enough to house a really generous double bed.

The longer she lay there, the more convinced she became that making love would make her feel better, however temporarily. But Maggie was a proud woman, and initiating love-making did not come easily to her. It was certainly not something she felt confident in doing all that often. But now the new basque lay neatly draped over the dressing-table chair – a sad contrast to the way it had been flung on the floor so passionately ten days previously. Over it lay her stockings, still showing traces of the three-dimensional shape they'd borne the night before. Maybe erotic underwear wasn't her scene after all.

Eventually, Jamie rolled over and opened his eyes. For a moment he looked mystified, then he seemed to realise she was crying. 'I'm sorry,' he said, stroking away her tears. It sounded heartfelt – as if he really meant it, and was upset to have made her so miserable. Uncertain how to repair things, he asked, 'Shall I make us a cup of tea?' This was hardly the closeness she craved, but it was a start.

'That would be nice,' she said.

Later that morning Jamie took Nathan to play football, and, hoping that it might help clear her head and improve her mood, Maggie went for a run. As it was Sunday, the village was packed with visitors to the regular antiques fair, but she fancied a change, so instead of heading out of Shere as usual, she followed Nathan and Jamie to the recreation ground. If she ran around the edge of the pitch, she could watch them play.

'Mum!' shouted Nathan, on seeing her. 'Watch me!' And with

that he focused seriously on the space between the two jumpers that had been laid out as goal and kicked with all his might. Jamie obviously sensed it was important for Nathan to score in front of his mother so he dived dramatically the wrong way. The ball rolled past his feet – not fast, but it was a goal all the same.

'Hurray!' whooped Nathan. 'Silly billy, Daddy.'

'Ouch,' said Jamie, getting up and rubbing his knees. These days he wasn't really fit enough to land with quite the same aplomb with which he'd dived.

'Well done!' called Maggie, stopping to jog on the spot and clap. 'Silly Daddy.'

Jamie threw the ball down to the far end of the pitch. Nathan ran after it, and began dribbling it back to the goal.

'Viera . . . neatly picks the ball up from defence,' roused Jamie. Maggie recognised his mock-Irish as the passionate commentator from *Five Live*. 'Still Viera . . . he feints past Keane, now shrugs off Scholes. It's still Viera. Oh . . . this is impressive stuff from the Frenchman. He's passed Stam, it's just the keeper to beat now, *Viera* . . . Agggh!' Nathan kicked and missed. 'Obviously today he's on somewhat erratic form.'

Maggie laughed. She loved watching Jamie and Nathan play soccer, being such boys together. As she continued running and they continued playing, her spirits began to lift. She noticed that Jamie always allowed Nathan to remain a couple of goals ahead. And to even the odds, when Nathan was goal-keeping, Jamie encouraged him to move the jumpers closer together to narrow the goal area and make it easier for him to save. And when it was Jamie's turn and Nathan was out in the field, they moved the jumpers and widened the goal. Given her husband's competitive temperament, this was particularly endearing. Nathan was the only person he'd happily allow to humiliate him, she thought.

After ten circuits she was ready to return home, but she had an urge to go back via Georgie's, which was just by the church. As she ran up to her cottage, she saw Georgie in the garden, bent over pulling up weeds. A quick scan of the street revealed no sign of Alex's car. He'd either made an early-morning exit or hadn't stayed, she thought.

'Hiya!' she said, reaching the gate.

'Oh, hi,' said Georgie, straightening and attempting to scoop her dishevelled chestnut mop back into her hair clip. 'I just phoned you but there was no one there.'

'I was out running,' Maggie puffed, 'and Jamie and Nathan are playing football.'

'Gosh, you are good, going for a run after all that booze! How do you do it?'

'I enjoy it,' explained Maggie truthfully.

'Yes, but being so fit and such a wonderful cook! It's so impressive. You seem to have everything sorted. Not only are you talented and gorgeous, but you've a beautiful home and boy too. I'm quite jealous.'

Well I never, thought Maggie. If only Georgie knew how miserable she'd been feeling.

'Anyway,' continued Georgie, 'I was ringing to thank you. It was a terrific party.'

'My pleasure,' said Maggie. 'You seemed to get on especially well with Alex.'

'I thought he was lovely,' Georgie gushed. 'Nice-looking too, in a cheeky sort of way, don't you think? And, oooh, that voice!'

Maggie raised her eyebrows. Perhaps she'd underestimated Alex's appeal. 'I'd never really thought about it. Though now you come to mention it, I suppose it is rather nice and deep.'

'I'll say. In fact, I know I shouldn't have, but when he dropped me off I asked if I could see him again.'

'Really?' said Maggie, uncharitably pleased that the pass had come from Georgie rather than the other way round. 'What did he say?'

'He seemed pretty keen. We're supposed to be going to see something at the National Film Theatre next week. I said I'd give him a call.'

'That's great!' Maggie would never have dared to be so bold.

'Yes, isn't it? He seems a very nice guy.'

'He is. What you see is what you get with Alex. I expect you'll have a really good time. Anyway,' she turned, 'I'd better get back. I've got to put the lunch on. Let me know all about it.'

'I will,' Georgie grinned. 'And thanks again,' she called after her.

When Maggie got home there were three messages on the answerphone, from Georgie, then Fran, asking if she could come over to tap into Maggie's culinary expertise – apparently she was planning on doing some basic cooking with her class at school and was after some recipes for children – and finally Alex, to thank her for a lovely evening. First Maggie spoke to Fran, then rang Alex.

'Did you have a nice time, then?' she asked, hoping he would spill the beans.

'*Super,*' he said, then obviously remembered that maybe she hadn't. 'Did you?'

'Yeah, yeah.' Maggie brushed his concern aside. 'And I've just been for a run. Feel much better.'

'Really?' Alex sounded sceptical. 'I must say you looked as delicious as ever –' Maggie couldn't help laughing '– and as for the food, you surpassed yourself. *Fantastic* starter, those oysters.'

How ironic, she thought. Maybe the aphrodisiac had worked on him and Georgie.

After lunch Fran arrived. 'Are you okay?' she asked, the moment Maggie opened the front door.

Heavens, thought Maggie, do I look that bad? 'Yes. Why?'

'You sounded a bit upset on the phone.'

'Oh, well, I feel better now.'

Fran knew she had to push to get her sister to open up. 'Now you do. So you didn't earlier.'

'It's probably nothing,' said Maggie, leading her into the kitchen. Jamie and Nathan were in earshot, watching telly in the living room. Then the pressure of keeping things to herself finally got too much. 'Jamie doesn't want another child – he said so at this supper party last night. In front of everyone – it was awful. He said we can't afford it, and then, when we went to bed, I asked him again, and he said it's not that he doesn't want one ever it's just that he'd rather wait a bit. But, Fran, I'm thirty-nine next month. If we wait much longer – Nathan's seven in October and, well, I don't know if I can.'

'Hmm,' said Fran, and filled the kettle as if it were her own home. 'It's the other way round with me and Geoff. He wants one now, I want to wait.'

'Yes, but you're younger.'

'I know.' Fran enjoyed being reminded of this. 'But, still, isn't it funny? Even when you've got one, it's still not that easy deciding when or if to have a second. All the way through life, it seems everything comes down to timing. And I thought it only affected whether or not you could persuade a chap to settle down. How wrong I was.'

'I know,' sighed Maggie. 'Sometimes I feel as if Jamie and I are just a year or two out of sync.'

Fran tried to make light of it. 'Maybe it's because he's the same age as me.'

'Maybe.'

'I tell you what you need,' said Fran naughtily.

'What?'

'A little extra-curricular. That would take your mind of it.'

'Fran!' Maggie was shocked. 'You can't be serious.'

'Well, I'm not, entirely. But I think you're suffering from a severe case of being taken for granted. What you need is attention from another admirer. Nothing serious, of course, just a bit of flirtation.'

'Oh, I couldn't. Jamie would be so hurt.'

'I'm not suggesting you tell him!' protested Fran. 'And I'm not really meaning you should even *do* much, just enjoy being fancied by someone else. After all, here you are, stuck in this house all day on your own while Jamie's up in town. He probably gets to flirt with hundreds of girls at the office.'

'I'm sure he doesn't.' Maggie couldn't imagine it. Or could she?

'I promise if he does it's quite harmless. But I bet he does, you know. Even Geoff – he admitted it to me once. Not that he'd do anything either, of course, but he said good old-fashioned sexual chemistry can sometimes get clients to spend a little more . . . you know the kind of thing.' She noticed Maggie's worried expression. 'But we're not talking about our husbands, we're talking about you. And you need something to distract you.

When Jamie sees you're a bit less focused on him, believe you me, he'll come running back. Before you know it, wham, bang! You'll be pregnant, he'll be delighted and everything will be tickety-boo.'

'Gosh,' said Maggie weakly, taken aback that her sister should be so matter-of-fact. Even if she was only talking about flirtation, wasn't mental infidelity just as bad? Still, she was intrigued. 'So how am I supposed to meet this man, then? The village is hardly chokka with bachelors beating a path to my door.'

Fran paused to consider while Maggie got to her feet and reached up to the top shelf of the dresser for the teapot. 'Now there you have a problem. Let me think what I did.'

'*What you did?*' Maggie was amazed. Her sister was surprising her at every turn.

'Oh, yes, I had an affair. Didn't you know?'

'*Fran!* You *didn't!*' Maggie nearly overfilled the teapot.

'I thought you knew,' said Fran, knowing full well that Maggie did not. It was her way of having the upper hand in their relationship, keeping a few trump cards close to her chest, ready to be revealed when they'd have most impact. 'It was nothing major, you understand. At least, I realise it wasn't now, although I didn't see things that way at the time.'

Maggie carried two mugs to the table and suppressed a smile. Fran even seemed to need to get one up on *herself*, just as she did everyone else. Hence the older, wiser Fran always knew more than the younger, naive Fran.

'So who was he?' she asked, getting the milk jug out of the fridge. 'When did it happen? Why didn't you tell me?'

'You never tell *me* anything.'

'There's nothing much to tell. Anyway, tell me now.'

'Promise not to laugh.'

'I won't.'

'He was the postman.'

Maggie hooted.

'I knew you'd think it was funny. But he was really attractive. A six-foot-two Ryan Giggs type.'

'Not your average Postman Pat,' Maggie teased.

'If you're going to take the piss, I won't tell you,' said Fran huffily. They were nine and ten years old, all over again.

'Aw, go on, I want to know, honest. After all, even Shere has a postman. Maybe you can help me seduce him.'

Fran felt better for being cast as the expert, albeit in adultery. '*He* seduced *me*,' she continued, more buoyantly. 'We first met when I walked Dan to school. Tim, his name was. He was always very friendly, and we were headed the same way, him with his trolley. He'd let Dan push it, then give him letters, and show him where to post them. Dan loved it, loved him. You know what it's like – someone's nice to your child, it makes you warm to them.'

'I suppose so.' As far as Maggie was concerned, there was warming to someone and there was having the hots for them. The two were quite distinct. *She* certainly didn't succumb to the latter when some Tim, Dick or Harry was charming to Nathan. After all, she was married, wasn't she? And so, for that matter, was Fran. What about Geoff? Were things more sticky there than they seemed? She couldn't recall Fran having said that their marriage was anything other than perfect. But one never knew exactly what went on behind closed doors. 'I always thought you and Geoff got on so well,' she said. 'When was all this?'

'About two years ago.' Fran lowered her voice. She looked uncharacteristically embarrassed. 'We'd stopped sleeping to-gether.'

'No! I thought you two . . .' Golly, thought Maggie, was all her sister's swanking mere bravado?

'Well, we do *now*, but for a while, when Dan was younger, it tapered off a bit.'

'Why? There must have been a reason.'

'Do you think there's a reason that things have slowed down between you and Jamie?' retorted Fran.

The idea made Maggie distinctly uncomfortable. Might Jamie's lack of libido relate to some deeper issue? 'But our sex life hasn't died. It's just not as frequent as it used to be. After so many years together that's quite common, isn't it?'

'Yeah, it is,' agreed Fran. 'But things with Geoff and me had got worse than that. I think it started because he was having a dreadful time at work. It was when his agency merged with that other one – remember?'

Maggie did, all too well. Geoff had been nervous that he might be made redundant. At the time she had felt sorry for him.

'After a while he got anxious about sex too. Pretty soon it became a vicious circle. I felt he wasn't communicating so I wanted affection, he felt I was demanding, emotionally and physically, and he couldn't answer my demands. So he worried and I got more demanding.'

Maggie could just imagine how Fran's impatience could make a man – especially one as sensitive as Geoff – insecure both in and out of bed. Poor chap. But surely the solution was not to sleep with someone else?

'Anyway,' Fran, breezily recalling the excitement of her liaison, was oblivious to her sister's concern, 'in the end Tim the toyboy satisfied my desires, or at least for a while.'

'How old was he?'

'Twenty-four,' said Fran proudly. 'Showed me a thing or two, I can tell you.'

'So you did *sleep* with him?' Maggie was horrified.

'Of course I did. I said I had an affair, didn't I? It's hardly an affair if there's no sex.'

'I suppose not.' Maggie felt distinctly unworldly. Just how did one end up sleeping with a postman? 'What happened?'

'I'm not going to tell you *everything*,' said Fran, who relished withholding the very information she'd promised, 'but I will say that one day he had to get me to sign for something – a registered letter from the bank, I think it was. I'd already taken Dan to school, and one thing led to another, and he invited himself in, and we knew each other quite well by then and, well, almost before I could stop myself – he was *so* dishy – we were shagging in the hall. I think he had a bit of a thing for older women,' she added, as if this explained the entire episode.

'Good God!' exclaimed Maggie. Fran 'shagging' the postman! It was a phrase that made her squirm – it seemed so mechanical. In fact, it all sounded so unlikely – like the kind of thing men said to impress their mates in the pub, that she never thought was actually real. Let alone something her slightly too tall and skinny younger sister would confide in her, sat at her very own kitchen table.

Fran got up and opened the cupboard where she knew her sister kept the biscuits. She rummaged around in the tin and took the last of the Bath Olivers. 'The reason I'm telling you all of this,' she said with her mouth full, 'is because it helped my relationship with Geoff no end.'

'It did?'

'Yup.' She swallowed. 'For a while I stopped wanting to sleep with him so desperately. And I don't know if it was 'cos he sensed something was wrong, and it made him appreciate me more, or whether it was because the pressure was off, but things got better between us. We started making love again, and gradually I even introduced some more adventurous things into our sex life – things I'd learnt with Tim – a little mild S and M using silk scarves, stuff like that. Then, finally, I didn't need Tim any more so I finished with him, and now everything's just great. *That's* why you should have a fling.'

'And Geoff never found out?' Maggie was agog. Fran was attractive, but an affair with a younger man? And *mild* S and M? She wasn't sure there was such a thing. With silk scarves? Her sister! Her primary-school teacher sister!

'No, of course not.'

Somehow Maggie couldn't help sympathising with the men in Fran's scenario: Tim who had been unceremoniously dumped when Fran's marriage had got back on an even keel, and Geoff, her dear, sweet brother-in-law, whom she'd known for ten years, and was fond of, who put up with Fran's incessant one-upmanship and bossiness. No one deserved to be treated like that, least of all big-hearted, bumbling Geoff. For what sounded like months he'd been unaware that Fran had been satisfying her lust elsewhere. On the hall carpet, to be precise, maybe even in their marital bed. Perhaps they'd even tied each other to the headboard! And all the while Geoff hadn't known? Surely he must have had some idea. She would, she was certain of it. And what about Dan? Cavorting with the postman was not exactly the behaviour of a responsible mum. What if Dan had picked up on his mother and Tim's mutual sexual attraction while they'd been supposedly innocently posting letters? He might have only been three years old, but it was amazing what small boys understood.

Maggie shuddered. Infidelity – what a horrible, horrible idea. She'd never let things between her and Jamie get that bad. No, she thought firmly. A flirtation elsewhere was not the solution, not for her. Not ever.

## 11 Chloë

**By Tuesday morning** Chloë had convinced herself she wouldn't hear from James again; not in that way, at least. Anyway, today she was meeting Vanessa Davenport for lunch, and she had more important things to think about. Or so she'd persuaded herself until she pushed open the rotating doors to UK Magazines' Covent Garden offices. There he was, in the foyer, waiting with a couple of other members of staff for the lift.

True to form, Chloë went pink immediately. James, on the other hand, with his jacket thrown over his briefcase – it was hot outside – looked incredibly cool. She was struck again by how effortlessly well-dressed he was. In some ways men had it so easy, she thought.

'Hello,' he said, on seeing her.

'Hi,' she responded.

'How are you?'

'Oh, I'm okay.' Should she ask how he was? No – far too familiar.

Silence.

A bell signalled the arrival of the lift. The doors opened and all four of them got in. James took control of pressing the buttons. 'Which floor?' he asked the others.

'Two,' said a man in a pinstripe suit.

'Three,' said a middle-aged woman.

He didn't bother to ask Chloë, just pressed the button for her floor regardless. Then he stepped back. Did that mean he was getting out with her? Or at the second or third? Chloë's heart was racing. If they were getting out together, on the fifth, they'd have a few seconds alone. Help!

They all stood pressed against the walls, looking everywhere rather than at each other. What was it about lifts that made chatting to people – including those one normally got on with easily – so impossible?

Ping! They arrived at the second floor, and the man in pinstripes got out. He probably worked in Accounts. More silence. Ping! They were at the third, and the middle-aged lady disappeared.

James and Chloë were alone.

'I'm meeting Vanessa Davenport today,' said Chloë, thankful to have thought of something to say.

'I know,' said James. 'She told me.'

This threw Chloë again – he'd been talking about her. But before she had time to think of every possible reason why, James said: 'I couldn't stop thinking about you all weekend.'

There was no doubt about it: that was personal. Shit. What should she say? She just looked at him, straight in the eye, trying to be stern. But . . . pow! There it was again. Sexual chemistry. Chloë felt sure it would cause the lift to shoot way past the fifth floor and explode out of the top of the building.

'Me neither,' she said frankly.

'I'd like to see you again,' said James. He seemed a little nervous.

Chloë virtually came on the spot. 'Er . . .' she stuttered.

'Thursday night?' asked James, as the lift arrived at the fifth. The doors opened.

Bugger her diary. Though she knew she shouldn't, she'd cancel it if she had something arranged. 'Yes,' she said quickly.

He followed her into Reception. 'I've a meeting with your editor,' he explained. 'Good luck with Vanessa,' he added, giving her a broad grin.

'Thanks,' said Chloë, wondering what it would be like to kiss him again. Yet they were in the most public of places; there were several people she didn't recognise sitting waiting on the sofas and the receptionist's face was raised in anticipation, ready to greet James politely. He was a powerful figure at UK Magazines, after all, so a hushed 'see you' was the most Chloë could manage before heading round the back of Reception to her desk opposite Patsy.

Three hours later she was sitting across from Vanessa Davenport in the Soho restaurant Little Italy. Vanessa looked good, in a ghoulish kind of way, with her rather sharp, beaky nose and gaunt cheeks. She was elegantly dressed in head-to-toe black Gucci (UK Magazines must rate her for her to afford that lot, thought Chloë), and they were surrounded by a precarious mêlée of papers, side salads and glasses. It was a tremendous challenge for Chloë to eat pasta and present her documents while maintaining a semblance of decorum.

As Chloë went through a brief outline of her magazine, Vanessa was guardedly positive. She appeared to have a matter-of-fact, business-like attitude to the idea, but Chloë usually felt more at ease with people who were intuitive and impulsive in their reactions. As a result, some wicked part of her had an over-whelming desire to say casually, 'Did you know that after discussing this last Thursday James Slater spent the *whole* night with me? He and I appear to be on the brink of an affair – and he has a huge willy,' just to gauge Vanessa's reaction. She knew she'd never do it, of course, but she would have liked to see whether Vanessa could be so disconcertingly formal about *that*.

All morning Chloë had been going over what that second date meant. And the more she thought about it, the more sure she was: he was keen. One encounter and she could have put James's behaviour down to the heat of the moment, a one-night stand that had come about as a result of too much alcohol and too little self-control. But two after-work meetings – with him suggesting both – that was deliberate, planned, a different thing altogether, especially as this latest one had been arranged when they were both sober. She knew that Rob would think it a dangerous move, but Chloë was flattered and thrilled. Although she couldn't know his precise intentions towards her, she'd never had a man quite *this* attractive and successful interested in her before.

Lit up by the knowledge that James liked her, Chloë glowed throughout the meeting, despite occasional wanderings of her mind and Vanessa's daunting reputation.

Vanessa must have picked up her confidence, because by the end of their lunch she agreed tentatively to take Chloë's idea to the board. 'But it does need a title,' she said, somewhat crisply, as Chloë got up. (She'd cunningly suggested leaving after Chloë, lest they be seen returning to the office together.) 'As you must already know from working on *Babe*, that's not easy to establish. See if you can come up with something, if only just to work with for the time being. It's important, if people are going to take this seriously higher up the company. If I could have any thoughts by early next week, it would be to your advantage. In the long run, you'll need to find something really memorable.'

'Okay.' Chloë shook Vanessa's hand. Its long slim fingers were laden with silver jewellery and the nails were immaculately French-manicured: it was clearly the weapon of a woman who knew how to intimidate another. But Chloë could stand up to types like this – especially today – and said with genuine self-assurance: 'I'll come up with some ideas. And thank you for lunch and for seeing me.'

'My pleasure. I look forward to working with you.' Then suddenly Vanessa smiled. 'James was right. It's a great idea, and your enthusiasm is infectious.'

'Thanks again,' said Chloë. Everything seemed to be going her way, and leaving the restaurant, bouncing on her Miu Miu rubber soles, she felt as if she was walking on air.

Back at her desk, Chloë was checking a proof when the phone rang.

'Hello, Chloë?' It was Craig Spencer, one of her favourite freelance journalists. A warm, cuddly man with a background in counselling, he wrote regular pieces for *Babe* and promised to be a pleasant antidote to the brittle Vanessa. 'I've an idea for an article. Thought you might like it.'

'Hang on a tick.' Chloë folded the artwork and reached for her biro and notebook. 'Right. I'm ready now.'

'It's a bit of a personal one, this. I'm a stepfather, if you didn't know, and for a long time I've been thinking about children after their parents' divorce. Don't get me wrong,' Craig must have detected Chloë's immediate scepticism down the line, 'I'm not talking about some piece focusing on young kids or the parents themselves – that would be far too *Good Housekeeping*, and I reckon it's been done before. I'm thinking more of interviewing children who are now grown-up, asking them to consider in retrospect how the experience of their parents' rows, affairs, separation and so on has affected their adult relationships. I thought I could talk to a range of people, maybe one who's several times divorced, one who's managed to maintain a happy marriage of their own despite a traumatic childhood and one who's perennially single, that kind of thing.'

'You could interview me, then,' said Chloë, not entirely joking.

Craig, a consummate professional, grabbed this opportunity to convey the pertinence of the idea. 'Pity I can't, but it shows it's got universal relevance.'

'Hmm,' Chloë was doubtful. 'It just doesn't sound very *Babe*,' she said.

Valiantly, Craig tried to fight his corner. 'I'm convinced it could be, if we get the right sort of interviewees and tone.'

'I think that might be a shame. It's an interesting topic, I agree, and I'd hate to see you not do it justice because you were forced to make it too upbeat and simplistic.'

Craig obviously thought this was just a polite way of giving him the brush-off. 'I guess so, if that's how you feel.'

It was then that Chloë had a brainwave. She checked over her shoulder to make sure no one was listening. Luckily Patsy was away from her desk. 'Actually, I'm working on another project at the moment, but I'm afraid I'm not in a position to give you any details quite yet. This article might be far more suitable for that. Yes,' she grew more certain, 'I think it's the kind of subject we could put a spin on and really make work.'

'Oh?' Craig sounded happier.

'Do me a favour, Craig. Don't tell anyone else about this idea. Don't offer it to any other editors – not yet. Give me a week, and I'll come back to you.'

'I'm on tenterhooks,' said Craig. 'Shall I wait to hear from you?'

'Yes, please do. And thanks for ringing.' Chloë put the phone down. She could see it now. Engaging and emotionally provocative, dealing with real issues about real people in a way that was touching rather than titillating, and written by a psychiatric professional with personal insight. It was exactly the kind of feature she wanted for her new magazine.

Chloë had no plans for that night so she decided to work late to catch up on a few ongoing features she was editing for *Babe*. When she finally left the office it was gone eight o'clock, but at least that meant the number nineteen would be quicker getting home.

Propped up against the bus stop in Charing Cross Road, Chloë felt the energy high that had kept her keyed up all day finally wear off, leaving her strangely deflated.

Shortly her bus arrived. Chloë got on and mounted the hazardously steep spiral stairs to the upper deck, where she was pleased to find that her favourite seat was free. It was at the front, and allowed her to enjoy a prime view of London. Tonight it was muggy, so as the bus lurched round Trafalgar Square, she wound down the window ahead of her, hoping that perhaps the through-air would help to clear her thoughts.

She flashed back to her dialogue with Craig. He'd said he wanted to write about the damaging effects of rows, affairs and separation on children. Momentarily this had brought back uncomfortable memories. Yet paradoxically that was precisely what had attracted her to the article – she knew it could push other people's buttons, just as it had hers.

Chloë had been an adolescent when her parents began not to get on, and as the eldest she had taken it particularly hard. Indeed, she knew that her own fear of commitment probably stemmed from being caught for so many years between two arguing adults. As Rob had often observed, she'd frequently picked unsuitable partners – boyfriends who weren't good enough for her. Either she'd gone for men less strong-minded than herself and tended to walk all over them or, sometimes on the rebound, she'd gone for the challenge – men she had to win over – and ended up being the one who got hurt. As a result her longest relationship had lasted only a year – and a very off-and-on relationship it had been too.

Before they'd retired, Chloë's mum and dad had both been actors and prone to bouts of melodrama, with the kind of love-hate relationship that gave credence to the cliché 'They can't live with each other; they can't live without each other.' All in all, so intense were the peaks and troughs of their marriage that Chloë had heaved a huge sigh of relief when her father had finally announced that he was leaving her mother for another woman.

The bus stop-started down Piccadilly, on round Hyde Park Corner and headed down Sloane Street. Chloë gnawed at her lip. Even now she could hardly say that she felt warm towards the memory of her father's girlfriend, Julia, a TV producer twelve years his junior, who had been ditched a few months later. But equally she felt Julia could not ultimately be held responsible for the breakdown of her parents' marriage. It had been a mess before she came along and the fact her father had found another woman had merely precipitated some long-overdue decisions.

In fact, reasoned Chloë, thinking of how much happier her parents were now that they were both settled with new partners, one could almost say Julia had done them all a favour. She was forced to acknowledge, however, that Julia hadn't come out of it well. 'Pah! I always knew it was a transitional relationship. It was never going to last,' Chloë's mother had said with vitriol after her father had dumped Julia because he needed time alone 'to think'.

Chloë sighed. One never knew how things were going to turn out, although for the moment life seemed to be going pretty well for her. Yes, she reminded herself as the bus picked up speed over

Battersea Bridge and she got to her feet ready for her stop, she had lots to look forward to. Not least that on Thursday she was seeing James again. She recalled the intimate conversation they had shared, their steamy sex, his gentleness, the way he'd made her feel so wanted and wonderful, and pushed her negative thoughts aside. I should live for the moment, she decided.

Chloë enjoyed living life a little dangerously, or so she liked to think: as a child she had always liked the fastest, most vertiginous rides at funfairs, enjoying their scariness, though now her excessive appetite more often manifested itself in occasional bursts of wild partying and recreational drug-taking with her friends. But she'd never done anything quite like this before. This was new territory. And although she knew what her mother and Rob would say, there was no point in asking their advice for she wouldn't listen anyway. No, this was one roller-coaster she had to ride for herself.

## 12 Chloë

**Chloë was filling** the kettle when Rob staggered, bleary-eyed, into the kitchen.

'You're up early,' she said.

'Tell me about it.' Rob scowled. 'It seems the world and his wife are desperate to lose a few pounds before their bloody holidays so they're all booking in with me.' Rob was a personal trainer. 'I've got the world's longest day.'

'So, you'll be out tonight?' Chloë acted disinterested as she reached for the coffee.

'Yes, bugger it. My last appointment's not until nine.'

'You poor thing,' said Chloë, secretly thinking *Ooh goody*! That meant he wouldn't be back till after eleven.

'You look posh,' said Rob, his eyes now sufficiently open to take in her carefully assembled outfit – a flimsy Karen Millen skirt, and a satin shirt she'd picked up on Portobello Road, both in shades of green, which offset her dark colouring rather well she thought.

'Posh?' Chloë was disappointed. Ravishing was more what she'd had in mind.

'Yeah,' said Rob.

'What, posh-smart, or Posh Spice?'

'Darling, you'll never look Posh Spice,' said Rob. Chloë's curves were more Geri Halliwell in her Ginger days. 'But you look nice.'

'Good,' said Chloë, pouring milk into her coffee. Rob was usually a fine judge.

He stood back for a full assessment. 'Surprisingly sophisticated.'

'Not sexy?' asked Chloë hopefully.

Rob eyed her suspiciously. 'Why is it so important to look sexy on a Thursday?'

'Oh, no reason.' Chloë grabbed her mug and made a hasty exit.

'I hope you're not seeing that man again today!' he called after her. 'You know I think he's bad news.'

When James rang, Chloë suggested they meet for a drink in Clapham Junction.

'Good idea,' said James. 'It's easy for me to get the last train home from there.' It sounded as if he was planning on being out as late as possible.

And maybe I can lure you back to mine for some nookie, thought Chloë, living for the moment just as she'd vowed. It was all coming together nicely.

But when she arrived at the Slug and Lettuce, it was heaving. Perhaps it hadn't been such a good idea, after all. She bought herself a glass of red wine and looked around for a table. There wasn't one. The music was blaring – they wouldn't be able to hear themselves think.

'Hi,' said James, coming up behind her and surprising her. He grabbed her round the waist and *smack*!, gave her a firm kiss on the cheek. He was close enough for her to get a waft of his scent. That, and the sheer assertive masculinity of the gesture, was enough to bring heady recollections of the previous week flooding back. 'Can I get you a drink?' he asked.

Chloë shook her head. 'I've got one.'

She watched him make his way to the bar. He was undoubtedly

a little older than most of the clientele, but he had the kind of effortless ease that meant he looked at home wherever he was. It was odd, wasn't it, she contemplated, the way some people got more attractive the more one knew them, while others, who initially seemed drop-dead gorgeous, became plainer, more ordinary? She definitely thought James was better looking now than she had two weeks ago. Mm, she concluded, in a well-fed Heathcliff-meets-curvaceous-Cathy kind of way, they complemented each other. She wondered if anyone else would notice that they made rather a good couple.

They quickly agreed that it was too noisy and hot inside, so opted instead to join the crowd that had over-spilt onto the street, although the busy main road was far from the most romantic location.

'Did you get home all right last week?' asked Chloë, keen to avoid any pretence that nothing had happened.

'Yeah,' said James. 'A cab's amazingly fast at five in the morning, and my wife and son were out for the night, so I was able to grab an hour's sleep or so before schlepping back into town.'

*My wife.* Chloë flushed. She'd been avoiding thinking about the fact that he was married. Yet there was also something about his words that seemed a bit distant – made Maggie more of a label than a person. It made Chloë think of the kind of girl who referred to 'my boyfriend' rather than calling him by his name, as if he was more important as an accessory than anything else. But she wasn't really in a position to comment, so she let it go.

That Chloë allowed more than a split second's silence while she contemplated this was unusual, which obviously worried James. 'Chloë?' he said.

'Um?'

'I hope you don't think I make a habit of this kind of thing.' A particularly loud lorry thundered past, billowing exhaust and James coughed, whether from awkwardness or asphyxiation, Chloë wasn't sure.

'I don't know what to think,' said Chloë truthfully. She could swear James was trying to assess her feelings.

His hazel eyes looked anxious. 'I've never had an affair before.'

God! He'd called it an *affair*. Already! 'You haven't?' Chloë was surprised, not to say doubtful. She found him so irresistible that she couldn't imagine others didn't too. She knew Patsy did. Though she supposed that wasn't the point. Fidelity wasn't just a matter of being desired by others; it meant reciprocating that desire and, more importantly, acting on it.

'No, not really.' James appeared desperate to explain himself. 'To be honest, I haven't been so attracted to anyone this much before. Not for years.'

*Pah!* Chloë could hear Rob's voice. *Bullshit! I bet he says that to all the girls.* But instinctively she believed him – and her instinct was usually right. She said supportively, 'You don't need to justify yourself to me.'

'I don't?'

'No.'

'Why's that?'

'Because – um . . .' Chloë paused. Should she risk being so open? Why not? She'd nothing to lose. 'Because I've never done anything like this before either.'

'So you're not like the woman who wrote the book that was in the papers recently?' James seemed relieved.

'The serial mistress? Never goes out with anyone other than married men?'

'Yes, her.'

'Hardly!' Chloë laughed. 'I read about her too – thought she seemed vile. Totally without scruples. And you'd never have known she was such a goer, would you? She looked so *prim.*'

'Not my type, certainly,' said James. 'But I guess you know that.'

'In what way?' How she loved fishing for compliments from him. He always seemed to come up trumps.

'Well, *you*'re much more my cup of tea.'

'Cup of tea?' she teased. 'How tame!'

'I suppose you'd prefer to be my margarita?' He laughed. 'Boy! I had such a hangover last Friday.'

'Me too.' Chloë shuddered at the memory.

'It took me all weekend to get over it. I guess I'm not as young as I was.'

'We didn't drink *that* much.'

'No, but we didn't have much sleep either.'

Chloë noted the reference to sex. It made her feel intimate with him, and more than a little excited at the thought of doing it again. 'I lay in on Saturday,' she said.

'Not an option in my case. Nathan wakes up at eight. Bounce! Bounce! "Daddy's day to get breakfast!"'

'Ah.' Chloë didn't know what to say. For a moment she felt truly terrible. What was she doing fooling around with a married man who had a child?

Belatedly, James realised the tactlessness of talking about his family, so to make up for it he said, 'I love your outfit.' Chloë beamed. 'You wear such great clothes. They really accentuate your figure.' He was undoubtedly gazing at her breasts.

'Thanks,' said Chloë, not minding.

He adjusted his focus to her face. 'So, how was your meeting with Vanessa?'

'Weird,' said Chloë, glad to have the conversation on more secure ground. 'I think she liked the magazine concept, but she's a strange woman.' Oops! She was talking about a close colleague of his. 'Well, I mean – she's, um, a bit difficult to make out.'

'You didn't like her?'

'No, no, it's not that,' said Chloë hurriedly. That was a bit strong – Vanessa had given her the go-ahead, after all.

'Well, she told me she liked it,' James reassured her. 'And she even said she liked you.'

'Me? Really?' Chloë was surprised and pleased. Recklessly she added, 'Blimey, if that's what she's like when she likes someone, I'd hate to see her when she doesn't!'

'A total bitch, believe me.' James grinned.

Now a bus stopped at the lights, engine spluttering loudly. It really wasn't very pleasant standing on the street. 'I tell you what,' said Chloë, suddenly. 'I presume you've got to be home later?'

James looked at the pavement. 'The last train's at eleven fifteen.'

'Well,' she raised her eyes, 'we *could* always go back to mine now . . .'

'What about your flatmate?'

'He's out tonight.'

'Okay, then, let's.'

Chloë picked up her bag from where it lay between her feet (so as not to get nicked) and slung it over her shoulder. As they strolled up the hill, she said, 'If you don't mind me asking, where did you say you were going tonight?'

'I said I was playing squash. I play every Thursday.' James looked uncomfortable.

'Till midnight?'

'A bit lame, I know. But I told you, this is all kind of new to me.'

'So you've *never* been unfaithful before? Not once?'

James took her hand. 'Do you want me to be honest?' *Shit!* thought Chloë. What was he going to say? That she'd swept him off his feet? But he said, 'I have been, yes.' Her heart sank. So he was a philanderer, after all. 'Once, at a company do, in Paris.'

This didn't sound so bad. 'It was a one-night stand?'

'Barely that,' said James. 'We didn't even spend all night together. We were pissed. She dragged me back to her room – she was a Spanish ad exec, very attractive, from what I recall. It was a couple of years ago now. We had sex once, then I left. It was no big love affair.'

Chloë was thankful. It was one thing having an affair with someone she was beginning to really like and who seemed to think she was special, but quite another to be one of a series of lovers.

By now they were back at her flat. Thank goodness she'd spent fifteen minutes tidying up before work. It was a long way from pristine, but at least the washing-up was done and her dirty clothes were in the laundry bin. They went into the kitchen.

'Hey, this is nice,' said James.

'You think so?' Chloë was amazed – its haphazard style was hardly in keeping with his designer suits.

'Yeah.' He sauntered around, casually taking stock of it all, peering at the fridge smothered in photos of Chloë with her mates, examining the eclectic collection of knick-knacks on the window-sill, chortling at Rob's camp fifties B-movie posters.

Then he wandered through the double doors into the living room. It was less tidy in there, thought Chloë, worried. There were magazines everywhere, overspilling ashtrays she'd failed to empty after last Sunday's gathering with her girlfriends and stacks of CDs separated from their covers.

'Ah!' James kicked off his shoes. 'Sorry, old fella, my turn,' he said, as he shoved the cat off the sofa so he could stretch out on it lengthways. 'This is really great, you know,' he called through to Chloë. 'Just my kind of place. Reminds me of where I lived when I first got to London.' She came to the door and saw that, with his feet propped up on one of the arms, he looked as if there was nowhere else he'd rather be.

'Do you want some more wine?' she asked. Living hand to mouth as she and Rob tended to, they had far from a cellarful, but they always had a couple of cheapish bottles in stock for emergencies. 'I'm afraid it's nothing spectacular.'

'Please,' said James.

Chloë grabbed the red, two glasses and the corkscrew and followed him into the sitting room.

'Budge up,' she said.

He lifted his legs so that she could join him, then promptly put them on her lap. Oh, my God, there it was again – that whoosh of sheer, unstoppable desire. Chloë found it hard to concentrate on the corkscrew.

'Let me.' James reached for it. He opened the wine easily, poured them each a glass, and carefully placed the bottle on the coffee table. 'Come here,' he said, reaching for her.

Chloë shifted so that she was half lying on him, their faces level. With some men she worried at moments like this that she was ungraceful in the way she moved and too heavy, but not here, with James.

'What time's your flatmate back?'

'Not till eleven,' Chloë could feel his breath.

He stroked her cheek. 'You're lovely,' he said, and kissed her. Jesus – it was even better than before! Maybe it was because she was sober. Or because she was more relaxed. Maybe it was because she was now pretty sure he liked her – a lot. Maybe . . . Chloë's energies shifted out of her head, her brain went mushy, and . . . mmm . . . she could feel the bristles from his five o'clock shadow . . . Now she was being taken over by a divine sensation that kissing was making happen lower down. He undid the buttons of her blouse without a hitch – she'd known it was a good choice for that reason – and slid his hands into her bra. *Yes, please* . . . She was feeling very horny, and – mmm – certainly not like plump, clumsy Chloë now. With her satin shirt slipping off her shoulders, his own half undone – my! she'd forgotten how sexy his chest was – she felt wonderfully wanton, like a gypsy in the heat.

Confidently, she knelt up and looked at him.

'Take off your skirt,' he directed.

There was no way to achieve this and remain close to him other than for Chloë to stand on the sofa astride him, balanced precarious on wobbly cushions. Nevertheless she managed to accomplish the task by standing momentarily on one leg. Better still, because she was being watched by a thoroughly appreciative man, she did it with real grace.

'There!' she said, still standing. Thank God for her best bra and knickers. He ran his hands up her legs. And thank God she'd shaved.

She looked down at James, enjoying watching him taking her all in and relishing the sight of him, still in his trousers, his eyes full of lust.

'Jeez,' he said, spellbound. 'You look amazing. You are *all* woman.'

'This is where I like my publishers to be,' she laughed, and knelt down, still astride him, the flatness of her crotch directly above the bump of his erection. She gently rubbed herself against it, knowing full well the effect it would have.

'Chloë,' he groaned.

Slowly she undid the remaining buttons of his shirt.

'Thank God all features editors aren't like you,' he muttered, unzipping his flies. 'There wouldn't –' he slid down his trousers '– be a hope in hell –' he pushed her knickers to one side '– of me being remotely able to keep my professional –' he began to fuck her '– distance.'

## **13** Maggie

'**Open the cupboard** door,' said Jamie to Nathan. They'd just come home from playing soccer again, all tired and sweaty.

Nathan opened the hall cupboard and stood back, ready for the ritual.

'He shoots, he scores!' said Jamie, whacking the ball through the door and knocking a couple of coats off their hooks.

Nathan squealed, delighted.

'I wish you wouldn't do that.' Maggie sighed.

'Oh,' said Jamie, deflated. He rather enjoyed it.

'That cupboard's enough of a mess as it is.'

'Gee, I'm sorry,' said Jamie sarcastically, and winked at Nathan in camaraderie.

'Boring Mummy,' said Nathan, voicing Jamie's feelings precisely.

That only made Maggie more irritable. She, too, was tired and sweaty, but not from having fun: she'd been hoovering and scrubbing all afternoon – they couldn't find a cleaner who met her exacting standards so she did it herself. And it was the second day of her period – always the worst.

'Actually,' she said, with unusual forcefulness, 'I would really appreciate it if you could tidy it up in there. Today. It's full of junk. I don't know how you can ever find anything – the other day it took me ages to find my trainers. I felt like I'd worked out before I even started running.'

'Ooh, *dear*,' said Jamie, 'what's got into Mummy today? It's probably that time of the month.'

That he addressed this remark to Nathan *and* accurately pinpointed her physical condition was the last straw. 'I am not kidding,' she said acerbically. 'In fact, I'd like you to do it now.'

'What – *now*?' Jamie was incredulous.

'You might as well. Before you shower.'

'But the results are on in a minute! We've come back specially.'

'Nathan can tell you them.' In need of no further excuse to escape, Nathan scarpered into the sitting room and switched on the telly.

'Why do I have to do it now this minute? Why not tomorrow?' Jamie sounded just like a child.

'Because you *won't* do it tomorrow.'

'I will.'

'No, you won't. And, anyway, I want it done now. Then I can relax.'

'You can't relax when there's mess in the hall cupboard?' Jamie seemed determined to provoke her.

'No, I bloody well can't!' Maggie raised her voice.

'Jesus, Maggie. Sometimes I worry about you. You're obsessed with everything being so goddamn tidy!' It was incredible how he'd managed to turn failings of his (messiness, compounded by an inability to do his fair share of the housework) into a failing of hers.

'I am *not* obsessed,' said Maggie, anger bubbling up. 'Anyway, if I am, it's because someone's got to be around here.'

'Why? It's hardly as if the world would stop turning if I didn't tidy up your precious cupboard.'

'Because,' now she let rip, 'if I left it up to you the whole house would be a fucking pig-sty.' This was not a word Maggie used readily, and she checked herself as she said it to ensure Nathan was out of earshot.

'Well, why don't you just let it be for once? Then maybe *I* could relax.'

'Oh, that's rich. You know damn well you'd hate to live like that.'

'That's where you're wrong, Maggie.'

Ouch! The use of her name, so pointedly.

'Tell me,' she said, 'how *would* you like to live?'

'I just wouldn't have everything so anally fucking perfect. It's bad enough having my dinner plate washed up before I've even finished my pudding, but all our CDs arranged alphabetically! I mean *really*. It's rock and roll, Maggie. All my bloody underpants rolled in my drawers. My socks in colour-co-ordinated rows. I don't mind when you do it to your stuff, but I *hate* it when you do it to mine. Come to that,' now his fury was unstoppable, 'if you *really* want to know how I'd like to live, I wouldn't choose to live here at all!'

'Oh?' What on earth did he mean?

'You're the one who wanted some beautiful sodding period home out here in the middle of nowhere. I'd much rather be still living up in town. All this commuting, it's wearing me out. If I don't have any energy for housework, that's damn well why!'

Maggie was shaking. 'You've got the energy for football.'

'It's not the same and you know it! Look, we've got this huge bloody house with a huge bloody mortgage. I take care of the mortgage—'

'So the least I can do is take care of the house?' Maggie couldn't believe he could be such a pig.

'Yes.'

'You do *not* take care of the fucking mortgage!' She was close to screaming now. 'We both do!'

'Hmph,' said Jamie, implying that he took care of the lion's share. 'And I've told you before, if you need some help, get a cleaner.'

'I can't *find* a cleaner!'

'If you weren't so snotty to them maybe they'd stay.'

That struck a nerve. Maggie knew she could be a tough task-master. 'I never knew you felt that way about the house,' she said, more soberly.

'Well you know now,' muttered Jamie, calming down too.

'You should have said before.' She was close to tears.

'I didn't know what it would be like until we moved here.'

'No, nor did I,' said Maggie regretfully. She missed her London friends – especially at times like this. Here she had so few people to confide in.

'And I wanted to make you happy,' added Jamie. By now Maggie was crying and Jamie looked as if he really hated himself. 'Though I don't seem to be very good at that.'

'Oh, it's not *you*,' said Maggie, too shattered to continue arguing.

## 14 Chloë

As she lay in bed on Sunday morning, Chloë dozily replayed Thursday night, carefully selecting the words and actions that made her feel good and skipping over the bits – James's family – that made her feel bad. She allowed herself to linger extra long on the compliments James had paid her, which made her feel all warm inside. He'd told her she was 'lovely', 'amazing', that he loved her breasts (she did too – they were her favourite part of her body) and even (mad man) her curvy hips, her belly. What was that phrase he'd used? '*All* woman.' She liked that . . .

My God! She was suddenly fully awake. *All Woman.* Wouldn't that be rather a good title for her magazine? All things to all women . . . every aspect of an individual woman . . . something for every kind of woman . . . the whole truth about women . . . It certainly had several meanings. It even sounded a bit *risqué*, but that was no bad thing . . . Yes. She liked it.

A week later she had a call from Vanessa.

'I've got you the go-ahead,' said Vanessa, not bothering with small-talk. 'And the board really like the name. You've got three months seconded to this department initially. You'll be working with me and another assistant.'

'That's *fantastic*!'

'It should prove very interesting.' Vanessa sounded a few degrees above freezing. 'I'd like to start at the beginning of October, as I'm going away for a couple of weeks next Monday. It would also help if you took any holidays owing to you before we start. That way we can get our teeth into it.' She probably sucked blood with hers, thought Chloë. 'So you'd better let your editor know, sharpish.'

So she had. Not a task she relished. 'Leave it with me,' said Chloë, trying to sound capable. 'I'll let you know when I've spoken to her.'

Having rung off, Chloë inhaled deeply. Well, she thought, there's no time like the present. She pushed back her chair and marched purposefully to Jean's office.

The door was open – it was one of Jean's I'm-one-of-the-girls practices (though, inevitably, being the boss, she wasn't – there was endless gossip from which she was excluded). Chloë stood on the threshold and tapped lightly.

Jean looked up and smiled. 'Ah, Chloë,' she said. She might have looked rather like a well-rounded version of Coco Chanel, but beneath her polished and elegantly-suited exterior, Jean was not a cold woman, just remarkably efficient. And although Chloë's unconventional approach sometimes frustrated her, she acknowledged that her features editor had her finger on the pulse and a way with words. *Babe's* regular contributors liked her too. Indeed, having nurtured her career from editorial assistant onwards and upwards, Jean considered Chloë her personal protégée and had a particularly soft spot for her.

Chloë knew that this latest news was not going to be well received, and she had no desire to scupper any future chances she might have with Jean. Thus diplomacy was the key. Flattery – that was the route to take.

'Ahem.' She cleared her throat, unusually nervous. 'I don't know where to start.'

'Sounds ominous,' said Jean. 'Have a seat.'

'You know how much I love working here at *Babe*,' began Chloë.

'Ye-es.' Jean sounded on her guard already – she was pretty shrewd.

'And you know how much I appreciate all you've done for me—'

'You're leaving,' said Jean bluntly.

'Not exactly.' She might as well say it. 'I've been invited to work in Special Projects for three months.'

'You have? They asked you? Just out of the blue?' Jean knew full well that this would not have been the case, but an immediate sense of betrayal made her snappish.

'No, I approached them,' Chloë admitted.

'I see. And why was that, if you're so happy here?'

There was nothing else for it, she would have to be honest. 'I've been developing another magazine concept.'

'A women's magazine?'

Chloë knew exactly what Jean was driving at. 'Yes, but it's not a competitor to *Babe*, Jean, honestly.'

'Okay, shoot,' said Jean, sitting back. 'I had heard rumours of this from Vanessa so I expected as much. I presume you kept it from me until it was verified. I want the whole story, beginning to end. And cut the flattery.'

How typical that she should want every last detail. But, Lord! As if she was going to tell Jean everything! So she related a highly censored version, omitting that she'd met James in *Babe*'s board-room and naturally (she wasn't bloody barmy) that they'd become lovers. She explained truthfully the amount of time she'd devoted to working on the idea, emphasising it had all been out of office hours, and played up Vanessa's role in the whole thing. (Vanessa would like that, so it would do no harm.)

When she'd finished Jean said, 'Well, it all sounds very exciting. But you do know a lot of these projects come to nothing, don't you?'

'Oh, yes,' said Chloë.

'I suppose I'll have to keep your job open for you.' Jean did not even try to disguise that this would put her out.

'That would be great.'

'Not for me it won't be. But it's UK Magazines' policy, so I've no choice.'

Chloë didn't know what to say. 'I'm sorry,' she ventured.

'No, you're not!' retorted Jean, spot on as usual. 'But I do understand. It's because you're good that I don't want to see you go. So, from a selfish point of view, I hope you fall flat on your face and have to come back to me. But for yours, I wish you luck. I can't begrudge you your ambition, given mine's got me where I am today. Now off you go, before I throttle you!'

Chloë knew when she wasn't wanted. Oh, well, she thought, Jean would get used to the idea, and she hadn't exactly expected her to be delighted.

Another fortnight, and a couple of snatched clandestine meetings later, Chloë was longing for the opportunity to spend more than just a few hours at a time with James. Especially as she was taking the next week off to use up her leave before starting work with Vanessa. She wanted to get to know him better, to see if the connection that promised so much ran any deeper. Despite struggling not to think of him too seriously, she was beginning to hope and believe that it did.

As they lay curled up together at her flat one Wednesday evening – this time James had used the hackneyed working-late excuse, believing he really ought to *play* squash with his friend the next day – he said, 'I'm afraid I'm not going to be able to manage this next week.'

Chloë could scarcely conceal her disappointment. She'd hoped to persuade him to take an afternoon off with her. 'Why not?'

'I'm going away.'

'Oh.' She supposed he was going on holiday with his wife. And while she knew it was only to be expected, the thought made her feel left out and rejected. It was a familiar emotion – she'd experienced time and time again in her teenage years, watching her parents bickering, too preoccupied with themselves to be aware of the impact on her. Because she didn't expect her feelings to matter to him either, she said nothing.

'Aren't you going to ask me where I'm going?' he asked, idly stroking her arm.

'Um,' she said quietly.

'New York,' he said. 'For a week.'

She couldn't help it. She was so jealous – it was somewhere she'd always wanted to go. 'You lucky thing,' she said, trying not to sound envious and turning her arm so that he could stroke it from a new angle. 'Where are you both staying? Do you know people out there?' Yes, of course he did – Beth. But she didn't suppose they'd be staying with her. Though one never knew – perhaps enough time had passed so that she and Maggie were mates by now.

'Both? Ah!' He laughed, realising her mistake. 'I'm not going with Maggie.'

'You're not?'

'I'm going on business, and Maggie's got to stay here and look after Nathan.'

'Of course,' she said, feeling stupid for not thinking of this.

'I'm going to visit US Magazines.' This was their parent company. 'It's the annual conference.'

It was obvious he'd be going. UK Magazines sent their key people every year.

'I'll miss you,' she said.

'And me you.'

'It's a shame, actually.'

'Why?'

''Cos I'm off work next week.'

'You are?'

'Yeah, I have to use up my holiday before shifting departments. I'd kind of hoped . . . you might have taken a day off to spend with me or something.'

'That would have been nice.' James sounded regretful.

'Oh, well, never mind.' Chloë changed the subject, unwilling to seem over-keen. 'Better make the most of this, then.' She kissed him persuasively. 'Fancy giving me a massage?'

The next day she was sitting at her desk, clock-watching, not something she was normally guilty of, but since she only had a couple of days left at *Babe* and had already briefed the freelancer who was covering her job while she'd be away she found it hard to motivate herself.

*Plip!* Her computer flashed up that she'd received an e-mail. She opened her inbox and scanned down. It was from James. They often used e-mail so they could communicate without being overheard in the office. She read it at once.

Have you opened your internal mail yet?

was all it said.

No, she hadn't opened any of her post. She hadn't been able to get excited about anything to do with *Babe* that day. She riffled through the pile until she located the thick brown manila envelope tied with string those at UK Publishing still found occasional use for. Her name was scrawled at No. 15, the last on the list. Inside was another smaller envelope labelled *Chloë Appleton* and underlined *Private and Confidential*. She tore it open and caught her breath.

Inside was a plane ticket. To New York. Economy, leaving the following evening (Shit! she'd have to leave work early on her last day at *Babe* – Jean would be even more cross) and returning a week – a whole week – later. Oh. My. God. Oh, my fucking God!!!

She screamed in excitement.

'What?' asked Patsy.

'Oh, er, nothing,' said Chloë.

Patsy clearly didn't believe her. 'What *nothing*? You're just screaming out of the blue?'

'I'm afraid I can't tell you,' Chloë apologised. She knew this would drive Patsy nuts.

'Tell me, tell me, tell me,' Patsy begged.

'I'm sorry. It's confidential.' Chloë thought quickly. 'To do with this new magazine. Vanessa would kill me if I disclosed it at this stage.'

'Oh,' said Patsy, pouting.

'When I can say, I promise you'll be the first to know.' Chloë simultaneously clicked on *Reply to Sender* on her e-mail.

# WOW!

she typed in 72 point, and then smaller

That is the nicest surprise I have ever had!

And quickly, before Patsy saw what she was doing, she pressed *Send*.

**Although that night** Jamie got home from squash a bit earlier than he had recently, he bolted his supper without asking Maggie how her day had been. Remembering their argument, she waited until he had finished both his dinner and dessert before clearing his plate and bowl away, but he didn't seem to notice. He simply raced upstairs to pack.

Maggie was left standing in the kitchen, reeling.

For the first time in nearly ten years, she was worrying about their marriage. Really worrying. What was going on? It wasn't just a question of normal day-to-day niggles – that was only to be expected in any long-term relationship. It was more than that, and she struggled to work out precisely what it was.

She and Jamie were very different, she knew. He was more impulsive, impatient, extrovert, light-hearted, socially at ease. At times he could be downright immature, she thought, but she had to admit that he had a way with people and his finger on the pulse of the media world. She, on the other hand, was perhaps sometimes a little over-serious, a self-disciplined hard worker with a passionate sense of aesthetics and a history of more radical political beliefs. It was true that she was less immediately gregarious, but nevertheless Maggie was a loyal and trusted friend to the few who took the time to get to know her well. She'd always thought these differences were precisely what made their relationship tick, that they complemented one another, and therein the attraction lay.

Certainly the idea of being with someone who was exactly like her was not one that she relished – Alex had also been different from her in many ways. And the thought of two people together like Jamie . . . Heaven forbid! What an overwhelming prospect that would be. But she was growing concerned that she and Jamie weren't spending enough time together, and that he seemed to be working harder than ever – though she expected that as he'd just taken on this incredibly responsible role. But their sex life was diminishing and, most worrying of all, he seemed increasingly distant. Not only had they had that huge row the previous weekend, but she'd also noticed that he was especially quick to criticise her; and he was most critical of those things where her behaviour differed most sharply from his own. It wasn't just tidiness that seemed to irritate him. It was the way she treated Nathan (apparently she was 'lacking in spontaneity and too traditional'); it was the work she did ('why don't you branch out and do something new and exciting? You've been doing this for years'). Given her own dissatisfaction with her writing and resentment of the pressure put on her to pull her weight financially, that had provoked another argument. He'd even been critical of what she wore. Maggie was proud of her taste in clothes and that day she had thought she looked especially elegant in her favourite Fendi suit, and it had really hurt. Again, he'd suggested she try something new and bold, 'sexier' was how he'd put it. But when she'd tried dressing up in that way on the night of the dinner party, he'd not even noticed!

And now he was going away on business. For a week. She'd known it was coming – he'd warned her of it months ago when he'd taken the job – but that didn't make it any easier to deal with now the time had come. She had a gut feeling that the last thing that would be good for their relationship at this point was time apart, and she desperately wanted to go with him. But she had to stay and take Nathan to school. And she certainly wouldn't want her son to feel that his parents would rather be off gallivanting alone than with him, so she didn't even venture to suggest it.

She sighed and mounted the stairs after her husband. He'd just finished packing when she entered the room.

'Phew, I'm whacked,' he said. 'I should go to bed – I've a long day ahead of me tomorrow.'

'Yes,' said Maggie, able to read the signs all too clearly. 'We'd better go straight to sleep, hadn't we?'

In bed, she lay awake, conscious that Jamie's back was turned to her. I wish we could be closer, more intimate again, she thought. But because she herself was quite reserved and the wedge between them seemed to be growing wider by the day, she wasn't sure how to broach the subject.

It was most troubling, and so far removed from the Maggie she'd imagined herself becoming. She remembered the visions she'd once had of her future. When she was a young woman she'd envisaged that by now she would be the Anita Roddick of the nutritional world, perhaps, a woman with both style and principles, who ran a chain of health-food shops, or the green queen of cuisine, with a string of beautifully written, informative vegetarian cookbooks to her name. But she wasn't even a proper vegetarian any more – these days she ate fish and chicken, albeit free-range. So here she was, to all intents and purposes a sexually frustrated housewife living in deepest Surrey with a husband who literally turned his back on her. Just how had it happened? Who was to blame?

# 16 Chloë

'**Oh, my fucking** God!' shrieked Rob. 'He's taking you to *New York*?'

'Yes.' Chloë was frantically emptying half her wardrobe on to the bed in a totally unfocused attempt at packing.

'For how long?'

'Just over a week.'

'A week! A fucking *week*? Why isn't his wife going?'

'She has to stay and look after his son.'

'Poor cow,' said Rob.

Chloë felt a sharp stab of guilt.

'Did it occur to you to say no?'

'Are you mad?'

'No, you're right. You absolutely have to go. It's a one in a million chance. So I take it this is a business trip. All expenses paid.'

'Yeah,' said Chloë. 'He's going to the annual conference at US Magazines. We'll be back next weekend.'

'He needs to be there over a week? And has to go on a Friday?'

'It runs Monday to Thursday but, hey, Rob, I'm hardly going to argue, now am I?'

'I guess not. But if I was his wife, I'd be a mite suspicious.'

'He said he hated being jet-lagged for meetings so he likes to arrive a day or two early to recover.'

'And shag you.'

'And shag me. But actually he was going anyway – I'm just going along for the ride.'

'Some ride!' Rob laughed. 'Well, firstly, I'm jealous as hell – 'cos you know I love, love, love that city, and September's a fabulous time to go. Secondly, let me help you decide what to take 'cos I know the scene there and you obviously haven't a clue – and thirdly, let me give you one piece of advice.'

'What's that?' Chloë was certain she wasn't going to like it.

'Don't, whatever you do, ask him if he is going to leave his wife for you.'

'What makes you think I would?' Chloë had studiously avoided anything too heavy so far.

'Because I know you, Chloë. You've been seeing each other – what? Once a week for a month or so? So far, it's been great fun. But it's been mainly about sex—'

'It hasn't!' protested Chloë.

'Aw, c'mon, hon – have you ever seen him without shagging?'

'No,' Chloë admitted.

'Right. So it's still at that rampant-sex stage, but when you go away together, you'll be entering a different phase. You'll talk more, you'll do things together, just the two of you . . . You'll develop your own set of romantic memories . . . You'll get closer . . . Then, *wham*! You'll fall in love with him.'

'How do you know?' asked Chloë, but she knew she was already more involved than she was prepared to acknowledge openly.

'Because all the ingredients are there. But just remember what your good friend Rob said to you: you're a long way from home, you're also a long way from reality. Back here, this man has a wife and kid. Whatever you feel while you're out there, this is where you live, where your home is, where your friends are but, above all, it's where *his* commitments are.'

'Yeah, yeah,' said Chloë, feeling distinctly uncomfortable.

'And remember, if it goes hideously wrong, I'm here, on the end of a phone for you.'

She wished he hadn't said that. It wasn't going to go wrong. There was nothing *to* go wrong. It would be fine. But she said, 'I'll remember,' just the same.

'Now, lecture over,' said Rob, his tone brightening. 'Let's decide what the girl's to wear! You'll need this.' He reached for the Spunky dress. 'Perfect for when you're wanting to hang out looking foxy in those groovy Greenwich Village coffee bars. You'd better take this,' he picked out the Whistles suit, 'because you never know when you might have to attend some smart business lunch, though I rather doubt he's gonna be parading you in front of his colleagues. Come to that, are you planning on doing some networking of your own while you're there?'

'I hadn't thought of that,' replied Chloë, 'but it's a good idea. You never know who I might meet.'

'And you'll need this, this, this and this,' Rob continued, rapidly selecting two slip dresses, a knee-length lace skirt, a short suede mini, some faded jeans, half a dozen tops and a couple of scarves, including her favourite black and red satin one. Finally, he darted off to his room, and returned, proudly brandishing a feather boa. 'From day . . .' he said, camply wrapping it round his neck ' . . . to evening!'

Chloë laughed.

'Now I'll leave you to sort out the most important thing in private.' He turned to go.

'What's that?'

'Your underwear,' he replied, shutting the door.

They met at the airport, having barely had time to speak since she'd agreed to join him.

Unfortunately, they were unable to sit together on the plane – James was travelling business class, which, when he came to book her ticket, was full. It was economy or nothing, so naturally he'd opted for economy, but he'd said he was worried she'd think he was mean. Chloë couldn't care less: she was far too excited to have a single negative thought. And while it meant they were prohibited from joining the Mile High Club by secretly having sex under the blankets (Patsy had told Chloë that this was how it was usually accomplished, not in the loos as Chloë had previously thought), it did mean they could both sleep.

'Chloë?'

She woke with a start. James had to stand in the aisle and lean over two other passengers to talk to her. 'Ye-es,' she said, sleepily coming to.

'We're nearly there. The plane's in a holding pattern. Look.'

There, out of the window, she could see it. Manhattan.

Teeny weenie from their height, but still enormous by comparison with the panoramic urban-sprawl and dense highways that surrounded it. Jesus – there was the Empire State, the Chrysler Building, and now she could see the Twin Towers, the Statue of Liberty. It was her first bird's-eye view of the fastest, most exciting, most intimidating city in the world – the ultimate fairground ride, an adrenaline queen's heaven, Chloë's Oz.

'Wow,' she said, not for the first time in twenty-four hours, nor would be the last. Configured from a thousand movies and TV shows, symbol of her passions and dreams, it was a familiar silhouette. Yet even though the baby pink clouds of sunset made it look more fairy-tale than ever, it was still somehow different from what she'd expected.

She prodded herself. Yes, that was why: because this *wasn't* a movie or a dream, it was real. Finally, at twenty-nine years of age, she was coming to New York. Or rather, and better still, she was being *taken* to New York by a man to whom she was more attracted by the minute. She was so overwhelmed by it all she thought she would burst.

No picture can do it justice, she observed, as the plane continued to descend. All the reduced scale flat images she'd seen until now simply couldn't convey the magnitude of the place in 3D. And that it was an island was somehow unexpected too. It appeared larger as the plane got closer. Fuck – if the buildings looked big from this height, they must be really *huge*! Coming in to Heathrow compared to this, coming in to Newark, thought Chloë, I mean *pur-lease*.

For a second she forgot James, carried away by her own imagination. But she wanted to share how she was feeling, so she struggled to put it into words. 'It makes London look so wimpy,' was all she could manage.

'Excuse me, sir,' said the steward, tapping him on the shoulder, 'could you return to your seat and fasten your seatbelt for landing?'

'Catch you later,' said James, clearly enjoying her reaction before he headed back to the front of the plane.

What would otherwise have been the drag of immigration and customs was far more fun because at last they could be together. Then there was more mythology made real – the exhilaration of her first New York taxi ride. James had ordered it specially.

'Can you open the trunk?' James asked the driver, immediately adapting his vocabulary to the environment. How worldly, thought Chloë. How cool. 'Here's where we're going.' He handed the driver the address, who grunted rudely in response. From the outset James had refused to tell Chloë where they were staying, wanting to surprise her.

They got in. A brutal black and white photograph, accompanied by the driver's ID number, was taped crudely on the dirty glass partition in front of them; the seating was functional black plastic. It was a far cry from the clean, spacious luxury of a London cab – more squalid, perhaps, but Chloë loved that. It had an air of de Niro danger that a black cab never would.

As they sped along the freeway through suburban New Jersey, Chloë was struck by the sheer *otherness* of it all. Not only were they on the wrong side of the road, surrounded by cars very much wider and more angular than their rounded little European counterparts, but the hoardings were bigger, brighter, brasher too. NEED THERAPY? screamed one in thirty-foot scarlet letters followed by a 1-800 number. The very idea that anyone could simply dial a freephone number for therapy – only in America, she thought. The way she was living at the moment, maybe she needed it.

Fortunately they'd missed rush-hour, so, although the traffic was heavy with people coming into the city to go out for the evening, they made it into Manhattan in just over half an hour. Through the Lincoln Tunnel and up into the city itself.

James tapped the partition. 'Can we make a detour via Sixth Avenue, please? That way we can see a little bit more before we get there.'

'So where are we?' asked Chloë, gazing in awe, up, up at the buildings towering above them.

'Midtown,' said James. 'This is 42nd Street.'

We're not *watching* a movie, thought Chloë, we're *in* a musical.

'On previous work trips I've tended to stay downtown, to be near the Village,' James explained. 'It's where Beth used to live so I know it well. And it's much more our social scene too.'

*Our* scene. He'd said 'our scene'! Linking them together, as an item, an 'us'. This was all so unbelievable. 'So why aren't we staying there this time, then?'

'I wanted to make sure we were well away from the rest of the UK Magazines brigade,' said James. 'They're all staying downtown – I think most of Editorial are at the Mercer and Sales have chosen the SoHo Grand. But I've somewhere equally special booked for us and, anyway, it's nearer the conference venue, so we can spend more time together, just me and you.' She looked over at him. Already he appeared far more relaxed, far freer than he was in London. Witnessing his delight in their surroundings she could just imagine what he must have been like as a small boy. So eager, so enthusiastic.

Chloë pushed the 'down' arrow to open the window, enjoying the exhilaration of the warm wind in her hair. The city even smelt different from home – the combination of food, people, steam was sweeter, more intense. Being here, with James, surrounded by phenomenal skyscrapers that juxtaposed to form an iconic urban jungle, Chloë again felt as if London was tame in comparison, that it lacked balls somehow. She felt so high it was as if she was on drugs, yet she'd had no more than mineral water to drink.

'Ooh, look, Times Square!' Chloë grabbed James's arm, as if he'd never seen it before. What a razzle-dazzle of pulsating neon lights – Piccadilly on acid. They turned back on themselves, west again, see-sawing their way through the night-time traffic. The crossings really *did* have signs that said 'Walk/Don't Walk', every building really *did* have a fire escape on the outside, vendors really *did* sell anything and everything on every corner, sirens really *did* scream all the time.

The taxi pulled up on 46th Street. 'We've arrived,' said James. He handed the driver fifty dollars and they stepped out on to the sidewalk.

Chloë looked up. But there was no hotel sign, only a Dean & DeLuca coffee shop to their right and a very dark bar full of hip New Yorkers sipping cocktails to their left. Confidently James picked up both suitcases and swept through the doors. Wide-eyed, Chloë followed him. She felt like Janet entering Frank 'n' Furter's castle in *The Rocky Horror Picture Show*.

'Blimey,' she said. Most unexpectedly, given the unassuming exterior, they were in one of the most gobsmacking hotel lobbies she had ever seen. Never mind the glitz of the Dorchester (she'd been to a few launch dos there), the old-fashioned polish of the Waldorf (a friend had once had a Sunday afternoon tea-party there) or even the art deco chic of Claridge's, this was more like Mezzo meets the Café de Paris: an architectural showpiece with the ambience of a nightclub, two of her favourite haunts rolled into one.

She stood on the checkered carpet and took everything in. The bizarre collection of seating had a playful humour that Conran venues lacked: an armchair with a ferocious-looking Rottweiler screen-printed on its back jostled alongside rotund ethnic stools and comfortable colonial-style sofas. A stone staircase swept down into the atrium, and in the Gothic candlelight it seemed as if it was suspended in mid-air.

'So what's this place called?' she asked at last.

'The Paramount,' said James.

'Ah,' said Chloë, 'of course.' It had been the haunt of the jet-setting *cognoscenti* for a few years now and its reputation in the media world was well-established not least because it wasn't *that* costly – accounts departments didn't get too uptight when it came to expenses. Yet those who insisted on being in the latest venue had since moved on to pastures new so they'd be away from prying eyes. Of *course* James would bring her here. They lugged their cases over to Reception, and James gave all his details to the nice-looking man behind the marble-topped counter. Indeed, the sleek young things who worked there – even the cleaners – were rumoured to dress head-to-toe in navy Armani.

Armed with their key, they took the elevator up to the fourth floor and made their way along the corridor, checking for their room number. Finally, when they found it, James turned the key and opened the door. 'There,' he said, plopping down the suitcases. 'At bloody last.'

The room was small but nicely decorated in white throughout, which ensured that the few unusual features created real impact. There was an asymmetrically designed marble-topped desk and a huge double bed, and where one would normally expect the headboard to be, Vermeer's *The Lacemaker* stared knowingly out of the corner of her eye on to the covers, as if defying Chloë and James to shock her with their antics. The bathroom was equally compact, but the cone-shaped chrome sink, with its sword-like point, was decorated dramatically with a single blood-red rose, lending the room a distinct S and M air.

'Aaah!' said Chloë, flinging herself on to the bed. 'Do you know what? For the first time since I met you, I feel as if my senses have gone into utter overload. For once, lover boy, I'm not sure I'm up to a shag.'

'Thank God for that,' laughed James, ''cos let me tell you, my dear, I ain't up for anything until I've had something to eat!'

'Hey, James,' whispered Chloë, at nine thirty the next morning, gently kissing the dip between his shoulder-blades. 'This is your rude awakening . . .'

He rolled over to face her. For a moment he looked confused, then he seemed to realise where he was, and – unless she was much mistaken – who *she* was.

'Hi.' He smiled at her. They'd been sleeping curled up together throughout the night, although James had said that he wasn't normally very good at it when she'd requested they go to sleep spoons style. But they'd both slept well, and Chloë concluded that he didn't have a problem with this kind of closeness.

Neither did he seem to have a problem in getting aroused, and they made love more slowly and sensually than they had before, enjoying the luxury of it being their first morning together and not having to rush. This time they sat facing each other, with Chloë on top, her legs wrapped around his, so they could rock gently to and fro. It meant they could see one another's expressions, heightening the intimacy of the experience, and that he could thrust deeper. It also allowed them to touch one another simultaneously, intensifying the pleasure to an almost unbearable degree.

'That was lovely,' sighed Chloë when they'd finished. Maybe it was because she was still getting to know him that it was easier to give more of herself away, but she certainly felt incredibly liberated sexually when she was with him – and this was just the start of their stay.

'Welcome to New York!' said James. As she got up he gave her bottom a mischievous smack. 'Now let's go paint this town red.'

They got showered and dressed and made their way down for breakfast. The dimly lit dining area was disconcerting first thing in the morning. Tables nestled in alcoves overlooking the lobby, allowing Chloë and James to people-watch as they ate, but tucking into coffee and croissants in such an evening setting made Chloë feel even more confused about the time difference than she already was. The choice of food was extraordinarily lavish – Chloë could have eaten enough to keep her going until breakfast the following day – and everything, bar the coffee, was topped with a single strawberry, the yoghurts, the fruit cocktails, the grapefruit halves, the pastries . . . The sensuality of this, with the surroundings and the secretiveness of their situation formed a heady concoction and Chloë felt quite intoxicated before they'd even left the building.

Next, they hit the streets. Down Eighth Avenue then heading

for pier 83 at West 42nd to catch the Circle Line boat tour around the island. 'This is the one totally naff touristy thing we're allowed to do,' said James. 'It will help you get your bearings and give you an overview of the city, so when you're wandering around next week on your own you'll know where you are.'

The colossal trucks that roared past them as they walked were so macho, thought Chloë, and so were the drivers, who honked at Chloë or James, depending on their sexual preference. On a corner they stopped to watch some evangelical singers with amps and mikes, performing in the street. It reminded Chloë of a Coke ad that had been on television when she was a child. It was a warm day – a crisp 72° Fahrenheit with clear blue skies and a light breeze.

As expected, the Circle Line boat was full of holiday-makers, but to Chloë's surprise and pleasure many New Yorkers too. Three hours later she understood why. It was the best 'touristy' thing she'd ever done – so good even the natives did it: the boat circumnavigated the island to the accompaniment of the most ironic guide she'd ever encountered. They passed Battery Park City, the World Financial Center and the World Trade, each making their mark on the unforgettable skyline of Lower Manhattan, and Chloë took photos of it all. They went round the Statue of Liberty and under all the bridges – Brooklyn, Manhattan and Williamsburg. They saw millionaires' mansions like the Rothschilds' and poor tenement blocks; the dominating presence of the United Nations alongside the Chrysler glinting in the sun; even a prison. The inmates, all out taking the air in their playpen cage on top of the building, rattled the wire mesh, crawled up it and shouted at them as they sailed past. Wild.

Three Americans were sitting in front of Chloë and James; initially Chloë – caught up in enthusiasm and loving everyone as much as everything – was happy to chat to anyone. But once she'd got over the excitement of talking to local people, she discovered they were right wing to an alienating degree. The leader of the trio – a self-confessed 44-year-old self-made man from the city – told her and James that they had better duck as they passed the bridge to the Bronx, lest the 'black animals throw bricks' at them. Chloë was shocked.

Later she persuaded James to make one more exception to his 'no naff touristy things' rule and they went up the Empire State. It was only a twenty-minute walk from their hotel, after all. Normally Chloë got vertigo at the top of high buildings, but she wasn't afraid of flying – her phobias had no logic. Up there she felt as if she was in a plane so she wasn't scared. At 102 floors up, Manhattan stretched out on all sides below; now she could see Central Park, the un-British regularity of the streets, the varying heights, shapes and architectural styles of the buildings. Momentarily she felt as if she could reach for the skies, achieve anything, be anyone she wanted to be. It was another unreal experience – Chloë had had several already that day and it was still only four o'clock.

But back at the hotel the receptionist brought them back down to earth with a bump. 'You had a message while you were out,' he said, handing over their key and a slip of paper.

James unfolded it and paled. 'Shit! Maggie!' he said. 'I never rang her to say I'd got here safely.' He glanced nervously at Chloë. The receptionist looked away tactfully. Doubtless, given that the hotel was a regular haunt of rock and movie stars, he'd seen far worse indiscretions before.

'Look, why don't I stay down here and have a coffee?' Chloë suggested graciously. 'You go and give her a call from the room.'

'Thanks,' said James. 'Give me fifteen minutes – yeah?' He charged off in the direction of the elevator, leaving Chloë not quite sure what to think, standing in the lobby. She made her way up the floating staircase to the bar and ordered a double espresso. Then she took a seat overlooking Reception just as they had at breakfast, and tried desperately not to think about James sitting on *their* bed talking to his wife, as she focused on the people coming and going below.

What an unlikely mix they were! There were golfing types in lurid trousers, diminutive Japanese businessmen and even more petite exotic beauties with pierced and bejewelled rockstar boyfriends. There was an entire family, complete with grand-parents and newborn baby. When Chloë eavesdropped she could make out they were Italian – trust them to put style over practicality even though they had little ones in tow, she thought.

But, try as she might, Chloë couldn't help wondering what James was saying to Maggie on the phone upstairs. In one way she was shamefully pleased that he'd forgotten to call her – the fact that he was too wrapped up in being here was surely a satisfying reflection of the amazing time they were having. But Chloë wasn't a bitch by nature, just occasionally thoughtless and often egotistical, and the bigger part of her heart went out to his wife at home. Maggie might have been worried, she pondered, I know I would have been. And all the while her husband was not only safe and well, he was having the time of his life with another woman. It wasn't nice of James not to have called. If he'd promised to phone at the first opportunity, he should have done so before they had gone out that morning. Then again, she reasoned, a woman with a husband as successful as James had probably got used to him spending time away from home. Especially because, from what she remembered James saying, Maggie sounded so capable and efficient. Doubtless she was good at dealing with his foibles and just took it all in her stride.

Chloë finished her coffee and checked her watch. At least twenty minutes had passed: she could go back to their room now. As she picked up her bag and walked round to the elevator, she thought, Oh, why, in God's name, does he have to be *married*?

## 17  Maggie

**Carefully Maggie edged** her way in through the kitchen door laden with four Waitrose carrier-bags, followed by Nathan, who was dutifully carrying the fifth. She looked over to the answering-machine and frowned. The light wasn't flashing; there had been no calls. She dumped the bags on the table, picked up the phone and dialled 1471 just in case. The irritatingly jerky voice of BT's computerised operator gave Fran's number. So no one had called since her sister had rung, long before she and Nathan had gone shopping.

Maggie checked her watch. It was 5.30 p.m. – gone midday in New York. Even allowing for jet-lag, she'd have expected Jamie to have telephoned by now. She'd said not to bother when he arrived, she'd be fast asleep at this end, but to call her when he woke up instead. Oh, well, she thought, maybe he's just having a lie-in. We so rarely get one. She resolved to ring him later and began to unpack the food.

'Can I have one now?' asked Nathan, grabbing a packet of

Wagon Wheels that Maggie had bought him in a rare moment of weakness.

'Yes,' said Maggie, 'but first help me put everything away.'

By seven thirty Jamie still hadn't called so, once she'd put Nathan to bed, Maggie rang the hotel.

'I'll just try for you, ma'am,' said the switchboard operator. Maggie listened to the phone with the distinctive single tone that differentiated American telecommunications.

'I'm afraid there's no reply, ma'am,' said the operator. 'Would you like me to pass on a message?'

'Yes, please. Could you tell Mr Slater that his wife, Maggie, called?'

Nearly two hours later Maggie was curled up on the sofa watching TV when the phone rang. Saturday-night television was so dull she'd found it hard to concentrate but the ringing still made her jump.

'Hi, Maggie.'

'Jamie!'

'I'm sorry I didn't phone you earlier.'

'I was so worried. I know it's silly, but you'd promised to call.'

'I know, I know, I'm really sorry,' Jamie apologised. 'I guess I completely forgot, what with jet-lag and all.'

'How was your flight?' Maggie didn't want to nag.

'Oh, fine,' he said. He sounded very far away. 'The usual, you know. All that drag of getting through customs and immigration – it seems to take longer each time. I didn't get in till really late.'

'Mm,' said Maggie. She did know. Before Nathan had been born she and Jamie had been to New York together a couple of times. He'd said he loved it, and although initially she had been uncomfortable with his passion for it because she associated it with a girlfriend of his who lived there, the more time she'd spent in the city the more aspects of it she found that appealed to her – the superb art galleries, the unparalleled choice of first-rate restaurants, the value-for-money designer clothes. Plus there was a liberal anti-establishment fervour that permeated certain areas like the Village around NYU and Christopher Street, which struck a chord with her, reminding her of the way she'd been as a student.

Nevertheless, if she'd gone this time with Jamie she probably wouldn't have had much opportunity to explore. Doubtless she'd have been roped into numerous business functions as his other half, and socialising as 'the wife of the publisher' was her idea of hell. No, it was better to leave him to it – he was much better at that stuff than she was. And Nathan needed her here, after all.

'So what have you done today?' she asked, tucking her feet snugly under a cushion on the settee in readiness for a long chat. She was so glad to hear from him that the argument of the previous night seemed light years ago.

'Oh, nothing much.' There was a pause.

'You must have done *something* – you were out of your room all afternoon.'

'I, er, went to Bloomingdale's,' he said hesitantly.

*Great!* thought Maggie. Perhaps he's bought me a present. 'Did you get anything?'

'Um, yes.' He sounded evasive. Maybe he had! 'I got something for Nathan.'

'You did? What?'

'Wait and see. It'll be a surprise.'

'You don't need to surprise *me* if it's for Nathan. Tell me, what is it?'

'It's hard to explain. It's the latest American gadget. You'll have to see for yourself.'

'I'm fascinated.' What could it be? 'Did you get anything for me?' she added hopefully.

'Yeah, a little something. But that will have to be a surprise too.'

'How exciting!' exclaimed Maggie. 'You are a lovely man!'

'Thanks.' Jamie sounded ill-at-ease – he'd always been bad at receiving compliments. 'So how's everything with you?'

The next day Maggie dropped off Nathan at Fran's on the out-skirts of Leatherhead to play with Dan, and drove down the A3 and along Chelsea Embankment to meet Jean at the Tate Gallery. There was an exhibition called *The Art of Bloomsbury* that they both wanted to see and then they were going for afternoon tea. They'd arranged to meet on the steps to the museum overlooking the Thames and – typically – Jean was already waiting among dozens of other art-lovers when Maggie arrived.

'Well,' Jean lifted her sunglasses to air-kiss Maggie's cheeks, 'how are you?'

'I'm fine,' replied Maggie, as they entered the foyer and headed for the ticket booth.

'Are you sure? I thought Jamie was a bit of a prick when we all came to supper the other night.' As ever, Jean didn't pull her punches.

That was weeks ago, thought Maggie defensively. 'Oh, we're over that now,' she proclaimed, joining the queue. 'Water under the bridge, you know. I spoke to him last night and he's already bought me a present in New York.'

'How sweet,' said Jean. 'So . . .' she nudged her friend in the ribs ' . . . been having lots of hanky-panky to conceive a sibling for Nathan, then, have we? I've noticed Jamie's been looking pretty good recently. Glowing, I'd say. And I thought it was only women who so clearly conveyed when they were getting some action.'

'Oh, er, yes.' Maggie was too embarrassed to contradict her. Jamie didn't look any different to her. If anything, he just seemed more exhausted. Maybe he was putting on a front at work – it being a new job – driving his energies into impressing his new colleagues.

'Ooh, I *shall* enjoy teasing him at the conference later this week,' Jean ploughed on. 'Meanwhile, I await the happy news. And remember, this time *I* want to be godmother!'

'Of course,' said Maggie. 'I wouldn't dream of asking anyone else.'

As they wandered around the exhibition, Maggie found herself unexpectedly moved by the work of Vanessa Bell. Before, she'd identified with the more serious, sensitive Virginia Woolf, especially as Alex – the sweetheart – had always said she looked like a prettier version of the author, and Maggie's gift was with words too, not painting. But now, reading the captions and examining the sketches and paintings, she appreciated that the sister had talent and had coped with a lot as well.

There was one striking portrait of Vanessa Bell, by Duncan Grant, where she looked both stoic and vulnerable. It was accompanied by a quote from Virginia Woolf: 'A spirit given to contemplation and self control. Decision and composure stamped her.'

Jean came up beside her. 'She reminds me of you in that,' she said, echoing Maggie's thoughts.

Her lover's bisexuality couldn't have been easy to bear, Maggie pondered, moving on to the paintings of naked men by Duncan Grant. The passionate strokes of paint over the muscular forms suggested that he was far more interested in the male physique than in that of a woman like Vanessa. Yet Maggie sensed that she seemed always to be yearning for him, even when she was married to Clive Bell.

What a weird triangle that had been – Vanessa, Duncan, Clive – with Vanessa having children by both of them . . . God, that Bloomsbury bunch had got themselves into terrible muddles, Maggie thought. What shaky foundations their relationships were built on. They might have produced great art, but at what cost to their children? Apparently Vanessa and Duncan's daughter had not been told who her real father was until she was seventeen.

Maggie stood in front of a self-portrait of Duncan Grant as a young man and looked deep into his eyes. The self-love was evident. Quite what Vanessa had seen in him Maggie wasn't sure. And how she'd put up with living in such close proximity to him throughout his various affairs was beyond Maggie's comprehension. Perhaps it was because these affairs were with men and she was married. But it must have hurt all the same. And he wasn't even that good-looking. Maggie was most indignant. Heavens! If Jamie managed to be faithful, and he was ten times more attractive – why couldn't Duncan be – if not to Vanessa, then to one man?

As she turned to look at the next series of sketches, she caught her breath. A man was standing with his back to her, examining a landscape. The way he was holding his head, coupled with the line of his shoulders, was Jamie to the life. A woman came up beside him and he placed a hand on her bottom in a manner that was both friendly and sensual. Now there was a hot-blooded heterosexual man, thought Maggie. She moved to get a glimpse of his face. He was remarkably handsome. Even if the woman was his wife, Maggie could see that endless other women must throw themselves at him.

Then a wave of nausea overtook her as, in a flash, she recalled Jean's words that Jamie had been 'glowing' recently . . . But he wasn't doing it with *her*, was he? And while she was sure he wouldn't sleep with men . . . *Oh, Christ*, she thought, feeling really sick. All the Bloomsbury portraits seemed to be crashing in on her. Surely Jamie couldn't be sleeping with another woman?

She looked round desperately for Jean, who was standing a little way off. She went up and tapped her friend's shoulder. 'Jean,' she whispered, 'you don't think Jamie's having an affair, do you?'

'Goodness!' Jean laughed. 'I know it's powerful stuff, but this exhibition's really getting to you, isn't it?'

Maggie wondered if she was just being silly. She didn't reply.

'Why on earth would you think that? asked Jean.

'Oh, I don't know.' Maggie couldn't face putting it into words. It was as if saying it might make it real. And if he is having an affair, she thought, I'll kill him.

'Don't be ridiculous!' cried Jean, causing a few people in the gallery to turn around. Then she added more quietly, 'You were only just telling me that things between you are fine at the moment. And this lot were far more experimental in their sexuality than most, I assure you.' She gave her friend's shoulders a comforting squeeze. 'Sometimes you worry too much, Maggie darling.'

'I know,' Maggie acknowledged. 'Perhaps I spend too much time on my own.'

'I'm sure that's what it is. I know Jamie adores you – and Nathan.' She laughed. 'And I'll tell you one thing, if he *ever* messes you around he'll have me to answer to!'

Maggie felt cheered. If there was one person she could rely on to poke fun at her it was Jean.

Jean seemed to sense that further reassurance wouldn't go amiss. 'Look, if it will make you feel better I'll have a word with him,' she said. 'I'm flying out tomorrow for the editorial presentations, and we'll be in the same venue for much of the week.'

Maggie hesitated. Jamie would be furious if he found out they'd been talking about him. 'Don't tell him I was worried.'

'Trust me, I won't. I'll just hint that he's so wrapped up in his work that he might be forgetting to pay you enough attention, that's all.'

'Okay,' said Maggie nervously. 'But only if it comes up without looking forced. And be subtle, won't you?'

'Leave it to me.' Jean winked conspiratorially. 'Now then, my dear, I think we should give this last room a miss. What we need is a nice cup of tea and a huge slice of cake.'

## 18 Chloë

Chloë listened at the door. It sounded as if James had finished on the phone. She knocked gently and went in. He was sitting on the bed, his head in his hands.

'James?' she said softly.

He looked up. She could swear there were tears in his eyes.

'Are you okay?'

'Mmm.' But he didn't sound it.

She sat down next to him on the white counterpane. The weight of the two of them propelled her closer to him. She took his hand.

James sighed unsteadily. 'I feel such a prick,' he whispered.

It was a tone she'd not heard before. Oh dear, she worried, here we go. He's going to get cold feet. Regret the whole thing. Finish with me. And we've only been here a day! The prospect of rejection was more than she could bear.

He looked at her. 'Have you got a cigarette?'

'No,' said Chloë, immediately wanting one too. 'Shall I go and get one?'

'It doesn't matter,' said James. She'd never seen him look so sad.

They were silent.

After a while she said, 'It's Maggie?' trying control her voice.

James nodded. 'Kind of.'

'Tell me.' Chloë didn't really want to know, but they were in too deep now.

'And Nathan,' said Jamie, putting his hand to his mouth as if he could hardly bear to say what he was saying. 'Oh, Chloë!' he said desperately. Then he squeezed her hand hard, as if to emphasise their connection, and to establish that she was definitely there.

Chloë was caught in a maelstrom of emotions. Part of her wanted to end this conversation right now, to move on to something lighter, less serious. They'd been having such fun, and she didn't want it to finish. Part of her wanted to make him feel better. To take his pain away, at no matter what it cost her. But some part of her wanted to run as fast as she could back to England, to Rob, her flat, her friends, Patsy, her job, before it was too late, before she, too, got hurt.

Instead she just sat there, saying nothing, paralysed.

'I don't know what to do,' he said, after a while.

'Do?' Chloë stroked his hand. 'You don't have to *do* anything.'

'I don't?' He stared up and into her eyes. He looked lost, vulnerable. Just like a small boy.

Oh, my Lord, thought Chloë, her emotions all over the place. Perhaps she was really falling for him, after all. She didn't want to lose him, or to curtail the time they were sharing. 'No,' she said, keenly wanting to reassure him. 'You don't.'

James sighed again, but this time he sounded a little relieved. 'You're quite a woman,' he smiled in acknowledgement.

'Thank you,' said Chloë, and smiled wanly. 'I try.' She had a mad, impulsive desire to tell him she loved him.

'I don't want you to get hurt,' he said.

Ouch. Not a good sign. She pushed away the thought of potential pain. 'I won't.'

He started fidgeting with the bedcovers, pulling at a loose thread. Then he took a deep breath, 'It's just . . . I have a son,' he said, finally.

'I know,' said Chloë, the full force of his words hitting her like a truck at ninety miles per hour. 'I'm not asking you to leave him.'

'I know . . . I know . . .'

Chloë's thoughts rushed back to that conversation she'd had with Craig, the journalist, a few weeks ago about the damaging effects of divorce. She felt a sudden jolt of identification with Nathan, remembering that twenty years ago, she had been helpless in the face of her parents' preoccupation with their own affairs. Incapable of making them behave any differently, incapable of understanding them.

'I don't expect you to leave them,' she whispered. And this time, when she looked at him, she was aware that her eyes were full of tears. Before she could stop them, they were coursing down her cheeks.

'Oh, Chloë,' he said again, and kissed her.

It was the only thing that could possibly, possibly make her feel better, so she kissed him back, blotting out the sorrow and the confusion, the future and the past.

'I'm so sorry,' he said, brushing away her fringe so he could look into her face.

'Me too.' She sniffed. And they kissed some more, falling backwards on to the bed. She giggled through her tears. 'I guess we're both just being a bit over-emotional . . .'

' . . . and jet-lagged . . .'

' . . . and jet-lagged . . .'

James began to kiss her again, more deeply, their lips locked together as if they couldn't bear to be apart. Then Chloë was swept up, up, and once more the future didn't matter – neither did she, nor Nathan, nor Maggie, nor anything other than being on the bed, in the Paramount, in New York, at that moment. And as they made love she thought of the view from the Empire State of the huge, huge city and the tiny, tiny people, all in their apartments, all with their own lives to live and their own paths to tread. And she thought that she and James were just two tiny, tiny ants in the whole scheme of things, and that the world would keep on turning regardless, and that she was powerless to stop herself, and what would be would be. Then, as she felt him move inside her, she started to come, softly, gently, at first, then on and on, as if it was never going to end.

## 19 Chloë

'**I'm going to** skip the conference this afternoon,' said James on Tuesday morning. 'I want to go to Bloomingdale's.'

'Fab!' exclaimed Chloë, kissing him enthusiastically. 'I haven't been there yet. Shall I meet you there?'

'If you like.' James hesitated. 'I was going to get something for Nathan.'

'Oh.' Not for the first time in the last couple of days, Chloë was unsure what to say. Should she go with him, and help him choose? No, that would be interfering. She ended up saying, 'Perhaps we can meet after you've bought something,' because she did *so* want to go Bloomingdale's herself – she had done little shopping thus far.

On Sunday in the morning they'd walked around Central Park, where she'd witnessed real New Yorkers running, roller-blading and power-walking around the reservoir and even a mother-and-stroller exercise class. On the edge of the track a group of women, complete with pushchairs and offspring, had performed a series of stretch-and-tone movements in response to whatever was barked at them by a fearsomely fit instructor. The elegance of a ballet class with *babies*? Was that what it was like bringing up children – or just in Manhattan? It was bizarre, and she couldn't imagine it at all.

Then they'd gone on to the Metropolitan Museum – there was something about art galleries on a Sunday that felt so *right*, Chloë thought. They wandered around together, discussing their likes and dislikes and pointing out their particular favourites. Sometimes Chloë appreciated James all the more for sharing her opinion, at other times she disagreed with him vociferously. But it was stimulating arguing with someone else whose opinions were as strong as her own.

In the evening they dined at a restaurant James knew of in the grimly named 'meat-packing district' of the West Village. When she stepped out of their taxi into a street full of bleak warehouses and rubbish skips and saw a transvestite hooker on the corner, Chloë thought that maybe 'meat-packing' referred to some weird sexual kink and James had got the wrong address. But no, in through a dark doorway was Fressen, with its understated Mondrian-meets-Japanese-minimalist décor and those-in-the-know clientele, sitting enjoying pre-dinner drinks at a huge horseshoe-shaped bar. The food had been delicious, and the conversation even more so.

To the accompaniment of lemon grass soup followed by sole with almonds (James) and Thai salmon fishcakes followed by duck (Chloë) they'd talked of their pasts – childhood memories, school successes and failings, first relationships, their siblings, their parents. They'd talked of the first time they'd smoked pot, and discovered a shared appetite for champagne and cocaine. And as they'd talked, freed by being a long way from anyone who might know them, they'd finally exchanged saucy tales of their fantasies in hushed whispers. It had been the most romantic, sensual day, and were it not for the underlying concern she had about their increasing involvement and its implications, Chloë would have thought she'd died and gone to heaven.

On Monday, while James had been at the conference, Chloë

decided to broaden her cultural perspective on the city. She had gone to the Tenement Museum on the Lower East Side to learn at first hand about the tough living conditions of immigrant workers and had come out of the experience duly chastened, for a while. Afterwards, she had wandered through the Financial District, and eaten a late lunch in Battery Park, nobly munching salad and less nobly eyeing up the wealthy bankers. (Not seriously, mind.) By the end of the day Chloë was in love with New York in all its diversity – the attraction of the metropolis only serving to enhance her feelings for the man who had introduced her to the city, and vice versa.

By Tuesday morning Chloë felt justified in being frivolous and hedonistic again and indulging in some retail therapy. Bugger if it's shallow, she thought, I might get run over by a bus tomorrow. She persuaded herself that she had to experience everything she possibly could, given the few days she had there, including narcissism New-York style. In the name of research for her magazine, she believed it was *essential* to sample some beauty treatments, so booked herself in for a makeover at the Mac counter at Bloomingdales at two thirty, and told James to find her there at three.

In the meantime, she decided to begin her day with a luxury manicure at one of the numerous Korean-run salons just off Times Square. The woman who did her nails could barely speak a word of English, yet through a series of gentle yet firm gestures managed to communicate exactly which finger or thumb she needed when and where. With the help of cuticle remover and nail clippers, orange sticks and cotton buds, files and fixative, nourishing cream and base coat, ultraviolet light and fans, she transformed Chloe's somewhat bitten nails into polished perfection. Chloë was even allowed to choose from a range of particularly manic-sounding colours including 'Snappy', 'Hasty', 'Chop Chop', 'Fast Lane' and 'Move Out'. In the end she opted for 'Supersonic', a metallic silver polish that reflected her present live-fast/die-young mood.

From there it was up to 59th Street and Lexington Avenue to the world-famous department store. After testing a dozen different perfumes and concluding that she didn't like any of them as much as Paloma, Chloë located the Mac counter. Here her face was stripped of its usual makeup and her hair clipped back while a thickly powdered beauty set about transforming her attractive but far from supermodel features into *femme fatale* flawlessness.

And that is exactly where Chloë was – one eye half made up, the other bare – when there was a screech from across the counter, a screech that made her blood run cold.

'Chloë! It can't be! *Chloë!* Is that you?' Out of one eye – she couldn't move her face – Chloë verified that the voice matched the person to whom she feared it belonged.

Jean.

Oh, fuck. Fuck. *Fuck!*

Now Jean was at her shoulder. After years of working together, she'd recognise Chloë anywhere.

'Hi,' said Chloë weakly, the powdered beauty still determinedly dabbing at her eyelid.

'Have you come to the conference?' asked Jean.

Jesus, never mind being in a live-fast/die-young mood; now Chloë had to think at supersonic speed. 'Er, no . . .'

'Gosh, really? How strange. Well, what a coincidence!'

'I'm on holiday. If you remember I had to use it up before starting work with Vanessa.' When lying stick to as close to the truth as possible, she'd always been told. And deflect: 'How about you?'

'Oh, I'm here for the conference, of course,' said Jean. 'You should know that!'

If she thought about it Chloë did, but she was playing for time.

'So,' continued Jean, 'where are you staying?'

'With some friends in the Village.' Chloë spoke as best she could with her jaw wide open as the powdered beauty lip-lined her mouth. God, being made up by this woman *and* grilled by her ex-boss – it was like being Dustin Hoffman in the torture scene with the dentist in *Marathon Man*. 'How about you?' Oh, please God, not the Paramount.

'The Algonquin,' said Jean. 'I know it's not trendy like some of the others but I like it there. I can kid myself I'm almost literary.'

Phew, thought Chloë. Maybe this wasn't so bad. But – oh, heavens – James! James was meeting her here! If she squinted sideways she could just see her watch: 2.55. She had five minutes to get rid of Jean, if she was lucky.

But Jean seemed to have no desire to go. 'So, if you're here anyway,' Jean continued, in her most I-mean-business voice, 'you should come to the conference, Chloë. Or at least come tomorrow. They're talking about Special Projects, I believe. I can arrange for you to attend. Ring me in the morning at the Algonquin before nine and we can meet up and go together.'

Aargh! Worse and worse! 'That would be great,' said Chloë, opening her eyes extra wide in horror. The powdered beauty misread the signal, and leapt at the chance to attack her with another layer of mascara.

'Then afterwards, if you like, we could go out for supper.'

No, no, no! thought Chloë. James and I have only got a few nights left. 'I'm afraid I've arranged to meet my friends,' she said instead. Then, in case Jean decided to invite herself to join them, she added, 'They've booked at Nobu for a birthday bash.' Thank Christ James had told her about this exclusive TriBeCa restaurant where you had to reserve a table three weeks in advance. There was no way Jean could gatecrash that.

'Really?' Jean was clearly impressed. 'What a hip crowd you must know here.'

'Oh, I do,' said Chloë. In for a penny. 'My friend Matt is a playwright. Lives in the East Village.'

'Is that where you're staying?'

'Um, yes.'

'Where, exactly?'

Addresses! 'It's on Spring Street,' she said, pulling a subway stop out of the air.

'Gosh, how *trendy*,' said Jean. 'But I'd call that SoHo.'

'SoHo, East Village, NoHo . . . it's all the same,' laughed Chloë, desperately. 'Eh?'

'If you say so,' Jean agreed.

At that moment, just when she thought she was winning, Chloë saw James weaving his way through Lancome, Chanel, Urban Decay . . . And Jean had her back to him so he was bound not to realise who she was talking to . . .

Drastic action was called for.

There, on the side, was a huge bottle of eye-makeup remover. Hideously oily, but . . . 'Oh, my God, *Jean*!' Chloë shrieked theatrically, as she sent the bottle flying. The liquid spilt all over Jean's Jil Sander suit. Then again, to make doubly sure everyone in the vicinity heard the ruckus, '*Jean!* I am so sorry!'

James was virtually upon them, only ten feet away, armed with a Bloomingdale's bag signifying success on the Nathan front. Jean was bent over frantically sponging her jacket with some tissues. The powdered beauty was mopping the counter – it needed one more shriek.

'Oh, JEAN, how can I make it up to you?'

And – thank *God* – all at once James realised what the commotion was about. He did a sharp right behind a pillar, just before Jean stood upright again, and fled. Fled as fast as he could (without running), through Christian Dior and Trish McEvoy, past women's belts and gloves, and out of the first door he could find on to Lexington Avenue.

Leaving Chloë sitting there, wanting the ground to swallow her up, thinking this was surely the closest shave of her life.

Half an hour later she was back at the Paramount. Believing that James would have returned immediately too, she was surprised – and disappointed – to find the key to the room behind Reception.

Once upstairs, she sat on the bed and tried to calm down. She was still shaken.

That was pretty nifty footwork, she congratulated herself. But now she was lumbered with going to the conference – probably not just tomorrow but on Thursday as well. And while Chloë had a passionate interest in magazines and her job, her experience of such events had taught her that one normally had to sit through hours of mind-numbing facts, figures and forecasts to obtain the merest morsel of interesting information. She would far rather be exploring New York, and moreover, she thought huffily, doing so would probably have been a more useful way for an up-and-coming magazine editor to spend her time.

Not only that but James would be at the conference too, and they'd have to ignore each other in a way that they hadn't had to before. Until now their professional encounters had been one-to-one, so they'd been able to relax and be themselves, and she didn't fancy faking not knowing him well. And Jean had insisted that Chloë ring her, so they could go together, and there was a distinct possibility that Vanessa would be there. How *stupid* of her not to have realised this was where she might be going too – and God knows who else besides.

As minutes ticked by and there was *still* no sign of James, she grew increasingly pissed off. Although she understood why he had fled she was none too impressed that he hadn't come back at once to sing her praises for being so quick-thinking and getting them out of a nightmare situation.

As New Yorkers would say, they were *all* pouring rain on her parade.

Eventually, about an hour later, James returned.

'Where have you been?' she asked. 'I was worried.'

'Sorry,' said James. 'I had some other things to get.' He plonked several carrier-bags on the bed.

'Wasn't that awful? Imagine if she'd seen you!'

'It doesn't bear thinking about,' James shook his head. 'It really doesn't. And Jean of all people. My God! She's Maggie's best friend!' He looked as shaken as Chloë felt.

Chloë, though she knew it was unreasonable, felt hurt. She'd suspected it – now she knew: James was ashamed of their affair, of her. Immediately, she pushed the thought aside. 'And now I've got to come to the bloody conference,' she said crossly, projecting her frustration with him onto something else. 'Jean's insisted I go along tomorrow as I'm here anyway. But I wanted to see more of New York.'

'Maybe it'll be useful,' he said, with equanimity. 'You could find out some stuff for this new magazine.'

'Pah!'

'Well, there are a lot of interesting things happening right now in the American market – especially in women's magazines. It might not be such a bad idea to learn more.'

'I suppose so.' This was *not* what Chloë wanted to hear. She wanted him to be grateful to her, while instead he was coming over all pragmatic and professional. 'So,' she changed the subject – her usual ploy when things got sticky, 'what did you get? Anything for me?'

'Er, no,' said James. 'I had to get some stuff for Nathan . . .' Then he added, as if being honest would alleviate his guilt, '. . . and I thought I ought to get something for Maggie.'

'Oh.' This upset Chloë further. Clearly it was Maggie who had been foremost in his thoughts over the last hour, not her. But, punishing herself, she had to find out more: she wanted a better idea of the woman. Just what *would* he give her? 'Can I see?'

James looked surprised. 'I suppose so, if you want.'

She emptied the bags on to the bed. For Nathan he'd got an American football shirt and some computer games, and for Maggie – Chloë unfolded several layers of tissue, shook out the contents and gasped. He'd bought a beautiful hand-printed silk chiffon scarf. In soft shades of blue and grey and pink, it was very, very elegant, the kind of thing Chloë would never wear. She checked the label. Fendi. It must have cost a packet. 'God. It's lovely.' She tried not to sound bothered.

But James obviously picked up her vibes. 'I was going to get you something,' he said, ruffling her hair. Chloë flinched – for a second she imagined him ruffling Maggie's hair in the same way and despised him. 'What I have in mind I need to meet someone for.' He looked at his watch. 'In fact, I've got to go to meet them pretty much now.'

'Oh. *Right.*' Chloë could scarcely keep the sarcasm out of her voice. She didn't believe him. He's trying to dig himself out of a hole, she thought. I can see through it.

James had already got to his feet again and picked up his wallet. 'I won't be long,' he said, and left before she could protest, banging the door behind him.

## 20 Chloë

**While James was** gone, Chloë got herself into something of a state. This was their first row – or it nearly had been. On one hand she was worried she'd been too stroppy, but on the other she felt she had the right to be demanding. So that she shouldn't start biting her newly done nails, she smoked three cigarettes. (They'd bought a packet to share when out for dinner one night.) She started writing a postcard to Sam to distract herself, but gave up after one line. She hadn't even told him she was seeing a married man, let alone in New York, and she was aware that brotherly concern might lead to disapproval of her behaviour, and that was the last thing she wanted. After a few minutes of chewing the end of the pen, she decided she really wanted to talk to Rob. He knew the scene after all, and five o'clock was a good time to ring the UK. He called her straight back – it was far cheaper that way.

'How are you getting on?' he asked.

Propping her head on the pillows and stretching out on the bed, she told him about the excitement of being in New York ('I want to come and *live* here one day,' she said exuberantly). She told him the things she and James had done, their romantic evenings, how she'd got to know him much better, everything they had in common, the lovely sex. ('Sounds fabulous!' he commented.) Then she told him about the encounter with Jean (which, to her irritation, he found funny) and finally about the near-argument.

'Hmm,' said Rob when she'd finished. 'Well, honey, what did you expect?'

'I don't know!' wailed Chloë.

'I did warn you . . .'

'I know.'

'Right, then. Let's have a moment's pause for thought here.'

'Okay.'

'I want you to be honest.'

'Okay.'

'Question one. Do you love him?'

'I think so.'

'Oh dear. I knew as much. Question two. Have you told him?'

'No.'

'Good. Question three. Has he told you?'

'No.'

'Fine. Question four. Have you asked him to leave his wife yet?'

'No.'

'I give you till Friday.'

'Rob! I won't! You told me not to!'

'Chloë. Darling. When have you ever done half the things I tell you to?'

'Sometimes,' protested Chloë. She racked her brain. 'I ditched Bob Andrews 'cos you told me to.'

'Well, I'm flattered you see it that way, but as far as I recall, you ditched boring Bob 'cos he wasn't bright enough for you. It's just I was the only one honest enough to tell you so.'

'Okay,' agreed Chloë. 'But, anyway, I promise I won't ask him to leave Maggie. He's got a son – I couldn't do that to him!'

'Couldn't do it to who? James or his son?'

'His son, Nathan.'

'*Now* you say so,' said Rob.

Eeek. That observation pained her. Rob might as well whip her and be done with it.

'Look,' said Rob, 'you know what I think.'

'What?' said Chloë. She supposed he might as well tell her it like it was. This was why she'd rung him, after all.

'I think he sounds great, to be honest,' Rob continued, obviously keen to express his take on the matter at last, 'absolutely right for you in many, many ways. He's successful, he's bright, he's funny, you like the same kind of things. He says he doesn't make a habit of affairs, which – if you believe it – means he might be serious. And from what I glimpsed of him from behind my net curtains that time –' Rob had sneaked a look a couple of weeks previously when James had been leaving '– I've got to concede he's pretty damn gorgeous. Infinitely fuckable, I'd say.'

Chloë purred.

'But,' he continued, 'you silly, *silly* girl, the man is married!'

'I know,' said Chloë, in a small voice. 'I just couldn't seem to stop myself.'

'You're too much of an adrenaline junkie for your own good,' said Rob. 'And if anyone knows, I should. It's just I don't want you to get hurt.' His words echoed James's ominously.

'Me neither.'

'And from my experience – which admittedly isn't quite the same – if a man is married, or committed to someone with a child, the commitment runs much deeper than might seem to be the case.'

'I realise that.'

'Has he ever, for instance, told you he doesn't love his wife any more?'

'Um, no, not exactly . . .'

'Well, then, I'm sorry to say that my guess is he does.'

'Oh.' Chloë hadn't really faced this idea. James's behaviour had seemed to suggest otherwise, but it was true he'd never said he didn't love Maggie.

'Which means one of three things. Either he's going to string you both along until he sorts his head out – in which case he *may* finally decide to leave her for you but it could take a long time, trust me. Or he's going to leave her eventually, but you may just end up being the relationship that instigates that, the rebound one, not the one he ends up in. Or he'll stay with her because he loves her and because of Nathan.'

Yee-ouch! Chloë felt her parade had been swept away by a hurricane. But she also knew he was right. 'So what do you suggest I do?'

'Quite frankly, my dear, I think you should probably just go to the conference, glean all you can about magazines, shag him senseless till Saturday and then quit while you're ahead.'

'What? Finish it? I can't. I'm in too deep now.'

'I know you can't. And, if it's any consolation, I'm not sure I would be able to either.'

'So what else, if I can't do that?'

'Prepare to ride it, my girl. Like a wild stallion. See where it takes you. But you're gonna have to hold on tight! This is by no means the worst it could get. But you'll know when you've had enough, I promise.'

'Okay,' said Chloë, now knowing that this was what she had been unconsciously prepared to do all along.

At that moment there was a soft knock at the door, and James breezed in, looking surprisingly chuffed with himself. Chloë pulled herself together and sat up. 'Rob,' she said quickly, 'I've got to go.'

'Is he back?' said Rob.

'Yes.'

'Did he get you a present?'

'I don't know.'

'Ask him – I wanna know!'

'Okay.' She put her hand over the receiver and looked up at James. 'Did you get me a present?'

'Yes,' James grinned. First he handed her an Astor Wines and Spirits carrier-bag. She opened it – inside was a bottle of Bollinger champagne. 'I had to go to the East Village,' he explained.

'Ooooh,' she said appreciatively.

Then, from his pocket, he pulled out a tiny, carefully folded packet of paper.

'Oh, my God!' said Chloë. 'You didn't!'

'I did.'

She opened it. From its glistening white colour and lumpiness it looked to be very high quality.

Cocaine.

She removed her hand from the mouthpiece. 'Rob,' she knew to be discreet over the phone, 'let's just say that what he's got here is sufficient to keep us going for quite a while longer. I think we may have a night to remember ahead of us. In fact . . .' she winked at James ' . . . there may well be no stopping us.'

Chloë might have been a hedonist, but she also knew the benefits of postponing gratification, if only for a few hours, so she and James held off on doing a line until after dinner. Apart from anything else, the coke would put her off her food, and Chloë didn't want to miss the opportunity to savour yet another New York eaterie.

They went back to the East Village for the evening – James had said that he'd spotted an interesting-looking venue on First Avenue he thought they might try. They could eat upstairs, then dance downstairs later.

The moment they'd finished their main course, Chloë wrinkled her nose excitedly and said, 'Go on, give it to me, then.'

Quickly he handed her the packet under the table. Holding it tight lest anyone see it, she got up and made her way to the restroom. She had to wait for two women to go before her (they went in together – a dead giveaway they were doing drugs) before a cubicle was free. Inside, she double-checked that the door was locked properly, had a pee and opened the wrap. It would need a considerable amount of chopping first, but she'd done this before – not often, but enough to know what she was doing. She took out a credit card, thinking how very New York this all was, shook some of the powder on to the top of the toilet cistern and broke up the lumps. Then she racked out a line – long, thin, elegant, the promise of pleasure to come. She rolled up a twenty-dollar bill (*dollars*, how wild!) and sniffed half up one nostril, half up the other, flushing the lavatory simultaneously so no one would hear.

Oooh, yum. She could taste it in the back of her throat. She licked her index finger and picked up the remainder from the cistern to rub on her teeth, vaguely conscious of potential germs. No point worrying about that now, she decided. I'm a bit pissed already, and soon I'm going to be off my trolley on Class As. What's a few germs compared to that?

She sniffed again, wrapped up the cocaine and left the cubicle.

Back at the table, she handed it back to James, who left to follow suit.

While he was gone, she looked around her at all the groovy East Villagers, contemplating what they each did. An off-beat, creative-looking ensemble, she wondered if they were writers or poets, musicians or painters . . . Then – whoa! There was a delectable whoosh as the chemical hit her brain. She had the same feeling she'd experienced at the top of the Empire State – a strange combination of powerlessness and omnipotence. It was as if because she was just one small person on a very huge planet she could do anything, behave how the hell she liked.

When James came back it seemed he was feeling similar. Sitting down, he looked across at her, and asked, 'Don't you sometimes feel that what counts is the good time, the experience, the sensation?'

'Yup,' agreed Chloë, 'sometimes I do.'

'You make me feel like that a lot.' He grinned.

'It's mutual.' She grinned back.

'It's kind of dangerous . . .'

'That too,' she nodded, 'but so irresistible.'

'Totally.' He laughed, wickedly. 'We're probably very bad for each other.'

'Oh, without doubt.' The coke gave her the guts to be more provocative. 'Do you think I'm worse for you than Maggie?'

'Yeah, definitely.'

'Do you really?'

'Yeah, for sure. She'd never do anything like this. She doesn't even know I still do.'

'Do you? How often?'

'Oh, I've only done it a few times since we've been married. But I did it at that conference I told you about.'

'The one where you met the Spanish girl?'

'Yeah. And at a couple of parties we've been at. Actually,' he paused, knowing he was going to shock her, 'I did it with Jean once.'

'You didn't!'

'I did, one New Year. It was a little treat I got for us both. Not that you'd know with Jean – she's so hyper and talkative she hardly needs it, but she likes it very occasionally.'

'I'm surprised.' Perhaps there was more to Jean than she'd realised. And perhaps, given Jean was Maggie's best friend, there was more to Maggie too. 'So how come Maggie's not into it, then?'

'Oh, I don't know, it's just not really her scene. She's quite clean-living, really. Likes to look after herself. She eats well, exercises a lot. I guess . . .' he paused, searching for the right words ' . . . she likes to be in control of things.'

'She doesn't seem to be very in control of you . . .'

Again James stopped to consider. 'No, I guess not – not at the moment.'

'You mean she has been?'

'I suppose, in some ways, yes. Not in a bad way . . . it's just she's provided me with some stability, some roots. She's kind of looked after me – I feel safe with her. Probably, if I'm being honest, I'd have to admit I couldn't have got as far as I have today without her support.'

'I see,' said Chloë. 'Do you feel safe with me?'

'No.' James was categoric. 'That's what I love about being with you.'

The coke had numbed Chloë's brain a little: now this all seemed fascinating rather than painful. 'So,' she said blithely, 'do you think you'll stay together?'

James looked at her. For too long, in the same way he had all those weeks ago at Aurora. There, along with the difficulty of the question, was that same, unstoppable desire. Only now it had more meaning. And danger.

'Chloë, I don't know. I really don't know. If someone had asked me six months ago, I'd have thought they were mad. Wild horses wouldn't drag me from her. But now . . . I've met you . . .'

'Do you still love her?' My God! She'd asked it!

'Yes, I do.'

Shit. Even through the coke, that didn't feel so good. Let's try this tack, then. 'Are you still *in* love with her?'

'No, not after nine years or however long it's been, not in the way you mean.'

Go on, Chloë, ask, ask! 'Are you in love with me?'

Again he looked at her. 'Boy! You're not mincing your words tonight, are you?'

'No.' Chloë felt very empowered.

'Okay, okay. Yes.'

She sat back, vindicated, thrilled. There. It had been said. There was no going back. 'Good.'

'Good? Is that all you can say? *Good?*' His eyes were wide, incredulous.

'Yup.'

'So, you pick up my heart, string it out to dry, fuck with my life, do my head in, totally confuse me about my relationship with my wife, let alone my child, and you say it's *good?*'

'Don't be so stupid!' Now she held his gaze. He was making it sound like she'd done it deliberately. 'I don't mean it's good for all those reasons. Do you think I feel good about that? Jesus, James, I might be wicked from time to time but I'm not a complete cow. No, I mean it's good because I feel the same way.'

'Oh,' he said, laughing at himself, 'I see.'

'So, you're not going to leave her, then?' *Hey!* She could hear Rob's voice. *It's only Tuesday!* But the coke had gone to her head and, hell, she could say anything now.

'Chloë.' He took her hand. 'I don't know. I really don't know. I haven't known you long – there are lots of things to consider. There's Nathan for a start – and things between Maggie and me . . . it's not that simple . . .'

'Right,' said Chloë. Although it wasn't the answer she wanted, she did understand.

'Is that what you want?' he asked.

Heavens! So two could play at this honesty game. 'I don't know,' she said frankly. And she didn't. 'I suppose . . .' Now it was her turn to think. 'I suppose I want you to make up your own mind. I don't want to force you into anything. And I do understand your situation.'

'You're very sweet.' He stroked her wrist.

'Really? You think so?'

'Um,' he said. 'In some ways, yeah. Anyway,' he signalled for the waiter to bring the check, 'I think that's enough seriousness for one evening. We're here now so we might as well have a good time. I'm going to take you downstairs and we're going to dance our socks off.'

It was nearly two by the time they got back to the hotel, but both of them were still buzzing.

'Let's have another line,' encouraged Chloë.

'And open the champagne.'

'Oooh, we are so evil! We've got to go to the conference tomorrow.'

'Fuck it, Chloë. You only live once. Conference, schmonference. We're in New York.'

She leapt on the bed and started dancing around. 'We're in love!'

'Exactly. Now,' he staggered slightly around the room – they'd had quite a bit to drink already, 'what are we going to drink this from?'

Chloë jumped off the bed (pity the people on the floor below) and ran to fetch two glasses from the bathroom. 'Here.'

He uncorked the bottle with the deftness she'd noted before and poured them each a glass.

'To us,' he said. Clink.

'To us.'

He racked them each another line. As the sublime I-can-do-anything high hit her again, she took another swig of champagne. Fuck it, why not?

'Lie back,' she said. He did as he was told. She leant over him, her mouth still full of champagne, and half parted her lips so the liquid gently seeped on to his. He parted his lips. Then she slowly, slowly released all the champagne into his mouth. He swallowed.

She took another swig, this time swallowing it for herself, then another for him.

'Now,' she said firmly. 'I'm going to blindfold you.' She dimmed the bedside light to create a more seductive atmosphere.

'You are?'

'I am.'

'What with?'

'This.' She produced the black satin scarf shot with scarlet she'd brought with her – there was nothing pastel, elegant or Fendi about it. She pulled him to a sitting position. 'Turn round,' she said.

He slid on the white counterpane so his back was to her, and swiftly she tied the scarf.

'I can't see!' He stated the obvious.

'That's the point.'

Then she began to remove his clothes. She undid his shoelaces, pulled off his shoes. Then his socks, and threw them recklessly to the other side of the room. 'Lie down again,' she ordered.

Swiftly she took off her dress, but she kept on her underwear, her stockings and swapped her dancing sandals for her foxiest shoes. Finally she threw the feather boa round her neck. Fuck! She felt so, so horny! Momentarily she was grateful to Rob for making her plan her underwear so rigorously. During the lunch-hour on the day that she and James had left, she'd flown out of the office to buy matching suspenders for her favourite bra and knickers, stockings too. And now she knew for certain that this – not just the stockings and suspenders, but the blindfolding – was one of James's fantasies. He'd said as much over dinner last night. As far as she knew it was something he'd only ever shared with Beth, and that was a long time ago, and he'd had to ask her: she'd not initiated it of her own accord.

'Ha!' She ran her hand over his crotch. Judging by the way she could feel his cock jerking through his trousers, all this seemed to be working already.

'You bitch,' he said.

She dug her heels gently into his calves. 'That's me. Got it in one.'

She undid his shirt, slid it first off one arm, then the other – he lifted himself up to help her – and ran her fingers down his chest. Gently at first, then harder. Hey, so this was why women got their nails manicured. What fun!

'Chloë . . .'

'Bet Maggie doesn't do this for you, does she?'

'No, not exactly—'

'Or . . .' she unzipped his flies, eased him out of his trousers and Calvins and took another swig of champagne ' . . . this?'

She took his cock in her mouth, and swept the liquid over it with her tongue.

'No, she's never done *that*!'

But Chloë didn't care. Now she was completely into what she was doing, sucking and flicking, her lips wet with champagne and saliva. Fascinated by the feeling, submerged in the pleasure she was giving, she felt she could do it for ages, forever, if he liked. Then, to intensify the sensation, as she could feel him get more excited still, she started to use her hands, one to play with his balls, the other running up and down his shaft. And gently she played her tongue around the most sensitive bit just below the tip . . .

Finally, inevitably, with a burst like the cocaine high, he came in her mouth.

'Hm.' She swallowed (it went with her wicked, wicked mood). 'Nice.'

She got up. 'My turn.' But she didn't blindfold herself. No. Now she took his hands and the feather boa, and with it tied his wrists together above his head. *So what do you make of this?* she challenged *The Lacemaker* portrait. The old woman didn't seem remotely perturbed.

She took off her knickers, and discarded them, and sat astride him, ready to lower herself on to his mouth.

'Now,' she said, 'you have to do this for as long as I want you to, and exactly the way I say. So, you can start softly, softly . . . But first,' She got off him again, 'here. You need some champagne.' She poured a little in his mouth, he swallowed, and she straddled him once more. And as he began to kiss her, the champagne made his tongue feel all cool and wet and wonderful – his lips were more sensual than ever, the pleasure was so intense. Christ! There was something about the fact that he was so in her power, with his hands tied and his eyes blindfolded . . . And there was something about the perversity of this when she was so in his power, too, when she was so incredibly hooked on him, that made it all the more enthralling, all the more erotic.

Gently Chloë moved herself to and fro, her hands propped on *The Lacemaker* for support.

'Harder, you can suck me harder, now . . .' And so he did. His tongue moved, deeper, faster, more assured. Incredible. 'Now you can fuck me with your tongue . . .' In and out . . . Mmm. How she loved this man for doing what she asked. 'There, like that, yes, there . . .'

There was something so, so sexy about watching him unable to watch her, and watching herself gyrating on him that slowly, building in the fantastic way the best orgasms did, right from the tippy tips of her toes, up, up her legs and at the same time down from her breasts, in a wave to the peak that was at her core, with a mind-blowing, never-to-be-forgotten rush, she came.

When she'd finished, she lifted herself off him and lay alongside him.

'So, do you still think I'm sweet?' she enquired.

'Yeah,' he said, trying to reach for her but unable to. 'You taste gorgeous.'

'Guess you still have a lot to learn,' she scolded, running her nails across his chest so that they left a mark.

'What do you mean?'

'I'll have to leave you like that till you figure it out,' she said, getting up from the bed. 'I'm going to take a shower.' And with that she went into the bathroom and turned on the taps, leaving James to extricate himself from the entanglement she'd created.

## 21 Maggie

**Although Maggie continued** to feel uneasy, by Sunday night she was more or less okay, thanks to Jean's comforting words, and by the time she had returned from picking up Nathan and put him to bed, she had convinced herself it was unnecessary to ring Jamie so soon. Monday evening she left it too, thinking he would be busy on the first day of the conference and might go out to some networking dinner. By Tuesday after a bad night's sleep, she was anxious that, once again, it was longer than usual since she'd heard from him. Normally when he went away on business, he called her every other day, at least, and often every day. Now it had been three days. Wanting to reassure herself, she called him at midnight when she went to bed, but there was no reply. Rather than face increased suspicion, she persuaded herself it was still early in New York, and decided to try to sleep. She wasn't ready to think too hard about what else he might be up to, but it took her ages to drift off, and when she eventually did, her fears emerged in her dreams.

She dreamt that she and Jamie were each on an island, separated by a strait of hot water. She was desperate to get across to him, but she couldn't because he had the one and only boat and the water was too hot for her to swim in. She was shouting and shouting for him to come and fetch her, so that she could go and pick up Nathan from school, where he would be waiting for her. But Jamie was surrounded by rock and roll CDs, chaotically scattered in the sand, and was too busy listening on his headphones to hear her.

She woke up in a cold sweat, and looked at the clock radio. It said 04.47, nearly midnight New York time; he was *certain* to be back now, and she really wanted, *needed*, to speak to him. So she turned on the light and reached for the number to ring the Paramount again. She didn't have to wait long for the operator to answer, and he said he'd try the room at once. There was no reply.

*Perhaps he's asleep*, Maggie kidded herself, although she knew it was unlikely that Jamie wouldn't wake up to a phone ringing on his bedside table. Unless he'd had a lot to drink, he was a light sleeper – that was why he'd insisted that they needed a super-king-size bed. Perhaps the operator had rung the wrong room by mistake. Yes, that was probably what it was. Oh, well.

She put the phone down without bothering to leave a message and turned out the light again. But it took her hours to fall asleep, and as she lay there, tossing and turning, she began to question whether perhaps Jamie's lack of consideration was her fault, the result of something she was doing wrong. Was she being over-demanding emotionally? She'd always tried not to be. Jamie had once told her that it was partly this that had caused him to split up with Beth, and the fact that Maggie was so much more self-contained was partly what had attracted him to her. So, if she wasn't being too pushy emotionally, was she being too pushy sexually? She doubted it – she wasn't comfortable initiating things like that, despite the raunchy underwear. She didn't believe that she could be accused of coming on too strong. So was she boring him, being too wifely and not enough of a lover? Had she been too wrapped up in Nathan recently? Perhaps she *should* have found a way to go to New York – sent Nathan to Fran's or something. But how would he have got to school? Shere Infants was pretty much on their doorstep, but it would have been too much to expect Fran to drive him there all the way from Leatherhead every day. Perhaps it's Jamie's muddle, she thought, finally. But even if it is, I'm his wife. Shouldn't I help him sort it out?

Maggie didn't know the answers, and as the questions mounted so her anxiety grew. By the time she phoned the Paramount in an attempt to catch Jamie before he left in the morning, she was shaking with nerves. Thank God, he picked up the phone.

'Jamie?' she said.

'Oh, hi.' Was it her imagination or did he sound particularly rough? By now it was hard for her to separate paranoia from reality.

'I was just calling to see if you were all right.'

'Of course I'm all right. Why shouldn't I be?'

How defensive he was being. 'Well, it's just I called you last night and you weren't in, and it was a few days since I'd heard from you.'

'Oh, er, what time was that?' It seemed he'd been caught off guard.

'I suppose about midnight your time.'

'I unplugged the phone – I was really tired.'

'Right.' Of course, sleep was so important to him. How stupid of her not to have thought of that. 'As long as you're okay, then.'

'Yeah, yeah, Maggie, I'm fine. Look, can I call you later? I'm running a bit late today and we have an early start.'

Maggie felt rebuffed. She wanted a proper chat to make her feel better; he seemed to be hurrying her off the phone. But she was too caught up in blaming herself to say anything that might be perceived as negative. So all she said was, 'Okay, if you prefer.'

'It would be better if we could speak tonight.'

'Fine. Speak to you then, then.'

'Yeah, 'bye, and say hi to Nathan.'

Maggie put down the phone and looked around the kitchen. She took in the fridge where she'd neatly stuck two of her favourite Nathan paintings, the dresser with its antique blue and white china, the Aga with its traditional kettle on the hob, and the huge oak table she'd inherited from her grandmother, marked by decades of use. It was as if these familiar surroundings might help ground her, provide some consolation. But they didn't, so she decided to do something she found most hard: phone Jean for help. If she rang now she might just catch her before she left her hotel too. She could ask her to have a word with Jamie at the conference that day.

Where was it Jean always stayed in New York? Ah, yes, the Algonquin. She found the number in an old travel guide.

The extension in Jean's room barely rang once. 'Chloë!' Jean cried, before Maggie had a chance to speak. 'About bloody time! I've been waiting for your call – I was just about to leave.'

Maggie was confused. Who was Chloë? 'It's not Chloë, it's Maggie.'

'Oh, I'm sorry, I was expecting someone else.'

'Is now a bad time?'

Jean picked up on the concern in Maggie's voice. 'No, no, no, it's fine – it's really nice to speak to you.' Although Maggie's call must have been unexpected, Jean's delight at hearing from her was in marked contrast to Jamie's put-out tone, Maggie mused. 'I've got to hang around for this colleague of mine,' Jean explained. 'I can't call her – I haven't a clue where she's staying.' Then, straight to the point as ever, she added, 'Were you calling for a chat, or is something up?'

Maggie sighed. 'It's probably nothing.'

'Um?'

'But I'm, well . . . you know . . . We were talking about Jamie the other day . . .'

'Ye-es . . .'

'And I know you said I was being silly . . .'

'I don't think that's what I said exactly, but go on.'

'Anyway, the thing is, he's still being a bit odd, and I'm rather worried about it.'

'Odd in what way?'

'It's hard to explain,' Maggie wasn't happy going into specifics, though she knew it would help Jean to understand, 'just more distant, really. He hasn't been calling me like he normally would, and when I do get to speak to him he's always in a hurry.'

'Well, it *is* very frantic here, honey. And you know what New York is like. It's so easy to get caught up in the mania of it all.'

'Oh, I know, I know,' said Maggie. 'But, it's not just that. It's how he was before. You know I said things haven't been that great for a while? Well, I suppose it's over the last couple of months that things have been noticeably bad. And now I'm having real problems sleeping – especially since he's been away.'

'I see.'

Maggie could tell that Jean was beginning to appreciate that there might be a genuine cause for concern. She went on, 'It's not just the child issue, but generally. I can't put a finger on it, but he's just not as communicative. He's been very busy at work, and I know when some people get stressed they do withdraw into themselves, but with us, I'm the one who tends to do that. Jamie's the more expressive one, and he's fine with Nathan. It's me he's different with.' She caught her breath. This was so hard to say. 'It's just I feel it's as if he's not quite *here* for me, really, it's as if he –' she gulped to hold back tears '– he, doesn't *think* about me, or me and him, in the same way.'

'Um. I didn't realise things were so serious.'

'I was wondering,' Maggie hated to ask, 'could you have a word with him, possibly?'

'Would you like me to?'

'I think so. I wouldn't normally involve you, but—'

'I'll talk to him today,' said Jean briskly.

'Would you? Are you sure you don't mind?'

'Of course not. I offered before, didn't I? I'd like to do what I can to help. I'm very fond of you both and I hate to hear you so upset. I'll see if I can find out what's up.'

'You don't think it's anything major, do you?' Maggie hoped Jean would say not, but was aware that the picture she had just painted was far from rosy.

'I do agree his behaviour sounds out of character,' said Jean gently, 'and if I can help in getting to the bottom of it, then I'm glad to do whatever I can. I very much doubt it's anything to do with you, or you and him. It's probably his stuff – some mid-life crisis or something. But if it is, you've got a lot going for you, and don't ever forget that. You'll ride this, I'm sure.'

'Thanks, Jean. You're a good friend.'

'Oh, here's another thought,' Jean added. 'If you're feeling anxious, perhaps it might be worth you having a chat with your GP.'

'Really? What could he do?'

'He could provide a sympathetic ear for starters. Is he nice?'

'Yes, he's lovely, actually, but . . .' Maggie was hesitant ' . . . I wouldn't want to waste his time. Still, I suppose he's always been really helpful about Nathan.'

'And you never know, maybe he can recommend a short spell of counselling or something for both of you. Relate or whatever it's called these days.'

'I hadn't thought of that.'

'You won't be the first person to ask for support, so why don't you ring today? I know all doctors are pushed for time, but it's a good place to start. Ask for a double appointment so he's got more than five minutes for you – that's what I'd do. After all, better to do it sooner rather than later.'

'Before things get worse.' Maggie read Jean's mind.

'Maybe worse, maybe better. Who knows? But it won't do any harm. And I speak from experience. Remember how helpful I found my doctor when I was having those anxiety attacks?'

'True.' Maggie recalled how Jean's fast-paced life had caught up with her at one point, and she'd started getting panicked about travelling on the tube.

'Anyway, I'd better go, my dear,' Jean said apologetically. 'This damn woman's probably trying to get through. But I'll call you later, when I've had a word, honest. And you take care now.'

'I will. And thanks again.'

As she rang off, Maggie was aware that one issue she'd brought up on Sunday had remained unexpressed this time. She hadn't felt able to ask Jean what she thought about it because she didn't want to face thinking – let alone talking – about it, again. Jean hadn't brought it up either. But that didn't mean it didn't exist, didn't figure in the equation, or that it wasn't the possible key to Jamie's behaviour. Certainly, it was the one thing that would explain everything, the emotional distance, the preoccupation, the absence, the lack of sexual interest . . . She put the thought behind her. No, better not even entertain *that* possibility.

## 22 Chloë

**Chloë was woken** by a loud ringing, and at first it seemed as if it was actually inside her head. But it wasn't. Disorientated, she wondered if she was at home, yet it didn't sound like the continuous tone of her alarm, and anyway, she usually had that switched on to the radio. Then, as she gradually came to, she realised that she was in the Paramount Hotel, and that the ringing was the phone on the bedside table. Even in her hung-over state she knew it wouldn't be a good idea to answer it herself.

'James.' She shook him. He was dead to the world. 'You'd better get the phone.' She shook him again.

'Eeuaarghblugh . . .' he said groggily.

'*Phone!*' she said more urgently and jammed the receiver to his ear. She could hear a woman's voice.

'Oh, hi,' said James. The woman said something else. 'Of course I'm all right.' He sounded much more awake suddenly. 'Why shouldn't I be?'

*Shit*, thought Chloë. James wouldn't speak like that to most people. It must be Maggie. Chloë felt awful. Maggie was clearly worried about something. Even though she sounded all tinny down the phone, it was the first time Chloë had heard her voice – and sensed her presence as real. And she, Chloë, was in bed with this woman's husband.

If that wasn't dreadful enough, Chloë felt terrible physically – she'd hardly slept a wink. Wanting to prolong the high of pleasure, she and James had consumed all the champagne and caned virtually a gram of cocaine. They'd been up till God knows when and – partly as a result of these intoxicants – she'd been happy to have her body contorted into all sorts of adventurous positions. Judging from her aching limbs this morning it must have involved using muscles not normally exercised at the gym. And, today she had been bullied by Jean into feeling she had to go to the conference. How typical of her ex-boss not to consider holidays sacrosant. Crikey, it was nearly nine so she'd better phone her. Chloë wanted to hide her head under the pillow until everything went away.

However, she didn't want to listen to James talking to his wife, so she hauled herself out of bed and into the bathroom.

Seconds later he joined her.

'That was quick,' she said, squeezing toothpaste on to her brush. Perhaps a thorough scouring session would take away the ghastly furry feeling in her mouth.

James stood naked next to her at the basin, checking his complexion to see how rough he looked. 'I asked her to call back later,' he explained matter-of-factly. 'I wasn't really up for a chat.'

'Me neither, but I've got to phone Jean at the Algonquin.' Chloë rinsed her teeth with water and spat it into the sink.

'Jesus!' He almost jumped out of his skin. 'Is that where she's staying?'

'Yeah. Why? Is it very posh?'

'It's not that it's posh, it's near!'

'Oh, really? I didn't know. Where is it?'

'It's on 44th Street – a bit further east than we are, but still . . .'

'Oops! Guess we've been pretty lucky, then. There's no way she'll be able to work out where I'm ringing from, is there?'

'No, not if she's in a hotel. I think here you can only tell if you've got caller ID.' James, quickly calming himself, turned to stand at the loo to have a pee. This was something Chloë was sure he'd have been too self-conscious to have done previously. They were definitely more intimate as a result of this concentrated spell away together.

Once Chloë had showered – which she did with impressive speed, given her fragile state – she located the Algonquin phone number through the operator and dialled. 'Jean MacDonald,' she said. 'I'm afraid I don't know which room she's in.'

'The line's busy,' replied the woman on the switchboard. 'I put through a call about a minute ago.'

'Bugger!' said Chloë, then realising that the operator might think this aimed at her, added, 'Sorry. I'll call back later.'

'What's the time?' asked James, emerging from the bathroom. He looked around. 'This room's in a right state.'

Chloë took it in: the overflowing ashtray, the empty champagne bottle and the rucked-up sheets were one thing – all in a day's work for the average hotel cleaner, even ones who dressed in Armani, she thought – but the cocaine-smeared marble table-top, the discarded underwear and the ripped stockings were predilections best not shared with the world. Moreover, it looked as a crow had been massacred: James's attempt to escape from the boa had left black feathers everywhere.

'Hmm,' she winced, 'we'd better tidy up.'

James began by picking up his watch from the bedside table. 'Fuck! I'm supposed to be having a breakfast meeting at the Millennium Broadway right now.'

'How convenient,' she said, a touch sarcastically. 'Who with?'

'Adrienne Sugarman, the US Special Projects Director.'

'Better get your skates on, then. Good job we're so near. Look, you go on ahead – I can't get through to Jean at the moment, and we can hardly arrive together anyway.'

'Are you sure?' James rummaged in his suitcase for a clean pair of Calvins.

'I'm sure.' Chloë couldn't afford to waste time either. So as James got dressed, she shelved any inclination to indulge herself in poor-me-I've-got-a-hangover self-pity or whinge about how he should lend her a hand, and switched instead into efficient-magazine-editor-able-to-handle-any-crisis mode, emptying, picking up, folding, putting away.

Within minutes James was in his suit and poised at the door – it was at times like this she envied men their ability to get ready so quickly. 'You're an angel.' He kissed her shoulder.

'I'll see you there,' she said, turning to peck him on the cheek. *That was almost wifely,* she thought as she wiped the smears from the table with loo paper. Then again, given what she was wiping up, maybe not.

Luckily it was only a couple of blocks to the Millennium Broadway Conference Centre – it was just the other side of Times Square on 44th Street – so Chloë was able to finish making both the bedroom and herself presentable and still make it there within the hour.

As she pushed her way through the rotating doors, she was thankful for the Whistles suit. The short tan skirt and jacket made her look much more together than she felt.

'Ah, Chloë!' She had barely had time to take in the polished marble, rich mahogany panelling and sleek leather chairs of the art-deco lobby before Jean had breezed up to her, checking her watch pointedly. 'You've just made it. We'd better go in at once.'

Inside, the Hudson Theatre was packed. However lousy she was feeling, Chloë had to admit that it was a fantastic venue. It was a proper theatre, with a circle and an upper circle too. She gazed up. The ceiling, with its floral plasterwork, was breathtaking. And the stage, with its sweeping deep red velvet curtains, was enough to make Chloë hanker to be up there speaking herself.

'C'mon,' said Jean impatiently.

They took two seats on the end of a row and Chloë looked around for James. Just before the lights dimmed for the presentation, she caught sight of him a few rows ahead of her, chatting animatedly with a group of older colleagues she didn't recognise. My, she thought, they all look very important. Come to that, in his smart navy suit James did too . . . She'd thought she knew the work side of him, but she realised this was yet another aspect of his life she'd barely touched.

You can certainly tell this is an American organisation, she thought a few minutes later, listening to the Chief Executive banging on about company ethics and 'publishing personalities' in accompaniment to her thumping headache. All this corporate stuff wasn't Chloë's bag at all. And in spite of the air-conditioning, with so many people, the auditorium was very warm. She felt her attention drifting, drifting . . . her eyelids drooping, drooping . . .

'*Chloë!*' Jean nudged her. 'You could at least have the courtesy to stay awake!'

'Sorry.' Chloë felt like a naughty schoolgirl, but the previous night was catching up with her. Luckily, there was a particularly pointy Pentel in the conference pack she'd been handed on the way in and she spent the next hour surreptitiously prodding her bare knees with it to stop herself falling asleep again. It was exactly the same ploy she'd used in maths classes at Chiswick High, only then she'd used a compass pin. The pen left daft dots of ink all over her knees but it was a small price to pay for maintaining appearances in front of her ex-boss.

At last they broke for a much-needed coffee. Chloë got to her feet. 'Can I get you one?' she offered Jean, hoping to make up for her rather unprofessional performance so far.

'That would be great,' said Jean. 'I've got to have a word with Jamie Slater about something personal, so I'll meet you back here.'

'Right.' Chloë's heart beat fast at the mention of his name, even without the aid of caffeine.

'Black, no sugar.'

'Fine,' said Chloë absent-mindedly. But her brain was already racing ahead. Just what sort of 'personal' matter did Jean want to discuss with James? Jean was one of Maggie's closest friends, and it didn't take Inspector Clouseau to work out that Maggie had been distressed about something when she'd phoned that morning. Maybe she's found out about us, Chloë panicked. Maybe she's told Jean! No, she reassured herself, Jean would never have been so normal with her just now. Jean was one of the most outspoken women Chloë had ever known. Even if she'd been sworn to secrecy, there was no way she'd have been able to hide her opinion about Chloë's behaviour over something so major.

She watched Jean make her way down the steps towards where James was sitting, and gently pulled him away from his colleagues, as if she didn't want anyone else to overhear what she was saying. Chloë watched his face – he hadn't yet seen her a few rows above him. He looked serious, and nodded, as if to show his tacit agreement. Jean carried on talking for quite a while. Whatever it was about, it seemed she had a lot to say.

Oh dear, thought Chloë, flooded with guilt, misery and self-concern. This doesn't look good. It doesn't look good at all.

## 23 Maggie

**The doctor's receptionist** clicked on the mouse and consulted the computer screen. 'Mrs Slater,' she muttered to herself, moving the cursor down. 'Ah, yes. Remarkably lucky we had a double appointment.' Maggie felt that she eyed her as if to say: *You don't look sick; you should be extremely grateful.* 'Go on up.'

The surgery occupied a tiny picture-postcard cottage on Gomshall Lane opposite Nathan's school. Ramshackle to the point of tumbling down, it was one of the many houses in the village to which a worn wooden sign 'Drive Carefully Overhanging Buildings' applied. But despite their low-tech accommodation and all the demands made on them, the three doctors dealt efficiently with reams of local people. And over the years of bringing Nathan, Maggie had found that one doctor in particular had a sympathetic, understanding approach. Now she always asked for Doctor Hopkin.

She mounted the creaky stairs, ducking to avoid a hazardous beam, and took the last seat in the waiting area. Around her was the usual cross-section of village society. Two elderly women in the corner were sharing a moan about their ailments – a visit to the surgery appeared as much a chance for a gossip as for treatment. Opposite was a sulky-looking teenage boy with appalling acne and an overweight man whose pale, blotchy beer gut was protruding in a rather unsavoury way from under his T-shirt. He really should invest in something large enough to cover that properly, Maggie thought. Despite her tiredness, her aesthetic sense still protested loud and strong. Lastly, next to Maggie, a harassed-looking mum was trying to keep her two small children amused with the surgery's uninspiring selection of toys. Of course the practice wouldn't be able to justify the budget for any more, Maggie thought ruefully. Toys were bound to be seen as unnecessary extravagances. She resented the way that everything to do with the NHS these days came down to a matter of funding.

Maggie picked up a well-thumbed three-year-old copy of *Babe* and began to flick through it, but as she skimmed the pages of tips on beauty, boys and orgasms, she soon realised she wasn't taking in a word. Her thoughts shifted from those around her to herself. Why was *she* here? There wasn't anything wrong with her physically, unless you counted the insomnia – which seemed to be getting worse. She looked down at her hands. Her shaking hands. Maybe the trembling was just a sign of growing older, something she'd have to get used to. She'd had it for a couple of months now.

'Mrs Slater,' the doctor boomed from down the corridor.

Maggie got up. As she braced herself to speak to him, she had a horrible surge of anxiety. I shouldn't be here, she thought. There's nothing wrong with me. I'm wasting everybody's time. Some people are genuinely sick, and here I am, worrying him over worry itself. I really should be able to get over it on my own. She was tempted to leave, but somehow her feet propelled her into Dr Hopkin's room.

'Hello.' The doctor beamed at her. 'What can I do for you?' He was a genial-looking man, whom Maggie estimated to be in his fifties, with grey hair, ruddy cheeks and a comforting taste in muted shades of elephant cord and brushed cotton.

'I'm not sure,' said Maggie, as she took a seat next to his paper-smothered desk.

'Oh.' The doctor sounded surprised. Then he looked at her, frowned, and propped his half-moon spectacles up so that he could focus on his computer screen. 'I see you have a double appointment.' He added gently, 'So we've plenty of time.'

'Um.' Maggie looked down at her hands. They were really shaking now. She thought she could sense Dr Hopkin looking at them too. He probably thought she was a junkie or something. She decided the most disabling symptom would be a good place to start. 'I'm not sleeping very well. In fact, I've been sleeping really badly.'

'How badly is badly?'

'I guess about half the hours I normally would, and this last week or so maybe even less than that. It's not been right for a while.' Maggie could feel waves of support emanating from the doctor. 'I feel exhausted now, and I find it hard to concentrate. And I suppose . . . I've been feeling pretty . . . um . . . worried generally.'

Suddenly, she was crying. It was as if she'd released some terrible floodgate of all her pent-up emotions since Jamie had been away, and once she'd started she couldn't stop.

Damn it! How silly of me, she thought, but the tears kept falling. I seem to be doing so much crying at the moment. How pathetic. What a wimp!

At home before she'd left, she'd put on mascara and a little grey eye-liner to make herself look more presentable. What a waste! She fumbled in her handbag for a tissue, but her hands were so shaky it was as if she couldn't control them, and just talking about being anxious seemed to be making her worse.

'Here.' Dr Hopkin handed her a box of tissues.

'Thank you,' Maggie blew her nose.

'Is there any particular reason that you feel so miserable? Anything major upsetting you that might be keeping you awake?'

Maggie was silent. It was against her nature to discuss personal issues, and she didn't want to be disloyal to Jamie either. But she took a deep breath. 'I'm lonely,' she said, thinking that if she didn't mention Jamie specifically the doctor might be able to help without her betraying her husband.

'Oh?' The doctor sounded surprise again. 'I thought you were married. Loneliness is not something I normally associate with happily married working mothers like yourself.' He adopted a more cheerful tone. 'They normally complain that they could do with more time to themselves.'

Oh dear, thought Maggie. Deflecting him didn't appear to be working. 'Well, my job isn't especially sociable,' she said. 'I work from home most of the time.'

'I see. I suppose that's different, then. Would you rather be working more with other people around? In an office, perhaps?'

'Ummm.' Again Maggie paused. She knew this wasn't the answer, because it wasn't the main problem. 'I didn't used to mind working on my own – I'm usually pretty happy with my own company.'

'So it's not that, then? The work?'

'No,' she said, growing more decided. In the safe haven created by this fatherly figure, she felt that she could be more open. She was also aware the doctor didn't have much time. 'I don't really think that's the solution . . . Though I suppose I would like to write something more challenging, more exciting.' She stopped to consider, a lot less tearful now. 'I'd like that. Maybe it's something I could look into.'

'Yes, but,' the doctor prompted her, 'you just said you don't think that's the solution. May I ask why it is that you feel lonely now when – unless I misunderstood you – you said that you didn't before, if you've always worked from home and enjoyed your own company?' He seemed determined to get to the root of why she was there.

'I think it's because I'm not getting on very well with my husband,' Maggie admitted finally. Instantly she felt the anxiety lift, just a little. 'We've not been talking as much as we used to, and when we have, we've tended to argue. He's away at the moment, but this has been going on for quite a long time. I just don't feel that he appreciates me the way he used to, and I'm not sure why. I don't think I'm any different.'

'Oh dear,' said Dr Hopkin sympathetically. Then he added, 'Silly man! You're lovely.'

'Thank you.' For the first time in days, Maggie smiled. It was so nice to have a compliment.

'Anyway,' Dr Hopkin coughed, a bit embarrassed by his own frankness, 'I'm afraid I don't have any miracle pill I can give either of you to make you get on better. Might make me a wealthy man if I did! Dr Hopkin's Miracle Marriage Mender.' He chortled at the thought.

'No, I realised that.'

'Sure you did, sure you did.'

'It's just, I was wondering, maybe about some . . .' now it was Maggie's turn to be embarrassed ' . . . counselling or something. My friend suggested Relate. What do you think?'

'Good idea, good idea.' The doctor nodded, as if saying things twice would underline how much he agreed with her. 'I've found it helps many of my patients. Many couples find it useful to talk to a third party, get an objective angle on things. Would your husband be willing to go with you, do you think?'

Maggie hesitated. Would he? She wasn't sure. But not wanting to confess this, she said, 'I see no reason why not.'

'It's just that sometimes men can be a little less willing to discuss things like this than their wives.'

'Um,' said Maggie. She could understand that. Yet Jamie was normally the more outgoing one in their relationship, and if she was willing to talk, surely he would be too?

Dr Hopkin seemed to pick up on her uncertainty, even though she was trying to disguise it. 'Well, you have a talk with him and see what he says. Remember, you can always go on your own initially if need be.'

'Can I?'

'Oh, yes, of course. And we usually find the men come round in the end. Can't bear to think their wives are talking about them behind their backs, and all of that. We've sensitive egos, after all.'

'Indeed.'

'We have an arrangement with the Guildford branch,' Dr Hopkin continued, 'so I can refer you to them through the practice and you pay what you can afford. Here,' he got out his pad, 'let me give you their address so you'll know where to go.' He wrote it down. 'Now I'll write to them too, and you should hear within the next few weeks about an appointment.'

'In the next few weeks?' Maggie was disappointed. Now she'd got this far, she wanted to be able to go along with Jamie as soon as possible.

'I'm afraid there's a bit of a wait. But you should get something in the next month, no longer than that.'

'I suppose it's not as bad as some waiting lists.'

'No, and maybe you could set yourself some fresh challenges with your work, like you mentioned, to take your mind off things until then.'

'That's a good idea.' Maggie got to her feet with a great deal more enthusiasm than she'd had when she'd sat down. 'In fact, you've given me an idea. I know *just* the person to talk to about doing something more inspirational. She's away on the same business trip as my husband at the moment, but I can have a chat with her soon.'

'You do that,' Dr Hopkin encouraged her. 'Come back and see me in a month, let me know how things are going.'

'I will, and thank you.'

'Any time, any time.'

Maggie closed the door to his room and went down the stairs. She was feeling much better at having taken some positive action. When Jamie gets back from New York, I'll talk to him about coming for this counselling, she vowed. And I'll find out who's working on Special Projects at UK Magazines at the moment. Perhaps there's a way I can write some sample pieces for a new magazine as it's being developed. *That's* the way to change things. I'll get involved in something really different and radical again.

She strolled back down the street, smiling at the prospect. She felt more positive than she had in weeks. The sun was shining, and even though it was September, it was warm. She stopped for a second to gaze at the river that ran through the heart of the village, with its resident white-feathered, yellow-billed ducks. They quacked up at her joyfully, hoping for a snack. There was no doubt that Shere was the place to be on a day like today. Surely things could only get better from now on, couldn't they?

## 24 Chloë

**Occasionally Chloë wished** that her legs were longer. Then they'd be able to propel her at the fast pace her lifestyle often demanded. As she raced back across Times Square and along 44th Street, she resented her mesomorphic frame more fervently than ever. She barely noticed the shops full of up-to-the-minute, must-have technology, so temptingly priced; the huge hoardings advertising films as yet unheard-of in London; the endless theatre posters begging her not to miss the best shows in town. She was as determined to get where she had to go as the locals all rushing home in their sneakers. She was a virtual New Yorker now.

She grabbed some chewing-gum from the kiosk on the corner to freshen her breath and cut through, past the glitzy lights of the Marriott, barely checking as she crossed the road to the Paramount. She charged through the lobby and threw herself into the elevator.

'Blimey!' exclaimed James, as she whirled into the room.

'What's the rush?' He had got in moments before her, and was standing, looking relatively relaxed, loosening his tie.

Chloë caught her breath, then blurted, 'What was Jean talking to you about?'

James didn't seem to know what she meant. 'When?'

'This morning, at the conference. She said, "I've got to have a word with Jamie Slater about something personal," and then went and grabbed you. She hasn't found out about us, has she?'

'No, no.'

'So, what did she want to talk to you about? And does she always call you Jamie?' Chloë could barely get the questions out quick enough.

'Yeah, all my old friends do.'

'Really?'

'Yeah. It's what I was called when I was young.'

'Oh.' The wind was knocked out of Chloë's sails. Yet again it was apparent that there were aspects of James she knew little about. 'Would you rather I called you Jamie too?'

'No, I like you calling me James.'

Maybe he likes me calling him something different, she thought. Perhaps he prefers being called James. She fished for confirmation. 'Why?'

Pushed like this, James replied bluntly, 'Because Maggie calls me Jamie.'

'Oh.' That was a horrid reason for him to want her to call him James. Chloë sat down on the bed, utterly deflated. Yet she was bent on getting to the bottom of his conversation with Jean, no matter how much the revelations distressed her. 'Anyway, what *did* you talk about?'

'Do you really want to know?'

'Yes.' As Rob had often observed, there was a masochistic side to Chloë.

'She wanted to have a word about Maggie.'

'Oh.' Chloë had thought as much. 'What did she say about her?'

James looked torn. It was as if he knew his honesty was hurting Chloë but that he hoped being cruel to her might take away some

172

of his own angst. 'She said she thought Maggie was pretty unhappy at the moment.'

'Really?' Chloë had suspected this too – she'd got that impression from Maggie's phone call earlier. 'You don't think *Maggie* knows about us, do you?'

'Not from what Jean was saying.'

'So why's she so miserable, then?' Chloë felt lousy. Naïvely, she had hoped Maggie's upset was nothing to do with her. After all, she kidded herself, she hadn't ever consciously set out to hurt someone. It had all just . . . happened. But now, just as Rob had predicted, she, too, was heavily involved with James.

'Well, Maggie really wants another baby. And Jean was there when we had this conversation about it.'

'Oh.' Chloë was shocked. While she hadn't worked out exactly what she wanted from James, it hadn't occurred to her that someone else might want something from him too – something so tangible. 'You had this conversation recently?'

'No, not that recently. Several weeks ago.'

Chloë's mind raced back. Was that when he had started seeing her? Could that possibly be *why?* But almost before the thought had formulated, Chloë shunned it. 'What did you say?' She braced herself to hear the worst. This discussion was taking some truly nasty turns. For God's sake, another *baby*. If James said he wanted a second child with Maggie, how was Chloë supposed to feel? Where would it leave her?

'I said I didn't really want one.'

Chloë couldn't help but be relieved. 'Why not?'

James sat down on the bed next to her and said quietly, 'I should have thought that was obvious.'

She felt a bit better.

He continued, 'But aside from my relationship with you, I had my doubts before anyway. I adore Nathan, as you know, but I'm not sure I'm ready to be a father again.'

'Really?'

James shook his head.

This was fascinating – even more revealing than the conversation they'd had the night before. But without the cocaine to numb the pain, it was difficult to take in. She was discovering things about James that she hadn't expected, and it was all rather muddling. She already knew he hadn't wanted the first baby initially, and now he didn't want a second. Unless she was much mistaken, he was something of a commitment-phobe. And of all people Chloë should know the signs – it took one to know one. But perhaps he and Maggie weren't really suited, she rationalised. At least, it didn't sound like they were, not from the way that James had described their relationship to her.

Then, to her surprise, a totally new thought hit her. *What if I want children?* If James left Maggie, does this mean he would never want them with *me*? She recalled Rob's warning that James might be attracted to her on the rebound. If he'd started seeing her because Maggie was pressurising him to have another child, it looked ominously likely. Chloë couldn't voice all this, of course. Nevertheless, it seemed that not only was she gaining new insight into James, she was also discovering new aspects of herself.

Before she had a chance to consider this any more deeply, James collapsed on the bed. 'I'm exhausted,' he said, clearly wanting to end the conversation.

Chloë was thankful. These revelations were causing her emotions to go up and down like a yo-yo. 'Me too. Shall we just stay here tonight?'

'That would be great. Let's go and get a bite to eat downstairs now, then come back and crash out.'

'Perfect.' Chloë got up and pulled him to his feet. 'I could do with a major dose of carbohydrate.'

'You go on down. I'll phone Maggie – I promised I would.'

Chloë frowned, not bothering to conceal that she was put out.

'Don't worry, I won't be long.' James obviously wanted to appease her. 'I'm bloody starving.'

'What are you doing tonight, then?' asked Jean, taking a bite of her sandwich.

It was the next day, and she and Chloë were eating a stand-up buffet lunch. They'd just been in a seminar about how Spanish was shortly to become America's most widely spoken language, followed by a discussion on how this would affect US Magazines. Chloë had to admit that her second day at the conference was proving far more interesting than the first. Although maybe that was because she and James had gone to sleep at nine o'clock the night before.

Chloë struggled to think of an excuse. A meal with friends at Nobu wouldn't do – she'd used that up already. But it was Thursday, her last night with James, and she'd been looking forward to an intimate evening. She was starting to feel depressed at the thought of having to go home. What was going to happen when they got back to London? Would things between them be any different? They were so much closer now – their relationship couldn't go back to what it had been before. Did the phone calls from Maggie and the quiet word from Jean suggest that things were coming to a head there? If they were, Chloë had mixed feelings about it. On one hand, she felt like an A1 bitch. She could hear her mother's voice: 'I can't believe you're stealing another woman's husband and breaking up a happy home, just like that awful woman, Julia, your father ran off with.' On the other hand, Chloë could argue that fidelity to Maggie was ultimately James's responsibility, not hers. She believed, looking back on it, that her father had been more culpable than Julia.

But Jean, naturally oblivious to the twists and turns of Chloë's mind, continued, in all innocence, 'I've arranged to go out for dinner with Vanessa and I thought I'd ask Jamie Slater too. You've met him, haven't you?'

'Er . . . um . . . yes.' Chloë was thrown.

Fortunately Jean was concentrating on not smudging her lipstick while she struggled to consume a particularly generously filled pastrami on rye and didn't notice.

*Lord!* Chloë thought. How *did* Jean manage to scupper her plans so successfully all the time?

'So, would you care to join us?' asked Jean.

What a prospect! Dinner with her lover, her ex-editor and her new boss! It was such a frightful scenario that it was almost farcical. Still, given that the alternative was probably sitting alone in the Paramount biting her nails and wondering what the three of them might be saying, perhaps she'd better go.

'That would be lovely.' If she could cope with the incident at Bloomingdale's, she could cope with anything. At least this time she and James were forewarned and thus forearmed.

'I've arranged to meet Vanessa at eight,' Jean elaborated, 'so we'll have time to go back to our hotels and freshen up first. I'm meeting her in a little restaurant on the Bowery in the East Village called Marion's. That'll be nice and easy for you.'

For a moment Chloë wondered why, but just as she was about to pipe up, 'Would it? Wouldn't somewhere Midtown be better for all of us?' she remembered that she'd told Jean she was staying on Spring Street. 'Of course it will,' she lied. 'I'll nip back to my friend's apartment for a shower and see you there.'

## 25 Maggie

**Maggie was still** feeling chirpy when Jean called her. She'd had been heading for bed when the phone had rung and had just got out of the bath.

'Hold on a mo.' She was dripping all over the carpet, so wrapped a thick cream towel around herself before sitting down at her dressing-table.

'I've got to be quick,' said Jean. 'I'm meeting Jamie and some others from work for dinner in less than an hour and I've just nipped back here to change, but I thought I'd let you know that I managed to have a word with him.'

'What did he say?' Maggie was suddenly nervous.

'I think he knew he was in the wrong. He seemed pretty sheepish.'

'Really?' Maggie thought this unusual for Jamie. Humility was not his style.

Jean paused to consider. 'Yeah, he was definitely a bit . . . well, sort of *guilty*.'

'Oh,' said Maggie, not sure what to make of this. Did that mean he had something to be guilty about? The idea of an affair recurred but she denied the thought before it could take hold. Instead she decided it was a sign that he knew he'd not been as nice to her lately as he might have been.

'I told him I didn't think he appreciated you.'

Maggie laughed. How like Jean not to mince her words! 'What did he say to that?'

'I think he knew he'd been a bit cold and distant, though of course he wouldn't admit it outright to me. Anyway, I did get him to agree that he'd try to sort things out between you. He said he'd have a proper heart-to-heart with you when he gets back.'

'Good!' cried Maggie. 'And not before time!'

'Quite.' Jean was glad to hear her friend sound more herself. 'My feelings precisely.'

'Well, I was going to have a heart-to-heart with him anyway, because I saw the doctor today.' She was proud of this achievement.

'That was quick.'

'I got a cancellation.'

'How lucky. What did he suggest?'

Maggie briefly recounted the conversation. 'Anyway,' she finished, 'apparently we should get an appointment with Relate within the next month, so I need to have a serious chat with Jamie to see if he'll agree to come. Sounds like he might, though, from what you've just said.'

'Yeah.' Jean sounded noncommittal.

'And, in the meantime, the doctor suggested that I try to focus on my work a bit more, take my mind of things. It'd kill two birds with one stone, actually, because I'd really like to do something more challenging – more like they do in the broadsheets. Make more use of my qualifications. At the moment I feel it's all going a bit to waste. Which reminds me – you don't have to answer this now, but if you could have a think. Do you know anyone who would be interested in something a bit different at UK Magazines? I know what I want to do isn't right for *Babe*, but I was thinking more of Special Projects. Maybe I could help steer the way a magazine covers food and nutrition from the outset, rather than have to fulfil someone else's brief.'

'What a *great* idea!' exclaimed Jean.

'Do you think so?' Maggie was delighted to have her friend's backing. After all, Jean was one of the most successful women in the industry.

'I do! I really do! In fact . . .' She paused to think. 'Now you've given *me* an idea.'

'Really?'

'Mm. Just leave it with me, my dear, and I'll come back to you.'

# 26 Chloë

**Back at the** Paramount at 7 p.m. James was clearly terrified that he and Chloë would give themselves away over supper. Indeed, if he hadn't been so anxious about exposing their affair Chloë would have seen the funny side of all the intrigue. Instead though, she saw James's usual relaxed demeanour replaced by wariness, and she found his jumpiness annoying, even cowardly.

'You'd better get your taxi to drop you near Spring and walk across to Third Avenue,' he advised her, buttoning his one remaining clean shirt.

Chloë was focused on finding something presentable to wear other than her Whistles suit. 'Mm.'

'It would be awful if Jean saw you coming from Uptown.'

'Mm.'

'She'd be bound to wonder why.'

'I suppose so.' Rebelliously, Chloë wanted to ask if it would be so dreadful if Jean or Vanessa did work out they were having an affair. Maybe not right now, admittedly – obviously it wouldn't be good for James and it wouldn't be good for her professionally. But if James was ever going to leave Maggie – and secretly Chloë was wishing more and more that he would at least *consider* it – they'd have to find out sometime. Otherwise, as she knew all too well from her own parents, this sort of thing could drag on for years.

At half past seven, they caught separate cabs from outside the Paramount. Chloë asked hers to take her north of Spring Street to Washington Square, but it still meant that she had to walk a couple of blocks along Great Jones Street to the restaurant. When she arrived, Vanessa, Jean and James were already there, having a drink at the bar.

'Ah, Chloë,' exclaimed Vanessa. 'You found it.'

'And on time,' said Jean drily.

'What'll it be?' James asked, in an-acquaintance-from-work-turns-on-the-charm kind of way.

'A margarita,' said Chloë.

'Salt?'

'No salt,' she said. James already knew this, of course. They'd had margaritas at Fressen only the other day. How clever he was being. She relished being in on the game. And how she liked seeing him being so suave in front of two such powerful women. She almost forgave him for irritating her earlier.

She turned to look around the restaurant. In some ways it reminded her of Aurora: it was only a little bigger, and it had a similar quirky, casually elegant charm. But the colour scheme was warmer and, with its mix of chintz and red velvet, and the assortment of antique plates and old photographs that covered the walls, it seemed more dramatic, more arty, in keeping with the off-off Broadway locale.

'This is fab!' she said, unable to contain her enthusiasm.

'Do you like it?' asked James.

'Ooh, yes. It's just my kind of place.'

'I discovered it,' he said, visibly pleased that she approved, 'then told Jean about it when she came to the conference here last year.'

Chloë wasn't surprised to learn that it was James's find. She knew his taste quite well by now, and that the East Village was a favourite haunt of his, though of course she had to feign ignorance.

'Anyway, cheers, girls.' James raised his glass. 'What a lucky man I am to be out with not one but *three* lovely ladies!'

Hmph, thought Chloë. He needn't sound quite so bloody happy. For all his seeming confusion, perhaps there was a side to him that enjoyed having more than one woman.

James poured them each another glass of wine. So far they were doing pretty well, Chloë thought. She and James were sitting next to each other, knees surreptitiously pressed together under the table, though to all outward appearances they were just professional acquaintances. James had steered the conversation away from personal matters, and Chloë, who was equally adept at separating business from pleasure, had done the same. They were helped by Vanessa's presence; she didn't know any of them well.

But then Jean said, 'I spoke to Maggie just now,' and Chloë's heart leapt into her mouth.

God, I hope she's not going to have another go at James, she thought. I couldn't bear that. It was one thing to hear about his marriage from him; that way, at least, he could safeguard her feelings to some extent. Yet to hear it from *Jean*, or to hear Jean say how wonderful Maggie was, was more than Chloë could stand.

Jean carried on, 'I thought it might help her if I had a word with you two.'

*Oh my God!* Chloë gulped. Was Jean really prepared to expose their affair in front of Vanessa?

'About Special Projects,' Jean added.

Chloë realised that 'you two' referred to her and Vanessa but by now she was as scarlet as the velvet décor. Luckily the lighting was low so hopefully no one would notice.

Jean addressed Vanessa. 'She's a talented cookery writer, Jamie's wife, you know,' she explained. 'You probably know her stuff – she works under the name Margaret Wilson.'

'Of course I do. She's been around for some years. One of the best in the business.' Vanessa turned to James. 'I never knew she was your wife.'

'Yes. She writes under her maiden name. Always has.' Unless Chloë was mistaken, James sounded proud.

'Gosh. What a small world!' said Vanessa.

'Isn't it?' Chloë reached for her wine. Worryingly small, she thought.

'Well, if you think she's good *now*,' Jean continued loyally, 'you'll probably be very interested in our conversation.'

'Oh?' said Vanessa, James and Chloë in unison.

'Yes. She's keen to write something a bit different, more controversial, something that draws on her training. She's got a great academic background, you know. Did a degree in English at Manchester, then trained as a nutritionist. If you think what she does already is okay, I'm sure she could produce some stuff that's *really* stimulating. So, I thought maybe – though God knows why I should help you out, Chloë – you'd be interested in her doing some writing for your magazine.'

Chloë's jaw dropped.

'That sounds very interesting,' said Vanessa enthusiastically. 'Don't you think? Chloë?'

For once in her verbose life, Chloë was gobsmacked. Fucking hell! The idea of working hand in hand with Maggie! With ex-bosses like Jean, she thought, who on earth needs enemies?

## 27 Chloë

**It seems only** seconds ago that we had dinner, Chloë thought morosely, as she watched the flight attendants wheeling the trolley down the aisle towards her. Eventually they were parallel with her row, and stopped and proffered her breakfast on a plastic tray.

'No, thank you. Just a coffee.'

It was most unusual for Chloë to reject any form of calorific intake (when she was little, other children's mothers had loved having her over as she always ate everything), but right now she really couldn't face it. It might be 6.30 a.m. GMT, but they couldn't fool her.

She pushed up the blind and bright sunlight flooded in. The plane was high above the clouds, but Chloë could see them down below, layer upon layer, from the darkest, rainiest shade to the palest, most ghostly grey.

England, she thought gloomily. Today she really hated it. Oh, yes, she was looking forward to seeing Rob again, and Potato, their couch-loving cat. She would be pleased to be in her own flat once more and have a nice, long bath instead of a shower. She was also happy at the prospect of a major ring-round of her friends – arriving on a Saturday morning had some advantages. And she *had* been looking forward to starting work on Monday with Vanessa. But since Jean had introduced Maggie into the scheme of things, it wasn't looking such a brilliant career move after all.

It's *my baby*! thought Chloë indignantly. I've spent months working towards this! And now some other woman is muscling in on my act. The irony was not lost on her.

Maggie was unaware of this, Chloë had to acknowledge, but things were fast becoming hideously emotionally and profession-ally tangled. She was too fuzzy-headed to consider all the consequences then, so she took another sip of coffee and resumed her position, nose pressed up against the glass.

As the clouds thinned, she could make out the patchwork fields of Berkshire far, far below. They were nearing Heathrow. If she was going to go to the loo before they landed, she'd better do so now. The people next to her had also rejected breakfast, but getting out involved some tricky manoeuvres with coffee cups, flip-down tables and legs. Out in the aisle, the trolley was blocking the way to the nearest toilet, so Chloë decided to go up to business class, and say hello to James. His was an aisle seat.

'Hi,' she said, crouching to speak to him.

'Oh, hi!' He seemed pleased to see her, and ruffled her hair affectionately. 'Did you manage to get any sleep?'

'A bit. Did you?'

'A bit.' He looked past his fellow passengers and out of the window. 'It seems we're nearly there.'

'I know.' Chloë was unable to keep the sadness out of her voice. 'I don't want to go home.'

'You're not the only one.' James sounded equally sad. He stroked her cheek. 'I've had a lovely time, you know.'

'Me too.' Chloë could feel tears pricking behind her eyes. She stroked his face in return, a particularly soft bit of skin that she'd discovered, just on his cheekbone. It's funny, she thought, you get to see a lover's face far more close up than anyone else's. Now she knew every contour, every line, even the way his stubble grew.

'Whatever happens, we've had this time, haven't we? No one can take that away.'

'No, they can't.' James smiled, then sighed. 'I need to have a chat with Maggie when I get back.'

'Mm,' said Chloë. Did that mean James was going to tell her? Chloë was about to ask him what he was going to say, but thought better of it. That was between the two of them, and she wasn't sure that she wanted to know. So she said, 'I'd better leave you now,' and got up instead.

Once she'd been to the loo, she made her way back to Economy, squeezed past the couple in the seats next to hers, sat down and looked out of the window again. The cars were little and rounded, the roads winding and irregular, the houses depressingly suburban and samey.

The 'fasten seatbelts' sign flashed on.

They were coming down now. After all the excitement, intrigue, intimacy and romance of the last week, they were really coming down.

## 28 Maggie

'Is that Chloë Appleton?'

'Speaking.'

'You don't know me but my name's Margaret Wilson, Maggie. I'm Jamie Slater's wife –'

'Oh!'

'– and a friend of Jean's.'

'Yes.'

'She suggested I might give you a call.'

'Yes. So she did . . . Er, could you hang on a second?'

'Sure, sure.' There was the sound of rustling papers, then silence.

Maggie waited. She'd always hated cold-calling. Thankfully, these days, she didn't usually have to phone strangers to drum up work any more because her professional reputation was well established. Ringing this colleague of Jamie's, whom Jean had described as 'phenomenally talented but prone to liking to have things her own way', was the first time she'd had to do it in years.

A few seconds later the woman came back to the phone. 'Sorry about that. Hi.'

By now Maggie felt certain she was interrupting something awfully important. 'Hi. I'm sorry, is this a bad moment?'

'Er, no, no.' But the woman sounded as if it was. 'Sorry, I only started in this department yesterday, and things are a bit chaotic round here.'

'I can call back if you like.' Maggie didn't want to begin on a bad foot.

'No, it's fine, honestly.'

Maggie was convinced the woman must be thinking, *Blast Jean for getting the publisher's wife to call me*, so was pleasantly surprised when Chloë continued, 'I understood from Jean that you might be interested in doing some pieces for Special Projects. What kind of things did you have in mind?'

'Actually, I wondered if I could come in and see you – show you some of my work.'

'Well, I have seen lots of your features over the years.'

'You have?' Her heart sank. If Chloë meant the typical articles that Maggie felt guilty of churning out for UK Magazines, doubtless she would already have typecast her as an uninspiring writer of conventional recipes.

'Yes, I have – you're very prolific. I'm sure it's not really necessary for us to meet face-to-face.'

Was it Maggie's imagination, or did Chloë sound as if she'd prefer to chat it through there and then? Did this mean that she had indeed made up her mind about Maggie and had already written her off as a waste of time?

But Chloë continued, 'Actually, I particularly liked that feature you did, "Pulling Dishes", in this month's *Men*.'

'You did?' Maggie was pleased. If she was going to be judged on what she'd been producing lately, at least this was one of her more amusing pieces.

'And Jean speaks very highly of you, so I'm positive you don't need to bother coming in. What kind of articles were you thinking of?'

Oh dear, thought Maggie. She'd prepared herself to speak to

Chloë in order to make an appointment. Coming up with suggestions on the hop wasn't the way she liked to work, and as she was keen to stretch herself and undertake something new, she was loath to come up with immediate solutions to an ill-understood brief. She knew all too well that this kind of pressure was what made many writers rehash the same old stuff time and time again.

Instead, she'd planned on meeting Chloë and presenting her with a portfolio containing a well-laid-out selection of the writing she was proudest of. (She'd spent that Sunday painstakingly putting it together, while Jamie, just back from New York, had volunteered to spend the day with Nathan.) She'd also been planning on handing Chloë her newly typed CV and explaining her particular areas of expertise and the direction she wished to take. Finally, she'd envisaged a full verbal debriefing on the new magazine so that she could go away and come up with some original and appropriate concepts.

As she contemplated this, Maggie was silent. Presumably conscious of the pause, Chloë said, 'I suppose it would help if I gave you an outline of how I see the magazine?'

'Um,' said Maggie, hesitantly. Oh, damn it! she thought crossly. It really *would* help if she could meet this woman in person! Come on, Maggie, she berated herself. Say what you mean. 'Actually, I really do think it would be useful if we could meet up,' she asserted. 'I'm sure we *could* come up with some ideas together over the phone, but from what I understand from Jamie and Jean, you're trying to do something a bit different, something less clichéd, quite radical. I believe it would be an enormous help if I could meet you, see the dummy, get a feel for who the magazine is pitched at, understand what you're really after, and talk you through where I'm coming from too.'

'Oh, okay, sure. I see your point.' There was another pause. 'So, when would you like to come in?'

'How about tomorrow?'

'Tomorrow!' Chloë sounded taken aback.

Maggie was keen to get moving. She might not have managed a heart-to-heart with Jamie yet but she was determined not to procrastinate about everything, and in comparison this meeting was less daunting. 'Yes. I've got to come into town anyway.' This was a lie, but she hoped it might make her appear to be someone who was constantly in demand. She didn't want Chloë to think that she was coming in specially.

There was more rustling of paper. 'Er . . . yes. I suppose that would be fine. Shall we say about twelve thirty?'

'Lovely. I'll see you there.'

'Do you know where to come?'

Maggie was more relaxed now that she'd swung things her way and laughed. 'Of course! My husband works there.'

'Oh, yeah, of course. Silly me. Er . . . Special Projects is on the third floor. Just ask for me, Chloë.'

'Okay. I'll see you tomorrow, then.'

'Yeah. Half twelve.'

'I look forward to meeting you.'

'And me you. 'Bye.'

''Bye.' Maggie put the phone down.

Poor woman, she thought. She sounded a bit distraught. Thank goodness I don't work in-house any longer – it's so much more stressful than being freelance. I might be bored with what I've been doing recently work-wise, but at least here at home I can run things the way I want to and, other than Jamie, I haven't got anyone standing in the way.

The next day, Wednesday, it was Maggie's turn to take the children to school. After she'd dropped them off, she headed straight out of the village on a run – she'd pulled on her running gear when she'd got up.

As she ran, she planned what she was going to wear to meet Chloë. Her Fendi trouser suit, with a white T-shirt so as not to look overdressed, and that scarf Jamie had brought her back from New York. That way I'll look smart but not intimidating, she thought. I've no idea what this woman's like, but a cream suit is bound not to offend anyone.

Unlike her husband, Maggie didn't enjoy meeting new people, so she wasn't looking forward to the encounter. Especially as when she'd mentioned to Jamie that she was going in to see Chloë he had seemed negative about it. 'Is that a good idea?' he'd said. 'I'm not sure you'll see eye to eye.'

But, then, he's always wanted me to stick with writing the same old stuff as it's a guaranteed money-spinner, she reasoned. Sometimes he can be so unsupportive.

She carried on running round her usual circuit, picking up speed as she hit her stride. She was a great deal fitter now than she had been a few weeks ago and, as the surrounding scenery energised her and the endorphins released by exercise gave her a lift, she pushed any resentful thoughts away and told herself firmly to think positive.

And when I've got over this hurdle, she vowed, I'll talk to Jamie about going to Relate. I'll feel stronger when I've given my self-esteem a bit of a boost, so I'll sort this career thing first.

Once home, she showered and got ready. She spent ages doing her makeup, and by the time she'd finished, she looked as if she had none on. But her skin seemed clearer, her eyes brighter, her cheeks rosier and her lips fuller. Next, she carefully selected a flesh-toned bra and G-string that would leave no tell-tale lines under either the T-shirt or her trousers. She always avoided underwear that would be visible, believing it made her look cheap. Standing in her T-shirt and knickers, she pulled out from under the bed the portfolio she'd put together at the weekend and checked that everything was in order. It was. Having carefully sifted through years of work, she'd found a reasonable cross-section of features with which she was genuinely happy. Then she put on the suit and knotted the scarf on one side, French-style, around her neck. Finally, she pulled on a pair of white canvas deck shoes and stood back to examine the effect in the mirror.

'You look *okay*,' she reassured herself. No matter what Jamie had said about the Fendi suit, she loved it.

It took Maggie just over an hour to get into town but, being a perfectionist, she'd allowed longer so she was early. She decided it couldn't be a bad thing to show that she was keen, so after browsing round the boutiques of Covent Garden for a while, she headed for UK Magazines ten minutes ahead of time.

In the event, it simply meant that she had to wait in Reception.

'I'm afraid Chloë's nipped out for some lunch,' explained the receptionist.

While she sat there, many women came and went, and Maggie wondered if each was Chloë. Some were very glamorous. She was just remembering her sister's observation that there must be lots of opportunities for Jamie to flirt at work, when a dark-haired girl came up to her and said, 'Hi, you must be Margaret Wilson.'

'Yes.' Maggie jumped to her feet. 'But people call me Maggie.'

'I'm Chloë,' said Chloë, and held out her hand.

As she shook it, Maggie thought, *She bites her nails.* It was the kind of detail she noticed, and it made her warm to Chloë. A woman who bit her nails must be something of a worrier too.

'I'm sorry, I just dashed out to get a sandwich. Have you been waiting long?' asked Chloë.

'No, no,' Maggie lied. Well, she'd only been waiting twenty minutes, and half of that time was her own responsibility.

'Come with me,' said Chloë, leading the way. 'I'm afraid we'll have to sit at my desk. There aren't any meeting rooms free.'

'Oh, that's fine.' Maggie followed her. It was several months since she'd had to bother going into a magazine in person, and the open-plan office seemed very busy and noisy. There were dozens of people, mainly women, and most of them looked rather younger than Maggie. Some were click-clacking away urgently at their computers, others were talking nineteen to the dozen on the phone, a few were chatting to each other, whether legitimately 'bouncing ideas' or simply gossiping Maggie couldn't tell. In contrast her freelance lifestyle didn't appear so perfect after all: her comfortable kitchen seemed terribly quiet and parochial.

Perhaps I'm very out of touch, wondered Maggie anxiously. Sometimes I go all day without talking to a soul.

When they reached Chloë's desk, Maggie noted that it was smothered in even more paper and magazines than Dr Hopkin's. Goodness! she thought. I could never work in such chaos. And didn't Chloë say that she's only been working in this department for a couple of days? How on earth has she managed to amass so much stuff in such a short time?

'Have a seat,' said Chloë, grabbing a chair from a colleague's desk and wheeling it over.

Maggie sat down. She was partly relieved to be in a less formal setting than she'd imagined, partly concerned that she wouldn't have the space to show her portfolio property.

'Can I get you a coffee?' Chloë asked.

Maggie couldn't face the thought of an office instant. 'Water will be fine.'

'Back in a mo.' Chloë rushed off.

Maggie watched her go over to the kitchen area on the other side of the office and make herself a quick coffee, then fill a glass from the water-filter machine. As she did so, Maggie was able to get a full view. What a fantastic outfit! she thought admiringly. Chloë was dressed in a bias-cut green skirt, a vest that enhanced her cleavage and one of those trendy angora cardigans that constantly seemed to slip off her shoulders. It wasn't the kind of thing Maggie would ever wear, let alone to the office, and she could see Chloë's bra straps even from this distance, but she had to admit it looked good. As Chloë walked back with the drinks, Maggie observed her shoes. They looked fashionable as well – they were those amazing sandals that Maggie had admired in all the magazines but knew would make her look too tall.

'Here,' said Chloë, handing Maggie the glass.

She's very pretty, thought Maggie. Then corrected herself. Well, attractive maybe, not conventionally pretty. She's wearing far more makeup than I ever would, but she's got the kind of face that looks good with obvious eyeliner like that. *And* she's got the kind of curly hair I've always wanted – sort of naturally tousled. She reminds me of someone, but I can't think who.

Then Chloë said, 'So, where shall we start?' and Maggie pushed all thoughts other than strictly professional ones to the back of her mind.

'I've brought some stuff to show you,' she said. The cut-and-thrust environment had made her feel more self-conscious about her work, and she was keen to get her presentation out of the way.

193

Maggie had had a hunch that Chloë would be the kind of adrenaline-driven young woman she'd met before in magazine publishing – a hunch that, from yesterday's phone call and what she'd seen so far today, was proving correct. Chloë did look rather on edge, Maggie observed. She was probably stressed.

With this in mind she had put a feature called 'Fast Times' at the front of her portfolio. It showed a number of snack and supper recipes that she'd described as 'perfect dishes for the end of a busy day – quick, simple and full of flavour'. She liked the photography too. Some of the weekly magazines she worked for insisted on using such dated shots, but this particular monthly was stylish and modern.

'Mmm, yum,' said Chloë. Judging from her well-rounded physique, Maggie guessed she enjoyed her food. Chloë peered closer and started to read. Maggie was silent. Fortunately this piece hadn't been too hacked about by subs, and she was still happy with the way that it flowed.

'This is very interesting,' concluded Chloë. 'I like the way everything can be done so fast.'

'Yes,' said Maggie, pleased she'd created the impression she wanted.

Chloë turned the page. Next, as a contrast, Maggie had put a short and punchy article entitled 'Supermarket Spy: the lowdown on GM'. It summarised which stores were still stocking genetically modified products and, although it was far less informative than she'd have wished due to confines of space, she'd selected it because it demonstrated her ability to research more topical subjects. 'Most people in the business seem to think of me as a home economist, a writer of recipes, but this is the kind of thing I really like doing,' Maggie explained.

Chloë flipped over some more pages, pausing to read the occasional spread. Maggie kept quiet, wanting to leave her time to absorb it properly. When she'd finished, Chloe said, 'Well, it's a very impressive range. So why do you want to work here in Special Projects with us? I'm sure you know this already, but a lot of things we do in this department never see the light of day.'

'Yes, Jamie said that,' replied Maggie. 'And it's not because I'm short of work – I've got more than I can handle some of the time. It's just that I feel . . .' She looked at Chloë's expectant face. Could she risk being perfectly frank? Yes, she decided. If I can't speak my mind now, I'm never going to. 'I feel that women's magazines have got stuck in a bit of a rut when it comes to cookery writing and I'd like to move them on in some way.'

'You do?' said Chloë.

Unless Maggie was mistaken, she sounded as if she agreed. 'Yes,' Maggie affirmed. 'I do.'

'Really?'

'Yes, really.'

'Oh,' said Chloë. 'I wouldn't have expected you to think that.'

'You wouldn't?' Immediately Maggie worried that she shouldn't have been so honest.

'No.'

'You don't agree?'

'Oh, no,' Chloë spoke hurriedly. 'I do. In fact, that's been my thinking exactly. You're very much coming from where I've been at with this new magazine. It's just . . .' Her voice trailed off, as if she was struggling to think of how to express herself. For a moment she said nothing. Then she said, 'I'm not sure it would be a good idea my involving you.'

'Oh.' Maggie was mystified. Then she thought, If they saw things similarly, why was Chloë giving her the brush off? Was it because she looked too strait-laced and conventional? Dearie me, she thought. I've got it all wrong. I should *never* have worn this cream suit. I look so different from the rest of these girls. They're all so trendy and interesting – Chloë probably thinks I'm dead boring. I bet she thinks I'm really old.

Maggie frowned. She'd felt quite confident until that point, but maybe Jamie had been right and she'd been wrong to come and see Chloë. She wished she could change what she was wearing and get dressed all over again. But of course she couldn't do that, so the only thing she could say was, 'That's a shame. Couldn't you tell me a bit about the magazine anyway?'

'No,' said Chloë abruptly. 'We have a policy not to discuss new projects with freelancers at this stage.'

But I'm the wife of the publisher! Surely you can trust me, thought Maggie indignantly. Still, she didn't want to use her husband's power to get her work; she never had before, and she wasn't about to start now.

Chloë continued, 'Anyway, I wouldn't want to waste your time.' Her tone was much brisker than it had been hitherto.

Maggie was sure that Chloe had offered to tell her about the magazine the day before. She couldn't understand her change of heart. Puzzled, she decided that she had probably been expecting too much. She knew what it was like in magazine journalism: unless an editor knew your work it might incur unnecessary expense to commission a feature from an untried source, no matter how experienced the journalist, in case they missed the mark. Maybe initially it would be worthwhile to offer her services for free. 'If it makes any difference, I could do you a couple of sample pieces on spec. You wouldn't have to pay me unless the magazine takes off.'

'Oh, I couldn't ask you to do that.'

Maggie was bitterly disappointed. 'If you're sure.'

'I'm sure.'

'Oh, okay.' Maggie took a gulp of her water and zipped up her portfolio.

'I'm afraid I really must get on.' Chloë stood up.

'Yes, of course.' Maggie picked up her things and together they walked back through the office. At the lift she held out her hand. 'Well, thank you very much for taking the time to see me. And if you'd like me to do anything for you at some later stage, then I'd be more than delighted.'

Chloe shook her hand. 'I'll let you know.'

'It was nice meeting you anyway.' Maggie smiled. Despite feeling rejected, she wanted to part on a friendly note.

'And you,' said Chloë. Then she added, as if she'd thought better of being so dismissive, 'Who knows? You may be right. Just from the little you've said, I do appreciate that we might see things in a similar way, so perhaps we can work together at some point in the future. It's just that I don't think now's the right time, that's all.'

Maggie felt slightly comforted. 'That would be great.'

Ping! The lift arrived, and Maggie stepped in. As the doors slid shut she could see Chloë standing there, biting her lip. She looked lost in thought already.

Oh, well, Maggie thought, as the lift whisked her down to the ground floor, maybe Jean had hit on something when she'd observed that Chloë liked to have things her own way. Maybe she wasn't very good at sharing things, and she simply didn't want anyone else treading on her toes.

## 29 Chloë

**Chloë stomped into** the kitchen and threw down her bag. On top of starting a new job, not being in New York any more and meeting Maggie, she'd had to wait ages for a bus to get home. Rob was in a familiar attitude, stirring home-made soup at the stove, glass of wine by his side.

'So, what was she like?' His voice had a distinct note of glee at the prospect of a good gossip session, but it made Chloë uncomfortable. Her meeting with her lover's wife might provide Rob with a cheap thrill but it had been a traumatic experience to her. She'd tried to persuade Vanessa to see Maggie instead, but Vanessa had had an appointment elsewhere. Then she'd phoned James but, although he was as anxious about them meeting up as she was, he couldn't see any way out of it.

How could she sum up all the feelings meeting Maggie had given rise to? She hadn't managed to work them out for herself yet, let alone for someone else.

She'd liked her; she'd hated her.

'What did she look like?' prompted Rob.

Pacing round the kitchen, Chloë tried to put it into words. 'Sickening.'

'Sickening?'

'Yeah. Stylish, beautiful, tall, slim, great skin . . . you know.'

'Blonde, brunette, what?'

'Blonde,' sighed Chloë, feeling very mousy. 'Looked bloody natural, too.'

Rob tried to provide solace. 'Bet she's not as sexy as you, though.'

'Thanks.'

'What was she wearing?' Rob had a true gay male's appreciation of fashion. When it came to revealing characteristics, it came far higher on his list of priorities than first impressions of personality.

'Some sort of classy cream suit, posh whiter-than-white deck shoes – all very understated and elegant.'

'See?' said Rob. 'She doesn't sound half so horny. Whoever heard of a sex kitten in white deck shoes?'

'Mm.' Chloe wasn't convinced. At the end of the day, Rob fancied men. '*And* she was wearing that scarf James bought for her in New York.'

Rob couldn't think of a response to this. Best move on. 'So, what was she like?'

'Actually, she was very nice,' she said regretfully.

'Nice? You're not supposed to like her!'

'No, I know.' Chloë nodded. 'But she was. I wish I could say she was a complete cow, but she was perfectly, utterly nice.'

'*Nice?* Who wants to be "nice" anyway?' Rob snorted. 'She obviously can't have any idea about you and James, then.'

'No, of course she hasn't. There's no way she'd have been that shy and sweet.'

'I thought you said the woman's one of the best-known cookery writers around. How can she possibly be shy with a high-profile career in the media like that?'

'Yeah, well, I dunno, but I thought she was a bit. Though, I suppose . . .' Chloë realised that her confidence was something that might make her attractive in comparison ' . . . James isn't shy at all.'

Rob agreed. 'My thoughts exactly. Because neither, my dear girl, are you.'

'Maybe.' Though next to Maggie, Chloë had felt loud and gauche.

'So, what was her work like, then? Was it as boring as you said you thought it would be?'

The night before meeting Maggie, Chloë had stayed late at the office and pored through back issues of various magazines to glean an idea of Maggie's work and, with the occasional exception, she had found to her glee and relief that most of the articles were more conventional in approach than she wanted for *All Woman*. But seeing the selection that Maggie had put together in her portfolio had convinced her that Maggie was a more interesting writer than she might at first appear.

'No, it was much better.' She sat down heavily at the kitchen table.

Rob seemed to realise that the meeting must have been hard for Chloë and handed her a glass of wine. 'Here. This might help.'

'Thanks,' said Chloë, taking a far-larger-than-some-people-would-think-seemly swig.

Of everything, it was Maggie's portfolio, paradoxically, that had made Chloe resent her the most. She'd been taken aback by Maggie phoning her so soon after she'd returned from New York, but had prepared herself well for the face-to-face encounter. At the start of the meeting she'd been able to be charming and friendly, because she'd convinced herself beforehand that Maggie wasn't going to have anything to offer her. In the first few minutes she'd decided that she might be beautiful and polite, a bit shy and surprisingly sweet, but this had only underlined how different they were. Everything that James had said about his wife had also led Chloë to believe this, and until that point she hadn't wanted to challenge it. Thus Maggie wasn't right for James; and she certainly wasn't going to be right to work on *her* magazine.

But when she'd looked at the portfolio and Maggie had said that she thought women's magazines were stuck in a rut, Chloë saw that they might have something in common. This had made her question her assumptions and left her doubtful of her analysis of Maggie's relationship with James, and very unsure of herself. So she'd been horrid. Then she knew she'd been horrid, so she felt guilty, and briefly – just before she'd bidden Maggie farewell – been pleasant again.

Not that my being pleasant would count for much if she knew I was having an affair with her husband, she thought.

'Hello . . . Chloë?' Rob waved a hand in front of her face to get her attention. She had been uncharacteristically silent. 'You're miles away. Come ba-ack . . .'

'Sorry.'

'Anyway,' Rob continued, 'bet she can't be such a go-getter as you – you're about to launch your very own magazine.'

'True.' The great thing about Rob was that, although he thought her affair with James a mistake, he was always on her side.

'You're not going to have to work with her, are you?'

'No, no. I managed to get out of that.'

Rob chuckled. 'Thank God! Not even you could cope with that.'

'What do you mean "not even me"?'

'Aw, c'mon, love, you tend to seek out messy situations a bit, don't you?'

Chloë began to bite her lip as she often did when she was uncomfortable. 'Do you think so?'

'Yes, honey, I do.' Rob always used endearments like 'honey' or 'love' whenever he was saying something Chloë might not like to hear, as if to soften the blow. 'It's the drama queen in you. But don't worry about it. It sounds to me as if you handled the situation remarkably well.'

'I suppose I did, in some ways. I certainly don't think she had any idea about me and James, and I didn't give her any evidence.'

'And you didn't cause any terrible scenes. I mean, some women in your situation would have spilt the beans to get things out in the open. Fantastic opportunity, after all, a one-to-one with his wife.'

Maybe Rob thought Chloë capable of this, but she was much too professional and proud to expose herself in that way, especially in front of her colleagues. Anyway, she wasn't that stupid: it might mean she'd lose James for ever.

Rob began to lay the table. 'Shift.'

Chloë, who'd been propping up her chin mournfully in her hands, obediently lifted her elbows to make room.

'In fact, what with so many crises in one week, I'm quite proud of you.' He laughed, hoping to tease her out of despondency. 'I mean, it's not every woman I know who could cope with having a lover who's her boss.'

'He's not my boss!' protested Chloë.

'Okay, a lover who's got some sway over her career, then.'

'Not much.'

'But you get my point. Your lover works with you and gives the go-ahead to your pet project—'

'That was up to Vanessa, not James.'

'Okay, okay. Let me finish, anyway. So you resign from your job and secretly go away on a business trip together. Meanwhile your ex-editor is his wife's best mate and you bump into her in Bloomingdale's when you're not supposed to be there, and – let me get this right – then she unwittingly suggests you work with the wife, so you end up interviewing the wife to work on your pet project.' He paused for breath. 'It makes the plot lines of Albert Square look positively mundane! But my point is that not every woman could handle that lot as well as you have.'

'I see what you mean,' acknowledged Chloë. When he put it like that, it did sound rather a lot to manage, and she had to agree that she'd surpassed herself so far. Yet was this an achievement she should be proud of – a reflection of her belief in the rightness of her relationship with James? Or was she in danger of being damaged in some way if she continually put her emotions through the wringer like this? Should she stick at things in the hope they would get better, or try to get the hell out, if – and it was a very big 'if' – she still could?

She didn't know the answers; clearly Rob didn't, either. There was only one person who could sort out this muddle, she decided, and that was James.

## 30 Maggie

**Maggie was home** from her meeting at UK Magazines earlier than she'd expected. She had half an hour before she had to collect Nathan from school so she decided to drop in on Georgie. As luck would have it, she was at home.

'Hi!' Georgie opening the door, looked pleased to see her.

'I wasn't sure you'd be in,' said Maggie.

'You must have got a psychic vibe – I often have Tuesdays off because I have to work Saturdays. Come in. Coffee?'

Maggie stepped into the tiny hallway, which looked even smaller thanks to the numerous watercolours that smothered the walls, and followed Georgie through into the kitchen. 'I hope I'm not interrupting,' she apologised, seeing books and papers piled high on the table.

'Oh, no! It's always like this. I'm not very good at leaving work at the shop.' Georgie reached for a jar of instant. Maggie flinched, but was too polite to say she'd changed her mind and could she have tea. 'And I suppose I've been trying to keep myself busy –

take my mind off things.' She launched straight into the situation on which Maggie was keen for an update. 'I split up with Alex last week.' She sighed.

'Oh dear,' said Maggie, who also felt the pain of troubled romance all too keenly just now. 'Are you okay about it?'

'I guess.' Georgie held her unruly hair off her face and frowned. 'I mean, it's not as if it had been that long or anything. It's just, when you get to my age . . . Sometimes I wish *something* would work out. But he was very decent about it.'

Maggie smiled to herself. Typical Alex, she thought. She tried to offer comfort. 'Well, he only parted from his wife a few months ago. Maybe it was a bit soon.'

'Mm.' Georgie nodded. 'Maybe.' Then she added, 'All I want is a nice man of my own. Someone to appreciate me. A chap like Jamie, perhaps. I mean, you two seem happy, well suited. How did *you* do it?'

Maggie was unsure what to say. Then she decided that being frank might make Georgie feel better. She could see that her friend looked paler than usual and was standing more rigidly. All in all she seemed down. Perhaps it was because Maggie felt like that herself that she could quickly recognise it in another. 'It's not that great always, you know, being married. Jamie's not quite as wonderful as you might think.'

'Really?'

'No. In fact, we've been having a bit of a difficult time recently. I'm sure we'll get over it, but still . . . it might surprise you to hear that sometimes *I* envy women like you who have their freedom, who can do what they like, who only have to answer to themselves. Believe me, marriage isn't one continual mutual-appreciation society.'

'Oh.' Georgie sounded astonished. Then she smiled. 'Isn't it funny? We always think everyone else has it so sorted but then, once you get a bit closer, you find that everyone's the same. We're all pretty vulnerable sometimes, I suppose.'

'Indeed.' Maggie remembered how she'd come to a similar conclusion when talking to Fran, then laughed with a touch of sorrow. 'I've certainly been feeling a bit vulnerable lately.'

'You surprise me.'

'Well, as you say, people aren't always as resilient as they seem.'

Georgie's face exuded understanding, and now she said, 'Well, anyway, I know one person who really appreciates you.'

'Who's that?'

'Alex.'

'Alex!'

'Oh, yes.' Georgie leant back against the counter-top, more relaxed now. 'If you ask me, never mind his ex wife, I think he's still a mite in love with you.'

'Surely not?'

'I might be wrong . . . but whenever he talks about you, he sounds so, well, fond of you. I mean deeply fond.'

'Oh!' Now it was Maggie's turn to be taken aback. But she was comforted, too.

'So there you go.' Georgie took a large gulp of coffee. 'Just you remember that. There aren't many of my exes who still hold a candle for me after fifteen years, or whatever it's been, I can tell you.'

'Mm . . .' Maggie *was* flattered. But however nice it was to hear that her old boyfriend might continue to hold her in high regard, the man she really wanted to appreciate her was Jamie.

As he ran to greet her in the playground, fair hair catching the sun, socks around his ankles, Maggie observed that now Nathan had plasters on every extremity – knees and elbows – whereas that morning he'd had only two.

'How did you do these?' she asked, examining his latest wounds.

'Football,' he said. 'I scored two goals!' His love of soccer never seemed to be tempered by tripping over, she thought tenderly. He was carrying a large roll of paintings. 'Here,' he said, handing them over. 'They're for you.'

'Thank you. I'll have a look in a moment.' It was only a few minutes' walk back through the village from Shere Infants to their house, so Maggie tucked the pictures under her arm and they set off, Nathan chatting away animatedly about his day. They stopped en route to feed the ducks. This was a frequent ritual. Maggie often had crusts left over from creating breadcrumb toppings for her recipes, and today she'd brought some in an old Waitrose carrier-bag.

'*I* want to do it,' he said, so she handed him the bag and took a seat under the weeping willows by the river. While Nathan busied himself throwing the crusts as far as he could to test whether the white ducks were quicker than the mallards, she unrolled the paintings and held them at arm's length so she could see the top one.

*Mummy*, it said, and was signed, with some letters back to front, *Nathan Slater*. She caught her breath. She'd seen Nathan's interpretation of herself many, many times – blonde hair the same bright shade of powder-paint yellow, triangular dress, big circular hands with digits carefully attached like rays of the sun, long thin legs, big feet. But this picture was different. Normally Nathan painted her with her mouth upturned in a happy semi-circle, smiling. Here her mouth was unmistakably turned down. She put the picture to the back, and moved on to the next. It was a different version of the same subject – but her mouth was down-turned in this one too. There were four paintings in all, each showed the same sad Mummy.

It didn't take Nathan long to learn that all ducks were equally fast when motivated by food and he returned to her side.

'But I look so sad in all of these!' she protested, holding out the top painting.

'You *are* sad,' said Nathan.

'Oh dear,' said Maggie, rolling up the pictures. 'Do you think so?'

'Um,' said Nathan, looking down and scuffing his shoes on the path. Clearly he didn't like talking about it.

'Well, we'll have to do something about that, then.' Maggie slapped her thighs cheerily and got to her feet. 'I know what'll make me a happy Mummy again. Shall we pop into Nell's Country Kitchen and buy some of their delicious home-made fudge?'

'Ooh, yes!' said Nathan excitedly. Nell's was the tea-room close by on Middle Street.

They pushed open the door with a merry tinkle of the bell, and Nathan cantered over to the baskets on the pine dresser by the till, where he knew that the fudge was displayed.

'Now, let's see,' said Maggie, picking through the different flavours. 'Which one of these is special magic fudge with Cheer-up Mummy potion in it?'

'This one!' Nathan gleefully selected the vanilla and nut.

'That'll definitely make a happy Mummy,' agreed Maggie. She handed over the exact money and they went home and had it for tea.

Well, that does it, Maggie decided, once she'd put Nathan to bed and had sat down in the living room with her feet up and a gin and tonic to await her husband's return from work. It was quite common for Nathan to draw the same thing again and again when he was particularly interested in it, but repeated images of a sad Mummy were worrying. Clearly things were beginning to affect him. And if she had got to the point where she was confiding in her neighbours, they must be affecting her hugely. I've got to talk to Jamie tonight, she vowed. She took a sip of her drink, and braced herself.

Suddenly, she had a idea. I know what would cheer me up, she thought, and give me strength: a chat with Alex. Get the lowdown on him and Georgie.

Luckily she caught him at home.

'It's me,' she said.

'Mags! I was meaning to ring you. How are you?'

'I'm okay.' She didn't really want to talk about herself. 'More to the point, how are *you*?' There was no reason to beat about the bush. 'I've just seen Georgie,' she explained.

'Oh.' Alex sounded worried. 'Is she okay?'

'Yeah, yeah.' Maggie didn't want to be disloyal to her new friend. 'Or, at least, she will be soon, I guess.'

'I feel a bit bad,' Alex confessed.

'Oh?'

'Well, it's never easy, finishing things, is it?'

Momentarily Maggie flashed back to when Alex and she had

split up. She'd just started working in magazines and, consumed by her new job, was unwilling to settle down so soon after graduating, though Alex had wanted to. But she'd never been sure she was doing the right thing in ending it, and it had meant, for once in her life, that she'd probably been a little heartless.

'No,' she said.

'I think Georgie was a bit of a rebound thing,' Alex continued. 'I was still getting over Stella.'

'Do you think?'

'Now I do, yes.' Alex was always straight with Maggie. 'It really helped – we had a lot of fun, and she's a lovely woman, but I don't feel she's quite right for me. You won't ever say that to her, though, will you? I've tried to part from her on reasonable terms, but that's often easier said than done.'

'Of course I won't say anything.' Maggie would never dream of being so tactless.

At that moment the front door slammed, and she heard the familiar rustle of Jamie slinging his jacket over the banister.

'Oh dear,' she said hurriedly. 'That's Jamie. I'd better go.'

'Already?' Alex seemed disappointed.

'I'll call you soon,' she promised, hung up, then called out to Jamie, 'I'm in here.'

A couple of seconds later he appeared at the living-room door.

She decided to open on something that didn't involve the two of them. 'I saw Chloë today,' she said.

But even that seemed to disconcert him. 'Um . . .' He paused. 'How did it go?' He went over to the drinks cabinet, got out one of the decanters they'd been given as a wedding present and poured himself a whisky.

'Actually, it was a bit odd.'

'Odd?' Now he sounded concerned.

'Yes. Well, rather, *she* was a bit odd.'

'Really?' He turned away from her to replace the decanter. Why was it, these days, that he barely ever looked her in the eye?

'You've met her, haven't you?'

'Yes.' He took a gulp of his drink.

'Did you think she was odd?'

'No, not particularly.' Another gulp.

'Moody?'

'No.' He took a seat, opting not for the sofa next to her but one of the armchairs. They were sitting at right angles to each other, both with their feet propped on the coffee table, relaxed yet unrelaxed, poles apart.

'Oh, well, maybe it was me, then.' Typical Maggie, quick to blame herself.

'Why? What did she say?'

'Nothing I could put my finger on.' Maggie frowned, wondering how she could explain. 'At first she was really friendly, charming, even. Then, when she saw my portfolio, she turned cool.'

'Maybe she didn't think your work was right for *All Woman*.'

'Maybe . . .'

Jamie took a third sip of whisky. He seemed to be drinking it awfully fast. 'I did warn you that you might not be of a like mind.'

'I know,' Maggie agreed. But years of being the observer frequently in social situations meant that she was a good judge of character and people's reactions, and she was pretty sure that Chloë had liked her work. Moreover, deep down she was confident that when she was stimulated by what she was doing, her work was exceptional, and she knew that what she'd shown Chloë was as good a selection of cookery writing as she was ever likely to see. She explained, 'You can tell me I'm imagining things, but I don't think that's what it was.'

'So what *do* you think it was?' Yes, she was right: he *was* perturbed. But maybe it was because he was more bothered about what was going on in her life than she was giving him credit for.

'Something Jean said . . .' Maggie struggled to find the words.

'What did Jean say?' Unless she was mistaken, he was angry now. God, he was so confusing these days! Then again, he'd always been defensive about Jean, and more than a little threatened by the closeness of Maggie's friendship with her.

'She said something about Chloë not liking to share things . . . so I wondered . . .'

'What?'

'Whether she was being possessive.'

'*Possessive?*'

'Mm, that she didn't want to share working on the magazine project with me or something.'

'Do you think so?'

'I can't think of any other reason why she'd be so funny. Can you?'

'Er . . .'

'After all, my work's okay, isn't it?'

Jamie hurried to reassure her. 'Of course! It's fine! In fact, it's more than fine, it's great!'

'Anyway . . .' Maggie couldn't think of anything more to add. 'I didn't want to talk about Chloë.'

'Didn't you?'

'No. It's no big deal, I suppose. I'll just have to look to someone else for the kind of work I want to do.' Maggie's took a sip of her gin for Dutch courage. 'I wanted to talk about us.' To show she was serious, she tried to look at him directly. But Jamie looked down at his feet and avoided her gaze in a way that was reminiscent of Nathan earlier that day. Or maybe Nathan was reminiscent of Jamie. Son like father, father like son – it didn't really matter. The important thing was that Nathan's upset had opened Maggie's eyes. As his room was directly above, she dropped her voice. 'We can't avoid this for ever.'

'No,' said Jamie gruffly.

'Don't tell me you hadn't noticed.'

'No,' Jamie agreed. 'I had.'

'Well?' Suddenly Maggie felt herself shaking again. How she hated emotional confrontations!

Then he surprised her. 'I'd kind of thought I should talk to you.'

Perhaps this was good: if he was prepared to acknowledge they had problems and wanted to talk, surely he would come with her to Relate. 'What did you want to talk about?'

'To be honest, I wasn't sure what to say.'

'Um?'

'That's why I didn't say anything.'

'I see.' Though she didn't. He seemed to have lost his bottle. Silence.

Then Jamie ventured, 'So what did *you* want to say?'

It occurred to Maggie that Nathan's pictures might be a good place to start. 'Hang on a minute.' She got up. 'I've something to show you.' She went into the kitchen and collected the loose roll from the top of the fridge, then returned to the living room. She handed them to Jamie. He looked through them without saying a word. 'Notice anything?' asked Maggie, finally.

'They're all of you.'

How selfish that his first concern was for his own standing in Nathan's eyes! But perhaps that was significant too: absent-father syndrome.

'Yes. Anything else?'

He stopped, and examined them again. 'You look miserable?'

'Yes.'

More silence. At last Jamie said, 'Is that true?'

Maggie was bottling up so much resentment that she didn't know where to start, or how. As she sat there, on the huge chesterfield, gin and tonic in hand, feet up in a way that was supposed to indicate she was 'at ease', although she was far from it, her emotions manifested themselves physically. She could feel her heart thudding in her chest, her cheeks burning, the gin glass cold and clammy in her sticky palms. All at once Maggie felt fury, stirred up by protectiveness of Nathan – misery was far too passive. Eventually she spat out – she was both fierce and bitter, 'I suppose you could say that I'm pretty fucked off, yes.'

Then out it poured. 'I'm fucked off with you working late. I'm fucked off with you not helping more around the house. I'm fucked off with you not supporting me in public. I'm fucked off with you not ringing me from America. I'm fucked off with you for not talking to me any more. You've hardly spoken to me since coming back from New York, for God's sake! Not properly, anyway. And I'm fucked off with you for making me – yes, *making* me – compromise my standards and slave away writing articles I hate, just to alleviate your neurosis about money. And, above all,

I'm fucked off with you for not being willing even to discuss having another child.'

He could be in no doubt as to the level of her wrath and pain. But he merely stared down at his feet, which made her angrier still.

'You're pathetic,' she said.

Jamie was shocked: now at least he looked at her. 'Oh?'

'Or, rather,' she corrected herself, 'your recent behaviour is pathetic.'

This made him blush, whether with anger or guilt she couldn't be sure. 'I just . . .' he stammered ' . . . don't know how I . . . er . . . feel about things right now.'

'You surprise me,' she said venomously. 'About what, precisely, don't you "*know how you feel*"?'

He tried to explain: 'It's not you, it's me.'

'Well, thank you for that insight.' It was such a hackneyed excuse but she was relieved that he had acknowledged it wasn't her fault. But it didn't help her understand things any better – she didn't know what 'it' was. The half-formulated belief that he was being unfaithful had remained with her since the day of the exhibition, but she certainly wasn't ready to articulate it. Instead she asked, 'What is it with you? Some mid-life crisis or something?'

'Perhaps. I've been feeling a bit claustrophobic lately. I guess I'm just not sure quite where I'm at.'

'How original.' Again she couldn't resist saying it with heavy irony. He sounded so juvenile, like a teenager, and she resented being made to feel that she was hemming him in. So she added, knowing it would really annoy him, 'Jean was right, then.'

'Fuck Jean.'

Wow, that really pushed a button. 'How dare you talk like that about my friend!'

'How dare you talk to your friend about me!'

'Well, *you* won't talk to me! Who the hell else am I supposed to talk to?'

'No one.'

'No one? Oh, get real, Jamie! I may keep things to myself a lot of the time, but I'm not a bloody robot! We've hardly made love for three months, and when we do I can tell your heart's not in it – probably because you're petrified of getting me pregnant. We've not spoken, you're hardly here, you don't help me, you nag me about money, you go away, you don't call – what the fuck am I supposed to do? Not breathe a word? Jesus, I had to go to the doctor I was so miserable. The doctor, for heaven's sake! And let me tell you, I found him a whole lot easier to talk to than you!'

'You went to the doctor?'

'Yes.'

'You talked to the doctor about us?'

'Yes.'

'Oh, great. So now everyone in the village will know about our marital problems.'

Maggie had a flash of guilt about how she'd confided in Georgie earlier, which enhanced her indignation. She wouldn't *need* to confide in these other people if he talked to her! And, anyway, she'd not said *that* much to Georgie, had she? She justified herself to him: 'In case it had escaped your notice, Jamie, doctors are sworn to secrecy, so you needn't bloody worry that he'll go round spilling the beans in the goddamn supermarket.' Shit. Maggie realised this conversation was not going the way she'd intended at all. She was supposed to be persuading Jamie to come with her to counselling, not driving a wedge between them because she had spoken to other people. She was also aware that there was only the ceiling between them and Nathan, so she halted for a second to think and calm down. 'Anyway, I think that's the point, isn't it?'

Jamie looked bewildered.

'Well, we haven't been talking, so I've had to talk to somebody else.'

'More than somebody. Somebod*ies*.'

'Somebody, somebodies, whatever.' Golly, thought Maggie, thank God he *doesn't* know about Georgie. She moved on, more calmly. 'My point is that I'd much rather be discussing things with you.' She took a deep breath. 'So I wondered, would you come with me for some counselling?'

'Counselling?'

Clearly this was going to be really hard work. 'Yes. Marriage-guidance counselling.'

'I don't need bloody counselling!'

'*You* might not. *We* do.'

'No, we don't.' She knew Jamie in this mood. Stubbornness personified. For the time being she was sure he wouldn't budge, but she forced herself to give it one last stab. 'It's not a bad thing, Jamie, you know, counselling. Hundreds of couples do it.'

'And we're not one of those couples.'

'If we're not one of "those couples", who are we?'

'Now you're being ridiculous. I just don't want to go and talk to some stranger about my marriage. All right?'

She inhaled deeply. 'Well, will you at least think about it?'

'No.'

God, sometimes she wanted to shoot him. If she'd had a gun, she'd have put a bullet in his brain there and then. Sitting so smug and self-righteous and self-obsessed on the sodding seat nearby. The uncompromising son of a bitch. The bastard.

'I'd rather sort things out my own way,' he said.

He clearly meant in a way that suited him. This decided Maggie. 'Fine. I'll go on my own, then.'

'You can't go on your own!'

'Oh, can't I?' she said. 'Just watch me.'

# **31** Chloë

**Summer eventually gave** way to autumn, and just as in Battersea Park a patch of mild weather kept the leaves hanging on branches in a semi-browned state of suspension, so a certain reluctance permeated Chloë's mental state regarding her affair. She sensed that James was as unwilling as she was to leave behind September's reckless behaviour and face the more sobering consequences of their actions. So instead of making demands or precipitating confrontations, she let their relationship drift on as it had before they'd been away, much to Rob's dismay. He was convinced that if she let things slide now, she would always do so, and would end up in a triangle indefinitely. 'You're letting him have his cake and eat it,' he said, time and time again, until it barely registered with Chloë. Heedless of his warnings, she continued to see James once a week – twice if she was lucky – but at least this left her free to focus on her professional life, which, if truth be told, might otherwise have suffered.

As well as asking Craig Spencer to write a piece on children and divorce as promised, she commissioned several journalists to produce a variety of articles. She asked one writer known for his investigative ruthlessness to produce the most dangerously provocative feature he had to date, and another known for her brazen interview technique to go one step further than she ever had before with a profoundly soul-searching star profile. She invited a favourite freelancer to come up with his sharpest, wittiest column, another to give vent to a biting series of reviews and a third to write an up-to-the-minute social exposé. 'I want you to stretch yourself,' she said to each. 'Pull out all the stops. Leave no holds barred. Write what *you* would like to read, as if there was no editor or advertising director limiting what you're allowed to do.'

But she couldn't brief all the work out to others and, anyway, she wanted to write some of the features herself, so one morning, a month or two after returning from New York, she decided she could do with a hand from Patsy. Given that Patsy wasn't supposed to be working on *All Woman* and that she had no wish to antagonise Jean by stealing her during working hours, she arranged to meet her for lunch. 'It's a bit embarrassing explaining this in an open-plan office,' she said tantalisingly over the phone.

'Blimey!' exclaimed Patsy. 'It must be hush-hush – I didn't think you ever got embarrassed!'

'You'll see what I mean soon enough,' said Chloë darkly, and they arranged to meet in the foyer on the ground floor.

'So what's this all about?' Patsy squealed. There was nothing she liked more than a little intrigue – she and Rob were soul-sisters in that way.

'Wait and see.' Chloë winked.

'Oooh!' Patsy was infuriated but thrilled.

They made their way down Long Acre, crossed into Endell Street and headed straight up to Shaftesbury Avenue.

'Where are we going?' panted Patsy. A combination of dysfunctional footwear and legs a good few inches shorter even than Chloë's made it hard for her to keep up.

Chloë tapped her nose knowingly. 'Patience.'

Along Denmark Street, with its funny little music shops that had been there for ever, over the pelican crossing on Charing Cross Road and they were there.

'*Ann Summers!*' Patsy giggled. 'Are you sure this isn't somewhere you should be coming with your man, not me?'

But Patsy doesn't know I *have* a man, thought Chloë, momentarily flummoxed. Still, this wasn't the moment to ask what she meant, so she moved on, saying firmly, 'No. This is a project, Patsy. Work. Not play. Research.'

'You're having me on!'

Chloë grabbed a basket and strode purposefully past the underwear, nurses' uniforms and maids' outfits, and up the steps into the back. Here the lighting was less harsh. She noted there were no lone women shoppers, only couples, and men, presumably buying for their girlfriends or wives. She scanned the shelves – no, not the videos or magazines, or the handcuffs, and certainly not the rather tacky 'play' whips or masks. (Far more creative to improvise, Chloë believed.)

'This is what we're after,' she said, halting in front of the biggest display.

Patsy was following close behind. '*Dildoes!*' she whooped.

'Vibrators,' said Chloë, mock-sedately. 'They call this the Vibrator Bar.' They peered at the samples lined up like giant lipsticks before them. There were small pink ones and huge black ones, ridged ones and ribbed ones, ones with curved ends and straight ones, ones with rather alarming prongs and ones that looked more like massagers. There was even a rather pretty butterfly-shaped device that didn't resemble a penis at all. Patsy switched it on and jumped back, alarmed, as it sprang to life in her hand. 'Now, then,' Chloë directed, 'decide on six different kinds.'

'*Six!*'

'Yup, six.'

'Bloody hell, Chloë, I always thought you were a bit of a goer, but six? You're insatiable!'

'They're not all for *me*,' laughed Chloë. 'One's for you.'

Patsy pouted. 'Are you implying Doug's not enough for me?' Doug was her long-suffering boyfriend of several years' standing.

'Far be it from me to criticise the prowess of your one true love, Patsy dear. I wouldn't dare.' Doug was six foot four and built like a brick shithouse. 'No, my faithful assistant, this is a little project for girls, *toutes seules*. You know those consumer panels they have in the Sunday papers and some magazines? "Tried and Tested", they're called.'

Patsy nodded.

'Well, you, my sweet, innocent Patsy, are going to head up my specially selected panel for *All Woman* to put six of these lurve machines through their paces!'

'No!'

'Oh, yes. I'm sick of reading about bottle-openers and baked beans – they're hardly the most important thing in a girl's life. And as for stay-on lipgloss and waterproof mascaras, give me a break. I mean, how unadventurous! *All Woman* is going to be about testing those things that you always wanted to know about but never dared to ask.'

'But we can try them out *here*.' Patsy switched on one with an intriguing extra prong.

'Not where it counts, you can't.' Chloë grinned wickedly.

Patsy giggled. 'They'll never let you!'

'Who's they?'

'Advertisers. UK Magazines. You know.'

'It all depends on how it's done. Okay, so maybe Estée Lauder won't buy the space opposite, but I'm sure somebody will. Black Lace novels or Durex, for instance. We just have to make sure it's written with humour –' Chloë scooped up a mammoth chocolate-coloured vibrator, aptly titled "Throbbing Muscle," and put it in her basket '– and grace.'

They decided to stop off for a sandwich at Prêt à Manger before returning to the office. Perched on high stools at a window table so that they could play spot-the-trend on passers-by, Chloë had her regulation Prêt Salad sandwich and Diet Coke, convincing herself that they couldn't be too fattening, which she wolfed at ninety miles per hour. Patsy picked pathetically at a vegetarian sushi and left half.

Part-way through, however, Patsy ventured, 'I'm glad we did this.'

'I told you you were in need of a little more buzz in your love life,' Chloë teased. 'You and Doug have been going out way too long.'

'No, it's not that. I meant I'm glad I've got the chance to have a chat just us two. There's something I wanted to ask you.'

'What's that?'

'Are you seeing anyone at the moment?'

Chloë swallowed a particularly large mouthful. She felt herself colouring immediately. 'No.'

Patsy looked at her carefully. 'Are you sure?'

'Of course I'm sure!' That was probably just a touch too defensive. 'Why do you ask?'

'I thought maybe you were.'

'What on earth should make you think that?'

'Lots of things.'

Chloë took another bite. She couldn't possibly be seen to be put off her food – Patsy would be sure there was something up. 'Like what?'

'Like . . . talking on the phone opposite me in hushed whispers during your last few weeks at *Babe* . . . your increasingly sexy wardrobe of workwear . . . your general glow . . . that mysterious "holiday" when you wouldn't tell me where you were going or who with . . . Do you want me to carry on?'

Blast Patsy's gossip radar! And she thought she'd been so discreet! 'Um.'

'Look.' Patsy took a deep breath. 'You don't have to tell me if you don't want to. I have my suspicions but, actually, in this case I'd be happy to keep them to myself.' Chloe raised an eyebrow. It was uncharacteristic of Patsy to *volunteer* to keep mum. Normally she'd only do it if asked. 'It's just I'm not the only one with them.'

'What do you mean?' Now Chloë paled.

'I might as well get to the point. You always were bollocks at lying. And now your every gesture is giving you away. Are you having an affair with James Slater or what?'

Chloe felt her face turn from white to scarlet.

'Obviously you are.'

In vain Chloë tried to bluff her way out. 'I am not!'

'I've *told* you, I've known for ages that you're seeing someone. I wasn't sure who it was but then Jean said something and I put two and two together—'

'And made five!'

'And made four. You're playing with fire, you know.' Patsy looked at Chloë as sternly as she could. The effect was somewhat diminished by her tiny stature and crazy pixie hairstyle, but Chloë knew she was genuinely concerned.

She didn't see the point in denying it any longer. It seemed more important to find out who else knew, and what they knew, than keep up the pretence. After all, if she begged, Patsy *would* keep it quiet. If there was one thing Patsy liked more than gossip it was to be privy to a nice juicy secret. 'If I tell you, will you swear not to tell a soul?'

Patsy nodded solemnly. 'Cross my heart.' She made the age-old schoolgirl gesture across her chest to indicate her sincerity.

'And will you tell me everything Jean said to you?' This was what really worried Chloë.

'My foremost allegiance is to my old features editor, natch.'

'Okay,' said Chloë. 'Here goes.' And as quickly as she could – she was aware that the minutes were ticking by and that they were due back at work – she gave Patsy a brief outline of her liaison with James.

'Well, I'll be damned!' said Patsy, when she'd reached the end.

Chloë tried to explain. 'I do really like him,' she said quietly. 'I like him a lot.'

But Patsy ignored this. 'Just one question. Then I'll tell you what Jean said, I promise.'

Chloë checked her watch. 'Okay, but only one. I've got a lot to do this afternoon.'

'Is he a good shag?'

'Patsy!'

'Ooh, go on, tell me . . . I'm the one who spotted his potential!'

'I'm not sure I should reveal that,' said Chloë haughtily.

'For goodness' sake!' Patsy jigged up and down impatiently.

'You take me to Ann Summers to buy vibrators and then you go coy on me!'

'Yeah, I s'pose so . . .' Chloë felt uncomfortable all over again. Joking aside, she didn't like reducing her relationship with James to such a low level. She could see that dragging out her colleague on a shopping trip to buy sex toys had done little to enhance her image as an old-fashioned romantic, but she would have liked Patsy to know that she and James cared deeply for each other. She was too self-conscious to reveal that she was in love with him however, so what she said was: 'It's great – he's great, if you must know, but that's the most you'll get out of me. So, go on, your turn. Jean. Shoot.'

'Well, so far, you're safe. And,' Patsy lifted her chin proudly, 'you've me to thank for that. I've batted off every suggestion she makes with a categoric denial.'

'Thank you. You're a star.'

'But you ought to be careful. Bloody careful. That woman,' here Patsy leant close to Chloë for effect, 'has eyes like a hawk and a nose like a bloodhound.'

'No need to tell me that. I worked under her needle-sharp editorship, after all. Nothing escapes her. So what did she say?'

'Well. Obviously she doesn't have access to your feeble attempts at "secret" phone calls like me,' Patsy said, 'and she hasn't said anything to me outright. I'm not sure she even realises that it's James you're seeing – at least, she's not told me she thinks it's him. Then again, I don't think she would, what with Maggie being her friend. But she does think you're seeing someone on the sly. She asked me point blank the other day but I hotly refuted it, of course – and she *did* see you in New York, remember? She said to me that she thought it was odd you hadn't told her that was where you were going when you knew she'd be there.'

Chloë felt rather foolish. 'Actually, I'd forgotten she would be. It was all so last-minute for me.'

'She's getting bloody close to sniffing you two out, that's what I reckon. It was only last week I heard her bitching to Vanessa that she couldn't understand why on earth you hadn't agreed to Maggie Slater doing some cookery writing for *All Woman*. That was when I worked out for sure that it was James,' she added smugly. 'I know what you're like, and you're a tight cow when it comes to commissions. So I couldn't think of any other reason why you wouldn't want to work with someone with such a good reputation who was prepared to write for you free of charge.'

'Oops.'

'Yes, "oops" indeed. Anyway,' Patsy got to her feet. 'We'd better go.'

They grabbed an Ann Summers carrier-bag apiece, slung their empty sandwich packets in the bin on their way out and raced back up Long Acre, just as it began to rain.

'Next time she asks, pretend you know who I'm seeing, and that it's someone else.' Chloë gasped for breath, her bag of vibrators bouncing as she ran.

'Will do,' said Patsy. Part of her was clearly relishing the chance to act adviser to someone more senior than she was. 'But just you watch your step, you *femme fatale*, you.'

Although things with James hadn't moved on apace in the last few weeks, one important development was due to take place that night: he was going to meet Rob.

Using the by now well-worn Thursday-night-is-squash-night excuse, James had agreed to come round to their flat and Rob had even offered to cook. He was a lot better at it than Chloë, as he told her in no uncertain terms. 'If you do it, it's –' he made a dramatic slicing gesture across his throat, accompanied by a choking sound '– to your affair. His wife's Margaret Wilson, girl!' Chloë could hardly have felt less like pulling on a pinny and dusting off her one cookery book.

She made sure she was home at a reasonable hour – if she wasn't permitted to help with the meal, she wanted at least to create the right ambience. On her way she stopped at Asda – it was the biggest nearby supermarket – and bought candles, paper napkins, three bottles of wine – more expensive ones than normal – and some cat food.

The bags weighed a ton. As she staggered up St John's Hill to the flat in the dusky drizzle, they sliced into her hands, and when she finally dumped them on the kitchen table, they'd left cruel red marks on her palms. One of the tins of Whiskas rolled on to the floor and nearly tripped up Rob, who was in the midst of slicing onions with tears streaming down his face. He glanced down impatiently at the offending object, took his eyes off the knife, cut his finger and swore.

She was nervous enough about Rob meeting James as it was and this didn't help. Other than her dad and her brother, they were the two most important men in her life. 'Sorry.' She winced. 'Are you okay?'

'I'll live,' growled Rob, running his finger under the tap. 'This man had better be worth it.'

'So,' said Chloë gaily, 'what are we having? It smells gorgeous.'

'Roast halibut with spiced lentils and coriander.' Rob was making a big effort. 'I hope he's not going to be late. All this needs timing to the minute.'

Chloë was confident. 'He's never late.'

'No, I'm sure every minute counts when you've a wife to get back to.'

She let the jibe go. 'Do you mind if I just freshen up before laying the table?'

'You go right ahead.'

Chloë disappeared into the bathroom for a speedy shower. *Swoosh!* under her arms with the powerful jets of water, *whoosh!* and a rapid soaping everywhere, then a hurried rinse and she was through. Back in her room Potato was mewing pitifully at the door, keen for a share of the fish. Ignoring him, she struggled to pull on a clean pair of knickers though she'd barely allowed herself time to dry. Rummage, rummage, rummage – where was that top? Ah, yes! Rush, rush, quick, quick, pull on her shiny black trousers – ugh, they were sticking to her thighs – and those mules, James hadn't seen them before, two minutes on her makeup, a few seconds scrunching her hair with the dryer – it had gone a bit frizzy in the rain – and, phew, she was ready.

She breezed back into the kitchen and began setting things up. There was just enough room to entertain at the small table if she cleared it of gubbins, so she swept up the piles of magazines and unpaid bills and dumped them in a corner of the living room. She grabbed the broken chair from the hallway and banged the leg back into place – it might just take her weight for the evening if she was careful. Next she hunted for three matching wine-glasses – in vain. Oh, well, two out of three isn't bad, she decided. Once she'd placed a folded napkin in each you couldn't really tell. She had the same problem when it came to crockery – one of the drawbacks of rented accommodation was that landlords were disinclined to provide anything of any value, so she and Rob boasted a pretty motley collection of plates. But the mix 'n' match look is supposed to be in, she persuaded herself. Finally, she ran round the flat scooping up every candlestick she could find and jammed a candle in each.

'There,' she said, turning out the main light so that they could have quick look. It was amazing how a little subtlety could enhance the atmosphere.

'It looks wonderful,' Rob praised. 'Almost wouldn't recognise the place. Now stir this. It's my turn.'

Obediently Chloë took her spot at the stove while Rob disappeared into the bathroom. While he was gone, her anticipation mounted. She did so want them to get on. She knew that Rob was prejudiced against James, but was convinced James's charm would win him over face to face. Then the phone rang. With one hand, she reached over and picked it up.

'Hi.' She tucked the receiver under her chin so she could carry on performing her culinary duties. Well I never – she was surprising herself – she was really enjoying this.

'Hi,' said a familiar voice, muffled by the sound of trains. 'It's James.'

'Oh, hi!' Chloë could scarcely contain her excitement. 'Where are you?'

'Waterloo.'

'Ooh, good – you'll be here any minute!'

A particularly loud train thundered past. 'I'm afraid I'm not coming,' he said.

Chloë thought she must have misheard. 'What?'

'I can't come. I'm terribly sorry.'

'Oh.' Chloë was so disappointed, she didn't know what to say. There was a long pause. 'Why not?'

'It's Maggie, I'm afraid.'

'Oh.' She knew she sounded pissed off. But, hell, she *was* pissed off. Gutted. She *hated* being let down. For all her impulsiveness and impatience, Chloë was very reliable. She might be late occasionally, but she loathed it when people didn't turn up at all.

James elaborated: 'She went to see this woman today, and now she wants to talk.'

'What woman?' Chloë wanted a cigarette, badly – anything to diminish the upset.

'Some marriage counsellor or something.'

'Oh.' Stunned, Chloë struggled to take this in. She had no idea Maggie was going for marriage guidance. What did that mean? That Maggie and James were going to work things out together?

'I'm sorry, I really am.'

'Um.'

'I promise I'll make it up to you.'

'But we've made everything for you! I've bought the wine! Rob's cooked something specially!' She looked at the beautifully laid table, the three chairs, the bottles of wine, one of which Rob had opened to breathe while she'd been getting ready. She felt an absolute idiot.

'I know, I know.' Even through the background noise, Chloë could sense his guilt down the line. 'Can't you eat it, you and him?'

'No, we can't. Well, I mean we can, or Potato can have it, but it's hardly the same.'

'I feel a complete shit.'

By now Chloë was so pissed off she was trembling. Should she say it? Yes, fuck it, she would. 'Well, you are,' she said, and slammed down the phone.

## 32 Maggie

**The drive along** the A25 into Guildford was so familiar that, although the day was damp and dark, Maggie could focus her thoughts elsewhere.

In one way the last few weeks had been good, in another bad. They had been good because of her work: her attitude had shifted, and she was no longer prepared to settle for second best. She'd had the courage to approach a couple of editors she particularly respected with feature ideas that she thought were refreshingly different. Both had been enthusiastic (much more so than Chloë, Maggie noted) and given her the thumbs-up, so she was currently in the midst of drafting the first commission. Indeed, that afternoon she had been so wrapped up in what she was doing that she'd been taken by surprise when she'd looked up at the kitchen clock and seen that it was time to go, and had had to leave her notes strewn over the table.

Speeding through the countryside in her Mégane, Maggie's head was still full of the article. She'd given it the working title 'Is your money where your mouth is?' and in order to research it had accompanied half a dozen professionals from the food industry on a weekend survival course. There, as well as having to forage for edible berries, mushrooms and plants in the wilds of Wales, she and the others – who had included a chef, a supermarket buyer, a dietitian and a butcher – had had to kill a couple of chickens then eat them. Inevitably those who had previously been happy to sell or serve meat weren't quite so comfortable when faced with the stark reality of slaughter.

The experience had tested her too – not just because, after years of eating chicken with Jamie and Nathan, she'd found she couldn't even attempt to strangle a live bird and so had been forced to reassess her own dietary habits, but also because she'd had to deal with several people she'd never met before. In the event she'd enjoyed the weekend, and found it a challenge. Also, it had been especially gratifying to leave Jamie to take care of Nathan and the house for once.

The fact that she'd been so busy also meant that to a certain extent Maggie had been able to bury her worries about Jamie. He hadn't been best pleased when she'd returned from her weekend away, insisting that she was only going to serve her family fish, vegetables and dairy products from now on, and it had precipitated yet another argument. 'But I *like* chicken!' he'd protested. 'I don't want to eat bloody seafood all the time!'

'Then cook it yourself,' she'd said.

Their frequent rows increased Maggie's nagging suspicion that he was having an affair. However, as she drove into the outskirts of Guildford, dutifully dropping her speed to thirty, she acknowledged that if she was totally honest she'd been happy to have the distraction of work because she couldn't face dealing with these fears on her own. Maggie dreaded asking him outright if he was seeing someone else, or talking to Jean again in case she told her something that she would rather not hear. But knowing that at last she was going to have the opportunity to talk in confidence to someone objective gave Maggie strength.

Today I'm going to begin tackling this mess, she resolved. I can't bury my head for ever. This is not just about me: it's about Nathan too.

Maggie knew roughly where the building to which she was headed must be, so she parked the car in a little side-street. She got out, checked the front wheels of the vehicle to make sure she wasn't overlapping a double yellow, flicked on the alarm and walked back on to the main road. It was that kind of horrible October weather when it couldn't seem to decide whether it was worth raining properly or not, and a grey mizzle hung in the air, getting into her hair and under her skin.

'341, 339,' she muttered to herself, counting down the door numbers, eventually stopping outside a modern office block with a distinct ring of municipal services about it. She unfolded the typed sheet. Number 335, this was it. She went up the path to the porch. There, among the signs for voluntary services and family planning, was the word Relate. '3rd Floor,' it said.

She pushed open one of the wire-glass double doors and looked in vain for a lift. Evidently she was expected to take the stairs. As she climbed, her navy loafers echoed against the linoleum, and by the time she reached the top she was a little short of breath. How was someone in a wheelchair supposed to get all the way up here? she wondered. Clearly the disabled never suffer from marital problems.

On the third floor, there appeared to be only one way to go so she tapped lightly on the door. There was no reply, so she went in. The small waiting area had the same minimum-expenditure feel as the rest of the building, but someone had done their best to make it more inviting with pot plants and magazines. There was a desk with an electric typewriter, but no receptionist; the chair was empty.

All of a sudden Maggie felt overwhelmed with uncertainty and apprehension, just as she had been in Dr Hopkin's surgery. What am I supposed to do now? she wondered, standing there awkwardly

At that moment one of the doors opened, and a woman popped her head round. 'Margaret Slater?' she asked.

'Yes.'

'Sorry,' said the woman, nodding towards the empty chair. 'Lorna's off sick today. I heard you come in. Is it just you?'

Maggie felt conspicuously alone. 'Yes.'

'No matter,' the woman said warmly. 'Give me five minutes and I'll be with you. Make yourself at home.'

Maggie didn't feel relaxed enough to sit down, so she stood at the window, looking out over a rain-soaked Guildford, wondering what the next hour would hold.

That must be the counsellor, she thought. From what she'd glimpsed, the woman was older than she'd expected, probably in her fifties. This impression was confirmed a few minutes later when she invited Maggie into her consulting room. 'My name's Nina,' she said, sitting down in a well-worn swivel chair, which creaked: Nina was not by no means a small woman.

There were two armchairs opposite her, one mustard, the other brown.

'Er, where should I sit?' asked Maggie, hovering.

'Whichever,' said Nina.

Maggie plumped for the brown one. Now she could take in the woman opposite more fully: she had grey hair – 'salt and pepper' – well cut, in a short style that not that many women as large as Nina could take. But Nina had a strong face, with a big, broad mouth and fantastic cheekbones so the style suited her. She was dressed equally confidently, in a rust-coloured bouclé jumper and olive green velvet trousers, offset by huge chunks of ethnic jewellery that rattled when she moved. She had what Maggie thought of as an apple figure: most of her bulk was centrally placed. She had a big bosom and a lot of tummy, although Maggie could see that she had small wrists and elegant ankles. The effect was impressive, and Maggie thought she looked marvellous, but it did little to lessen how intimidated she felt.

Nina leant back. 'Well,' she said, 'I often think it helps if I start by telling you a little about how this works.'

Maggie was relieved. In spite of her resolution to talk openly, she felt overwhelmed with shyness.

'First, I need to check that this appointment is okay with you on a regular basis?'

'Yes, it is,' said Maggie. 'I have a son, Nathan, but I've arranged for him to go to his friend's in the village after school for an hour or so.'

'Good. And I should explain to you that the session is always the same length – an hour – and we can't overrun, even if you're late, because I see someone directly afterwards.'

Maggie couldn't imagine that she would wish to prolong the agony of talking about emotional issues a minute longer than necessary, but didn't feel she could say so. 'I understand that.'

'Next there's the issue of funding.' She handed Maggie a form. 'You'll need to fill in your details here and bring them with you to the next session. Then we can see if you're eligible for a subsidy, or what.'

'Fine,' Maggie took the form, 'but to be honest I doubt I will be.'

'Finally, I wanted to ask,' here Nina adopted a more sympathetic tone, 'whether it's just today that your partner couldn't make it?'

Maggie found herself blushing. She was both disarmed by the directness of the question, and ashamed. Would Nina think it a failing on her part that Jamie had so steadfastly refused to join her? Would she consider it a sign that their relationship was in an irreparable state? Perhaps there was a limit to how many sessions she was allowed to attend on her own: this was supposed to be marriage guidance, after all. Maggie didn't know what to say, and the silence seemed interminable. 'I don't know,' she said eventually.

'Um?' It seemed that Nina wanted her to elaborate.

Maggie felt as if she was about to launch herself off a precipice. She was acutely aware that once she'd spoken, she couldn't go back on what she'd said. The doubt continued, and the questions came thick and fast. Would Nina think her a disloyal wife? Demanding? Unreasonable, even?

Go on! she exhorted herself. Dive in! You're the one who wanted to do this!

'Well . . .' she hesitated. 'He hasn't exactly been receptive to the idea of counselling so far, no.' She gained momentum. 'In fact, I suppose it's fair to say that he's been completely against it.'

'So it was your idea?'

'Yes.' Maggie was beginning to feel a little more at ease. 'Or, rather, it was my friend Jean's suggestion, but it seemed like a good one to me.' She sighed. 'We've been getting on so badly, though, me and Jamie – my husband – that sometimes I feel as if any attempt I make at communicating is met by a brick wall.'

'And how does that make you feel?'

'Desperate,' Maggie answered simply. 'That's why I'm here.' She was silent again. At that moment it seemed as if the room was filled with her troubles; the walls were dripping with her disappointment, the air was heavy with her unspoken fears.

Then something snapped.

Every bit of evidence – both in terms of Jamie's emotional behaviour and his physical response – pointed to it. In some ways she had been certain of it for ages, but it was only now that she was ready to confront it.

'I think Jamie's having an affair,' she said.

My God, she hadn't been expecting herself to *say* it. Not in her first session. But she couldn't bear to keep it in a moment longer. All at once it was as if the shutters had been lifted from her eyes, and her vision had been restored. And it wasn't a good feeling, being able to see so clearly. It was terrifying. Sick-making. Vile. *Her* husband, *her* Jamie, sleeping with someone else! How could he? How could she – the other woman, whoever she was? Maggie was beyond hurt. She was revolted, repulsed, shaken to her very core. In that minute she wanted to die. She felt as if part of her *had* died.

And bizarrely, as this ghastly realisation took shape, Nina was still sitting opposite her, plump, capable and knowing. The chair next to Maggie, where Jamie should have been sitting, remained exactly the same, with its worn mustard covers that must have borne witness to a hundred similar heartbreaks. Indeed, the whole room was just as it had been five minutes before.

Yet Maggie's whole world had changed.

Several minutes passed without either of them saying a word. It seemed like an aeon. Maggie could hear the clock ticking on Nina's desk. She was acutely conscious of it; of the fact that she had only an hour.

231

'What makes you think Jamie's having an affair?' asked Nina gently.

'Everything,' said Maggie. 'Everything.'

Then she told Nina how Jamie was out late a lot, how he'd been so odd and elusive when in New York the month before, how he'd been withdrawn from her generally. Once she'd started she couldn't stop. It wasn't that it was easy to say – it wasn't – and she was trembling with emotion throughout, but she had to, she was *burning* to, get it off her chest. 'And we row all the time now,' she added, finally.

'What do you row about?'

'Oh, everything. Anything. What we eat,' she explained, because it was still at the front of her mind, 'the house – his mess. Nathan – how we each are with him. Where we live. His work, my work. Money. Whether or not to have a second child . . .'

'Ah.' Nina frowned. 'So he doesn't want one?'

Maggie nodded and looked at Nina. 'How did you know that?'

But Nina encouraged Maggie to continue.

Maggie considered. 'I guess he's never been that happy with the idea. In fact, he wasn't that happy the first time either when he found out I was pregnant. It was an accident, you see. But there was no way I could even think about getting rid of it. I just couldn't.'

'Did he want you to?'

'Yes, he did, initially. But it went against every principle I've ever had. I really do think it was my right to choose. So I said I was going to go ahead regardless. And a few months into the pregnancy he came round. I think it was when he saw the scan . . . At last he seemed able to see it was a little person, a little us . . . Whereas I'd felt like that all along, it being my body. After that he was completely different about it. And then, when Nathan was born, I suppose he came round so wholeheartedly to being a father – he's great with Nathan, really great – that I'm sure he'd do so again.'

'Maybe he's not so sure,' Nina observed.

Maggie was shocked: she'd not thought of this. 'Maybe . . .

Hmmm . . . You might be right . . . There is a side of him that's a bit reluctant to grow up . . .'

'Maybe he doesn't feel ready to.'

'Well, I *do*!' said Maggie vehemently. 'I'm nearly forty! And I want another child!' At this point, strangely, she began to cry. It was all too much.

Tentatively Nina ventured. 'And now you think there's reason to believe he's having an affair?'

'Yes,' Maggie whispered. 'I do.'

'Have you asked him?'

'No.'

Again there was a long pause. Nina passed over a box of tissues that lay ready on her desk. 'But you're sure?'

'Mm.' Maggie drew her breath. 'I'm not *sure*. But I'm not totally stupid. And he's been very preoccupied.' She stopped crying.

Nina looked at the clock. It was obviously nearly time to finish.

'I'm going to ask him,' Maggie decided. 'Outright.' She stopped, then said, 'Yes. I'm going to ask him tonight.'

Back in the car, Maggie pressed the Lloyd Cole track again. God, that haunting song she loved, about a man who ceaselessly chased women – his thoughtlessness, his lack of contentment, his cruelty. It might have been Jamie he was singing about. She played the track four or five times, hoping to gain insight, consolation, some sense that she was not alone. She even stopped for a few minutes in the car park on Newland's Corner and looked out at the panorama stretching below, listening to the lyrics, again and again, but she gleaned no comfort from them or the breathtaking beauty of the richly coloured autumnal landscape. She wept, soundlessly at first. Then she began to howl, deep down from the base of her gut, with the pent-up grief of months of worry, with an anguish that she couldn't recall experiencing before, not even when she was an unrestrained little girl. And she didn't care if the people in the car park could hear her, or what they thought. She didn't care about anything, except Jamie, and herself, and Nathan, and what was going to happen to them all.

## **33** Maggie

**'But I'm playing** squash tonight.'

'Cancel it.' Maggie wouldn't budge. If she chose to be, she could be just as stubborn as Jamie. And she sure as hell chose to be today. She might be utterly miserable and scared of the outcome, but she'd decided to confront him that night, and nothing was going to get in her way. She'd even stood up to phone him to make her more bold.

'I can't.'

'What do you mean, you can't?'

'I promised Pete I'd play.'

'Don't lie to me, Jamie.'

'I'm not lying to you. Why on earth would I lie to you?'

'I don't believe you're playing squash tonight.'

'Of course I am!'

Maggie detected the note in his voice that came to Nathan's when he was caught doing something he shouldn't be. 'If that's all you're doing, playing squash, surely it's easy enough to rearrange. Just phone and tell him you can't play.'

'I can't get hold of him.'

'Why not?'

'I don't have his number.'

The tension made Maggie's throat so tight that she could barely breathe. Jamie's frequent long evenings out had given her cause to doubt him before; now his unwillingness to come home seemed to underline just how right she was to distrust him. If he was having an affair, presumably he was planning on seeing whoever he was messing around with that night.

'Jamie, I'm not a fool. Of *course* you've got his number. You must ring him all the time.'

'I do not.' Jamie paused, as if thinking of a reason. 'He's out at a meeting all day.'

His lies were so blatant that Maggie was insulted. Jealousy was gnawing at her, but she didn't want to confront him over the phone. 'Ring his mobile.'

'That's the number I don't have.'

'Leave a message at his work.'

'He's not going back to the office – he's going straight to the club.'

Maggie found it hard not to scream. 'Just don't turn up, then. Ring Reception at the club and tell them to explain.'

'I can't do that – Pete's my mate.'

'And I'm your wife, Jamie. Your *wife*. Or had you forgotten that?'

'Of course I hadn't.'

'Just say it's a family crisis or something. If he's such a good mate, he'll understand.'

'What? He'll understand that my wife's been to see some stupid counsellor who's put a whole load of ludicrous ideas into her head? That's some sort of crisis, is it?'

There! He was doing it again, turning his shortcomings into her failings. Jealousy or no jealousy, she despised him for it. 'Now you're being an arsehole.'

'C'mon, Maggie.' He tried being more soothing. 'This is a bit melodramatic, isn't it? Why do we have to talk right now? Can't it wait till I get back?'

'No, it can't. You won't be back till midnight – if your recent Thursday nights are anything to go by – and I certainly don't want to sit up waiting for you. Anyway, this isn't the kind of conversation that's going to be over in a couple of minutes. And you're hardly likely to want to stay up talking till three. I mean, heaven forbid, you might miss some of your precious beauty sleep.'

'Can't we talk about it at the weekend? We'll have loads of time then.'

God! How was she going to convince him this was serious? What was he doing that night that was so important? 'Jamie, I mean this. I. Need. To. Talk. Face-to-face. Now. If you don't come home at a reasonable hour, then you might just find me and Nathan not here when you do.'

'Oh. Okay.' At last he seemed to get the message. 'I'll be there.'

'Good,' she said curtly.


So, for the first time in months, Jamie was back by seven.

'Daddy!' Nathan ran downstairs to greet him joyfully. He was half dressed in a white vest and underpants – Maggie had been poised to put him into the bath.

'Wa-hey!' Jamie took off his coat, put down his briefcase and scooped Nathan up in his arms.

Nathan tugged his father's hair as they mounted the stairs. 'You can read me a story!'

At the top, Jamie put him down. 'I'll read to you in the bath,' he offered.

Maggie was standing on the landing. Jamie caught her eye for a split second, then looked away.

'Come with me.' Nathan dragged him into his room to choose a book.

Doubtless Jamie's glad to have an excuse to put me off for another few minutes, Maggie concluded. But it tugged at her heartstrings to see the two of them together. Nathan worshipped him.

Forty minutes later Jamie had finished putting Nathan to bed. As she stood in the kitchen, Maggie fondly imagined Nathan tucked up under his duvet in his room above her, all clean and pink and shiny. She heard Jamie descending the stairs to join her.

God, give me strength, she prayed, leaning against the Aga for support. How shall I start this?

If their recent conversations were anything to go by, she'd been doing an appalling job of steering things the right way.

Sure enough, their opening gambits propelled them in opposite directions, and within a few sentences they were firmly entrenched in separate camps.

'So what's all this about?' he said, entering the room and standing several feet away from her.

'I'll come straight to the point.' Her heart was racing. 'Are you having an affair?'

'*No!*' he exclaimed indignantly, without the slightest hesitation. Then added, 'What makes you suddenly say that?'

Maggie drew breath. 'Where do you want me to start?' she asked. 'It's almost a cliché, the way you've been acting. Out till midnight a couple of times a week, "working late" or "playing squash"'. She imitated his voice with acid sarcasm – a tone she was adopting more and more. 'Forgetting to call me from New York . . . What do you take me for? You've not been at the office or meeting Pete these last few months, have you? You've been shagging someone else.' She spat the word.

Jamie said nothing.

'You have, haven't you?'

'That's crazy.'

'Is it?' In some ways she was desperate for him to say that. There was still a massive part of her that just didn't want to know or, better still, didn't want it to be true.

'Yes. You're imagining things.'

'I am?'

'Of course you are!'

She was far from a hundred per cent convinced, but she was relieved all the same.

Jamie continued, 'You've been spending too much time on your own cooped up here.'

Bloody hell! He was doing it again. It was *her* fault.

'Let me get this straight.' Jamie was sounding more assured now. 'What are you talking about? Just a few late nights and the fact I forgot to ring you one day when I was away on business?'

Although she was tempted to leave the conversation there, Maggie was damned if he was going to get away with putting that spin on what she was trying to say. 'That's just the obvious stuff,' she said, struggling not to lose her temper or – God, please no, that would be even worse – cry. 'What's really made me wonder is how you've been towards me.'

'And how have I been towards you?'

'Cool. No, more than cool, cold. You've barely touched me since earlier this summer.'

'Jesus, Maggie, who's counting? Can I help it if I don't feel like sex at the moment?' Jamie shrugged. 'You know I'm not very up for it when I'm under pressure – I never have been.'

Maggie knew that wasn't true. Until the past few months their sex life had been fine. In fact, it had often been more than fine, it had been great. 'You've never been like this before. Not even when you were really overworked at IPC. We've had the odd patch where one or other of us hasn't felt much like it for a few weeks, I agree, but this . . . It's been months. And anyway,' she felt they were focusing too much on sex, when she could see that the real issue ran much deeper, 'that's just one aspect of things. I wouldn't mind about that if you still talked to me.'

'Jesus, not this one again. I talk to you all the time! I'm talking to you now!'

'You know what I mean. Oh, yeah, we talk in passing. We talk about day-to-day things – who's going shopping, who's going to collect Nathan from football – but we don't talk, properly talk, just me and you, other than to argue.'

'Hmph.' Jamie snorted. Then he seemed to relent, just a little. 'Well, I'll try talking to you more.'

She pounced. 'Will you come to Relate, then? The counsellor says it's not too late for you to join us.'

'No.'

'Why not?'

'I've told you! I just don't want to, okay? Fuck, sometimes I feel so *got* at! I'm simply trying hard to earn money to make a nice home for us, working every hour God sends, and here you are, accusing me of who knows what exactly.'

Maybe he was telling the truth, Maggie thought, and it was merely his job that was causing all this friction, and if that were so, she would be a fool to push things any further. She took a deep breath.

'Look, it's just not my thing, therapy,' he was saying. 'You should know that. In fact, I'm rather surprised it's yours.'

'It wouldn't be, in the normal scheme of things,' Maggie conceded. 'But you just don't get it, do you? I've told you before, I want to sort this out. This isn't just about me or you, is it? It's about Nathan. It can't be good for him to have parents who are at each other's throats the whole time.'

Jamie appeared to have another touch of remorse. 'I'm sorry. I guess I have been pretty wrapped up in my own stuff recently. It's just – you know what it's like – I've never had so much professional responsibility before. But I'll make more of an effort, I promise.'

'You will?'

'I will.'

'Thank you.' She smiled at him. She knew it took a lot for him to say this; perhaps he wasn't quite such an arsehole after all.

He smiled back, somewhat wanly. But it was a smile just the same.

'Shall we have a glass of wine?' she asked, realising they were both still standing there, in the middle of the kitchen.

He let out a long breath. 'I think we deserve it.'

'We certainly do.' Then she, too, relented a little, went over to him and kissed his cheek.

It seemed to work. 'Oh, Maggie,' he sounded sad, 'I don't mean to be horrible to you, honestly. It's just sometimes I get all muddled . . . and I suppose I take it out on you.'

'I know,' she said forgivingly, though she did wonder if she was being too much of a softie for her own good.

'Come here.' He reached out and pulled her to him to hug her.

She snuggled into his crisp white shirt and inhaled his familiar scent. 'Are you hungry?' she asked, remembering they'd not eaten.

'Not really . . .'

And before she knew it, they were kissing – properly. A thought flashed through her mind that maybe he'd been doing this with someone else. Ugh. She shoved it away before it had time to take hold. Gradually, she found herself becoming aroused despite her upset – or maybe it was because of it – because she was thankful that Jamie had denied so vociferously having an affair. And, lo, it seemed that he was turned on too. Then, having supper didn't seem a priority to her either any more. What she really wanted was to be intimate with him again – and it seemed he must want it as well – they grabbed a bottle of wine from the rack and the corkscrew, and went upstairs to bed.

In the middle of the night Maggie woke up in need of a drink of water. She got up quietly, but on her way to the bathroom she was hit by a dreadful, unexpected impulse. She still couldn't shake off her conviction that Jamie had been going to see someone else that evening, even though they'd made love so passionately. The thought of his infidelity sickened her yet again.

She filled a glass of water, gulped it down, refilled it and left it by her side of the bed. Jamie stirred but didn't wake. Then, as if sleepwalking, she glided down the stairs. Mesmerised, she picked up Jamie's briefcase from the hall where he'd put it down when he'd come in. She carried it into the kitchen, turned on the light and laid the briefcase on the oak table.

Click. Click. She opened the catches.

Yes, there it was – his mobile phone. She flipped open the protective cover. She hated herself for doing it, but she had to know. She had a *right* to know. She shuddered. They'd only just been making love, for God's sake. Was it really possible that he'd been going to see someone else that night? That he'd been going to have sex with her?

Maggie looked down at the little piece of technology in the palm of her hand. So tiny, so innocent-looking. What secrets did it hold? She had precisely the same model herself – a Motorola –

which Jamie had insisted on buying for her. She knew exactly how it worked. She pressed the menu, then the phone-book key. A couple more beeps and she had what she wanted displayed on the LCD screen.

*Last Ten Calls.*

Her heart was in her mouth. She wanted to know; she didn't want to know. She pressed OK, then the forward arrow. *Last Calls Received.* No, not that one.

She pressed the backwards arrow. *Last Calls Made.* That was the one.

She pressed OK again. *0207,* she read. Inner London. Not Jamie's mate, Pete, then. She knew he lived in Wimbledon. She read on, *924,* and tried to remember what part of London the code represented. Someone else she knew had the same one. Ah – Jean. Jean lived in Battersea. But it wasn't her number. As far as she could remember, they didn't know anyone else who lived there. She was petrified now. But having come this far, she couldn't stop. She looked up at the clock. It was five past four, but she didn't care. She pressed the OK key. Within seconds the phone was ringing at the other end.

Three rings, and an answerphone clicked on. Whoever it belonged to was obviously asleep, or hadn't had time to wake up and get to the phone.

'Hi, this is Chloë,' said a voice Maggie recognised. The sound made her retch. 'I'm afraid neither Rob nor I can get to the phone right now –' Rob? Who was Rob? Was Chloë married too? No, Maggie was convinced she hadn't seemed the married kind. '– so if you'd like to leave your name and number after the tone, we will get back to you as soon as we can.'

Maggie ran over to the sink and retched again. She felt hot and cold and sweaty all at once. She puked into the stainless steel bowl, but all that came up was a pathetic remnant of the wine she'd drunk earlier, diluted with water, and it made her feel no better. She thought she might faint. She sat down at the kitchen table, her head spinning.

Chloë . . . Chloë . . . Chloë . . .

It fitted. Chloe's strange behaviour when Maggie had been to see her that day a few weeks ago. Chloë's refusal to give her work. The fact that she was a colleague of Jamie's. Christ, hadn't Jean even said that he'd been in to see her once, months ago? And he'd claimed he was introducing himself to all the features editors at UK Magazines. *I bet he was*, Maggie thought. How long had this been going on? Had Chloë been with him at the conference in New York? Maggie closed her eyes, as if to shut out the world, the truth. But an image of Chloë flashed into her mind. The obvious sex appeal. The hour-glass figure. Maggie had always suspected this was more Jamie's type. And she must be ten years or so younger than Maggie. How hackneyed. How *obvious*.

She shuddered. Then remembered. That was who Chloë reminded her of. And if she had any remaining doubts, this made her absolutely sure.

Beth.

Chloë was the spit of Beth, who Jamie had been seeing before her, with whom he'd been so in love. Maggie had always hated her. She'd seen a picture of Beth once. She'd insisted Jamie show her one in the hope it would make her feel better, but it had only made her more jealous, because she couldn't see the slightest physical resemblance between them.

The phone still lay on the kitchen table, almost staring back at her. The key to his secrets. A twenty-first-century Pandora's box . . . Maggie turned it off. It had told her what she needed to know.

Jamie . . . Jamie . . . And they'd been making love only a few hours before . . . She was still so shocked that she didn't know what she felt. She was numb.

Eventually, it must have been an hour later, she got up and made her way back upstairs. Then, strangely – because she was at a loss as to what else to do – she got back into bed. The marital bed. Again Jamie stirred but didn't wake.

She edged herself as far away from him as she could, and curled herself into a tight, protective ball with her back to him. She lay like that for the rest of the night, unable to sleep, unable to move, unable to do anything.

## 34 Maggie

**When Jamie got** up and went to work, Maggie pretended to be still asleep. Then, in slow motion, she got up, got Nathan dressed, and took him to school. When she returned home, she reached up into the top of the wardrobe, pulled down two suitcases and began to fill them with clothes. She didn't stop until she'd packed them both.

Later, around mid-morning break time, she rang Fran at work. Luckily her sister was in the staff room and answered the phone.

'I'll keep it brief,' she said, knowing that Fran would be busy, 'but I need to get away. Something's happened with Jamie, and I was wondering if Nathan and I could come and stay.'

Fran detected the urgency in her voice. 'Of course,' she said at once. 'What's up?'

'I'll explain when we get to you.' Then, considerate for Fran and not wishing to impose, Maggie added, 'I just need to get out of here for a bit – have a think. We won't stay long, only a couple of days, while I decide what to do.'

'Sounds serious.'

Maggie didn't want to make a drama out of things, though if this wasn't serious she didn't know what was. 'It is,' she choked, her voice breaking.

'Do you need us to come and pick you up?' offered Fran.

'No, I'm fine. We'll drive over straight after school, if it's all right with you.'

'What time will you be here?'

'Probably about five.'

'Can't you tell me what's wrong?' Fran sounded terribly worried.

'I'd rather explain in person,' replied Maggie.

'Okay. We'll see you later, then.'

'Okay . . . And, Fran . . . ?'

'Yes?'

'Thanks.' Maggie let out a long breath. 'I really appreciate this.'

'No worries,' said Fran.

Naturally Maggie didn't explain to Nathan why they were going to Fran's, but they went so often he didn't seem to think there was anything odd about it. When they arrived, Fran swept Nathan and Dan off upstairs to play, and sat Maggie down at the antique pine kitchen table with a cup of Earl Grey.

'What's happened?' she asked, pulling up a chair close to her sister.

Maggie felt safer in these surroundings, and there seemed little point in beating about the bush. 'Jamie's having an affair,' she said.

'I wondered whether that was what it was.'

Maggie shivered. Had Fran known about this before? Did anyone else know? She felt so stupid. 'Did you?'

'Yeah. I couldn't think what else would make you pack your bags in such a hurry.'

Maggie was comforted at this explanation. 'So you didn't know, then?'

'No!' Fran exclaimed. 'How should I?'

'Oh, I don't know,' said Maggie, not wanting to say, *Because you always know everything.*

'So who is she? Has he told you?'

Maggie flinched. 'A girl he works with.' She certainly wasn't going to call Chloë a *woman*. To Maggie that implied someone mature, someone sisterly, someone with integrity.

'*Quelle surprise*.' Fran was bitter on Maggie's behalf.

'Why do you say that?

'Oh, because it's so *easy*. Men are so bloody lazy when it comes to affairs. They like it all laid on a plate for them. Somebody on their doorstep.'

Maggie wondered whether Fran's affair could be seen any differently, given she'd found her postman literally in the same street but she didn't say so. It was hardly the moment – she needed Fran's support.

Maggie continued. 'Chloë Appleton, she's called.'

'I suppose she's younger than you, too.'

'Yes,' said Maggie. The obviousness of the whole situation made it even worse. More tacky somehow. Sordid. 'I suppose she's sort of up-front looking. Blatant. Displays her assets to the world. Dead trendy. You know the type. Magazines are full of them.' Envy racked her. She was far less inclined to view Chloë in a positive light now.

Fran was perplexed. 'Did Jamie tell you all this? Doesn't sound as if he likes her that much, if that's how he describes her!'

'No, of course not. I bet he thinks she's bloody gorgeous. She's just his type.'

Then Fran clicked. 'You don't *know* her, do you?' She was incredulous.

'I have met her, yes.'

'God, how *awful*! When?'

'I went in to see her, to try and get work.'

'Jesus! Did you know who she was then?'

'Of course not.'

'Did Jamie know you were going in to see her?'

The memory stung. The fact that he hadn't stopped her made Maggie abhor him. 'Yes. I remember him saying he didn't think it was a good idea –'

'I'm sure he fucking didn't!'

'– but I suppose, to be fair, I was pretty determined . . .' Maggie frowned. When she looked back on the whole episode, Jamie's behaviour had been despicable.

'So, how long's it been going on, then?'

Maggie noted that Fran didn't question whether it was true. Maybe Jamie was a more likely candidate for infidelity than she'd realised. 'I don't know exactly, though my guess is about four or five months.' Then she explained what had happened the day before, how she'd been to see the counsellor, how she'd confronted Jamie when he'd got home, how he'd denied everything and she'd believed him. She told Fran that they'd made love – hard though she found it to talk about such personal matters and even though she knew it would make Fran judge Jamie harshly. Finally, she recounted how she'd got up in the middle of the night, still full of suspicion, and how Jamie's mobile had ultimately condemned him.

Despite her husband's immoral actions, Maggie was worried Fran would think her own conduct had been far from exemplary, but when she'd finished, Fran said, 'Well, I have to hand it to you. It's damn clever of you to figure it out like that.'

Through all her anguish, Maggie was mollified. So far, it seemed that her sister was behind her all the way. This gave her the courage to ask, 'Fran, you don't think this is my fault, do you?'

'No!' Fran was most indignant. 'Why would you think that?'

'I'm not sure.' It pained her to say this. 'I just thought that it was never one person on their own who was to blame for this sort of thing . . . I wondered whether I'd been boring him or something. Not given him enough attention, you know.' Her feelings seemed to come in waves. One minute she was strong, resolved, fired up by anger; the next unsure, insecure, full of self-blame.

'Well, that's bollocks for starters.' Fran topped up both their cups of tea. 'If you ask me, *he* hasn't been paying *you* enough attention, not the other way round.'

'That's what Jean says. But I don't really understand why, then . . .' Maggie trailed off, and she blinked away tears.

'Hey,' said Fran, grabbing her hand, 'it'll be okay . . .'

'I don't think it will.'

'Of course it will! I told you about me and Geoff, didn't I? We went to hell and back, really.'

'You did?' Maggie was surprised. Fran hadn't given her this impression when she'd been telling her about her affair. But Fran was a proud woman, just as Maggie was, and she liked it to appear that she had everything in life sussed.

'Yeah; it was awful . . . awful . . . for a while. Both of us were miserable as sin.' For a moment Maggie thought she was going to get the real version of events. 'But you know – I explained before – it all came out okay in the end. Look at us now – things have never been better. I'd even go so far as to say that in the long run it was no bad thing.'

'Mm.'

Fran stopped, seemingly aware that she must sound rather sanctimonious and that Maggie was crying, and asked, more gently, 'Does Jamie know you've found out?'

'No. No. I couldn't face it right away – I just had to get out. I couldn't get hold of him at work – I was rather glad not to have to speak to him – so I left a message on his voicemail, saying we were coming here.'

'You are going to tell him, though, aren't you?'

'Yes.' By now Maggie was sobbing uncontrollably. 'Oh – Fran!'

'I know, I know . . .' Fran muttered, standing up and putting her arms round Maggie's shoulders. Maggie hugged her back, hard, gleaning comfort from the warmth of her sister's fleece. She couldn't remember the last time they'd done this, and it made her feel better.

When Maggie had almost stopped crying, Fran burst forth, 'Just wait till I get hold of him! I'd like to chop his prick off!'

Although she was stunned by her sister's vehemence, Maggie laughed through her tears. 'What do you think I should do?'

For once Fran resisted the opportunity to tell someone what was best for them. 'I think you should take your time. There's no hurry. Wait till you've worked out what you want to say. You're welcome to stay here as long as you like.'

'I can?'

'You can.'

'But you think I should confront him?'

'Yes, I do. As long as he thinks you don't know, you're stuck in this God-forsaken status quo.'

Maggie could see what she meant. 'Okay. Perhaps we'll go back and I'll do it on Sunday. I don't think we should stay beyond that, or Nathan'll think there's something going on.'

'It's up to you,' said Fran.

'I think that's what I'd prefer. Hell, though, Fran, how could he do this? Not just to me, but to Nathan. It's not just that he's been seeing someone else, it's all the lies. He completely denied it, even when I asked him outright! And then he had the nerve to make love!'

'Don't ask me,' said Fran. Then, she said, 'Are you going to leave him, then?'

Raw with the memory of the night before, Maggie felt so hurt and betrayed that her immediate reaction was to grip the edge of the table ferociously and say, 'I tell you, if it was just up to me, I'd leave now.' Then she recalled Nathan's excitement when Jamie had got home. 'But I can't just walk out. We've got a child.'

'That's exactly how I felt when things got really bad between me and Geoff.'

'Aside from what he's done to me, I'm just not sure I could take Nathan from his dad. Not without trying to get to the bottom of this thing first.'

'But you'd insist he finish it? Stop seeing this Chloë?'

'Of course I would!' Maggie couldn't conceive of any other possibility.

Fran nodded. 'Then I suppose it all comes down to one thing,' she said philosophically.

'What's that?'

'Do you still love him?'

Maggie put her head in her hands. Jamie was a liar, a cheat, a selfish pig. He'd been leading her a miserable dance for months. Heaven only knew the precise ins and outs of it all. She recoiled at the thought of him and Chloë together. Making love. Shagging. Screwing. But he was the father of her child. Her husband. And part of her believed – was desperate to believe – that deep down he must still be the man she had married, bright, charming, sociable, successful . . . Muddled, by his own admission, very muddled. Having some sort of mid-life crisis. But he was still her Jamie, not a total bastard, surely. The man she'd sworn to love till death parted them. The man she'd believed was the love of her life.

'I suppose so,' she said at last.

# 35 Chloë

Chloë was so hacked off with James for standing her up and humiliating her in front of Rob that the next day she threw herself into work with a vengeance. After two cups of coffee and no breakfast, she was racing through the day's tasks like there was no tomorrow. By eleven o'clock she'd chased up all the journalists she'd commissioned to find out how they were getting on, seen two photographers' portfolios, had an argument with the art director and written the introductory paragraph to 'A Buyer's Guide to Vibrators'. She was in the midst of drawing up a flat-plan of the magazine when her PC plipped to tell her she'd received an e-mail. She looked up. It was from James. There was no subject – presumably he feared that someone might be peering over her shoulder.

Typical, she thought. Safeguarding his privacy as always.

Still fuming, she carried on with what she was doing for a few more minutes. Not that he'd know, of course, but she was damned if she was going to do him the courtesy of reading it at once. Eventually curiosity got the better of her. She fumbled for the mouse, located it under a pile of transparencies, and clicked to open the message.

What can I say? I am so, so, so sorry. I feel absolutely terrible. Please, please forgive me.

She ignored it. An hour later she got another.

:- ( Are you still speaking to me?

She hit *Reply*.

:- { No!

Then, ten minutes after that, she got a third:

Please don't be cross. I can explain. I could come over tonight instead and make it up to you. I can even stay over, if you'll have me . . .

James xx

If he was wanting to see her so soon after what Chloë had assumed was a heart-to-heart with his wife, maybe they hadn't patched things up between them, after all. As she'd drifted off to sleep the night before, Chloë had had nasty visions of the two of them immersed in conversation. She'd seen James coming round to whatever Maggie was saying, and agreeing that the two of them should make a go of it. Chloë had even pictured them making love – which, until then, she had preferred to think they couldn't be doing any more.

Her sense of damaged pride had been compounded by Rob's disgust with James, but in spite of all this she was desperate to see him. She typed,

Okay then. But it'd better be fucking good!

though she had mixed feelings. But he was offering to spend the night. Perhaps this indicated that he'd told Maggie he needed space or something. Maybe they were having a trial split. Or possibly – Chloë found this idea rather alarming – he'd told Maggie he was in love with someone else. After all, he'd said in his e-mail that Chloë could have him if she still wanted him, even that he could stay the night. This was a new development. Other than when they'd been away together, he'd always had to go home. Could it be that he'd told Maggie he was leaving her? The thought made her shudder. Was that really, really what she wanted?

If our affair becomes public, everyone will hate me! she panicked.

No, she convinced herself. He wouldn't write an e-mail like that if things were coming to a head. His words didn't display the signs of a man who'd had enough. Thanks to her father, she knew only too well what they looked like.

Fuck it, she resolved, still seething. He can explain tonight, just like he says.

In the meantime she made herself another cup of coffee, and got on with her work.

Fired up by fury and caffeine, she spent the rest of the day putting together the flat-plan of the magazine, and then, thrilled by how it was panning out and keen to share it, she presented it to Vanessa late in the afternoon. Naturally Vanessa had plenty of suggestions, and by the time they finished it was gone seven. But in some ways Chloë was pleased.

Tough shit if James has to wait on the doorstep, she thought.

Yet when she arrived home, she was surprised to hear male voices coming from the kitchen. She hadn't expected this. She stopped in the hallway and listened.

'Chloë?' called James.

'Is that you?' Rob shouted.

Bollocks. Rob had got back before her and let James in. The thought of the two of them meeting without her there to supervise made her nervous. She tried her best to breeze casually into the room.

James and Rob were sitting at the table, an opened bottle of wine in front of them.

'Hi.' She was a little embarrassed. 'How long have you been here?' she asked James. Judging from the nearly finished bottle, it was quite a while.

'Ooh, I don't know – at least an hour. I thought I'd better not be late. But it didn't matter – Rob was here.'

An hour! Lord knows what Rob had said in that time. When called upon to defend his friends, he was rarely backward in coming forward. She wouldn't have put it past him to give James a real piece of his mind after the charade of the night before. She glanced at Rob, hoping to detect a sign of what he'd said. But his face gave nothing away. It would have to wait until she got him alone.

'Look what James has brought you,' he said, nodding in the direction of the sink.

There, standing on the draining-board in their own globe of water, was the biggest bunch of flowers she'd ever seen. They were wrapped in cellophane and hand-tied with a huge white bow. Stargazer lilies. There must have been a dozen. The head of each flower was as big as an open hand, the stamens a rich, golden yellow, each petal tinged with pink. Chloë leant down into the midst of them and inhaled. They smelt pungent, heavenly, out of this world.

Her heart skipped. How romantic! It was *ages* since a boyfriend had given her flowers. It seemed that James really did want to make it up to her, that he really cared.

'I'm sorry about last night,' he said, coming over and slipping his hands round Chloë's waist. That oh-so-irresistible whoosh of desire hit her once more. 'Am I forgiven?' he whispered, wiping off the pollen she'd got on her nose.

'Hmph.' Chloë pouted, but his physical presence made it difficult to be cross.

Then he added, turning to Rob, 'And I'm sorry if it pissed you off too. I gather you cooked something specially,' and Chloë was even more inclined to let him off. James continued, 'So I was thinking, to make it up to you both, I'd like to take you out to dinner.'

Chloë melted. First the e-mail, then the flowers, an apology, now supper. Her legs were buckling. If it hadn't been for her yearning to impress Rob, she would have dragged James off into her room there and then.

'Never one to turn down a free meal, me.' Rob grinned.

'Where would you like to go?' asked James.

'Let's stay local,' said Chloë. 'I'm knackered.' She'd had a busy week, working late on *All Woman* every night except yesterday.

They went to Café Spice, a posh Indian restaurant on Lavender Hill where Chloë often went with her father, who loved curry. It was too expensive for her, but her dad was usually happy to pay. And now, with James offering to take both her and Rob, she wasn't going to forgo a treat.

The restaurant was bright and boldly decorated, with a sophisticated menu of beautifully presented dishes. Its primary colours created a jolly backdrop to their upbeat conversation. James was on fine form, and Chloë was particularly chuffed that he and Rob seemed to get on so well. Given that they came from two very different worlds, Rob a personal trainer, and gay, James in magazine publishing, and straight, things might have been quite sticky. Especially because Chloë knew that, with a few drinks inside him, Rob could be outspoken to the point of tactlessness. But this was far from the case: instead he asked James about his work, particularly keen to know what had attracted James to an environment chiefly populated by women and queens. All in all he kept well away from difficult subject areas, and was utterly charming. Half-way through their main course it dawned on Chloë why.

Shit! He fancies him!

In return, far from being threatened by Rob's sexuality and different philosophy of life, James appeared to find it stimulating. He seemed flattered; indeed, unless Chloë was mistaken, he was flirting back.

This is a turn-up for the book, she laughed to herself.

By the time they'd got home, they'd had an awful lot of wine, topped off with brandy, and Rob was on a roll discussing his various sexual exploits. He relished having an audience, especially one as attentive as James, who was clearly fascinated by the number of notches on Rob's bedpost.

'I must say,' said Rob, slapping James on the back as they stumbled into the hall, 'you're not half so bad as I'd thought you'd be.' Oh, help! Chloë winced. Rob's directness could be mortifying at times. 'I wasn't really too sure what to make of you before. What with your being married with a child.' For a split second James, even though he was drunk, looked aghast but Rob pressed on: 'Although, hey, I guess I understand you a bit better now.' James smiled, if a little half-heartedly. 'So, my two love-birds,' Rob winked camply at Chloë, 'I think this is when I make my exit and leave you to it.'

After such a successful evening, Chloë was on the biggest high she'd enjoyed in weeks, and was horny as hell. She'd been longing to leap on James since he'd arrived, and the anticipation had only made her worse. With no further ado, she shoved him into her bedroom and, for what must have been two or three hours, shagged him senseless.

The next morning James didn't stay late. Much as Chloë would have liked the chance to lie in with him, he was up and gone before ten, leaving her to wonder if he was racing to get home before Maggie after all. In the end she'd not asked what he and Maggie were up to – she and James had been with Rob till gone midnight the night before and by the time they'd gone to bed James's problems were the last thing she'd wanted to talk about.

But nothing could mar the pleasure of thinking about the evening they'd shared, and although she lay in bed trying to get back to sleep after James had left, in the end she decided she was too excited for that. She was desperate to know what Rob had thought of him, and when she heard the tell-tale sounds of Virgin Radio coming from his room, she couldn't resist bouncing out of bed, pulling on her dressing-gown and rushing to tap on his door.

'Tea?'

Rob looked at her out of one eye. 'You must learn to be quieter,' he said sternly. 'I can hear everything through that bloody wall. Ooooh . . . Aaah . . .'

'Oh dear. Sorry.' Still, it was a bit too late to do anything about it now.

She made tea, carried it carefully into Rob's room and sat on the end of his bed. By now Rob was sitting up, looking decidedly morning-afterish, his peroxide hair standing in unkempt Tin-Tin tufts.

'So?' she asked impatiently. 'What did you think?'

'Well, I'd shag him,' said Rob frankly.

She knew it! 'You thought he was sexy, then?'

Rob was very positive. 'I'll say.'

'What about the flowers and everything? The fact he took us both to dinner?'

'I know.' Rob nodded. 'Very generous. He seems like a nice guy.'

Basking in his approval, Chloë felt confident to push for more. 'And what about us? Do you think we make a good couple?'

But here Rob paused. 'Mm.' He looked perplexed, as if wondering what to say. Suddenly Chloë feared that maybe he wasn't going to be so positive. 'I'm not so sure.'

That hurt. 'Why not?' Chloe was really disappointed.

'It's not that I don't think you're well suited. I think you're great together – I've never seen you so happy with anyone – and he's obviously dead keen on you. It's just,' now he sighed, 'to be perfectly straight with you, I don't think he's ever going to leave his wife.'

'You don't?' Surely he couldn't be right about this.

Rob rubbed his forehead. It was clearly hard for him to say so, but he felt obligated to: 'No, I don't. I had a rather revealing conversation with him last night.'

'When?'

'Before you got home.'

After the intense up of the night before, Chloë could feel herself rushing headlong down. 'What did he say?'

'It's not so much what he said as what he didn't say. I think he was disconcerted to have found me here without you, and he seemed to feel he had to explain himself a little. Especially since he knew I'd cooked for him and everything. Anyway, I suppose I led him into it, without realising, but I was pretty cross with him at first. I said something a bit bitchy about my cooking not being up to his wife's standard.' Chloë could hear it all too easily. Rob was a master of the snide one-liner. 'Then he said something about her cooking being amazing, and I said something about how it must make it impossible for him to leave such great home-cooking behind.'

Oh, fuck. 'And what did he say to that?'

'He didn't really say anything.' Rob ruffled his hair, causing it to stand up even more bizarrely. 'That's what I mean. He just grunted, and said that was probably true. Which, I have to admit, doesn't really seem like the kind of thing he'd say if he was planning on divorcing her tomorrow.'

By now the happiness had been drained from Chloë's day.

'Then he tried to justify what was going on with you. He knew that I know about the two of you, and that I must wonder what he's playing at.'

'So what did he say?' Chloë wasn't sure she wanted to hear, but she had to ask.

'He said he felt irresistibly drawn to you. He asked me if I knew what that was like, and of course I said I did but that I'd never been seriously involved with a married man. I said I'd had my casual flings, but nothing major.'

'I see.'

'Then he said he felt torn between the two of you, that he'd never done anything like this before, and that he didn't really know how to handle it. Or . . .' Rob appeared extremely hesitant now, as if he couldn't bear to hurt Chloë so, but he also believed it was for her own good '. . . how to finish things with you.'

'Did he say that?' Chloë felt as if she'd been smacked in the jaw. She'd been imagining that James was on the verge of committing to her, but he was actually trying to work out how to end it! The pain was all the more intense because it came hard on the heels of such hope.

'Not that I think he *is* going to finish it with you,' Rob added. 'He said he just couldn't stop seeing you, and that it was even harder because you work together.'

Chloë felt tears welling. 'So you don't think we'll end up together, then?'

Rob tried to be kind. 'I might be wrong.'

'Do you think *I* should end it?'

'It's up to you, honey. You've always known what I think. This whole thing's got tragedy written all over it.'

Chloë was silent, and bit her lip. 'I suppose so,' she said at last.

# 36 Maggie

**With a scrunch** of gravel, Maggie pulled the car into the drive and turned off the ignition. Nathan was asleep in the seat next to her; it was past his bedtime, but she'd wanted to be able to tuck him up the moment they got in so that she could talk to Jamie. She got out of the car, and lifted Nathan into her arms, all floppy and sleepy. The electric security light in the porch came on as she approached the house, and clutching Nathan to her left breast, she opened the door with her right hand. She didn't bother to shut it behind her – she had to return to the car for their bags.

Jamie had heard them come in and came to lend them a hand. Unaware of her discovery, he'd been mystified as to why she'd chosen to stay away the entire weekend, but she'd refused to discuss anything, explaining over the phone that she wanted to speak to him face to face. 'Oh, not that again,' he'd moaned. 'I thought we'd sorted that one. Haven't we had enough serious chats?'

'Seemingly not,' she'd said. The gall of him!

'You can get the bags,' she ordered, without saying hello. As he passed her on the stairs, she'd a good mind to kick him or, better still, stick out one of her legs and send him tumbling headlong. Right then just the sight of him made her feel murderous.

Five minutes later everything was safely inside. Sitting on the bed, watching her unpack, Jamie was defensive. 'So now what is it?'

'It's not what,' her words stabbed the air, 'it's *who*.'

Jamie blanched. 'God, Maggie, you're sounding like your needle's stuck. Can't you leave it alone?'

'Seems like you can't.'

'I don't know what you're talking about.'

She threw her clothes viciously into the laundry bin. His denials were infuriating, and she had a good mind not to unpack at all but to turn round and drive straight back to Fran's. But he was in the wrong and she was damned if she was going to leave her own house. 'Try this, then. Here's a clue. Her name's Chloë.'

'I don't know a Chloë,' he said, way too fast.

'Crap! Crap! Crap!' She hurled her books on to the bedside table. 'You are one helluva liar, Jamie. Have you forgotten that I *know* you know a Chloë? I even know her myself, for God's sake! Though not as intimately as you seem to, that's for sure.'

'So where's this suddenly come from?' The colour was draining from his face. 'Jean said something to you, didn't she?'

Maggie was horrified. Did Jean know? Was this common knowledge at UK Magazines? Was she the last to find out? But surely Jean would have told her, if she knew. 'Does she know something I don't?'

'You tell me.'

'No, actually, Jean didn't tell me. You gave yourself away with no help from anyone. I found Chloë's number on your mobile while you were asleep. You called her the night I made you come back here last week – Thursday.'

'You sneaky bitch!' Now he got to his feet, fired up.

'Not half as sneaky as you.'

'But that doesn't prove anything!'

Maggie stopped unpacking, and turned to face him. 'Do you

want me to walk out of that door right now? Because you're sure going a great way about it. I know Fran world be more than willing to have me.'

'But I had to call Chloë about work! You know she's the editor on a really important project of mine!' He sounded desperate.

'Oh, yeah,' said Maggie. 'Very important project, I'm sure. You just had to call her at home, didn't you? In case you've failed to notice, Jamie, I am not a complete dunce. You were going to see her that night, weren't you, not to play squash at all? Then when I insisted that you come home, I threw all your plans so you had to phone her and cancel. In fact,' now she was really getting going, 'I bet you even saw her on Friday night, didn't you, just to make up for it? That's why you weren't here then when I called.'

'You called me here on Friday?' Distractedly he picked up her hairbrush and put it down again.

'Yes.'

'You never left a message.'

'Seemed rather pathetic. Wife leaving message while husband's out shagging mistress. Couldn't face that role, myself.'

Jamie said nothing and stood rucking and unrucking the rug on the floor by the dressing-table. His actions were clearly full of displaced energy, and he seemed to be battling with his conscience, trying to work out whether it was too late for him to get away with anything other than being honest.

After a while, with obvious reluctance, he brought it forth. 'You're right.'

Confronted with the truth, Maggie didn't feel sick or faint. She'd been expecting this: she knew Jamie well enough to know that there would come a point when he would no longer lie. Instead, she felt a ghastly sense of relief. At least she hadn't imagined it, at least her judgement was sound, at least she wasn't going mad. But there was one more thing she had to find out. 'Are you in love with her?'

Jamie looked at his shoes. 'No.'

'Look at me when you answer!' she snapped. 'I need you to look me in the eyes and tell me that. Because if you don't love her, then I'd like to know why on earth you would want to risk

261

jeopardising everything you've got. And if you do—' Here she stopped. What if he did? What then? Aside from the searing jealousy, it might mean that he didn't love her, Maggie, any more, that he'd want to leave her, Nathan, their home.

He looked up, with those horrible, beautiful hazel eyes that had cast such spells on her for so many years. To her surprise, they were full of tears. 'I suppose I do,' he said at last.

Maggie sat down on the bed, afraid her legs wouldn't hold her upright. This was it, then. The end. The end of her whole world.

'But I still love you,' he added, sitting down next to her, unsure as to how near was appropriate. 'I love you, too.' He looked as if he might take her hand, but thought better of it.

She didn't know whether to see this as a glimmer of hope, or as hollow words designed to soften the impact of what he'd just admitted. A consolation prize. There was only one important question left. 'Do you want to split up?'

'*No!*' He was vehement. '*No!* I couldn't bear it! I love you! I love Nathan! I didn't mean it. It doesn't mean half as much to me as you do. I couldn't bear to lose you. Please!'

'What do you mean you didn't mean it? Sounds like you bloody meant it to me . . . How long has it been going on, then? How often have you been seeing her? Is she a good fuck? A better fuck than me?'

'*No!* I told you! It's all been a terrible mistake. Once I'd started I just couldn't seem to stop.'

'Was she with you in New York?'

'Yes.'

'Did you see her on Friday?'

'Yes.'

'Did you fuck her?'

'Maggie, please.'

'Did you?'

'Yes.'

'The night after you made love to me.'

Silence. She was acutely conscious that they were sitting, with only a few inches between them, on the marital bed. Where they'd been so intimate. Now they seemed a mile apart.

She continued, 'Can you imagine how that makes me feel?'

There was a long pause, then Jamie cried, 'I don't know what got into me, Maggie, honestly. I've never done anything like this before. It's just something that happened, then, before I knew it, I was in too deep – I couldn't seem to stop, and she . . . she . . .'

'She what?'

Jamie seemed at a loss for words. 'She was so . . . so . . . up for it.'

'Up for it!' sneered Maggie. 'I bet she fucking was. An older man. Her boss. Someone else's husband. Every magazine editor ought to do it at least once. Great copy, after all.'

'It's not her fault,' Jamie defended her.

'Do me one favour, Jamie. Allow me to hate her. You might be in love with her, but excuse me if I'm not. She's done something I would never have done.'

'No, I know,' Jamie acknowledged.

'But see where it's got me.'

Now he was subdued. 'I really am sorry,' he whispered, his face contorted. He looked as if he hated himself.

'It's not just about being sorry,' Maggie said. 'It's about trust. I trusted you, Jamie, and you broke that trust. Smeared my trust over the whole of bloody New York. Jesus – you even allowed me to meet the girl and ask her for work! What a prat I feel about that now. No wonder she was so odd.'

'I didn't mean to hurt you, you know.' His voice was very quiet now; she could hardly hear him.

'But you have, and I don't know if I'll ever get over it. What's more, in the process you've turned me into something I hate – a paranoid, whining nag of a wife.'

'You're not, Maggie. None of this is your fault.'

'Well, it's *someone*'s. And if I'm not to blame, and neither is Chloë, then it's got to be you.'

'I know,' he admitted. 'I've fucked up.'

'You sure have.'

'What can I do? How can I make this better? Is there anything I can do to make you forgive me?'

'One thing is certain. We can't carry on like this.' Maggie was amazed at how together she was sounding, how matter-of-fact. Despite this dreadful knowledge, she was empowered by understanding the full picture. The not knowing, the suspicion, the anxiety had been worse.

'What do you want me to do?'

He was still sitting there, awkward, unsure. After everything, he was asking her to decide. To Maggie the answer was obvious. She'd had the entire weekend to think about it, and for all Jamie's muddle, the options were black and white.

'You've got to choose,' she said, getting to her feet once more to add impact to her words. 'It's her or me. You've got to finish it with Chloë and make a go of this marriage, and come to Relate, or that's it between us. It's simple.'

'And what about Nathan?'

'What about him?'

'You've said yourself this isn't just about me and you, it's about him.'

'You should have thought of that on Friday night when you were sticking your dick in someone else. It's a bit late to come over all moral on me now.'

'He needs a father.'

'That's precisely why I'm willing to give it one more go. If it weren't for him, I don't know what I'd do. But he needs a proper father, not a philanderer. He needs someone he can respect, learn from. And, come to that, he needs a mother who's not a doormat, someone he can be proud of, someone with principles. If we stay together, it's got to be on my terms, and we've got to do it properly. I'm certainly not staying around here like some other pitiful suburban housewives I could mention locally. Letting their husbands carry on with all sorts behind their backs, just because they've got huge houses in the country that – heaven forbid – they might have to forgo if what was really going on came out in the open.

'But this way, if he ever does find out – which I hope he doesn't have to – at least my son will see that I didn't just sit back and ignore everything. No,' she affirmed, 'I've had time to think about this, and I'm absolutely clear. I can't compromise any further. I feel like I've been letting things slip for years, but it's more than my sense of self is worth to carry on doing it any longer. If I catch you fucking around with Chloë – or anyone else come to that – one more time, I won't give you another chance. This is it, Jamie. No more Chloë. Or this marriage is over, and you'll be the one that has to go.'

## 37 Chloë

I was used as a punch bag for my parents' rows; their training equipment, the place they'd come to when they needed to get rid of some aggression. One minute I'd have my mum in tears, telling me what a worm my dad was; the next I'd have my dad telling me how my mum didn't understand him. I was ten at the time. And I don't agree that children don't understand what's going on. They understand more than people think. I knew these demands were making me grow up emotionally in a way most other kids at school didn't have to. But not in a good way – I felt ashamed of the situation at home, embarrassed by my parents' constant bickering. There's a lot more acceptance of divorce these days, but when I was young there was still a stigma attached. And that hurt, I suppose. In fact, I think that's made me very wary of commitment myself – because I associate it with pain. So here I am at forty, still acting the carefree bachelor, unwilling to settle down.

**Chloë was sitting** at her desk. It was Thursday morning, and she'd just received Craig Spencer's article, 'Broken homes, broken children?'. In some ways it might have been her talking here. So soon after her discussion with Rob, it was like pouring neat alcohol on an open wound. It forced Chloë not only to think about James but also about his son, Nathan, once more. Was he feeling the effects of all this? Was he aware of more than James and Maggie realised? He was only six, wasn't he? Poor little boy.

James didn't talk much to Chloë about his son – he obviously appreciated that she found it hard to hear – but now her conscience really disturbed her. Their affair was becoming appallingly messy and she was beginning to wonder if the good times were worth it. She knew she should talk to James, but the magazine was making increasing demands on her time, and she had been glad of that. After her experience with her parents, she tended to avoid heavy scenes like the plague.

For his part, James had responded to the one e-mail she'd sent him with the explanation that he was also too frantic to communicate at length but that he'd meet her on Thursday. Now it was Thursday, and if she was honest with herself, she knew she should try to cool things between them, if not finish it altogether. Yet knowing what she should do and what she would do were often two different things.

'So how's it shaping up?' Vanessa had come up behind her.

'It needs cutting,' Chloë didn't want to reveal the article's true impact on her, 'but it's very good. Craig's delivered a great piece.'

'I gather the research groups are all set up for next week. So you're positive we'll have a complete dummy magazine to show them?'

'Oh, yes.' Chloë was in no doubt. 'This is the last of the features to come in. We'll be raring to go.'

'Should be fun, then,' said Vanessa.

Chloë found it hard to imagine Vanessa having fun, but she agreed. She, too, was looking forward to seeing how the public responded to her baby. Secretly she was confident. Her love-life might be a disaster zone, but professionally everything was coming together brilliantly.

\*

In her heart, Chloë knew that if she was committed to the idea of breaking up with James it wasn't a good idea to meet him at her flat. It would have been less risky to meet him on neutral, preferably public, territory. She also knew that she shouldn't have replenished her lipstick, doused herself in Paloma perfume and she certainly shouldn't have put on a clean pair of knickers. But she wasn't convinced that Rob was right: she still wanted to believe that the passion they had shared was a sign of the potential for a more permanent relationship. In short, she wasn't ready to give up the notion that she and James were meant to be together.

Nor, it seemed, was James.

Rob would have been proud of the way Chloë kicked off the conversation when James arrived. She sat him down in the kitchen with a cup of tea, not wine, and took a chair opposite him, several feet away. She glanced across at him in his familiar Paul Smith suit: his shirt needed ironing and the dark hair she loved looked in need of a cut. He appeared worn out.

'I'm beginning to feel all this is a rather bad thing,' she said.

'Oh?' He looked up at her, his hazel eyes mystified. Then he seemed to realise from her expression that she was poised to say something serious and he frowned.

'Yes.' Chloë nodded. She'd rehearsed this bit, to help her come out with it more easily. 'I don't just mean in terms of your marriage, but also for me.' She bit her lip, then rushed on, 'I'm worried about Nathan. I suppose I'm even a bit worried about Maggie. I'm worried I'm going to get really hurt . . .' But just when she knew she should say, 'So that's it, it's over,' she began to cry.

Suddenly the thought of not being involved with him any more, of not being able to look forward to their evenings together, of not having any romance in her life, of not having anyone to daydream about, to share those special moments with, to laugh at her jokes, to banter with, to chat about to those few of her friends whom she'd taken into her confidence, seemed too much to bear. If she broke up with James, she'd never to go to Aurora with him again, or share dinner with him in any restaurant, anywhere. He'd never come round to her flat; she'd never go to New York with him, never do coke with him; they'd never swig champagne. She'd never get to see his face in such intimate close-up. She'd never make love to him, ever, ever again.

And it wasn't as if she could just cut him out of her life, which was how she had handled gut-wrenching break-ups in the past. Instead she'd have to see him every day, work with him and, as the launch of her magazine drew closer, she knew her professional dealings with him might well be more frequent, rather than less. What a dreadful prospect. At last she could see what Rob had warned her about: that the situation was too complicated, too much for her to handle. No matter what she did now, there was no way she could come out unscathed.

'Hey, Chloë,' said James gently. He leant over and squeezed her knee. 'Please don't cry. I can't bear it when you cry.'

'Sorry,' said Chloë, sniffing, aware that her eyeliner must be making its way down her face. She'd always striven not to weep in front of him, knowing how uncomfortable over-emotional women often made men feel. 'It's just – I can't bear not to see you again, ever—' She choked, her voice breaking as she fought against the tears. She looked up at him. His face was anxious, concerned. He was so lovely, she thought. She liked him so much.

'You will see me,' he said, trying to be consoling. 'You'll see me at work all the time.'

'That's not what I mean. We won't be close, we won't be able to talk, not in the same way.'

'We can still be friends, though, can't we? I'll always care about you – you'll always be really special to me, you know that.' He took her hand across the kitchen table.

This only made Chloë worse. 'But I don't want to be friends!' she gasped, knowing she should remove her hand but not doing so. 'You never were my friend. I never felt about you the way I feel about a friend – it's different, what we've had.'

'No, I know,' James agreed. He seemed *so* unhappy, too.

'I don't make love to my friends.'

'Glad to hear it,' said James, and smiled at her, trying to make her do the same. But she was too upset for this to work, so then, perhaps at a loss as to what else to do, perhaps as a farewell gesture, perhaps to try to heal things, she wasn't sure, James began to stroke her hand, gently at first, in a way that brought back memories of the very first night they'd spent together, of when they'd first seduced each other in The Player, on Broadwick Street. And then, of course, he didn't stop at stroking her hand, but moved up her arm, and she leant into him, and he kissed her, and soon, sure enough, she climbed on to his lap for comfort, intimacy, to be closer to him again in that unique, special way. And then he wanted to make love, and so did she, and she knew Rob wouldn't be back till much later, so she whispered this to him, and he lifted her skirt, and she unzipped his trousers, and he pushed aside those newly put-on knickers, and she pulled down his boxers, and they made out like that, in the kitchen, supposedly just one last time.

## 38 Maggie

**Maggie was rereading** a printout of her article, 'What the people of Britain really eat' when the phone rang. Following in the tradition of the 'Day in the Life' column in the *Sunday Times*, she'd written a full-length feature for the *Independent on Sunday*, covering a day in the diet of a cross-section of people from around the country. Her subjects included an MP, a homeless boy, a model, a doctor and a single mum living on benefit.

Great timing, she thought. She hoped it was someone she felt like talking to: she was ready to take a break, and in the mood for a chat.

'Hi, Mags.'

Although she could scarcely hear him (the reception was terrible – it was clearly a mobile phone), she knew that voice at once. 'Alex!' she exclaimed joyfully. 'I haven't heard from you for ages. It's a dreadful line. Where are you?'

'I'm on the M25,' he said, 'coming up to junction nine.'

'You're really near!'

'I know. I thought I'd call on the off-chance you'd be in. I've just had a meeting at a site in Tunbridge Wells,' Alex was a landscape architect, 'and I was going to go back to the office, but it hardly seems worth it now.'

Maggie looked at the clock. It was four fifteen. By the time he'd driven back into London it would be time to go home again. 'No, no, I'm here. Why don't you stop by for a cup of tea? We've got some cake I made for Nathan's birthday too. I'm sure he won't mind if you have a piece.'

'Oooh, goody.' Maggie could almost hear Alex's mouth watering down the phone. He had always been particularly appreciative of her desserts and cakes. 'I'll be with you in about fifteen minutes.'

Perfect. Just enough time to run upstairs and make herself more presentable. It was November, and a bit nippy, so she'd been sitting at the kitchen table in her oldest jeans and a snug red fleece. These were fine, and the casual look became her, but her rather daft pink slippers with pom-poms (well, she was working from home after all) would have to go. She pulled on a pair of Russell and Bromley boots instead, and put on some makeup. She'd barely finished dabbing her wrists with Chanel No. 5 when the doorbell rang. She charged back downstairs.

'Hi!' she said, not bothering to contain her pleasure.

'Hi.' Alex stepped into the hall. Dressed in a sweatshirt and muddy jeans, with a leaf in his hair, he was as scruffy as ever, she noted fondly. 'You look well,' he said.

'Do I?' She was surprised but flattered. She'd been worried that the strain of the last few months must show.

'Mmm.' He stood back to admire her. 'Slimmer? Fitter?'

'Well, I am a bit fitter,' she acknowledged, embarrassed. 'But I'm surprised you can tell in this old stuff.' She tugged at her fleece.

'You forget how well I know you.'

Maggie blushed, flashing back to their intimacy of nearly two decades ago. All these years later, there was still a little sexual chemistry between them. 'Tea?' she said brightly, too self-conscious to continue in this vein.

Alex followed her into the kitchen.

'Sorry about the mess,' Maggie apologised, waving in the direction of the table. There were papers and books everywhere.

'That's not like you,' Alex observed. Maggie's workspace had been tidy even as a student.

'No, I know. But I was so into this article I've been writing I seemed to forget myself.'

'That's great,!' said Alex, going over to her laptop and hitting a key to take it off screen-saver. 'Do you mind if I have a look?'

'Go ahead.' Maggie stretched up to the top shelf of the dresser for the guest tea-pot. She had a less precious one for everyday use, but Nathan was out with friends so she didn't need to worry that he'd break it.

Alex was silent while he concentrated on the article, and Maggie felt abashed. This was the first time anyone since Chloë had read anything she'd written in her presence. She felt a bitter jolt at the memory, but she was damned if she was going to think about that girl now.

As Alex continued reading, she took the opportunity to watch him, trying to imagine what it would be like if she was seeing him afresh. He was dark-haired, like Jamie, and tall, but there the similarity ended. He had a less angular, cheekier face, with big brown eyes and brows so thick and dark they were almost comic. He was naturally muscular, and in years gone by had been a great rugby player. These days, thanks to his penchant for puddings and cakes, his physique was perhaps a little more teddy-bear than Action Man, especially as he was approaching forty. Nevertheless he retained a boy-next-door charm that mothers – including Maggie's own – loved. When Maggie had been going out with him, she hadn't been particularly maternal and hadn't appreciated him fully. Instead she'd been attracted to more obvious good looks like Jamie's. Now that she was older, she could see what these more mature women had liked in him. Above all, he looked generous, kind.

'Why, this is really interesting', said Alex, relishing Maggie's witty exposé of the MP's excessive drinking habits. 'It seems quite different from what I thought you'd be doing, though. More of a feature, less a bunch of straightforward recipes.'

'I got sick of that. I'm trying to break into something new.'

'Like what?'

Maggie went on to explain further, concluding, 'I suppose I just felt some part of me had died since college. You of all people should remember what a stirrer I was.'

Alex laughed. 'How could I forget? You and me, marching for just about any cause that would have us.'

'I'm not sure that's entirely fair,' Maggie protested, handing him a generous portion of birthday cake.

'So,' Alex looked more serious, 'how does Jamie feel about all this? I wouldn't have thought such revolutionary zeal was quite his scene.'

'No, it's not – at least, not when it's me trying to challenge accepted views. It's fine if it's the people he works with,' here Maggie pictured Chloë again, though she didn't say so, 'but I don't think he really likes it in his wife.'

'I see,' said Alex.

Maggie could tell that he didn't approve of Jamie's lack of support, but she didn't really want to hear anything critical so she changed the subject. 'Have you heard from Georgie?' she asked. 'I've been meaning to give her a call.'

'I haven't, not for a while,' Alex admitted. 'We went out once for dinner as friends, but it was a bit awkward – and it's not like we dated for that long. With hindsight I'm not sure we'll ever be close – though don't get me wrong, I think she's a great woman.'

Although Maggie knew she shouldn't be, she was faintly pleased. A month had passed since she'd found out about Chloë, things with Jamie remained far from dandy, and if she'd had to listen to her ex rave about what great buddies he was with every woman he'd dated, it would have been more than she could stand. She liked to think that their relationship was unusual, special.

Alex leant back in his chair, his healthy weight causing it to creak a little alarmingly. 'How are things with Jamie? Any better than that night we all came for dinner?'

That had been the last time Maggie had seen Alex. My God, she thought, we've really been through the mill since then.

Alex continued, 'What about the baby issue? Has he come round?'

'Um, not exactly.' Maggie spoke softly, wondered whether to tell Alex about Jamie's affair. Somehow she just couldn't face it – it would take too long, it was too recent, too raw. And, anyway, that was all water under the bridge. Jamie had stopped seeing Chloë weeks ago. She took a deep breath. 'I don't want to go into the details, but things haven't been that great recently.'

'Oh, I am sorry,' said Alex, with feeling. She knew he meant this. Sympathy could have been his middle name. 'Believe me, I know what it's like, I've been there.' Maggie was sure this was true: Alex had taken the separation from his wife hard. 'I don't know if you're aware that the one of the reasons we split is that Stella didn't want to have children. Or not mine, at any rate.'

'No!' Maggie had had no idea. Like all their peers, she had observed that Alex and Stella had been together for years without ever talking publicly about offspring, but she'd assumed that the reservations must stem from Alex, not the other way round. How sexist of me! she scolded herself. 'You never said.'

'It didn't seem fair, somehow, to air our dirty linen like that. And I suppose I was a bit embarrassed, too proud.'

Too proud. Maggie knew how that felt. 'Didn't you talk about it before you got married?'

'I know it seems ridiculous now, but no, actually, we didn't. Not at any length. We were years younger then and it didn't seem such a burning issue. I guess, though I knew she wasn't into the idea, I just thought she'd come round.'

'I see.'

'Anyway, Stella's with someone else now,' said Alex philosophically. 'All water under the bridge.'

'Of course.' But Maggie knew there was pain behind his bravado. Funny how his choice of words about Stella even echoed her own thoughts about Jamie.

'May I?' Alex reached for the knife to cut himself another piece of cake.

Maggie nodded, happy to provide food in consolation.

'For you?' he offered her.

But she had been planning on making something special that night for herself and Jamie. 'No thanks, I'm fine.'

Alex spoke with his mouth full then looked up at her, straight into her eyes. 'Though you do know, of course, that Stella was convinced that I'd never fully got over you. When we split up, she even suggested that maybe I'd be happier if I found somebody more like you.'

Maggie was astounded. Although she had occasionally wondered if Alex still had some feeling for her – Jamie certainly suspected it and Georgie had stated it directly – she would never have expected him to come out with it so blatantly.

But Alex seemed unaware of the impact of his words, and was hell-bent on making the most of what he clearly thought was a fine example of Maggie's culinary skills. 'This is delicious.' He scraped his plate vigorously with his fork. 'Would a third slice be out of the question?'

'Yes.' Maggie laughed. 'I think Nathan might be a bit miffed.'

'Oh, shit.' Alex wiped his mouth with a napkin. 'Of course! How is the little bugger?' He looked around. 'Where is he?'

'He's playing football with his friends up on the recreation ground – he does it every week now. They've got a five-a-side team, the Shere Tigers.'

'God, so he's old enough to be in a team!'

'Yes, he was seven last week. We had a little party for him.'

'How time flies!' Now he'd touched upon his own desire to have a family, Maggie could see that Alex looked wistful. But she could hardly say so: she was in the midst of trying to repair things with Jamie. And when they had, she still hoped against hope that they might try for another child.

## 39 Maggie

**Although Maggie had** just come out of a productive meeting with the editor of *Marie Claire*, she was perturbed. Jean had been in touch the night before, and when Maggie had mentioned that she was coming into town the next day, Jean had said there was something she wanted to talk about, and was Maggie free for lunch? Maggie knew Jean well enough to recognise concern in her voice and she was worried that her friend was going to face her with knowledge of Jamie's affair. The thing was, now it was over and a few weeks had passed, Maggie had no wish to rake over old ground. She wanted to move on, put it behind her.

As it turned out, she was right on some counts, and wrong on others.

'Maggie,' said Jean, once they were sitting in Cranks with a bowl each of healthy salad, 'I may be completely out of turn—'

'It's okay,' said Maggie, wanting to put Jean out of her misery, 'I know.'

'You do?' She could tell that Jean was amazed.

'Jamie's been seeing that Chloë girl who used to work with you.'

'Gosh.' For once Jean seemed at a loss for words. 'How long have you known?'

'About a month.'

'Really?'

'Yes. We've talked about it. I'm just beginning to come to terms with it all.'

'You are?'

'Yes, I am. It's been hard, but I'm getting there.'

'Oh. Well, if you say so.'

This annoyed Maggie. *Yes, I do say so!* she thought. She hadn't taken Jean into her confidence before because she really hadn't wanted to talk about it. It was over now, and Jamie was coming with her to Relate, albeit he'd cancelled a couple of times due to work commitments, but he had promised to make an effort just the same.

Jean looked at her closely. 'Frankly, I'm surprised you're so cool about it. I'd never have put you down as so phenomenally tolerant, given a situation like this.'

'I wouldn't go so far as to say that,' explained Maggie, 'but we're sorting things out, honestly.' Perhaps she should never have agreed to meet Jean. It was going to be difficult not to explain everything to her: she was not going to be happy unless she had the full picture.

'So you don't mind that he's sleeping with someone else?'

Maggie's heart missed a beat. The use of the present tense was alarming. 'He's not any more.'

'Oh, shit.' Jean furrowed her brow, as if working out whether to carry on, then obviously decided not to, and was silent.

'What?' Maggie was scared.

Now she was pushed, Jean couldn't keep shtum a moment longer. 'It's just that I saw him in Battersea last week. I was on my way home from work, going up the hill from Clapham Junction. He didn't see me, mind, he was walking ahead of me, but I thought it was strange he'd be around there.'

'Was he with her?'

'No,' said Jean, 'but to be perfectly straight with you, I'd won-dered before if there was something going on between them – they seemed just a bit too chummy in New York. When I saw him walking in the direction of where she lives, I worked out that must be where he was headed. I followed him a bit, just to check.'

'I see,' said Maggie acerbically. Her tone was directed at an absent Jamie, not Jean. 'What night was this?'

'Tuesday.'

Maggie had been at Fran's. Jesus, she thought, the moment my back's turned he's there like a shot. She'd not even got in from Leatherhead that late, and Jamie had been home when she'd returned, so it hadn't occurred to her that he might have gone somewhere else first. She began to tremble. He must have gone straight round to Chloë's, fucked her, and come straight home. What kind of a person was Chloë that she'd put up with being treated like that? At that moment Maggie despised her more than ever, but she *loathed* Jamie.

So his promises that he'd finished it meant nothing. And as for what he'd said at Relate, it was a complete sham. No wonder he'd bloody cancelled last week. Obviously his conscience wouldn't let him live with himself and go. Clearly he didn't want to repair things with Maggie at all. Or maybe he just wanted to have his cake and eat it. Either way, it was foul behaviour. Weak. Selfish. Cruel.

'I'm sorry to be the one to tell you this.' Jean looked worried. 'Believe me, I had to wrestle with myself before I did so.'

Maggie reassured her. 'It's okay. I'm glad you did. I'd have found out sooner or later, anyway.' Then she explained exactly what she had known, and when, so Jean understood what was going on, and quite how big a deal Jamie's continuing to see Chloë was.

'What are you going to do now, then?' asked Jean, unsure as to whether Maggie's curt manner disguised misery, disappointment, anger or all three.

'I'm going to ask him to leave,' she said simply.

'For good?'

'I don't know about that. But certainly for a while, yes. I need some space – and not just for a couple of days. The thing is, it's not only that I don't trust him any more, it's that I don't know if I can love a man who behaves like that.'

'Bully for you!' said Jean passionately. 'I'm proud of you! And you know, my dear, that I'm always here for you, don't you?'

'Thanks,' said Maggie, more subdued now. She felt so utterly betrayed that she needed the loyalty of her friends more desperately than ever.

Jamie came home that night to find his suitcases packed for him. Maggie filled the two biggest ones they had to bursting. Never mind putting his socks in goddamn rows now: being organised was the last thing on her mind. Maggie just wanted to be rid of him, as quickly as possible, with minimum fuss. Only then would she be able to assess the impact of his actions. Only then would she know what, in the long term, she wanted from him.

In went the Calvins. In went the T-shirts he wore under his crisp cotton shirts in winter. In went these shirts too – no folding. In went the belts he always removed with that 'swooshing' sound. In went socks, then shoes. She didn't care that these should be on the bottom lest the other clothes get dirty. It would be a good thing if they did. On top of it all she threw the Paul Smith suit – the navy one she loved. She wondered if he'd worn it when he'd been with Chloë. She sniffed it. And, sure enough, she believed she could detect the traces of a scent that was not her own. She sniffed again, but couldn't place it. I bet it's Poison, she thought.

Once one case was full she moved on to the second. Into this she slung the contents of the bathroom cabinet that belonged to him: shaving foam, razor, aftershave, antiperspirant. On second thoughts, she left that out. It would be good to make him sweat. Next, down to the hall cupboard under the stairs: here was where he kept his precious sports equipment. Not much of it would fit inside the suitcase, but she forced what she could within the straining seams. Finally, she added a handful of his rock-and-roll CDs.

I should never have married a man who once liked Genesis, she thought.

'Mummy, what are you doing?' asked Nathan, catching her in the middle of the living-room floor, case wide open. She'd thought that he was playing in his room, but obviously the rumpus had disturbed him. 'Are we going on holiday?'

Maggie went over to him and crouched down to his level. She took his arms, and looked him in the eyes. 'No, sweetie, we're not. I'm afraid Daddy's going to have to go away for a bit, that's all.'

'Again?' asked Nathan. He'd missed his father when he'd been in New York. How was he going to find this more prolonged, possibly permanent departure?

'Yes, my love, again. But don't worry, this time you'll be able to see him, even when he's gone.'

Nathan frowned. 'How can I see him if he's not here? Where's he going?'

'I'm not sure yet,' said Maggie, fighting tears. She hadn't worked this one through. 'It's just that Mummy needs a bit of time on her own right now, and I think it's better if Daddy's not around.'

'Do you still want me around?' asked Nathan, sounding very small and lost.

'Oh, of course I do!' exclaimed Maggie, folding him into her arms. 'I want you around very much!' She gently pushed back his head a little, so she could see his face again, and tidied his fringe. 'You must understand this, darling. No matter what Mummy and Daddy think of each other, no matter what happens, none of this is your fault, and we both love you very much.'

'What's all this, then?' asked Jamie, standing in the hall examining the two suitcases. Luckily Nathan was in bed, but Maggie put her fingers to her lips, not wanting to disturb him, and gestured to her husband to follow her into the sitting room.

'I want you to leave,' she said directly, not bothering to sit down.

'Leave?' Jamie raised his voice at once. 'Why?'

'Because you're still shagging Chloë, that's why.'

'Jesus! Not that again!' he cried.

'Jean saw you,' explained Maggie.

'Jean!' spat Jamie. 'Where?' But she noted he didn't deny it.

'In Battersea, last Tuesday. You weren't with Chloë, but she knows where Chloë lives. They're virtually neighbours, remember? Or perhaps it hadn't occurred to you – you're so wrapped up in your own pathetic little world.'

'That *woman*!' Jamie was patently very angry with Jean – unjustifiably so. But maybe he was angry at being found out, or with himself.

'Don't you dare take this out on her!' Maggie said. 'You've no one to blame for this but yourself.'

'I tried to cool it, honestly.'

'You tried to cool it, Jamie? Or finish it? I asked you to finish it, and clearly you haven't. I told you there are no half-measures as far as this is concerned.'

'But you can't kick me out! I've nowhere to go!'

'Try Chloë's,' said Maggie drily.

'I wouldn't go there.'

'Why not? You go there all the time. I thought you liked it there.'

'I just can't.' Jamie found it hard to explain. 'It wouldn't seem right.'

'Right? That's rich! Who are you to tell me what's right? I don't think you even know what's right any more. But one thing's for sure, you can't stay here. I'm not the sort of person who can just let this go – not a second time.'

'But what about Nathan?'

'I've told Nathan you're going away for a bit. He understands.'

'I'll go to Pete's,' said Jamie, sitting down heavily, utterly despondent. Eventually he seemed to realise that he hadn't a leg to stand on, that Maggie wasn't going to change her mind. Not tonight, at least.

'Do what you like.' Maggie shrugged. 'You can come back at the weekend and see Nathan, though you'll have to take him out for the day. I don't want you hanging around here.'

Jamie looked shell-shocked, as if he couldn't quite take it in. 'Do you want me to leave now?'

'Yes. Now. You can make a phone call. Ring Pete, or find

yourself a hotel for the night. But that's it, Jamie. No more discussions for the moment. No begging. No pleading. I want you out.'

## **40** Chloë

**Chloë was really** excited. For the first time in two years, she was going to see her brother, Sam. It was mid-December and he was coming home from California to spend Christmas and New Year with their mum and stepdad, and New Year with their dad and stepmum. Chloë had even taken the first day off she'd had in three months in order to pick him up from the airport. She'd emailed:

> We can go back to mine. You can have a nap, get over your jet-lag, and I can take you out for supper! Then you can stay over on the sofa-bed with Potato, and catch the tube to Mum's when I go to work the next day.

She stood waiting at Arrivals, barely able to contain herself, scanning every luggage label to see if it was from LAX. At last his fellow passengers began to trickle through from Customs, out into the maelstrom of waiting families.

After what seemed an age, she saw him, pushing a trolley laden with far too many bags for one person. She was desperate to shout, knew that Sam would think it the height of uncool, so she waited until he'd rounded the corner into the airport proper and ran up to him.

'Sam!'

'Chloë!'

They flung their arms round each other, then stood back, faintly embarrassed. Such open displays of affection weren't normally their style. They were British, after all.

'So how are you?' he said – sounding faintly American, Chloë realised.

'Oh, I'm well – I'm fine! I've got loads to tell you – loads. But it'll keep. How are you?'

She looked him up and down, taking in his familiar yet unfamiliar form. His skin was browner, his hair lighter, he seemed a little leaner, fitter – probably thanks all those beach sports. But he still looked like her Sam – scruffy, with his chestnut curls, his 'sticky-outy' ears, as she'd always cruelly referred to them, and his impish, Puck-like charm. Though perhaps his face did seem a bit older now, she mused. Wiser.

'I'm great!' he responded, with equal enthusiasm. 'I love it there! You should come out and stay with us for a bit, Chloë, you really should.'

'I went to New York,' she retorted.

'Oh, yeah,' he said, remembering. 'I got your postcard. Not that it's anything like California, of course. But did you like it? What did you think?'

'I loved it!' Chloë raved. 'I had the best time ever! I'm dying to go back!'

'I can imagine. It's just your kind of city. In fact,' he reflected, as he pushed the trolley into the Heathrow Express ticket area, 'I can see it would really suit you. Have you thought of living there?'

'I'd love to!' For a moment Chloë forgot James. 'But how could I? I'd need a green card or work permit or something – it's so hard to get in.'

'Tell me about it.'

Chloë knew that Sam was still waiting for his to come through. 'Any joy on that score?'

'Shouldn't be long now,' he said.

By now they were at the platform, and within minutes a train drew in. They struggled aboard with Sam's bags, took two seats opposite each other, and leaned together to hear each other speak.

For some reason she didn't want to tell Sam about James straight away, perhaps because she was ambivalent about the current situation. Instead she dived straight into updating him on the magazine, which was going swimmingly. The research groups had come back with positive feedback, and they were all set to launch it properly in the New Year.

'I've got something to tell you,' he said, when he could get a word in.

'Ooh, what is it?' Chloë could tell by his expression it was something major.

'You know that Couples Weekend I mentioned months ago? Well, I went. Actually it was rather good, made me see things a bit differently. Made me see what's important.'

Fancy that, thought Chloë. I'd never have imagined Sam doing something so *Californian*.

But the revelations weren't over. 'Anyway, I'm getting married,' he said.

'Oh, my God!' cried Chloë. She could scarcely contain herself. All at once she was awash with emotion. Her little brother getting married! 'To Michele, I presume?'

Sam laughed. 'Of course – who else would it be?'

'Just checking,' said Chloë. 'You never know.' She stopped to think. Although on many levels she was delighted – she really liked Michele – she felt more than a touch envious and a whole load of other feelings that she couldn't quite place. Getting married, eh? But she was older than him! It should have been her first. She bit her lip. Although James wasn't living with Maggie at the moment, Chloë hadn't been seeing much more of him as a result. He'd told her he needed space, time to consider, and she didn't want to push things, though it made her miserable as hell not to. And now her baby bro was getting married, was going to be a husband, Michele's other half. Would James ever commit like that to her? A thought popped into her mind. If James offered to commit seriously – or in any way, come to that – would she trust him? He wasn't as trustworthy as Sam, she could see that. She was biased, of course, but everyone who met him agreed: Sam was a real sweetie. Oh, well. She pushed these observations aside. There was time enough to ponder that. Now she owed it to Sam to focus on what he was saying.

'So where are you going to have the wedding?' she asked. 'Here? Australia? California?'

While Sam was making up for lost sleep, Chloë took the opportunity to catch up on some housework. She disliked doing it, but it had to be done some time. She put a load of whites in the washing-machine, then set about doing the dishes. Dirty plates, saucepans and wine-glasses had piled up on the draining-board, and if she didn't do them soon, she and Rob would end up having to eat off the table. As she stood at the sink, wrist-deep in soapy water, scrubbing absent-mindedly at their one casserole dish, she thought once more about James.

Since he had left Maggie three weeks previously, he'd been staying with his friend, Pete, and Pete's wife, in Wimbledon. Apparently their house was reasonably big and, although they had two children, they had a proper spare room. Chloë might have hoped that James would have chosen to stay with her, but she could understand why he hadn't: he didn't want to leap into something so serious straight away. And, heeding Rob's words, she wanted to avoid him turning to her on the rebound. In the back of her mind, however, Chloë also wondered whether he might still be hoping to work things out with Maggie: if he moved in with her it would ruin his chances for a reconciliation. But she was too afraid to ask him in case it was true.

Increasingly there were things that Chloë was too scared to ask James, or mention, because she was wary of what he might say. Now she understood how vulnerable her own position was, and she was terrified. Turning a blind eye was her way of protecting herself. She no longer invited him to spend time with her, just accepted what little time together they had (usually one night a week) as the most he could give. She didn't ask him if he loved her, as she was petrified that now he was potentially available, he'd say no, or that he wasn't sure. She hadn't even asked him for the full details of his split with Maggie. He'd told her that they'd had a huge row and he'd walked out, but as to whether it had had anything to do with her, or if Maggie had found out about the affair, Chloë didn't want to know. She hated the idea that Maggie might despise her, that as the other woman she was the villain of the piece. So she remained oblivious to many issues, and for the moment she preferred it that way.

Equally, she'd not filled in her friends as to what was going on: a sure sign that she was uncomfortable with her own behaviour. She'd never given Sam the full picture either, although she normally confided in him, and she'd certainly not told her parents. The only person who was aware that James had left his wife was Rob, and that was only because, living with him, Chloë knew he would find out anyway.

'Ooooah . . .' At that moment her brother emerged from the living-room sofa next door, rubbing his eyes and yawning like Bagpuss. 'Blimey, Chloë, what's got into you?' He looked at the pile of clean dishes, stacked precariously on the draining-board.

Lost in thought she'd accomplished more than she'd realised. 'Impressive, huh?'

'You'll make someone a nice little wifey yet,' he teased. 'Any chance of a cuppa?'

'Of course.' Chloë jumped to attention. 'Tea? Coffee?'

'Got anything herbal?'

'Really?' Chloë was surprised. Her brother had liked his drinks so packed full of sugar and caffeine they were almost a match for class A drugs.

'Yup.' Sam nodded. 'I'm on a bit of a health kick.'

Well, I never, LA must be affecting him more than he'll admit. Chloë smiled to herself. On the train earlier Sam had been most scathing about the West Coast obsession with the body beautiful, yet he appeared to be embracing the lifestyle even so.

Cup of Bovril in hand (it was the closest Chloë could come to herbal anything), Sam returned to his spot on the sofa and edged his feet back under the duvet. Potato shifted grudgingly to make room.

'How's your love life, then?' he asked, doubtless noticing that his sister, most uncharacteristically, had not been forthcoming in that area.

'Bit of a mess, actually,' she said, wondering where to start.

'Oh? Why? You seeing more than one fellow?' Sam ribbed her.

If only! thought Chloë. But at least here was a way in. 'Not exactly . . . It's more like the other way round.'

Sam looked perplexed. 'You're seeing some guy who's seeing someone else too?'

Chloë nodded. 'You could put it like that.'

'Do you mind?' Sam examined her face closely. 'Yes, you do. You're too old for the double-dating game. Why don't you tell him you want to go out together properly, or he's got to sling his hook?'

'He's married,' stated Chloë, then hurriedly looked away.

Sam was stunned. *'He's what?'*

'Married,' Chloë repeated, conscious of his gaze but unable to return it. Then she added, believing it would make it sound a bit less dreadful, 'Though now he's not living with her any more.'

Sam seemed to see straight through this. *'Now* he's not – you mean he was?'

'Er . . . yes,' Chloë admitted. She might deceive herself, but she wasn't a liar. 'Until last month, he was.'

'So how long has this been going on, then?'

Chloë cast her mind back. 'About six months.' She felt hopelessly ashamed. Although Sam was younger than her, she desperately needed his approval. They'd always looked after each other, particularly during those times when their parents had been preoccupied with their own misfortunes.

'Are you telling me he left his wife for you?'

'Oh, I'm not sure about *that*,' Chloë said rapidly. 'I mean, he'd probably have left her anyway.'

'Hmm.' Sam was plainly dubious. 'I suppose next you're going to tell me he has children.'

Chloë squirmed. 'Only one,' she whispered.

'He? Or She?'

'He.'

'How old?'

She could barely say. 'He's seven, now.'

'Oh, *Chloë!*' cried Sam. Disappointment emanated from his every pore. 'How could you?!'

'But I love James!' she protested. 'You haven't even allowed me to explain! You don't understand!'

Sam said sternly, 'I think I do. Where did you meet him?'

'At work – he's the publisher at UK Magazines.'

'You mean he's your *boss*? Jesus, Chloë, what were you thinking of? This spells trouble through and through!'

'He's not my boss – Vanessa is!' Chloë began to cry. She reached out for Potato, picked him up and cuddled him close to her. He might be fat and lazy, but at least he wouldn't judge her; he wouldn't be so mean.

'Hey, I'm sorry.' Sam knew he had reacted a bit harshly. 'It's just that I'm surprised at you. You know, after everything Mum and Dad went through, I wouldn't have expected you to end up a marriage-breaker yourself.'

A marriage-breaker? The word was out there. Chloë had never felt so small. Still looking downwards, stroking Potato with one hand, she began to chew the nails on the other. 'But they're fine now. They're both really happy. It was good that they split, in the end, don't you think?'

'Yeah, yeah,' Sam agreed. 'But don't you remember how much we hated Julia. Horrendous woman. Ghastly.'

'But it wasn't her fault!' Chloë argued. This was true – it hadn't been, really. But she could see from Sam's face that he was still far from happy. 'So, do you think I'm truly awful, then?'

'I don't know, Chloë, I haven't met the bloke. I know you're nothing like Julia, actually, and if you say things between this chap and his wife were bad already, and they'd have split up anyway, who am I to judge? It's just, you're my sister . . .' His voice went gruff; he didn't like expressing affection to her openly ' . . . and I'd rather see you with someone more easily available, someone without all sorts of baggage like this. You deserve to have a nice time with someone who'll treat you well.' He paused, seeming to appreciate that maybe Chloë thought she *was* having a nice time. 'How much are you seeing of this guy?'

Chloë sighed, 'I s'pose we get to see each other once a week or so.'

'Oh, so it's not that serious, then?'

'No, it is,' she countered. Then wondered. If he was serious about her, shouldn't James be wanting to be with her more often than this? By now she felt the lowest of the low – unscrupulous, uncaring, unwanted. She sniffed loudly. 'Oh, I don't know, Sam, do I? That's what I mean – I've got myself into a bit of a mess, haven't I?'

## 41 Maggie

**Christmas was the** hardest. Maggie didn't feel able to refuse Jamie's request that they spend it together as a family, so she allowed him to come home for a few nights, but insisted he stay in the spare room. For Nathan's sake she tried to put a brave face on things, and cooked a huge dinner as usual. She invited Fran, Geoff and Dan, in the hope that additional people would ease the tension between her and Jamie. She even cooked a turkey, free range, of course, and made do with a rather unsuccessful nut roast for herself.

In the event, it was pretty depressing. Fran was so angry with Jamie that she could barely be civil to him, and to make up for his wife, Geoff over-compensated with forced joviality. Nathan and Dan seemed to pick up the vibes, and jumped down from the table the moment they'd finished the main course, refusing pudding, and galloped away from the adults to play together in Nathan's room.

All in all, when Jamie left on Boxing Day, Maggie heaved a huge sigh of relief. The whole experience had been monstrously testing, not least because being in such close proximity to her husband made her skin crawl. She was so disappointed in him that she was beginning to think she would never be able to feel the same way about him. This sense of let-down was compounded by her certainty that he was still seeing Chloë; she'd asked him directly and he'd said, 'Not really,' which she interpreted as meaning that he was. In some ways she might have understood better if he'd run into Chloë's arms more assuredly; it would have hurt more, but at least it would have seemed as if the angst they'd been through had had some purpose, some passion underlying it all. But this half-hearted 'not really', coupled with his repeated pleas over Christmas that she let him move back into the family home more permanently, left Maggie with a rather nasty taste in her mouth.

'I'm losing respect for him,' she'd said to Fran, as they carried the dishes from the dining room after lunch. 'I can feel that we're going in different directions, growing apart. It's as if the more I regain strength in my own convictions, and the more confident I become about what is right, the more woolly and muddled Jamie grows.'

'Or maybe that's just how he seems to you now,' Fran had responded wisely.

'What do you mean?'

'Well, maybe he's always been like that, but this particular set of circumstances has allowed you to see it, has highlighted that difference between you. Or maybe it's you who's changed.'

'Could be.' Maggie had nodded, scraping the left-over bread sauce into a smaller bowl and putting it in the fridge. 'Yet the trouble is, for me there's no going back. I can't compromise so much any more – I realise it was stifling me, draining the life from me. That's why I changed the work I was doing. What's more, I can't see our marriage in those terms either. For me, now everything is out in the open, it's an issue of right and wrong, and while I suppose I wish that Jamie would appreciate where I'm at, I don't see much evidence of that.'

New Year's Eve promised to be more fun. Jamie had offered to look after Nathan, and Maggie's friends William and Liz were holding a dinner party, with around a dozen guests. They preferred to entertain at home, having recently had their baby, and so it was agreed that Jamie would stay in Shere with Nathan, so that Maggie would stay overnight with them in Twickenham.

It was strange going out socially on her own, but as the evening progressed, and once Maggie had a couple of drinks inside her, she began to enjoy herself. And anyway, she argued, she'd known William and Liz long before she'd met Jamie, and the other guests had never met her before, let alone her husband, so there was no reason to feel uncomfortable.

At about nine o'clock, when Liz was muttering that they couldn't wait any longer and would have to start eating without him, Alex arrived. 'Sorry I'm late,' he said. 'Peace-offering.' He handed over not one but three bottles of champagne.

Liz had organised the seating so that Maggie and Alex were next to each other: as the two 'single' guests it seemed an obvious move. The irony of being planted next to her ex did not escape her, and secretly Maggie was pleased. It gave her a chance to update him on the situation with Jamie without having to yell it across the table, and also, as she rapidly realised, made it easy for them to flirt.

By the time it reached eleven o'clock she was feeling good – warmly, but not uncontrollably, drunk, and at ease, but not so much so that she didn't appreciate the spark that seemed to be developing between Alex and herself. Over the next hour the chemistry became more marked, until eventually Alex leant in close and asked, 'So, Mags, d'you think you'll get back together with Jamie, or is there any hope for an old flame like me?'

Maggie had never been very good at handling advances, especially when she reciprocated them. She couldn't think what on earth to say. Just then, as she was sitting there with her mouth opening and shutting like a goldfish, the countdown to midnight began.

'Ten!' shrieked William, poised at the head of the table with one of Alex's bottles in hand, his wrist tilted to face him so he could see his watch.

'Nine . . . eight . . . seven . . . six!' Everyone else joined in, standing up in excitement. 'Five . . . four . . . three . . . two . . . ONE!'

'Wa-hey!' There was the crack of a cork and champagne flew everywhere other than into the glasses. At that moment Alex grabbed Maggie's hand and led her out of the dining room into the hall. 'Only this once,' he said, 'for the New Year. May the next year be better for both of us than the last.'

And then he kissed her.

And, to Maggie's amazement, it was fantastic. Gentle and soft, but oh, so, so sexy. God, had Alex always kissed like that? She was sure he hadn't. In fact, once it had started, she didn't want it to stop, and were it not for a vague awareness that someone might come out of the dining room and catch them, she would happily have stood there, in the corner of the hallway, kissing him, so intimately, so deliciously, for the next few hours. She felt her whole body come alive, as if what was happening to her lips was a magic key, unlocking the sensual world of her entire physical being.

Suddenly, she thought about Jamie, about how she'd been judging him, about how she'd implied to Fran only a few days previously that infidelity was such a clear-cut issue. Was this what had got into Jamie? Was this what it had been like with Chloë, so heavenly, so tantalising, so irresistibly moreish?

She pulled away. 'Oh, Alex . . . I'm not sure we should be doing this, should we?'

'No, we probably shouldn't,' he said, but he didn't sound as if he meant it, and merely started kissing her again, more passionately.

Lord, it was so good!

He felt different from Jamie, smelt different. Yet he felt and smelt familiar too; briefly, Maggie was taken back to her youth, to the years they'd spent together before. How comforting, reassuring. And then again, as they continued embracing, touching, kissing, she grew increasingly aware that Alex wasn't the boy he'd been then, that he was different, somehow, somebody exciting, new.

'Maggie,' he said, softly, 'you do know I still care about you, don't you? I care about you an awful lot . . .'

'And me you,' she said, realising that she did, though unsure whether it was to quite the same degree. And as she was swept up into his kisses once more, and felt the solidity of his body against her, she was filled with yearning for him, for his uncomplicated kindness and humanity.

'Where are you staying tonight?' he asked, oh-so-quietly, a few minutes later. 'Have you got to go home?'

'Here,' Maggie whispered. 'I was supposed to be staying here, with Liz and Will . . .'

'Why don't you come back with me?' He pulled away from her a little, and started stroking her hair. She remembered how he'd always loved her hair, how soft and beautiful he'd said it was. 'It's not far . . .'

Maggie frowned. If she went back with him she knew what would happen. She was feeling far too turned on not to make love with him, if she ended up at his place. She battled with herself. She'd lose the moral high ground, there wouldn't be quite the clear distinction between her own behaviour and Jamie's that there had been. And she hadn't allowed enough time to elapse, she knew that too. It had been only a month since she'd kicked her husband out and she hadn't worked out her feelings about him, let alone another man. She didn't want to do anything she might regret. But then, she persuaded herself, would it really be so bad? She'd been so goddamn *good*. She'd been so much the Goody Two Shoes she'd almost been a bloody martyr! Wasn't it her turn to have some fun? And at least with Alex she knew he cared and she wouldn't get hurt.

Ultimately what swayed her was curiosity. As far as she remembered – but it had been over fifteen years since she'd slept with him – Alex hadn't been that great a lover, at least not as good as Jamie, and she wanted to see if this was still true. Because if these incredible long deep kisses were anything to go by, he might have changed . . . He might have changed a lot.

'Okay. What the hell? It's New Year's Eve . . .'

'I'll tell them you don't feel so good,' said Alex, knowing she wouldn't want it made public that she was going back to his place. 'I'll say I'm going to drop you home after all.'

'Thank you.' She smiled up at him. He was so generous-natured, a characteristic that was reflected in his big, dark brown eyes.

So it was that, an hour or so later, she found herself in Alex's flat in Putney. He poured them each a nightcap, and sat down next to her on the sofa. Maggie felt self-conscious all over again. What was she doing here? Was this really such a good idea? Would this scupper any chance of a reconciliation between her and Jamie, once and for all, or were they beyond that anyway?

Alex could see the doubt in her eyes. 'It's okay,' he took her hand. 'I'll look after you, I promise. You don't have to do anything you don't want to. And you don't need to worry – I've no expectations beyond tonight.'

But just as he said that, Maggie knew that she did want to – that she more than wanted to, she needed to, she needed him, needed his wanting her very much indeed. It was as if the lid had been lifted off all the unexpressed passion she'd harboured for months, and now she had a direction for it, with someone who reciprocated her desire.

Thus what started as a little tentative hand-stroking rapidly developed into something far less coy. Within seconds Alex had slipped his hands into her bra, was stroking her breasts and she'd unzipped his trousers and had her hand down his boxers. Soon they virtually ripped off each other's clothes and she pulled him on top of her so they could make love properly. They threw the cushions off the sofa and a few seconds later they tumbled on to the floor. Maggie could feel the carpet scraping her back, but she didn't care. Far from it – there was something about his wild intensity that made this mild discomfort turn her on even more. With one foot, Maggie pushed away the coffee table so she could lift her legs, allowing him to penetrate her more deeply.

Bloody hell! she thought, I am quite, quite convinced Alex did not do it like this before!

Half-way through he stopped and withdrew from inside her, then very gently, he, put two fingers into her, pushing slightly towards her belly, then away as he did so. *Jesus* . . . she'd not had that experience, ever – maybe it was that G-spot thing she'd never really believed existed . . . And then he withdrew his fingers, and started to kiss down her body, pausing to suck on her breasts, softly swirling his tongue around her nipples – wow, she had always liked that. Then he continued kissing her, lower down, too, so she wasn't sure what was what or where, only that it felt good – so, so good.

She opened her eyes and looked down at him, and as she did so she could see him tenderly watching her, seeing if she was happy.

'Are you okay?' he asked.

It made her long for him all the more. She nodded and, seconds later, she felt herself about to come.

'Alex,' she cried, 'come back inside me, now . . . I want to come with you . . .' So he stopped what he was doing and did as she asked. 'Can you feel it? she breathed. 'Can you feel me about to come?'

'Yes,' he whispered, and paused, inside her, so that he could feel the pulses of her orgasm. Then he began to move rhythmically again, and digging her nails into his back, she came with a fantastic shudder. Then feeling her do so, he gave in to his own desire, and came too, along with her.

## 42 Chloë

**On 14 February,** the first ever issue of *All Woman* was launched. The moment the magazine hit the news-stands, its controversial subject matter and provocative tone, offset by typography, illustration and photography that were stunning, stylish and shocking in equal measure, caused a furore. Chloë even found herself asked to talk about it on local radio and television. The first time she had to do so, she was nervous, but having done it once, she found she took surprisingly well to centre stage.

'You're more of an actress than you'll ever know,' Rob had observed, after watching her on *London Tonight*. 'Must be the theatrical family background, darling. You put me quite to shame.'

The main event of this frantic week was the *All Woman* launch party, due to be held – on Chloë's insistence – at the Café de Paris in Leicester Square. Although it was no longer quite the trendy night-spot it had been a few years before, Chloë was convinced that its opulent *faux*-Baroque interior would provide the perfect backdrop for a fancy-dress extravaganza. Guests were invited to come as historic figures they felt were 'all woman', and as word spread that it was going to be *the* media event to be seen at, invitations became highly sought-after, with style and media correspondents fighting to get on the list.

Rob could scarcely contain himself when he heard. 'You're going to have all these straight journos turning up in *drag!*'

'Exactly.' Chloë nodded. 'They won't get in otherwise. It'll be a scream, don't you think?'

'Oooh, I *wish* I could come,' he sulked.

'I'd love you to, but it's not really up to me, I'm afraid. Everything's organised by our PR department.'

Inevitably Chloë took ages to decide what to wear. In the end she left it so late that she was forced to make the outfit herself, running like a mad thing round the fashion wholesale shops of Soho's back-streets to find all the necessary accoutrements.

'So what do you think?' she asked Rob, when she was ready, twirling into his room.

Rob looked at her, mystified. He took in the white sheet, loosely swathed around her hour-glass form like a toga, exposing not unattractive amounts of curvy flesh. Her dark curls were gathered up like those of a Greek goddess, with a few tendrils framing her face becomingly. Her eyes were emphasised with copious black liner, to true Maria Callas effect. Her wrists jangled with gold bangles, and on her feet were thong sandals. The final touch, which she was proudly brandishing in front of her, was a large box.

'You look divine,' he acknowledged. 'But who the fuck are you?'

'Open it,' she ordered, thrusting the box into his hands.

He read the carefully hand-written label, 'A Gift from Zeus', and tentatively lifted the lid. Startled, he jumped back as half a dozen springs popped up, narrowly missing his face. But where one might perhaps have expected there to be a Jack-in-a-box, on the end of each spring was a different object: the figure of a little devil, a lipstick, a miniature bottle of tequila, a packet of condoms, and a scaled-down copy of *All Woman* . . . He scratched his head. 'Evil things . . .' he muttered, trying to work it out. 'You're some kind of wicked woman . . .'

'Ye-es?' she encouraged him.

' . . . a box . . .'

'Hmm?'

'You're Pandora!' he exclaimed at last.

'Appropriate, don't you think, that I should be the woman single-handedly responsible for bringing all the troubles into the world?'

'Ideal for the editor of such a contentious mag,' he agreed.

'Thank you,' said Chloë, as the doorbell rang. 'Eek, there's my taxi!' She snatched back her most crucial accessory and grabbed her coat, throwing it over her shoulders.

'You go, girl!' shouted Rob, as she bolted out of the door.

On arriving at the Café de Paris, Chloë deposited her coat in the cloakroom. In the foyer, she helped herself from the silver tray laden with glasses of champagne held by a waiter before he had the chance to offer it to her. She downed it in one to steady her nerves, and moved on to a second waiter for the next. Then she pushed open the double doors into the main body of the nightclub. The first thing she saw, straight ahead of her, was a giant poster of the *All Woman* front cover. At what must have been twenty feet high, it took up the entire stage, spanning the lower and upper levels of the club. Chloë was flushed with pride. She moved towards the edge of the balcony, where two symmetrical staircases swept in decadent golden spirals to the main floor below, and looked down.

She'd made sure not to be too early; there was nothing she hated more than waiting for guests to arrive and the fun to start, especially at a party where she was one of the hosts. When she and Rob entertained at home – which they did most years as they virtually shared a birthday – she had little choice in the matter, but here, at a work party where everything was set up already, she didn't have to sit around nervously biting her nails. The bar area was already thronged with people. Despite the dim, ultraviolet lighting, from her vantage-point Chloë could see many familiar faces. There was Jean, dressed as . . . yes, Anaïs Nin. She might have been all woman, true, but it was typical of her ex-boss to choose someone so literary. There was her co-host Vanessa – or Morticia, rather. Golly, thought Chloë, she'd barely had to dress up at all. And there, surrounded by three male Marilyns, clearly relishing an invitation to assess their fake cleavages, was Patsy – Holly Golightly to a T. Chloë scanned the rest of the dance-floor. There was a very masculine Nell Gwynn, a couple of Madonnas, a particularly chubby Mata Hari, half a dozen Cleopatras – three of each sex – and a riot of other amusingly costumed guests. But where, among all these people, was James? Chloë couldn't see him, so she decided to go down and have a thorough look. But no sooner had she reached the bottom of the stairs than she was cornered by Jean.

'Chloë! Long time no see!' She was tipsy already.

'Yes,' agreed Chloë, feeling at once that she was to blame. Despite working in the same building, she'd not been in to see her old boss in weeks. Although she knew it was always advisable to keep on the good side of a woman as influential as Jean, she'd not had a moment to spare. Also, since Patsy had warned her of Jean's mounting suspicions all those months ago, she was concerned that Jean would jump at the chance to delve into other, more personal matters. James had told her that Jean knew, and was hopping mad with them both. Rather than face her, Chloë had opted for what had lately become her favourite response to all matters emotional: avoidance. Obviously she said none of this, but simply, 'I've been rushed off my feet.'

'So I gather. Whenever I've caught sight of you around, you've looked rather preoccupied.'

Was Chloë being paranoid, or could she detect an underlying jibe? 'Well, you know what it's like, launching a new magazine. There are never enough hours in the day.'

'No, not with a life as full as yours, I imagine.' Chloë was convinced that this was barbed. Especially as Jean then drained her glass and added, 'Love the outfit – how very *risqué*,' eyes fixed pointedly on Chloë's exposed bosom, as if to say, how *unseemly*. Desperately Chloë scanned the venue for an excuse to talk to someone else. Out of the corner of her eye she could see Patsy giggling with the three Marilyns. How she longed to join them at the bar! But Jean had consumed enough alcohol to loosen her tongue and continued, 'I wanted to congratulate you on not one but two impressive achievements.'

'Oh, yeah?' By now Chloë had little choice but to hear Jean out.

'First the magazine. I must say, it's marvellous.' Jean swayed slightly, then took hold of Chloë's arm to steady herself. 'Goddamn marvellous. No, I mean that. It's very different, thought-provoking, great fun – I love it.'

Chloë blushed. 'Thank you.'

'You've achieved everything you set out to do, and I'd like to congratulate you on a job well done.' Jean clinked Chloë's glass.

'Cheers. I'm glad you like it.'

'And the other thing,' here Jean leant close, dropped her voice and spoke with thinly veiled sarcasm, 'is that I'd like to congratulate you on breaking up what, until you came along, was one very happy little family.' *Shit*. Chloë knew it. She just knew it. What the fuck was she supposed to say to that? There was no need to fear, however, because Jean hadn't finished. 'I gather Jamie's had to move out of the family home – away from Maggie and Nathan. I also understand that you're still seeing him. Though at least I hear he's had the sense not to move in with you straight away. Well, I hope that's what you wanted. Driving a father away from his son, a husband away from his wife. I hope you're satisfied.'

Chloë didn't know how to respond. She experienced the same stomach-churning guilt that she'd had on occasion when talking to Rob about James. Only this time her guilt was more pronounced, as it had been when she'd spoken to Sam at Christmas. Jean and Sam – her ex-boss and her brother: their moral judgement was heavier, less compromising. It weighed on her hard. Her shame was compounded because she was also aware that although she wasn't seeing any more of James than she had before she still hadn't had the courage to shift the status quo. She'd neither finished the relationship, nor tried to move it on into something more definite. She knew she ought to do one or the other, but somehow she'd been paralysed. Especially when she'd had so much else on her mind. It had hardly seemed the time to deal with something so difficult, so potentially painful. 'Maggie told you?' she asked, finally.

'Who else but Maggie?'

'Oh.' This was the first time Maggie had ever been mentioned directly by Jean in this context. It sounded strange, hearing her name, coming from a friend; someone who, other than James, actually knew this woman, doubtless knew her side of the story. It made Maggie seem more real somehow, less remote, and reminded Chloë that she wasn't the only one involved. This caused more discomfort than Chloë could bear. 'Jean, I'm not sure this is the right place to talk about this.'

'No, I'm sure it's not. But then where is? Indeed, I bet there are plenty of people who would consider it quite inappropriate to mention it but I'm not one of those people, I'm afraid. You know me, I have to speak my mind. And I don't know if you realise, Chloë – sometimes you can be quite naïve – but I've done a lot of listening to Maggie over the last few months – a lot of picking up the pieces. She's been to hell and back, you know.'

'I know,' said Chloë, stifling a desire to scream. *But so have I.*

'I also don't know if you're aware of quite what a woman she is, how remarkable.'

'Hm.' But surely, thought Chloë desperately, if she was *that* remarkable, James would never have been attracted to anyone else, would he? He would never have walked out on someone truly right for him.

Then, like a spear plunging directly into Chloë's heart, it came: 'I think Jamie wants her back, you know.'

At once Chloë began to shake. She felt her vision of the future rocking, her world crumbling. 'You do?'

'Yes, I do.' Jean seemed determined to put Chloë straight. 'Maggie tells me that he rings and hints prettily heavily at moving back in all the time.'

'But, but . . .' Chloë was fearsomely confused. 'He's the one who walked out! He could probably go back – if that was what he wanted?'

A waiter, dapper in his white dinner jacket, was hovering

helpfully with a tray of freshly filled glasses, oblivious to the shattering dialogue close at hand. Jean reached for another drink and Chloë, keen to take the edge off all these harsh words, followed suit. In the background she thought she caught a glimpse of James, glancing in her direction, then rapidly looking away.

'So that's what Jamie told you, is it? That he walked out on her?'

'Er . . . Yes, it is.'

Jean sighed. 'Sometimes I wonder about him, I really do. He surprises me. Seems to be telling you both a slightly different story. I wouldn't have put him down as so duplicitous, but I'm constantly amazed by what people will say or do when they're caught in the middle like that.' She shook her head. 'I guess I've not heard his side of it, and probably never will. But if that's what he told you about what happened with Maggie, take it from me, it's not true. She found out about the two of you – otherwise I'm not sure he ever would have told her. When she found out, she made him promise not to see you any more, and to try to work things through with her, and he didn't stick to that promise. When she discovered he was *still* seeing you regardless, she kicked him out.'

The bubble had finally burst. Chloë was crushed. She'd honestly believed that James had been the one to leave his wife, not the other way round. She'd persuaded herself that it had been a positive decision, albeit one made in anger. The fact that this wasn't the case only reinforced her concerns that he wasn't totally sure about what he was doing. It made her wonder whether, in the long term, James might indeed go back to Maggie, just as Jean was suggesting. Not only that, but Chloë could now see that there was little likelihood that he would ever commit unreservedly to her.

Seeing Chloë look so crestfallen, Jean appeared to appreciate that perhaps her former protégée wasn't in possession of a full set of the facts regarding what precisely had taken place between Maggie and Jamie. Maybe Chloë wasn't the total villain of the piece. 'How ironic,' she said, scanning Chloë's ensemble once again, less critically this time. 'Pandora, eh?'

'Oh, you know me . . .' Chloë faltered, feeling genuinely humbled. 'Nothing but trouble . . .'

'Hey,' Jean nudged her, acknowledging that she might have overstepped the mark. 'Look, I know you're not really that wicked. You must understand, this hasn't been easy for me, knowing you both like I do, being so fond of the pair of you – and I'm pretty fond of Jamie, too. I worry for you, Chloë. Aside from Maggie, I wouldn't want to see you come unstuck in all this. You've got such talent, and I should know that, more than anyone. It's more than just a passing thing, it's rare. I meant it, what I said about the magazine. It really is great. You ought to be very proud.' She drew breath. 'Anyway, I've said my bit. I don't want to spoil your evening completely, so I'll shut up now. Off you go, Chloë, scoot. This is a very special night for you. Enjoy it.'

Chloë needed no further encouragement to take her leave. James was deep in conversation with someone she didn't recognise and, anyway, she certainly couldn't approach him *now*. To add insult to injury, she noticed that he hadn't bothered to dress up. Probably thinks he's all things to all women just like that, she bristled. Instead she headed straight for the bar, and Patsy.

'Oops,' said Patsy. 'That looked heavy. You okay?'

Chloë exhaled. 'Only just.'

'Here. Let me get you a drink.' Patsy drew herself up to her full height in a bid to make her presence felt behind the counter. 'Margarita,' she ordered. 'No salt.'

On top of three glasses of champagne Chloë knew this probably wasn't this best idea in the world, but, Lord, she needed it. 'Thanks.'

A few minutes with Patsy and the three Marilyns, and Chloë had put a bit of space between her and that ghastly confrontation. Within half an hour she was back on an even keel.

'Ah! Just the woman I'm after!' exclaimed a familiar voice. It was Vanessa. 'Chloë, here's someone who's dying to meet you. Adrienne Sugarman, Chloë Appleton.'

Chloë wished her mind was less fuzzy. The name was familiar, though she didn't recognise the woman before her.

'Hi!' enthused Adrienne, shaking her hand with the iron grip customary in confident Americans. 'Special Projects Director. US Publishing.'

Ah, yes, of course. James had mentioned meeting her, and Adrienne's golden touch was well known throughout the whole organisation. Aside from the aura of success that surrounded her, with her deep honey-toned skin, wild Afro and sensational curves, she oozed sensuality. Although she held the equivalent position on the other side of the Atlantic, she was the antithesis of Vanessa physically, certainly, and quite possibly in temperament too.

'Fabulous magazine, Chloë. *Fabulous.*'

'Thank you.' Chloë warmed to Adrienne immediately.

'Can I get you a drink?'

'No, thanks. I'm fine.'

Vanessa moved off, leaving the two together. 'Gee, if I'd known, I'd have gotten dressed up like you guys, but I only flew in today and Vanessa invited me along. Anyways, I just had to say, I so *love* what you've done with the magazine!' rhapsodised Adrienne. 'It's so refreshing! So challenging! So very . . . *now.*' Chloë was feeling better and better. She needed a boost to her self-esteem. 'Talking of new,' continued Adrienne, 'I think us guys should get together while I'm over, just you and me, off the record initially, of course.' Chloë raised her eyebrows. 'It's only a thought, but if the magazine does as well here as it looks set to do – and we'll know pretty quickly, I reckon – have you thought about launching a US edition? I could see it going down just *fabulously* well.' Chloë couldn't believe what she was hearing, but Adrienne left her in no doubt. 'What I'm trying to say is, would you ever consider coming to work with me, at US Magazines in New York?'

## 43 Chloë

**Chloë picked up** Potato and cuddled him to her. 'How would you feel if I went to New York?' she whispered into the furry triangle of his ear. 'Would you be okay if I left you here with Rob?' Potato purred. 'And what do you think I should do about James, my fat friend? You think I should finish things, don't you? You never liked him – always on your bloody sofa.' Potato purred some more.

With a sigh, Chloë put him down and watched him make his way back to the dent in the cushions that was the hallmark of his favourite snoozing spot. He didn't appear to give a fig, merely bemused at being disturbed during his post-breakfast nap. She hunted for her handbag, located it under the kitchen table and cast her eye around the flat, briefly allowing herself a moment's nostalgia as she recalled all the good times she and Rob had shared there. It had been her haven (albeit a messy one) virtually since the day she'd left college, and she wasn't sure how she felt about someone else moving into her room, even though the plan was that it should be a good friend of Rob's whom she also knew well. Then there was Rob, too. Would he and Potato be okay without her? More to the point, would she be okay without them?

Hell, thought Chloë. I'll never know unless I try it.

She caught the bus to work as usual, conscious, now that the decision was taken, that it was one of the last times she'd travel this particular route. She took her favourite seat on the top deck and pondered on the previous few weeks. As predicted, the first two issues of *All Woman* had proved an unprecedented success, and US Magazines had made her a pretty irresistible offer. She'd not breathed a word about her transfer to anyone at the office other than Vanessa until it was all signed and sealed – not even to James. She'd seen him a few times outside work since the launch party but, with uncharacteristic patience, had held off on mentioning anything until she'd an offer in writing. Two days ago her contract had come through; today she was seeing him to break the news. And this time, significantly, she'd chosen neutral territory and arranged to meet him during her lunch hour.

They met in Soho Square. It was a bright, spring day; the daffodils were up. And although they needed to keep on their jackets, it was warm enough to sit on the grass with their sandwiches.

'You wanted to talk.' James unwrapped his panini and took a large bite. He sounded faintly worried.

Now that she was confronted with this situation, Chloë couldn't think where to start. A dozen voices were fighting to be heard in her head.

There was Jean, reminding her that perhaps Jamie still loved Maggie.

There was Rob, despairing because James had shown no sign of being able to decide between the two of them.

There was her mother, all those years ago, with her theories of rebound relationships, causing Chloë to wonder if this affair might be like the one her father had had with Julia.

Then there was Sam, who seemed so disappointed that she should be selling herself short.

And there was also another set of voices: Chloë's own voices.

There was the hedonistic voice of the rebellious teenager, which said, 'Hey, but you've never had such a good time! Surely you're not going to give up the most fun you've had?!'

There was the romantic voice, which recalled the flowers, the love-making, the passion.

There was the intellectual voice, which made her question whether she'd ever enjoy such sparky conversations with another man.

There was the lonely voice of the little-girl-lost who wanted a partner, who didn't want to be on her own.

And there was the voice of doom, which said she'd never get over it, that if she finished it with James she'd never meet anyone, ever again.

But the voice that finally spoke was none of these. It was the voice of self-belief, the voice of resolve, the voice of a grown woman. 'I'm leaving you,' she said.

James stopped mid-mouthful. He swallowed, hard. 'Oh.'

Chloë knew she needed to explain more fully. 'I mean literally leaving you.'

James looked puzzled. 'Literally?'

'Yeah. I'm leaving. Going away.'

'On holiday? You're having a break? You deserve it.'

Chloë laughed, slightly bitterly. 'You couldn't be more wrong. I'll probably end up working harder than I've ever had to work in my life. I'll have to learn a whole new market.'

'I don't understand.' His mouth was contorted.

'I've got a new job.'

'Oh? Gosh.' He sounded surprised. 'But *All Woman's* been such a success. I thought that was what you wanted, it's so much your baby. Would you really want to go and work on another magazine? And, anyway, even if you did, why does that mean you're leaving me?' She noticed he'd stopped eating altogether.

'I'm still going to be working on *All Woman*. But they've asked me to go to New York. Set up an American edition there.'

'What?' James was clearly stunned. In the normal run of events, as the publisher, he would have known about such a move.

'I asked them not to tell you, or anyone, until I'd thought it through,' Chloë went on, beginning to find the conversation harder now. He was plucking at the grass, little tufts of unspoken emotion. 'I know it was a bit out of turn . . . but I didn't know what else to do.'

'Oh. I see.' James looked up, into her eyes. He looked so wounded, so hurt, so lost, so like a little boy. It was a look she'd seen before, all those months back, in the Paramount in New York, just after he'd spoken to Maggie – the day before he told Chloë he loved her. Her guts wrenched. Oh God, this was so unfair!

'I'm sorry,' she said softly.

'Are you definitely going to go?' He was hoarse.

She nodded.

'Do you want me to stop you?'

'No, not really. I don't think it would be a good idea.'

'It's me who should be sorry,' he said. Bloody hell – he was crying! 'I know I've been . . .' he stumbled over the words ' . . . pretty useless, really.'

'No,' she said. 'No more than me, you haven't.'

'Can't I come and see you?' he pleaded. 'You know, I come over to New York a lot.'

'Well . . .' She hesitated, but then a voice reminded her of what she had pledged to do. 'By all means come in and say hello, put your head round the door of my office, or whatever . . . maybe even go for lunch. But as for more than that, no, you can't.'

'Oh.' James made the word sound like a cry of pain. 'I guess you're right. It wouldn't be a good idea.'

'It's just . . .' Chloë was getting tearful too, but fought against it, crazily aware that she had no hanky. 'I need to give myself another chance, you know, of meeting someone else.' Her resolution grew stronger again. 'Someone who wants me, and only me.'

'I guess.' The sadness of his expression suggested he was far from enthusiastic about the idea of her with another man. 'So when are you going?' he asked, in a whisper.

'Monday.' It was Friday. 'Vanessa's going to take over the

running of the magazine here, and I'm going to liaise with her from New York for this next edition. Then next month they've got a new editor here in the UK. Someone I know actually – she's very good.'

'But she's not you.' The miniature pile of grass was getting quite high now.

'No, she's not. But I'm not Maggie, either.'

'No, that's why I loved you.'

'I know.' Chloë sniffed. 'But you love her too – and I don't want only half of you.' Then she added, generously, 'You could go back to her, you know.'

'I'm not sure she'd have me, even if I was sure I wanted to . . .'

'But you're not sure.'

'I don't know . . . I don't know what I want any more.'

And although Chloe felt terribly sad, this convinced her that she was doing the right thing. 'But you're not sure you want me, my love, either.'

James was silent, then said, 'I hate goodbyes.' Right then he seemed a million miles from the successful, confident publisher that she'd first met less than a year before.

Suddenly Chloë felt old and wise. Philosophic, even. 'They don't matter. It's what's gone before.'

'It's what you're telling me can't come after. Nothing. No more us.'

'Yes,' she paused, pained. 'That is what I'm telling you.'

'I should never have got involved with you, dragged you into this mess.'

'But I knew what I was doing, James, really. I knew you were married when I went into this. I walked in with my eyes open. I may not have liked what I saw, I may have blinded myself. I don't really blame you, honestly. It's just . . . in a way, in a funny way . . . you've given me a taste of what I could have, had things been different. And now I want to see if I can find that properly. And it's easier for me – and it'll be much easier for you – if I can do that without you around, constantly reminding me.' She leant forward and very softly, kissed those still-contorted lips. 'I'm going to go now,' she said, standing up and dusting off her skirt.

'And please don't phone me or e-mail me or anything. Just let me go and do this my way.' She looked down at him one last time, sitting there on the grass of Soho Square, surrounded by all the other people with their little bags of sandwiches, enjoying their normal, everyday lunches. 'Part of me will always love you, and you know that. And I know that part of you will always love me. But part of you is not enough for me now, I want more than that. Maybe I want too much, who knows? But I've got to give it a try, because I've only got one life . . . And I know this might sound melodramatic, but I mean it. I want to be able to live with myself as I live it. So this is it. Goodbye.'

And before he had a chance to say any more, to protest, to beg, to tell her he loved her, to promise that he'd make a go of things with her, she picked up her handbag and turned and walked away.

Once her back was turned she started to cry. But she fought the tears and kept walking, determined, back for her final afternoon at UK Publishing, all woman at last.

**They were standing** on the edge of the football pitch together, watching the Shere Tigers versus the Godalming Lions. It was a typical March afternoon – neither warm nor cold, cloudy nor sunny, but it was particularly windy, and gusts kept catching Maggie's hair, swooping wisps in front of her face.

With only five minutes to go, the Tigers were losing one–nil, and Nathan was standing scuffing the turf with his boots on the edge of the pitch, bored. The play had been focused down at his team's goal end; as a striker, he'd had little opportunity to play. Suddenly, one of the Tiger's defenders snatched the ball in a rare moment of aggression, and kicked it away from the goal mouth, towards him. Startled, Nathan realised he had an opportunity at his feet.

'C'mon, Nathan, my son!' shrieked Jamie, caught up in a wave of excitement.

The Godalming defence, having had it easy the entire match, were taken unawares. Quick as a flash, Nathan shot down towards the goal, dribbling the way his father had taught him, with a virtuosity surprising in a seven-year-old. He nipped round the first defender. Now, other than the keeper, there was only one player between him and the goal.

Maggie couldn't contain herself. She jumped up and down and squealed, 'Oh, my God!'

'You're on side!' bellowed Jamie. 'Go for it!'

And with a decisive thwack, Nathan kicked the ball past the keeper, through the posts and scored the most magnificent goal.

'*Hooray!*' his parents yelped and, caught up in unanimous pride, threw their arms around each other just as Nathan's team-mates rushed to do the same to him.

A few seconds later, flustered, Jamie and Maggie broke apart, shocked at the first physical contact they'd had in months.

Maggie took a step back. 'He's very good, isn't he?'

'Brilliant,' Jamie enthused. 'Far better than I ever was.'

'Surely not – I thought you were the best in your class.'

'Hmm,' Jamie shook his head, disagreeing. 'I think he's got a perfectionist streak that I never had.' He turned to look at her. Her hair was still blowing in the wind. She'd grown it over the last few months, and it was longer than it had been in years. She looked different somehow, younger. 'Must have got it off his mum.'

Maggie blushed, but she knew there was truth in his words: she was more of a perfectionist than Jamie, an idealist, even.

'I miss him, you know,' said Jamie.

'I know.'

'I'm not seeing Chloë any more,' he added.

Presently Maggie looked at him, saying nothing, but her face must have expressed her scepticism.

'I know you've heard me say that before,' he added, with some urgency, presumably conscious that there were only a few minutes before the game was finished.

Again Maggie was silent.

'This time it's different. It really is over.'

Maggie sighed. Part of her so wanted to believe him, still wanted things to work out, if not for her sake, then for Nathan's.

For several months she'd held off on seeing anyone else, let alone beginning a new relationship, so that she could be sure. 'Why should I believe you? What makes it different this time?'

'She's leaving,' explained Jamie. 'Going away.'

'Oh.' Maggie felt a mix of emotions. Part of her was glad that at last this woman would be out of her life. But regardless of her relief, part of her still refused to give in to her desire to make up with Jamie, to reunite as a family. She realised that this was probably what he was asking her to consider – he'd pretty much said so before. Yet deep down something prevented her from feeling wholeheartedly at ease. She tried to put a finger on it, and, in the hope of gaining clarification, asked, 'Where's she going?'

'To New York. She's been invited to set up an American edition of *All Woman* there.'

'I see.' Maggie began to understand. 'So when does she go?'

'Tomorrow.'

There; there it was. That was what was bothering her. Maggie was sure she could hear regret in his voice. It was so subtle that someone who knew him less well might not have heard it. 'Tell me, Jamie, did you finish it?' She paused, then asked the crucial question: 'Or did she?'

Jamie looked down at his shoes. 'I suppose . . . she did.' He knew this wasn't the right thing to say. He knew it meant he would lose her, but he was sick of lying, sick to death of lying.

Maggie tucked her hair behind her ears so that she could see him properly. 'That's it, Jamie, don't you see? It was all I ever asked of you, for you to decide for yourself. And you never could. That was all I wanted – for you to come back, to try to make a go of things, of your own accord. But you couldn't do that, and even now that it's over with Chloë, you weren't the one to decide. That ceaseless fluctuating . . . Never knowing what you wanted . . . Always reacting to me or her, never taking the initiative yourself. You must see that I can't take you back. Not on those terms, not now.'

'Um,' His voice was small, disappointed, but resigned. 'I kind of thought you'd say that.'

She sighed. 'I guess maybe it's because I'm a perfectionist, like you said. But that's the way I am and, try as I might, I can't change that. I wouldn't be being true to myself.' She fought back the tears, struggling to express what she meant yet be kind. 'That's the irony, I realise. That might be one of the reasons you love me but . . . I don't know. Perhaps we're too different in that way. Your ambivalence, your pragmatism . . . I understand it, but living like that, it was killing me, all that compromise. And I ended up putting all my idealism into the wrong things – stupid things, shallow things – an immaculate house, the perfect bloody soufflé . . . I'm so sorry, but I've fought so hard to get it back . . . who I really am. It's not that I don't still love you, it's that I can't love you like I used to – or at least be with you – not in the same way, not any more.'

At that moment the referee blew the final whistle and the boys came running off the pitch. Nathan charged over to his parents, pleased as punch with his performance, happily unaware of the significance of their conversation. He bounced along between them, and they made their way back across the recreation ground.

When they reached the car park, Jamie headed for his vehicle as if to drive straight up to London.

'Hey,' Maggie touched his shoulder as he turned to go, 'why don't you come back with us, for a bit? Have some tea and biscuits?' This was her truce, her way of saying he was still a part of her life with Nathan, regardless of whether the two of them remained husband and wife.

'Really?' he asked, unsure if she meant it.

'Of course,' said Maggie generously. 'You'd like to have tea with Daddy, wouldn't you, Nathan?'

## 45 Chloë

**Chloë got out** of the yellow cab and checked her watch.

Bugger. She was early. It was only twenty to eight, and she was meeting Adrienne Sugarman in Nobu on the hour. She took a peek through the double doors of the famous restaurant. Every table was packed, but the bar was empty. It was in the centre of the room and she'd be most conspicuous, especially as she hadn't brought any thing to read.

Hmm, she thought, I can't face that.

To kill time she strolled a couple of blocks down Hudson Street. Soaring ahead of her against the clear sky of the June evening was the World Trade Center; on the corner was a tavern, Puffy's. Small to the point of poky, it was seedy in comparison with the impressive bamboo chic of Nobu – but then again it didn't have Robert de Niro's financial backing. However, several people were sitting at the bar and it was a darn sight less intimidating.

Chloë pushed open the door and squeezed herself in at the counter.

'What'll it be?' asked the bartender.

'A margarita. On the rocks. No salt.' That would help her meeting go with a swing.

As the bartender prepared her cocktail, the guy sitting next to her caught her eye. 'Are you English?' he enquired.

'Yeah.'

'Been here long?'

'About two months.'

'Not here on vacation, then?'

'No.' Chloë wasn't really in the mood to talk.

He seemed eager to chat to her, however. 'So you're here a while?' he insisted.

'As long as it takes,' said Chloë, and thought, *to get over a broken heart.* She was silent for a moment, contemplating how hard it was to be so far from home. She missed Rob and her friends and family, but at least e-mail allowed her to stay in touch with them on a regular basis, and Rob called her far more often than was healthy for his phone bill to check she was okay. No, the person she really missed was James. She'd stuck to her resolve and not been in touch with him, and it was getting easier as time passed, just as Rob kept on assuring her would be the case, but it was testing her new-found self-control to the full. She knew this was for the best, yet it was often when other men chatted her up that she missed James most keenly – they never seemed as special as he was, somehow.

'Huh?' The guy next to her interrupted her thoughts, sounding puzzled.

She realised her responses (or lack of them) must appear rather odd, so she pushed these thoughts away and explained, 'I've come for work.'

'What kind of work?'

'To launch a magazine.'

'Oh, really?' He appeared genuinely interested. 'Coool.'

There was nothing like flattery to bring Chloë out of an introverted mood. She beamed proudly. 'I'm meeting my new business partner at Nobu in a few minutes. She's bringing some potential advertisers.'

'*Nice,*' said the guy. 'Hey, I'm Peter.' He held out his hand.

As she shook it, noting his firm grip, she took him in properly for the first time. She judged he was a few years older than she was, and his clothes suggested that he wasn't short of a bob or two. Indeed, he was pretty good-looking in an Italian-who-likes-the-good-life kind of way.

Peter continued, 'And these are my friends – Ben, Brad.' Two other men leant around the counter and shook Chloë's hand in turn. They were decidedly leaner and scruffier than Peter. One looked like a dissolute rock star, while the other – if his paint-splattered hair was anything to go by – must have been an artist of some kind. But she had to admit all three had one thing in common.

They were gorgeous.

Suddenly she felt better still. 'I'm Chloë.' She grinned.

Then, for a split second, she wondered what it would be like to have sex with them all. Simultaneously. Better than the boys in the gym back home, that was for sure. But maybe they were gay. This *was* New York. And before she could stop herself, she said, 'So, are you straight, or what?'

Peter, the Italian-looking one laughed. 'Now there's a direct-to-the-point kinda girl. Far as I know to date, yeah, we are.'

She smiled wryly. 'Married?' No way was she going down that road again.

Each shook his head.

Wonders will never cease, thought Chloë.

She took a generous gulp of margarita.

What the heck?

Perhaps she was just *beginning* to get over James, after all.

## 46 Maggie

'**I guess I've** come to say goodbye,' said Maggie, checking her watch. It was nearly time to go. She looked around the room. With its view out over Guildford, glistening in the summer sun, it seemed less shabby to her than it had several months ago, more comforting, homely. It was a retreat she would miss, just as she would miss Jamie and their house in Shere. But she was ready to leave it behind, all the same. 'I wanted to thank you for everything you've done for me, really. You've been brilliant, a great help.'

'Do feel free to stay in touch,' said Nina, 'let me know how things are going. I'd like that.'

'Oh, I will.' Maggie nodded, knowing she would, just as she would stay in touch with Georgie – even if she only ever sent a Christmas card to Nina; she was good that way, loyal. 'It's a bit far to come here every week, now that Nathan and I are moving closer in to London.'

'I quite understand.'

'And I suppose I feel we're moving on in other ways, too, and I ought to draw a line under this whole affair, try to put it behind us.'

Now it was Nina's turn to nod. Her jewellery rattled accordingly. 'Well, good luck,' she got to her feet and held out her hand, 'I hope it all goes well for you.'

'Thank you.' Maggie shook her hand. It seemed strange, such a formal gesture, after all she had shared with this woman over the last few months. So, impulsively, she reached forward instead, and gave Nina a quick hug, around her broad shoulders. 'Thank you,' she said again and, with no further ado, turned and left the room.

Back in her car, she rummaged in her handbag for her mobile. She checked her messages. Golly, *three*. There was one from the *Independent on Sunday*, giving her the go-ahead on an idea she'd put to them that morning. That was a quick response – they must have liked it. There was one from Jean – very excited that Maggie was going to be living nearer to her again, and offering to lend a hand with packing. And there was one from Jamie, asking if he could have Nathan on Saturday not Sunday to be able to take him to a game. He wondered if it was possible for Nathan to spend the night with him. Now that he was no longer living with Pete's family but had his own rented flat this was a viable option.

Tip tap tip, Maggie keyed in his work number.

'About Saturday,' she said, when he answered, 'that's fine. In fact, it's quite good. I fancied doing something myself so that makes it easier.'

'Great! I'll look forward to it.'

She rang off without getting drawn into a long chat, but before starting the engine, Maggie decided to make one last call.

'Hi – is that you?'

'Course it's me.'

'It's Mags.'

'I know.'

She felt a bit funny, flustered even. 'I – er – um – you know you wanted to see me this weekend? Maybe go away somewhere?'

'Yeah?' Alex sounded hopeful, and a bit nervous too.

'Well, that's fine. I mean, only for one night, that's all I could manage. But I've decided I'd like to. Come, I mean.'